GRAFT

LI PEIFU

Translated by
James Trapp

SINOIST

ACA Publishing Ltd
University House
11-13 Lower Grosvenor Place,
London SW1W 0EX, UK
Tel: +44 20 3289 3885
E-mail: info@alaincharlesasia.com
www.alaincharlesasia.com
www.sinoistbooks.com

Beijing Office
Tel: +86(0)10 8472 1250

Author: Li Peifu
Translator: James Trapp
Editor: David Lammie
Cover Art: Renée Elizabeth Clarke
Interior Art: A. Bodrenkova

Published by Sinoist Books (an imprint of ACA Publishing Ltd) in arrangement with Guangdong Flower City Publishing House co., Ltd

Original Chinese Text © 平原客 *(Ping Yuan Ke)* 2017, Guangdong Flower City Publishing House co., Ltd, Guangdong, China

English Translation text © 2022 ACA Publishing Ltd, London, UK

Hardback ISBN: 978-1-83890-548-4
Paperback ISBN: 978-1-83890-534-7
eBook ISBN: 978-1-83890-535-4

A catalogue record for *Graft* is available from the National Bibliographic Service of the British Library.

Translator's Foreword

ONE OF THE LESS APPRECIATED but nonetheless important problems facing the translator and publisher of Chinese novels in English (and other foreign languages, of course) is the question of the title. A book's title may be thought of as encapsulating the essence of the author's understanding of their work, and as such, its full meaning and significance may take some time to emerge to the reader and translator. In other words, you cannot translate the title and then the book, it has to be the other way around. Even then, as often as not, the resonances and nuances of the Chinese are either impossible to render in English or lose their subtle power in the process. At this point, there is an element of hubris on the part of the translator and publisher as they effectively try to second guess the author with an alternative "essence" of the book which is both acceptable to the author and carries the same power as the original to readers in its new linguistic incarnation. Li Peifu's 平原客 *(píngyuán kè)* is a case in point.

So, how did we, at Sinoist Books, get from 平原客 to "Graft"? And why? The book's original title carries a host of historical, cultural, sociological and linguistic nuances in its three simple characters, one of which pretty much defies succinct translation on its own. 平原 means "plain" as in "flat land around a river" and here stands in for the more specific 中原 *zhōngyuán* or "Central Plain" which refers to the vast fertile area of the middle and lower Yellow River Valley Central Plain, including Henan, western Shandong, southern Shanxi and Hebei provinces. It is an area of huge cultural and historical significance, being known both as "China's Breadbasket" and the "Cradle of Chinese Civilisation". The use of the more general term in the title sits better with the enigmatic third character, 客 *(kè)*. 客, either by itself or in one of many combinations in which it occurs, carries respectful or honorific connotations in meanings such as "guest", "client", "customer" and "traveller". Perhaps its most common usage is in the combination 客气 (kèqi) meaning "polite, courteous, formal, modest". Here, in the title, its use seems to be something of a coining by the author, and as such, it is possible to get a feeling for its meaning without actually being able to pin it down in a different language devoid of all the Chinese cultural resonances. In the end, we gave up trying!

We did kick around quite a number of possibilities that were more or less directly connected to the original Chinese title, but while it was not that difficult to come up with something that was superficially acceptable, none of our suggestions really hit the mark. We tried several variations around "Man of the Plains", but eventually had to accept that none of them really captured the nuances of the Chinese, nor, more importantly, did they have any resonance or depth of meaning for an English readership. At this point, with the apparently easy option of a more or less direct translation proving a dead end, we began to cast around, with occasionally ludicrous results, for a completely different emphasis drawn from the themes of the book. In the end, it was the narrative structure of the novel that provided the key.

The story begins and ends with "Butterfly Transformation", a *bonsai* combination wintersweet and flowering plum (it is important to note that what we in the West call *bonsai*, using the Japanese pronunciation of the Chinese term 盆栽 [pénzāi], was a Chinese invention that was taken to Japan sometime from the late 6th century onwards). This tree is the pride and joy of Master Horticulturist Liu Quanyou, the father of one of the novel's protagonists, Liu Jinding. There is a detailed description of the huge amount of work Liu Quanyou puts into the creation of his masterwork, starting with a journey deep into the mountains to find a suitable root bole and the trials and tribulations of bringing it back home healthy and in one piece. Throughout his career, the corrupt political and commercial fixer, Xie Zhichang, uses Liu Quanyou's *bonsai* as "gifts" to further his business and political ambitions.

Almost out of the blue, three elements of the story of the *bonsai* "Butterfly Transformation" came into focus and condensed into a single word that also represented important themes of the novel as a whole. The three elements were the hard work Master Horticulturist Liu put into the creation of his masterpiece, the technique he used in that creation and the corrupt practices the tree was employed in. The single word was "graft".

CHAPTER ONE

ONE

THIS IS A VERY SPECIAL PLACE. Its name is Meiling.

Historically, it is an area of river silt, also called an alluvial plain. Some people say that this plain came "roiling" out of the Yellow River. In the old days, the Yellow River used to flood, year after year, spilling over and retreating, and in the process, roiling out this area of land. Others say the plain was scooped out by the Yellow River and the Huai River. Where the two rivers meet, the Yellow River thinks it can swallow up the Huai River, and the Huai River thinks it can spit out the Yellow River. After many years of this conflict and many changes of course as the waters rolled to and fro, neither side could declare victory and the only result was the silting up of this plain. The truth is, the plain was once the meeting point of the two rivers but there is no water to be seen any more. The water is three feet under the ground or even deeper. A few years ago, you could dig down three feet and see water, but not now. You have to dig deeper. But the water is still there, oozing through the soil. It is said that, right down below, there is an underground river.

Not only is this the meeting place of the Chu and the Han kingdoms, the mid-point between the north and south, it is also a land of softness. Even the sun, when it comes round to fall on this place, seems rather more amiable, like a little old man with slightly narrowed eyes and no rancour. The wind here is surprisingly soft, anodyne, neither fierce nor violent. When the wind blows, it is like an evil-looking but kind-hearted old woman. There are strong winds too, but the noise they make is greater than their actual speed. They roll slowly across with a throaty whistle and are gone without causing any damage. It is as though they are issuing a warning, telling people to watch out.

Meiling is an excellent place for growing plants. It is wide and flat with abundant rain and has an annual average temperature of 17.1°C with four distinct seasons. Even more important, the soil is unexpectedly soft, loose and breathable, of the kind that is called lotus flower soil or mid-weight earth. Sandy soil is known as light earth, clay soil as heavy earth. Sandy soil is highly breathable, but it doesn't hold moisture well. Clay soil is good at holding moisture, but it crusts up very easily. The lotus flower soil here falls between light and heavy and is particularly suitable for growing nursery stock. So from ancient times, the people of Meiling have entrusted their fortunes to the gifts of heaven and earth and the bounty of nature. The place is known for producing gardeners, and as well as growing wheat, almost every household plants, nurtures and sells flowers.

Gardener Liu, whose actual name was Liu Quanyou, originally came from Yakou Village in Meiling. Because they had been growing flowers for generations, several of his family members worked as gardeners in other parts of the country. As a result, they were often called the Hunchback Family behind their backs. Of course, "Hunchback Family" sounds rather derogatory, but originally it just meant to say that the family made its living pushing wheelbarrows and that they were flower sellers. Later on, the term simply came to mean that this family had produced generation after generation of gardeners, and Hunchback Family became the name of a well-known gardening company in Yakou.

Tradition has it that the Lius started growing flowers in the Song dynasty. However, the Liu clan had no recorded family tree. Remembered history only went as far back as the Liu family growing plants and flowers in the Qing dynasty, and that was just an oral family tradition passed on by grandparents about pushing wheelbarrows into Kaifeng to sell flowers. In those days, the family made their living pushing barrows along the eighty *li* of winding roads between Meiling and Kaifeng.

By Liu Quanyou's generation, the Hunchback Family Clan had dispersed across the country and only Liu Quanyou's branch remained in Yakou. At the beginning of Deng Xiaoping's reforms and opening up of the country, Liu Quanyou was invited to be the gardener at the People's Park in Huanghuai City, but for some unknown reason, he suddenly went back to the village to manage on his own. In appearance, Old Liu – or Lao Liu in Chinese – was thin and rather stooped, with deep-set eyes, drooping eyebrows and a face like ancient bronze. The blood in his veins gathered in patches of threadlike erythema, and the wrinkles on his face had been gouged into deep crevasses by the wind and frost. With the white sweat-cloth that hung year-round from his waist as he walked silently along, he looked like an old, walking tree stump. In general, he didn't have much to do with outsiders, and he was referred to by the other villagers as "Hunchback Liu". Many years later, when he was honoured by the city with the title "Master Horticulturist", no one dared to call him by his old nickname. Those who knew him well had another name for him: "Iron Hands" or "Master Iron Hands". Certainly, Lao Liu's hands were not the same as other people's: there was some kind of mystical quality about them. When he picked up a handful of earth and pinched some of it between his finger and thumb, he could tell immediately whether it was heavy, light or middle soil. For a period after the Cultural Revolution, he secretly went to do ornamental topiary on some pines and cypresses in a public park away from the village, and after so many years working with the thorns and prickles on such trees, his hands were as resistant to them as if they were made of iron. His thumbs in particular, which were affected by viral warts, had callused over into an iron nail-like hardness as the warts were continually slashed open by thorns and then healed up. Later on still, when he had become a famous grower of plums, and had his own plum tree nursery, he was still in constant contact with gnarled trees and steel wire, and he grew layer after layer of skin over his hands until the calluses were so hard even a knife couldn't cut them. Soil and blood, steel and blood, plum tree trunks and blood merged into one bloodline. It was said that if any flower was dying, a smear of blood from Lao Liu's hand would probably revive it. Of course, that was only a rumour.

After Liu Quanyou was honoured as "Master Horticulturist", the thing he was most widely known for was his bonsai "plum tree". This tree, which was in part a wintersweet, was Gardener Lao Liu's most treasured possession.

The bole was an ancient flowering plum. It had originally been dug up deep in the Daba Mountains of Sichuan and was at least three hundred years old. The grafts came from seeds carefully selected and optimised from wild root stock from the Tianmu Mountains in Zhejiang. After undergoing the hybridising grafting process, the new creation was lavished with careful nurturing. During this period, it died three times and was brought back to life on each occasion. In the winter of the year we are writing about, an icy north wind was blowing and seasonal snow was driving in outside the window when the tree suddenly burst into bloom, dazzling yellow as if freshly dyed, sparkling and limpid, like little golden bells, and incomparably fragrant. This first ever blossom on the three-hundred-year-old tree inspired a surge of tender affection, and ancient tears welled-up in Lao Liu's eyes. Spontaneously, he gave his tree a name, calling it Butterfly Transformation.

Old Gardener Liu lavished eighteen years of his heart's blood on this tree. Eighteen years is a long, slow journey, but in Lao Liu's eyes this was his child and he was watching it grow up, day by day. It was as the tree started its eighteenth year that it gained the name Butterfly Transformation and the shape of its blossom like little golden bells led people to give it the title "King of Chinese Plum Trees".

There was a period when the thing that gave Old Gardener Liu the most pride was not his flowering plum tree but his son. The child's name was Pa Cha, but his real name was Liu Jinding. When he was little, his name used the character 定 (dìng, meaning "certain") but on turning eighteen, he changed it to 鼎 (dǐng, meaning "a type of sacrificial bronze tripod vessel"). He was determined to make something of himself, and after graduating from university, he began his ascent from deputy village mayor to local government official, all the way up to becoming executive deputy mayor of Huanghuai City. Some people even predicted he would soon make it to full mayor. For a while, the residents of Meiling County could talk about nothing else: Gardener Liu's son is a top official!

At this time, when people introduced Lao Liu, they said: "This is Master Liu", or "This is the mayor's father."

TWO

MANY YEARS LATER, Deputy Mayor Liu Jinding still remembered the rumbling and clattering of the wheel on the road during that trip. He was sleeping in the second of the straw baskets on the right-hand side of the wheelbarrow his father was pushing. He had his head under a tatty old quilt and was lying on a cotton-padded mattress, half curled up in the basket like a monkey. He was lulled by the smell of flowers and the dull rumbling of the wheel until he woke up to hear his father saying to himself: "Here we are then! Weichuan!"

Weichuan is forty *li* from Meiling, or about twelve miles, and it was Liu Quanyou's chosen stopping place for a mid-journey snack. In another forty *li* they would reach Kaifeng, which was where he intended to sell his flowers.

At the time, Liu Quanyou was making these flower-selling trips in secret. In the middle of the Cultural Revolution, the authorities did not allow the growing of flowers, and all the flower growers had gone to the open countryside to grow cotton. In order to earn some money to supplement the household income, Liu Quanyou had built a partition wall in the inner courtyard of his house and was secretly growing flowers behind it. At the end of the year, he picked them and took them to Kaifeng to sell.

In those days, the poor could not afford women, especially pretty women. But at the time, Liu Quanyou did have a woman, and she was the prettiest in Yakou Village. He had brought her back from the mountains of Sichuan when he went there in 1960 to dig up his plum tree. He had paid for her with thirty *jin*-worth of national grain coupons, equivalent to about fifteen kilograms, plus an extra twenty yuan. For that, he was able to take home a woman who stunned the whole village.

This girl was strikingly beautiful and all the villagers' eyes were out on stalks when they saw her. She hadn't been there more than three days before a constant stream of folk came into the courtyard on the pretext of wanting to borrow something. However, she didn't even stay in the village for a whole year before running off. She came from the deep mountain country of Sichuan and it wasn't her fault that she didn't understand the local dialect, but the main problem was that she couldn't get used to eating the dark, bitter-sweet sweet potato doughnuts. She preferred to eat long grain rice, but there was no long grain rice in the village. Liu Quanyou once went out and braved the dangers of the black market to buy her a few *jin*, but it was all consumed within a few days, after which she said that there was nothing to keep her there any longer.

During the following days when he searched everywhere for his woman, Liu Quanyou was in torment. Within three short years, this beautiful woman from the Sichuan mountains ran away four times.

Liu Quanyou brought her back on each occasion. The third occasion, she was already pregnant with a swelling belly, and the villagers all reckoned that this time, when she had had the baby and was beset by all the cares a child brings, she would not run away again. But when the child was only a month old, off she went. This time she never came back.

After the Sichuan woman had run away, Liu Quanyou had a child to look after all by himself. This was the time in the planned economy era when people were striving to earn work points and there were perpetual shortages of oil, salt and cash. When the year-end came around, Liu Quanyou had no choice but to sneak out and sell flowers.

Deputy Mayor Liu Jinding could never forget Weichuan. Not only was it the place where his father stopped to rest his feet and have something to eat, it was also where he first tasted bread.

It was close to noon when Liu Quanyou pushed his wheelbarrow into Weichuan on the eighty-*li* journey to Kaifeng. Usually, he would sit down at a nearby tea stall, tip the dust out of his shoes, carry Liu Jinding out of his straw basket and let him stretch the stiffness out of his legs. Then he would spend two cents on two cups of tea and bring out the dry rations he had packed. He gave one half to his son, which comprised some softened oil breads, and the other half, which was sweet potato doughnuts, he ate himself.

From his youth, Liu Jinding remembered very clearly that there was a middle school behind that tea stall. The complex contained a huge enclosure with a sports field so big you couldn't take it all in in one glance, and row after row of school buildings. Both sides of the sports field were lined with willows and locust trees. What else was there? Groups of youngsters wearing red armbands were coming out of the school enclosure in twos and threes, looking very pleased with themselves. He remembered his father seemed much in awe of these children. He hung his head down, taking little sips of tea without looking at anyone. On that day, he ran over into the school enclosure. At the small snack kiosk by the gates, he smelled a wonderful, fragrant smell. It was the smell of bread. Those bread rolls were unbelievably fragrant and made his mouth water. He saw the youngsters inside the kiosk buying bread rolls. They were the size of chicken eggs, golden in colour, row after row of them. They cost five cents each. He was rooted to the spot by his greed for those rolls, and he stood in front of

6

the kiosk counter for a long, long time, unwilling to leave. When Liu Quanyou was anxiously searching for him and arrived at the kiosk, he saw his son transfixed by something, standing dumbly in front of the counter, saliva running down his chin. Liu Quanyou probably also smelled the fragrance of the bread rolls, but even more he saw the greedy look in his son's eyes. He immediately loosened his belt and took some cash out of the cloth lining. He spent fifteen cents on three bread rolls for his son, then hauled him away and set off on the road again.

Years later, as a city administrator in charge of investment, Liu Jinding went abroad many times and ate all kinds of foreign bread, but the delicious smell of the warm bread he had experienced at the snack kiosk of Weichuan Middle School was what lingered in his mind. Of course, he later came to realise that Weichuan was so small it could not be found on any world map, but Weichuan Middle School's name was known throughout the education world.

The fragrance of those three little bread rolls, which he ate mouthful by mouthful in the basket on the wheelbarrow, accompanied by the rumbling and rattling of the wheel, stayed with him all the way to Kaifeng.

Kaifeng is an ancient city. It was once the national capital of the Song dynasty, so we ought to be calling it an imperial city. But the ancient, genuinely imperial city has long ago been submerged under a hundred metres of water from the countless years of flooding by the Yellow River. All the precious objects and artefacts were carried away when the Song officials and rich merchants fled south to Hangzhou. The only things left behind for future generations were a few snacks and entertainments, like soup buns, double sheep intestines and peanut cake; or cock fighting, showing dogs and growing flowers. Of course, over the centuries of the Ming and Qing dynasties and into the Republican era, Kaifeng was the site of the provincial yamen and it gradually accumulated a bit of its own character and laid down some new foundations. During the Republican period, it was said that if an opera singer could make their name in Kaifeng, they could go on to achieve nationwide celebrity. This is why the place still had many traditional-style old streets, although they have been changed in recent times. They included Xiangfu (Opposite the Government Offices) Street, Xilou (Opera House) Street, Siqian (In Front of the

Temple) Street, Yahou (Behind the Yamen) Street and so on. Sometimes, if two people are having an argument over some deal or other in the market, Kaifeng folk may still roll their eyes with the look of an impoverished aristocrat, as much as to say: "Been there and done that, Granddad!" Whenever Gardener Liu Quanyou went to Kaifeng, he always rested up at a small public bath house behind Xilou Street. One reason for choosing this location was that it was close to the marketplace where he sold his flowers, but it was also because he had a friend there.

That friend was one of the back-scrubbers in the bath house. He was known as Hunchback Lin. The "Hunchback" part was clear enough, but where did the "Lin" come from? After all, his real surname wasn't Lin, it was Zhu. This man's hunchback was formed like two mountain peaks with his right shoulder higher than his left, so his neck also tilted to one side. He wasn't tall, but he always trotted along at a fair pace, carrying a towel that was wrung out and twirling like a twisted rope. He would keep cracking the towel like a whip over the plunge pool, giving off a series of loud, crisp detonations. Despite his crooked neck, his voice was high and clear like an opera tenor as he cried out: "Next one please... that means you!"

This public bath was originally called the Dehua Baths, but during the Cultural Revolution it was changed to the Hong Xing (Red Star) Baths. A pale-skinned, plump woman sat in the bath house ticket office. At first sight, this woman seemed tall, well-built and healthy, with a round face like a full moon and breasts resembling twin snowy mountain peaks. Nothing was visible below that, but if you did get a glimpse, you would see that she was sitting cross-legged and that her legs and feet were tiny and deformed, small as a baby's. At that point, you would realise she was a cripple. This woman, who was paralysed in her lower limbs, was Hunchback Lin's wife. Once through the doors of the bath house, Gardener Liu led his son over to the ticket window and called out: "Sister!"

The pale-skinned, plump woman in the ticket booth looked up at him, put down the wooden plaque with a bath house bed number she had just picked up, then hung it back in a little cupboard. All she said was: "You're here, then."

"I'm here," Lao Liu replied.

"In you go."

8

As a child, one of the very first people Liu Jinding ever got to know was this woman his father called "Sister". She never smiled, but her chubby beauty left a lasting impression on him. Many years later, when he was in a Turkish bath in Istanbul enjoying a skin scrape and massage in a room full of steam as thick as fog, he could still recall the plump, pale-faced woman because that had been his first experience of a bath house.

The bath house behind Xilou Street in the old city of Kaifeng wasn't very big. Inside, there were two thirty-metre-square hot pools and one twenty-metre-square warm pool but no separate room for back massage. Anyone who wanted a back massage either sat on the edge of the pool or lay on a small wooden bed waiting for their number to be called. Every year end, just before New Year, the pools looked like pots of dumplings, with boiled red buttocks of various shapes and sizes floating around in them. This fifteen-cent-a-ticket Red Star Bath House, with its simple wooden beds and its scalding steam, had its own "house god", and that house god was Hunchback Lin.

"Hunchback Lin" was what people called him behind his back. In the steam-shrouded, shadowy, people-packed bath house, what they called out was simply "Lao Lin" or "Lin, Number Eighteen", "Lao Lin, Number Twenty-Seven", "Lao Lin, over here in the corner". To which came the replies: "One for Number Eighteen", "One for Number Twenty-Seven", "Over in the corner, one for Number Thirty-Five", "In front of the counter, one for Number Sixteen." Hard on the heels of those cries, a veritable whirlwind of hot towels would go flying across the room to land precisely in the hands of each customer.

The back massages given by Hunchback Lin were even more abrupt. In his bath house, back massages weren't called "back massages"; instead, he called them "renewals". When Hunchback Lin gave someone a renewal, it was like a dramatic performance. As he twirled the dripping towel in his hand, it danced and flew, sometimes like a spinning top, sometimes like a flower hoop, sometimes like a bow stave, sometimes like a whistle arrow, sometimes like a plaited whip. From time to time, he would shake it out and snap it back with a whistling, cracking noise. Sometimes he would be flexing a customer's leg, sometimes kneading their neck. With his hand

9

wrapped in that white towel, wherever it went, it left behind its red marks. The last stage of his renewal was the back rub. In his hands, this was like someone beating a drum, from top to bottom, light and heavy, first like little raindrops and then like pearls, large and small, dropping into a jade dish. Finally, with the flat of his hands, he would beat up and down like on a drum: rat-tat, rat-tat, rat-tat-tat... with the power of a stampede of horses. And all the time, he was keeping up his replies to the customers: "Number Eight, you're done! Number Twelve, you're up next! Number Seven, just wait a moment!"

Hunchback Lin also did the pedicures. When he had the time, he would carry a little wooden chest over to the bed where his customer was lying, spread out a shiny black cloth mat across his knees and lay out a row of pedicure knives, some long some short, all different shapes and all looking incomparably sharp. He would give a shout of "Shai dan!", which seemed to be an approximation of the English "Lie down!" and was indeed an instruction to his customer to lie back. Then he could raise both the man's legs high in the air, above the top of his own head, and inspect them, studying them carefully in the gloomy lamplight. Then he would put the feet back down flat, cradling them on his mat, and only then begin to wield the knife...

In this brash, vulgar, baking hot bath house, the figure of Hunchback Lin, moving around like a mountain peak slipping in and out of the clouds, would appear intermittently behind one pair of glowing red buttocks after another. Now here, now there, yelling, shouting, leaping and gliding like a gambolling mountain goat. For every pair of buttocks he encountered, Hunchback Lin could respectfully address their owner by name: Section Chief Fan, Bureau Chief Liu, Secretary Wang, Department Head Qin, Director Ma... Occasionally the clients would give him a cigarette, which he would tuck behind his ear, and he would bounce around with even more enthusiasm. The twin peaks of his hunchback often glistened with strings of shiny beads of sweat that would drip down his back like a painting of a sparkling stream. He would be busy until beyond midnight, waiting for the last customers to leave before neatly folding all the towels that were left scattered over the wooden beds. Only then would he go over to the bunk in the furthest corner, sit down and take a deep breath.

That bunk, right up against the western wall and next to a tool cupboard, was his bunk. It wasn't normally available for rent, but now Gardener Liu Quanyou, his scarlet body wrapped in a bath towel, was sitting there.

Although he had been a friend of the bath house for many years, Gardener Liu did not stay there for free. On this occasion, he had already spread out two yellow paper packages on the bunk. Inside one was half a *jin* of soy-braised pig's head and in the other half a *jin* of fried peanuts. There was also a tin pot and two small wine bowls.

After midnight, the two friends sat quietly, drinking alternately. Eyes bleary with sleep, Liu Jinding got up in the night to piss, and he saw Liu Quanyou follow him out. He thought his father wanted to piss too, but that wasn't it. His father was carrying a mug of water as he walked over to the wheelbarrow beside the lavatory. First, he rinsed his mouth, gargling with the water that he then spat out onto the ground. After rinsing his mouth, he sucked in another mouthful of water, lifted the quilt from the flower baskets and sprayed the flowers with mouthful after mouthful of water. "The flowers stay a bit fresher like this," his father said. When he had finished his piss, Liu Jinding went back into the bath house and saw that the two men had continued drinking, alternately, just as before. There wasn't much wine, and they sat there, lips pursed, not speaking. From time to time, as his father drank, he would pick up a peanut and stuff it into Liu Jinding's mouth. Liu Jinding was wide-eyed, watching the two men. To him, at the time, they appeared like two piles of accumulated dirt and dejection. But looking back on these childhood memories, this annual trip to the bath house was Liu Jinding's greatest pleasure. It was in the Red Star Bath House in old Kaifeng that he gained his first experience of real life, naked, unadorned and shrouded in white, foggy steam. He decided, there and then, that Hunchback Lin's life was a very lowly one. He didn't actually know the word "lowly", but he was quite clear about what it represented.

THREE

GARDENER LIU QUANYOU once had a very remarkable dream.

In this dream, there was a blossoming plum tree that just kept growing. Normally speaking, plum trees blossom first and then put out leaves, but the remarkable thing about this tree was that it did the reverse, growing leaves first. Three leaves, six leaves, nine leaves... all like feathers and as big as fans. It grew and grew, then suddenly one day, it burst into bloom, and in among the stamens and pistils of one flower there grew a beautiful, coquettish woman. This woman leapt down from the flower and began to circle Liu Quanyou's bed, calling out: "Lao Liu, Lao Liu, I want some rice to eat. Lao Liu, Lao Liu, I want some rice to eat." After she had circled the bed three times, two dazzling beams of golden light shot from her eyes, blinding Lao Liu.

On waking up, he rubbed his eyes and was surprised to feel a sharp pain in them. The dream had him rooted in fear. He threw on some clothes, got out of bed, hurried into the courtyard and over to his greenhouse. He walked round and round his precious miniature wintersweet plum tree. Time and again he raised the pruning knife in his hand, but in the end, he couldn't bring himself to use it.

Liu Quanyou believed there was some malign spirit in this plum tree that he wanted to drive out, but at the same time, the tree was too precious to him and he had lavished so much of his heart's blood on it that he couldn't bear to harm it.

He really had spent a lot of love and care on that ancient tree. When he dug it up in the deep mountains of Sichuan, even though he had hired someone to help, he had put his back out and needed to recuperate in a grass hut in the mountains for some time, unable to stand up. In the end, he gathered up some earth to serve as incense, and kowtowed to the tree three times, saying: "Grandfather, I know you've been here for many years and don't want to leave. But where I live, the sunshine and scenery are very fine. Tell me, who knows about you, hidden away in these mountains? I want to spread your fame across the nation, Grandfather!" The amazing thing was that, after Liu Quanyou had made this entreaty, there were no more incidents.

After the ancient bole had been dug up, it still needed to be put out in the sun. This had to be done for three days, constantly keeping it moist, in order to stop the roots getting mouldy. During this "sunning" process, Liu Quanyou carefully trimmed the fine, hairlike roots known as the beard and covered them with soil. Then, he laid out a plastic bag on the south-facing mountain slope and draped it with a tatty old bed quilt for extra protection. Late in the night, when the stars were out and the humidity was rising, ignoring his own comfort, he wrapped the tree in some plastic sheeting he had brought with him. He waited for the sun to come out and repeated the whole process. After three days, when the beard was half dried out, he wrapped the bole in the old quilt, added another two layers of plastic sheeting, tied it up neatly and gave it to the hired help to carry down the mountain. All the way, Liu Quanyou kept repeating, over and over: "Be careful, be careful!"

Liu Quanyou collected the seeds deep in the Tianmu Mountains in Zhejiang. In fact, there were people at the bottom of the mountains selling them. This wasn't just to earn money; the important thing was they wanted customers to choose these wild seeds and protect the mature, mother-stock. In July, when the days were at their hottest, a sunburnt Liu Quanyou scrambled his way up the mountain side to collect his seeds. He was wearing a large pair of undershorts and a battered old straw hat, carrying a cloth bag and a water bottle slung over his shoulder. Coming back down the same day, he had been drenched in sweat, almost marinated in it, and the sweat had dried into salt under the fierce sun, turning his body shining white. He was also covered in red patches like fish scales, where tree branches had gashed his flesh. In his travels, east and west, there and back, he covered several thousand *li*. It goes without saying that it was hard going, "eating the wind and drinking the dew".

Although Meiling produced a lot of wintersweet trees, there was no readily available wild stock. All the flowering plum trees in the county were produced by grafting shoots collected elsewhere, and it was only by grafting on wintersweet that you could grow a high-quality commercial flowering plum tree. Everyone in Meiling understood this, and the locally grown, ungrafted trees were known as dog-tooth plum or just stinking plum. To make a rather infelicitous comparison, they were like the children born to the local women, uncouth and rustic with flat faces. By contrast, the children born to the women who had been bought and brought back from the deep mountains of the southwest, all looked fresh-faced and intelligent with bright, lively eyes. Perhaps this is the advantage of cross-breeding. This, at least, was the idle observation made at the village entrance by the primary school teacher in Yakou, indicating Liu Jinding as an example.

After the seeds were brought back, they first had to be sun-dried and air-dried, and then, before being transplanted, they had to be "sand-buried" for three days. The sand-burial was to promote germination by allowing the seed cases to soften slowly, and only after the seeds sprouted could they be transplanted into the fields. After that, the first year was spent tending the shoots and the second year was for setting the plants. Only then, after the beginning of the third year, were they ready for grafting. For those three years, it was as though Liu Quanyou was looking after a child as he went out every day to check on the seedlings. He even had to cook the chicken shit fertiliser he applied in order to kill off any parasites.

The grafting itself was a crucial time. The shoots had to be carefully selected, taking only the best of the best. He did the earliest grafting using a traditional method called "setting a fuse". A shoot was inserted into the old bole and wrapped in hemp cloth. The cut was smeared with a mud paste and sealed with earth, and after the new shoots appeared, the sealing earth was carefully pried apart a little. Three months later, the graft could be considered established. The great majority of these new growths were hunched over. Many of them were bent and twisted, and only a few of them grew straight upwards, so they were known as hunch and stoops.

Once the grafts had taken successfully, the next three stages were "retaining the head", "setting the trunk" and "fixing the shape". These three stages were the ones that needed the most careful thought and could even be said to be entering the realms of art.

The most amazing thing about this particular ancient bole wintersweet plum tree was that although the trunk was old and withered, the plums were colourful and abundant, hanging high up in the branches. The bole had three hundred years of natural growth, and when you looked at it straight on, there were two big dried-up holes in it, giving it the appearance of a mountain monastery gateway, or you might even say the entrance to a hidden world. Above, two hanging branches fluttered and danced in the wind, and when the blossoms opened, they were like a cloud of butterflies dancing above the monastery gate, with the bright yellow flowers looking as though they were flying, each one gay and lovely and incomparably fragrant. Viewed from the side, the trunk and roots were robust and strong, though on one side there was a patch of recently broken bark, above which was an old insect burrow. On the other side, there was a bulging knot shaped like a fist. Viewed from a distance, it looked from one side like a belly button and from the other like a reclining Buddha grasping a flower. The blossom on the "Buddha" was like its golden halo.

Fixing the shape of the hanging branches was the most difficult process. It required many years of manual manipulation, little by little moulding bends, stretching and circling to allow it to take shape, step by step. The final step, the "burning of incense and washing of hands", was to "invite" the ancient bole of the flowering plum into the purple clay pottery basin as though it was following its own innermost wish. Gardener Liu Quanyou had eighteen years of hard-won experience, and the better part of it had all gone into this ancient bole flowering plum known as Butterfly Transformation.

When Butterfly Transformation first appeared in public during its annual flowering, it caused a sensation in Meiling. Thereafter, a continuous stream of visiting merchants came trying to buy it. During that time, there were people who offered fifty thousand yuan and some even eighty thousand. One day, a Japanese came visiting. He had a camera round his neck and as well as bowing non-stop, he also kept repeating: "*Arigato, arigato gozaimasu...*" Liu Quanyou had no idea what he was on about. Later, an interpreter told him that the man was offering a Toyota car in exchange for the bonsai tree. Liu Quanyou just shook his head and refused the deal.

Later on, a painting academy was holding a founder's celebration and offered twenty of the master's paintings in exchange for the tree. Once again, Liu Quanyou shook his head and refused.

There was a conflict deep inside Gardener Liu. On the one hand, he couldn't abide the thought of being parted from this ancient-trunked flowering plum, but, on the other, he was afraid. He couldn't voice the hidden fear, but that dream of his was lodged deep in his breast, and he still felt that the flower witch was exerting an evil influence on him. During the night, whenever he sat in front of those blossoms, he didn't know how or why, but an ominous feeling always oozed up inside him.

That was the problem: he had no idea what this plum tree intended for him.

FOUR

IN THE COURSE OF HIS LIFE, Liu Jinding had met two important people. One was very important, the other less so. According to Liu Jinding, the less important person was Xie Zhichang.

This Xie Zhichang, nicknamed Big Mouth Xie, was what might be called a "flower man", a 花客 in the local dialect. On the Central Plain, the word 客 is used as a kind of honorific. In the upper register of its use it applies to anything from bureaucrats, to religious types and mystics and magicians of all kinds, to sons-in-law, to teachers. Lower down, it could be used for family and relatives, good friends and even street pedlars and the like. Anyone who comes through your door is essentially 客, which in standard use also just means "guest". In this case it denotes that the man was a middleman for the flower and plant trade, and really he could be called a 掮客, or agent. Its use here in 花客 or "flower man" is definitely a respectful title and not at all derogatory. Many years later, Big Mouth Xie turned into Boss Xie, president of the Flower World group of companies, and the chapter of his life when he was just a 花客 was over.

This first occasion Xie Zhichang arrived was at a time of worry for Liu Quanyou. His son, Liu Jinding, had just gone up into the second year of middle school and had been expelled.

Liu Jinding complained bitterly that the affair had had nothing to do with him. The boy he shared a desk with was a student called Feng Erbao. This boy's father was chair of the township's institute of industry and commerce and was always being given gifts of cigarettes. Feng Erbao often stole some of his father's cigarettes and brought them to school where he smoked them in secret. That winter, Liu Jinding and his desk-mate Feng Erbao were seated in the back row of the classroom, right next to the door. That door had been rotten for a long time and even with just a light breeze blowing, the cold was piercing. Feng Erbao's nose was running and he was hunched down secretly lighting a cigarette under the desk and cupping it in his hands to warm them. After a while, he couldn't resist any more and lowered his head to take a quick drag, blowing the smoke carefully, thread by thread, through a crack in the door. Then he nudged Liu Jinding with his elbow and whispered: "Have a puff. Go on, have a puff." Liu Jinding also lowered his head, so his forehead was resting on the edge of the table, looking at him. Feng Erbao whispered again: "Try it!"

Just at that moment, the form master, Teacher Cui Guoxiang, came charging down from the dais. He rushed to the back row of the classroom like a whirlwind and grabbed Liu Jinding's hand that was holding the cigarette. Lifting it high in the air, he shouted: "Look, students! What is this? How appalling!"

In the township's Tianbao Middle School, Teacher Cui's discipline was legendary. His most famous saying that year was: "Wake up! Students, now the country is opening up and reforming, there are a hundred things to be done, and it is talent and ability that the country needs now, talent and ability. How can you stay asleep! Which one of you seventy-two students wants to be a stinking dog turd? Raise your hand, and I'll scoop you up and throw you away!"

On the dais there was a cardboard box containing the marbles that Teacher Cui had confiscated from his students. Any time he saw a student not paying attention, he would take a marble from the box, grip it between his fingers and launch it like a bullet in whichever direction he wanted. Teacher Cui's "bullets" were never launched in vain, and any student who had nodded off or was wool-gathering, would find themselves his target. If the same student was the target three times, Teacher Cui would stride over to them and, in front of the whole class, shout out a stern "Please!" This was an invitation to the student to go over and stand facing the wall. This was called "wall-face".

In the school's other year groups, students were seated according to height, but Teacher Cui did it differently and seated his students according to their examination results. Tests of varying seriousness were held more than ten times a term, and after each test, Teacher Cui rearranged his class. Because of this battle for position, the students studied day and night, too scared to make any complaint. Every time the results were read out, the students at the front were covered in glory and the ones at the back in shame and disgrace, with the latter being publicly pronounced the lowest kind of creatures. The students at the very back were so covered in shame they almost didn't dare show their faces. Teacher Cui would make the announcements in a loud voice from the dais. For example: "Student Liu Jinding, you came second to bottom in the test. Please go and sit in the back row in the second-to-last seat. The lavatory is just outside, so it's a delightful spot..." At this point, the whole class would turn their heads to stare fixedly at Liu Jinding.

In fact, that year, in Teacher Cui's eyes, Liu Jinding was such a "stinking dog turd" that he shovelled him right out of the school gates.

Of course, Liu Jinding felt that he had been very harshly treated. He hadn't even taken a puff on the cigarette; it had just been shoved into his hand by his desk-mate, Fen Erbao. But he didn't dare tell on Erbao in front of the whole class because that would only be asking for more trouble in the days to come. So he kept his peace in the face of all the accusations and had no choice but to leave the school with his tail between his legs.

Gardener Liu Quanyou only found out about his son's expulsion three days later. Liu Jinding left home the same time as usual, with his school bag on his back, but then spent the day idling round the township. But he frequently found himself standing in front of the small flower-wreath shop, looking at the character 奠 (*diàn*, tribute) on the sample wreaths, and inwardly mourning his own life. Standing in front of the wreath shop, a train of thought formed in his head: why not just die and end all my troubles? He was only brought back to his senses by a shout from the old man who owned the shop: "What are you staring at, youngster? Are you stupid or something?"

In the end, however, it was his classmates who let the cat out of the bag. When Gardener Liu heard, he grabbed a whip but didn't use it. He just sighed heavily. He knew his son didn't smoke, and that the teacher had treated his son unfairly, but what could he do about it?

It was just then that Flower Man Xie Zhichang turned up. Big Mouth Xie saw the bitter, worried expression on Gardener Liu Quanyou's face and made a promise: "You just leave Old Teacher Iron-Fist to me. I'll get your Liu Jinding back in school in three days."

Gardener Liu looked at Big Mouth Xie in amazement. He knew what Xie Zhichang did, acting as a middleman between buyer and seller in the flower trade, and that he possessed remarkable abilities, but he wasn't aware that he could do anything like this. It would be fantastic if he could get Liu Jinding back into school, but...

"I haven't had any dealings with Teacher Iron Fist before," Big Mouth Xie explained, "but I promise you – don't worry, leave it to me. I'm on the case. We can't have children not going to school. It's no big deal. Just two bonsai trees' worth."

Then the penny dropped with Liu Quanyou and he pointed, saying: "Help yourself."

So Xie Zhichang went away with two trees that day: one was a *suxin* wintersweet and the other was a *xinkou* wintersweet, both of them expensive items.

"Are those enough? Take some more if not."

"No need!" Xie Zhichang replied. "What do they know about appreciating fine flowers? I'll fix it for certain."

He was a man of action, and sure enough, in the late afternoon next day he came riding up on his bicycle and said, with a big grin: "Teacher Iron Fist doesn't want to get you riled up, and I've got a message for you. I saw the head teacher and the director of education and they're both full of apologies. The boy can go back to school tomorrow."

Then what should happen but, on the afternoon of the third day, Xie Zhichang came hurtling up on his bicycle again. He was panting and gasping for breath as he said, with great discomfiture: "That man really is the world's number one bastard! Who the fuck does he think he is? The director of education went to see him and he gave him an earful in return on the spot. Then the head teacher showed up, and that bastard had the gall to ask him, right to his face: 'Is this a school or a smoking hall? Have you been taking bribes?' He put the head teacher right on the spot with no way to get out of it... I'm telling you, he's a real piece of work."

Liu Quanyou looked at him cheerlessly and said: "If there's really no way, we'll just have to leave it."

Xie Zhichang ignored his response and said: "No way! What right have they got to exclude a kid from school? Quite apart from the fact he wasn't smoking, even if he had been, would that make it right? What law of the land has he broken? I take this as a slap in the face. As for Teacher Iron Fist, you just wait for some news. There's no way I'm not going to get the better of him! I'm off to see my cousin's husband. He is the deputy county director in charge of education. I'll get him to come..."

Liu Quanyou looked at him in astonishment, then saw his eyes straying towards the bonsai. "Go on," Liu said. "Help yourself."

This time, Xie Zhichang took two "tiger paw" wintersweets.

In the nine days after Liu Jinding stopped going to school, Xie Zhichang spared no effort and came hurrying over eight times. The last time, he squatted down in the courtyard, foaming at the mouth from his exertions, and said hoarsely: "You're not going back there, son. Even if he kowtows a hundred times, you're not going back there. What does this one-horse town have to offer? You're going to one of the county schools. Number One County Middle School and Number Three are both pretty good... you choose."

When Teacher Cui Guoxiang was mentioned, Xie Zhichang began cursing him loudly: "That man is a slippery bastard and a cold-hearted shit. He's a posturing and pretentious wannabee! If you put a pisspot on an aeroplane, all it does is stink up the heavens! Look how arrogant he is! Just because he can parrot a couple of sentences of classical Chinese. He's a piece of shit with no right to look down on anyone. I booked a table at the Furong Restaurant and ordered the best wine and cigarettes. The deputy county director of education, the bureau chief, the head teacher and the director of education all came, but he didn't, even though he was invited three times..."

It was true. Cui Guoxiang, subject head in Chinese language and literature at Tianbao Middle School, was a very well-known teacher and it was said that Number One County Middle School wanted to poach him. So he was naturally conceited and arrogant. All he had to say was: "Even if God or Laozi asked, it wouldn't do any good. If anyone else wants to teach a student like him, they're welcome to it. But I'm not going to!"

"That bastard!" Xie Zhichang said. "I hope he dies a horrible death. The whole table was cursing him at that meal. So this is how it is, lad, I've agreed everything. You haven't been expelled from Tianbao Middle School, you've been transferred. Transferred to one of the county middle schools–"

"I'm not going to the county!" Liu Jinding suddenly blurted out.

Xie Zhichang was stunned. "In that case, child–"

"I want to go to school in Weichuan."

"Weichuan Middle School?"

"Weichuan Middle School."

"I understand. The kid wants some face. All right, I'll go the whole hog. You just wait a while."

Liu Quanyou made noises of agreement and was about to say something, but Xie Zhichang interrupted: "Forget about Teacher Iron Fist, we just have to live with him. I'll go and see to things." With that, he wheeled away his bicycle to do just that. Big Mouth Xie was certainly a man who knew how to get things done. Three days later, he came back, wheeling his bicycle, and personally escorted Liu Jinding the forty *li* to Weichuan Middle School. After that, Xie Zhichang became Liu Quanyou's agent in the flower trade.

(Twenty-two years later, Teacher Cui Guoxiang, known to his students as "the world's number one hard bastard", Cui Guoxiang, subject head in Chinese language and literature at Tianbao Middle School, Cui Guoxiang the "world-class marble marksman", was unexpectedly to be found in a queue of petitioners. At the time, Liu Jinding had just taken up the post of deputy secretary of the city legal and political committee, and the seventh petitioner he received on that "petitions day" was Cui Guoxiang. He was carrying a stack of material related to his case as he walked hesitantly up to stand in front of Liu Jinding. His hair was gleaming with hair oil and he was wearing a pair of spectacles repaired with sticking plaster. There was no trace at all of his former arrogance. He had only just sat down when the words came tumbling out of him: "It's not fair! My house, I reported it and reported it–"

"Do you recognise me, Teacher Cui?" Liu Jinding interjected.

Teacher Cui raised his head slowly and looked at him in surprise. "You, you are–"

"Teacher Cui, I am Liu Jinding. Do you remember?"

A thread of fear washed across Teacher Cui's face. "Liu, you are Liu, Secretary Liu–"

"Don't worry, Teacher Cui. I will put what happened behind us, so we can get on with the matter in hand properly." At this point, the once incomparably arrogant Teacher Cui grasped Liu's hand, tears springing to his aged eyes. He gulped and began to wail. Even now, the substance of Cui Guoxiang's complaint has not been settled and he is still on the petition trail.)

FIVE

IT WAS FOUR YEARS LATER THAT A VERY, very important person appeared in Liu Jinding's life. What is more, the VVIP came into play as a result of the LIP (less important person), Xie Zhichang. After Liu Jinding had gone up to university, he read the following sentence in a book: "In this world, whoever it is you are looking for, no matter where they are, you only have to go through six other people to make a connection. It is a question of probability." Liu Jinding profoundly agreed. In fact, when you drill down into to it, it is the study of connections, or *guanxi*.

Big Mouth Xie, Xie Zhichang, had a particular ability. In a very short space of time, he was able to turn someone he didn't know into someone he did know, and from someone he knew into someone he was on intimate terms with, a friend, someone he had "*guanxi*" with. This wasn't just achieved with a few honeyed words, nor was it simply a case of "hail fellow, well met" acquaintanceship, it actually amounted to an almost uncanny ability. You have to be particularly enthusiastic and meticulous, and have the courage and persistence to scramble up again with a smile even if someone kicks you down three times in a row. You have to have limitless patience and all the while be the embodiment of loyalty and respect – especially with those literary and intellectual types, where stressing respect for their eminence is always the most reliable way of winning them over. In Meiling, all this rich content could be encapsulated in the single word "rush", and Xie Zhichang used this method to rush Liu Jinding into Weichuan Middle School, forty *li* away. Liu Jinding worked this all out for himself later on.

Back then, the smell and taste of sweet bread swirled around all through Liu Jinding's time at Weichuan Middle School. So he naturally felt a special kind of closeness to that school. There is one approach to education that can completely destroy a person, and that is the "stinking dog turd" approach. There is another approach that can be the making of a person and turn him into a future mayor. Of course, while Liu Jinding was at Weichuan Middle School, he didn't think about such things. He just knew that it was more relaxed there, no one knew who he was, and there was no great emotional pressure on him.

The school had a huge sports field. Like his fellow students at Weichuan Middle School, Liu Jinding got up at half-past-five, ran three laps of the sports field, then washed and rinsed his mouth, ate breakfast and went to class. The days were like the script from a Soviet-era film: if you had bread, you had everything.

It should be said that Liu Jinding's motivation to study was roused in him by Teacher Cui Guoxiang. That's right, because who actually wants to be a stinking dog turd? Although he had changed schools, he could still feel Teacher Cui Guoxiang's contemptuous stare on his back. He had to make something of himself at school to prove that he wasn't a stinking dog turd.

He never saw his father during the days he was studying at Weichuan Middle School, but he felt his shadow everywhere. As winter arrived, Liu Jinding discovered that beside the desk in the head teacher's office, there was a tiger paw wintersweet bonsai tree. It had red blossoms with thick juicy petals, the whole flower in the shape of a tiger's paw, pure, limpid and pristine, and its branches and leaves looked like swallows in flight. In the winter sun, this ancient bole wintersweet was exceptionally fragrant and you could smell its perfume from twenty or thirty metres away.

Liu Jinding remembered one day catching sight of Xie Zhichang leading his father, Liu Quanyou, into the head teacher's office. It was after he had seen the ancient bole wintersweet, roots exposed, in the office. It lay under the sun outside the office door for three days. Later, his class teacher was heard to say that the head teacher treasured that tree like nothing else but had killed it by overwatering. It was only under the direction of a real expert, who took it out of its pot to expose the roots to the sun, that, against all expectations, it was brought back to life.

When the school's director of education saw Liu Jinding, he asked with a smile: "Are you fitting in all right here, Jinding?"

"Yes, I am," Liu Jinding replied.

The director continued: "If you study hard, you may earn yourself a high school recommendation." He later discovered two potted chrysanthemums in the director of education's office: one was a white chrysanthemum known as "jade guanyin" and the other was a black chrysanthemum known as "sky full of stars", both top-of-the-range varieties.

On the face of it, Class Teacher Xu did not show Liu Jinding any special consideration, but every time he saw his student on his own, he nodded to him meaningfully. Those nods were very significant. When Teacher Xu arranged the seating in class, he put Liu Jinding next to his female classmate Wang Xiaomei, who was the class student council representative and one of the top three students in the year group. Liu Jinding later also found out that, when it came to graduating from high school, Teacher Xu's son did not sit the national university entrance examination, but went up to Wuhan University, one of the National Key Universities, on the basis of a "school recommendation". Before that happened, Xie Zhichang accompanied Teacher Xu to Wuhan, taking gifts with them that included two ancient bole wintersweet bonsais. One was a "fragrant mouth" wintersweet and the other a "sandalwood scented" wintersweet. Both were top-of-the-range species.

In this comparatively relaxed educational environment, Liu Jinding's academic achievements improved conspicuously. From being second from bottom at Tianbao Middle School he leaped up to twenty-seventh out of sixty-five students in his class. So although his achievements could only be reckoned middling, he was certainly no longer a stinking dog turd. This had a lot to do with his sharing a desk with Wang Xiaomei.

At first sight, Wang Xiaomei was not an especially beautiful girl, but you had to give it time. She was pale-skinned, round-faced with arched-eyebrows and her eyes were clear and transparent. A glistening drop of sweat often hung from the tip of her nose, and she had two shallow dimples either side of her mouth. In summer, she wore short skirts that revealed legs like lengths of lotus root. There was a faint fragrance about her body, which was hard to describe but had a subtle charm. What is more, her father was a deputy county-level cadre. Her family wanted for nothing and she had been brought up with a sense of superiority. Such girls may appear cold at first sight with the kind of aloofness that means they don't often talk to strangers. But after you got to know her, or rather, once she trusted you, she was generous and giving with her affection. It helped that Liu Jinding was such a straightforward and honest sort, open-faced in the way that girls like. With the two of them sharing a bench in the classroom, their feelings for each other slowly became equally close.

To begin with, the two of them were a little bit distant. When Liu Jinding started sharing the bench, Wang Xiaomei shifted her body across to the left, leaving a six-inch gap between them, intentionally distancing herself from him. Since Liu Jinding had only just arrived there, naturally he didn't dare do anything rash, and the gap remained between them. Every time the lesson bell rang, as they stood up from the bench, whoever stood up most abruptly made it tilt upwards, jolting the other person... so it was really their buttocks that first got the pair talking. When the two of them were about to stand up, one of their backsides would give a kind of warning noise and shift towards the middle of the gap. Thereupon, the other one's backside would take notice and shift a little towards the middle too. This way, no matter who started to stand up first, neither one was jolted.

Wang Xiaomei was the class representative and her most important tasks were to clean the blackboard, and collect and distribute homework books. She was also responsible for answering any questions from the study groups during self-study periods, rather like a teacher's assistant. So Liu Jinding benefitted somewhat by association with such an important person. After their two backsides had come to their cooperative agreement, whenever Wang Xiaomei was handing out the homework books, she distributed the other students' books first, and kept two of them back and put them down together on the desk for Liu Jinding. Then, when it was time to go up to the dais to clean the blackboard – that is when Wang Xiaomei was cleaning the blackboard – Liu Jinding had the chance to open the two exercise books and systematically compare them. Wang Xiaomei's book was very neat and, of course, covered in red ticks, whereas in his own book, at least half those ticks were crosses. After comparing their homework, Liu Jinding was sure of all the correct answers. In some cases, he could see at a glance where he had gone wrong, but sometimes it wasn't so obvious, and he had to slowly work it out. Luckily, he was very bright and quick on the uptake. Being able to compare the correct answers with his mistakes naturally helped his progress.

The first time the two of them spoke to each other was when Liu Jinding got full marks in his maths homework. On that day, when Wang Xiaomei put the homework books on the desk, she looked at him and said: "You got full marks."

"No way!"

"It's true."

"It's all thanks to you."

"I haven't done anything for you," she said indifferently.

"When I look at your book, you've got everything right and I can see how I went wrong."

Seeing how honest and open Liu Jinding was being, Wang Xiaomei said: "You need to have a wash."

Liu Jinding sniffed himself and asked: "Do I smell?"

The next morning, after finishing his morning laps, Liu Jinding brought two bowls to the side of the sports field. Standing beside the water pipe, he doused himself with them in front of everyone.

After that, the relationship between the two became a step closer. During their self-study English class, Wang Xiaomei went up to the dais to write the English blackboard text for the teacher, then secretly slipped Liu Jinding her Walkman, which was loaded with a tape called *Three Hundred English Phrases*. A Walkman was a rarity at that time, and Wang Xiaomei's father had brought hers back from Hong Kong. With the machine in the tray under the desk and an earpiece in one ear, if you leaned forward over the desktop and listened quietly, no one else could see what you were doing.

That winter, the south-facing windowsill of the girls' dormitory sported an extra potted chrysanthemum. It was a top specimen called snow sea, with large flowers of the purest white. As the sun flooded through the window, the mass of snow-white flowers in full bloom were reflected in the glass, just discernible like a mirage or something in a dream. Immediately below the windowsill was Wang Xiaomei's bed.

Moving on, there was a friendly exchange of notes between the two that went something like this:

Note 1: The composition of water is two parts hydrogen to one part oxygen, hence H_2O.

Note 2: Why is Number 3 wrong?

Note 3: y is a function of x; x is called the independent variable.

Note 4: Why does Lu Xun's character Kong Yiji drag himself along with his hands?

Note 5: Because his legs are broken.

Note 6: "The Peach Blossom Pool is a Thousand *Chi* Deep" is by

Li Bai. "The Nation is shattered but the Mountains and Rivers Remain" is by Du Fu.

Note 7: You've got dark rings round your eyes, Wang Wang. Aren't you sleeping well?

Note 8: So you're calling me Wang Wang, are you? I'm fine, I've got some pills to help me sleep now. My father came back last night, and he brought some Daoxiang Village cakes from Beijing. I've put some in the drawer for you.

Note 9: They've got those cold mustard noodles in the canteen. I'll save a portion for you.

Note 10: Be careful. The others are beginning to talk.

Note 11: Is it that fat girl again? Take no notice of her.

Note 12: Teresa Teng's "Small Town Story" is a great song.

Note 13: I like "Wolf from the North".

If something hadn't happened at home with Wang Xiaomei, this note "conversation" might have gone even further. Indeed, if it had gone on, it might really have grown into something.

On the second day back at school after the Spring Festival that year, all the female students were wearing the new clothes they had received for the New Year, each and every one of them resplendent. Wang Xiaomei was wearing a trendy, waisted, corn-yellow windcheater and a snow-white scarf. She looked very natural and elegant, and even the dark rings round her eyes gave her a kind of melancholic beauty. The other girls clustered round her, twittering praise for her fashionable jacket.

But she just replied vaguely: "Is it? Is it all right? I wasn't too sure."

After that, the "conversation" stopped. Liu Jinding remembered that she looked at him then, but it was a very confused and confusing look. Could he look back or not? Liu Jinding couldn't make sense of it. When they sat down in class, everything felt as usual with the position of their backsides. Liu Jinding said: "Did you have a good New Year?"

"All right," Wang Xiaomei replied. The answer seemed very abrupt, lacking any warmth or enthusiasm. In the course of about a year, everything seemed to go into reverse. Those note "conversations" that had gradually brought them closer together seemed to count for nothing, and it was as if they were starting again as strangers. At the time, although Liu Jinding was a little put out, he didn't really give it much more thought.

On the third morning, at the crack of dawn in the bright, cold schoolyard, the sound of confused footsteps could be heard, first heading this way, then that. The only other thing that could be heard was the headteacher's voice: "Is anyone there? The school doctor! Hurry up and get the school doctor!"

As if in response, Liu Jinding, who was about to go to the sports field to do his laps, came hurtling out of the boys' dormitory and headed straight over to Wang Xiaomei's girls' dormitory. On reaching the single storey "A Block" where the girls lived, he saw a crowd of teachers and girls standing round the door to Wang Xiaomei's dormitory. They were all chattering away about something. At that moment, the school doctor arrived. Staggering under the weight of a medicine chest, he hurried in, calling out: "Who? Who is it? What is it?"

"It's Wang Xiaomei," the fat girl said. "She's taken something!"

After the doctor had gone in, Liu Jinding could see the dormitory was in an uproar. Some people were searching everywhere for the medicine bottle, others were looking for a suicide note and yet others were trying to revive Wang Xiaomei. The school doctor shouted: "I want the headteacher and the class teacher to stay. The rest of you get out!"

After a while, the class teacher Mr Xu came running out of the dormitory and gestured, saying: "Any boys in Upper Second Number One Class come over here."

Liu Jinding and two other boys ran into the dormitory where they saw Wang Xiaomei lying on her bed still wearing the corn-yellow jacket, her hair loose and what looked like tears in the corners of her eyes. "Quick!" said the doctor. "Carry her to the infirmary!"

Liu Jinding was the first over to the bed. He picked her up then turned round, gripping her by one elbow, hoisted her onto his back and left. At that moment, he felt how soft she was, and how light. She was almost floating, like in a breeze.

Two hours later, Wang Xiaomei, who had clearly taken an overdose of something, was driven away in an ambulance. The wailing of the siren alarmed the whole school. Afterwards, the school immediately put out an emergency announcement to the effect that staff and students were forbidden to discuss the matter of Wang Xiaomei's overdose; they must not spread rumours or believe any gossip. Anyone spreading gossip or causing trouble in any way would be severely dealt with, and so on and so on. The verbal information given to every class teacher was that Wang Xiaomei was taking a year out of school for health reasons.

This was a big event in Weichuan Middle School, and the teachers as well as the students secretly passed on every little titbit of news and gossip. Some people said that they had it from a reliable source that, during the New Year holiday, Wang Xiaomei's father had started shouting about divorce and smashed up the kitchen pots. Someone else said that Wang Xiaomei's father, the deputy county-level cadre Wang Tianen, had been having an affair with a female cadre in the County Statistics Bureau. Another said that it wasn't the Statistics Bureau but a maid at the county guest house and she was only twenty-two. Gossip about Wang Xiaomei was flying around everywhere. It was being said that Wang Xiaomei was firmly on her mother's side and opposed to any divorce so she had swallowed a bottle of sleeping pills to use her death to force the issue. Or else, because everyone was always at loggerheads at home, Wang Xiaomei had developed mental problems, become neurotic and committed suicide by overdose. And so on and so on. On top of all that, what the students and teachers at Weichuan Middle School all thought was that Wang Xiaomei was Tsinghua or Peking University material, and it was a real shame.

During that time, Liu Jinding often stood by himself in the huge sports field, looking up at the night sky. The hazy, shadowy image of Wang Xiaomei sometimes appeared to him there, walking across the star-filled sky, clutching her homework book, her head slightly tilted to one side, looking very serious. Occasionally, she would look back, smiling, and ask: "Is that so?" It was something she often said. He turned the phrase over on his own tongue countless times. All Wang Xiaomei's notes were still tucked into his textbook. He was to keep them for many years. Sometimes he couldn't resist the urge to take them out and read them. The elegant, pen-written characters seemed to dance in front of his eyes like tiny candy figurines. Were these the signs of first love? He wasn't sure.

After this, the fat girl in his class became his desk mate and the old backside sensation had turned into something completely different and much heavier. The fat girl wrote him notes but Liu Jinding didn't reply to them. He crumpled them up and threw them in the wastepaper basket.

Seven years later, when he saw Wang Xiaomei again, she was already a cadre in the Meiling County Agricultural Office. He heard that she had got married but then very quickly divorced and was single again. When they met, the first thing she said was: "I know how you carried me out on your back."

SIX

16 APRIL WAS A VERY IMPORTANT DATE.

It was on that date one year that Liu Jinding met the most important person in his life.

The days leading up to the university entrance examination, the *gaokao*, were a very gloomy time for Liu Jinding. Although he was hard-working, when he took the frequent mock exams, he always came outside the top one hundred in the two hundred and forty-six students (plus those re-taking the exam) in the graduating year of the school. Because of this, his classmates came up with a nickname for him: 101. Overall, this meant that he was at least twenty per cent short of the minimum admission score of previous years.

(Many years later, when he was acting deputy mayor of Huanghuai, he chose car number "101" for himself. He felt it was his lucky number. Also, as a student, he had read a well-known novel called *Tracks in the Snowy Forest* in which the platoon commander, Shao Jianbo, has the nickname "Captain 203". He also later read a book about the former vice-premier Lin Biao which said that when he was in the Fourth Field Army, his code name was "Captain 101". At the time, the car number he really wanted to acquire was "001", but he didn't dare since he was only deputy mayor. A lot of this was actually going on in his subconscious mind.)

In his heart, he was quite clear that this was a turning point in his life: if he didn't pass the examination to get into university, he would have to go back and grow flowers with his father. He would be busy from one year end to the next with barely even time to wash. It didn't bear thinking about. Even if he did all right in the exam, the best he could hope for was a second-string university or a professional training college, and that wasn't going to cover him in glory. Of course, there was another way, but it involved passing through a narrow gateway that very few people could negotiate. That was not to sit the *gaokao* but go straight up to university through "school recommendation". He knew that the son of his class teacher, Teacher Xu, whose academic level was about the same as his, had secretly used his father's connections to do this.

It was at this critical moment that Xie Zhichang came to his aid again. Getting into university through school recommendation required a whole series of endorsements, and it had to be rubber-stamped at every level of the Department of Education. In addition, not only did it have to be supported by the school, the desired university also required the candidate to undergo an interview and a written test. This time, Xie Zhichang couldn't do it all by himself. He said: "The sheer number of stages makes it difficult, son. I'll see what I can do."

Gardener Liu Quanyou was squatting down, not saying a word, just weeping. Over the years, although Liu Quanyou had made a name for himself around the place, he had never earned very much money.

Things were pretty good where Weichuan Middle School was concerned. Over recent years, Xie Zhichang had already smoothed the way considerably, but there remained one hostage to fortune on the education authorities' side: although the school could make a recommendation, the relevant university also required personal contact with the student's family. That is to say, if the university accepted you, the school couldn't block you, but if the university request you of its own accord, Weichuan Middle School couldn't openly push the recommendation. This was all something that had to be kept secret because if the students got to hear about it, it could cause the school a lot of trouble. Once again, Flower Man Xie Zhichang showed his almost magical ability. Six months later, on 16 April, he came hurrying into the school, calling for Liu Jinding: "Come on! We've got to make a trip to the provincial capital!"

"Where are we going?" Liu Jinding asked.

"The University of Agricultural Science and Technology. I've fixed it all, and we're going to meet the principal." Liu Jinding hesitated. He wasn't sure about going through all this just to go to an agricultural science and technology university. Xie Zhichang continued: "Son, I've kowtowed my head off to find somewhere like this that is willing to take you. Besides, it's a topflight university. You'll come out of it set for life."

Seeing Liu Jinding still hesitating, Xie Zhichang continued: "Son, this is the best you'll get, so don't chuck it away. I know you want to go to Peking University, but I asked around and it's not just Peking University and Tsinghua, even the Beijing Institute of Technology, if you haven't got twenty or thirty thousand yuan to splash around, you won't get a look in."

That day, Liu Jinding went with Xie Zhichang to the provincial capital.

This was the first time Liu Jinding had been through the gates of a university. The University of Agricultural Science and Technology is huge. It feels as though it is bigger than the city itself, with red-walled building after red-walled building. Its roads twist and turn so you get lost walking along them and don't know which way to turn. The library is a particularly imposing building. It is like a maze inside, with numerous arched doors and staircases as though you could go on reading books all the way up to the heavens. The avenues are lined on both sides with sycamore trees whose branches form a natural archway. The whole campus is full of luxuriant flowers, grasses and lush trees, just like a botanical garden. The students stroll along in twos and threes in the shade of the trees, every one of them clearly very pleased with themselves. Although it is called the University of Agricultural Science and Technology, there are no crops to be seen. Surprisingly, cars are allowed to drive through the campus and it has a very "Western" look to it.

Once they were on the campus, Liu Jinding began to feel rather intimidated. Even though it was known simply as Agricultural Science University, it was, in fact, a top-level provincial capital research institution and a national-ranked university. He followed Xie Zhichang exclaiming in amazement, turning this way and that through more than three *li* of scenery until they came to a single-storey courtyard complex at the heart of the campus. Xie Zhichang wiped the sweat from his forehead and said: "This is it."

When they pushed open the gate, Liu Jinding finally saw the

crops. It was a very large courtyard that contained a lush green wheat field covering an area of about a third of a *mu*. There were already ears of grain on the stalks. A little old man – actually maybe not that old – was half-kneeling in the wheat field, holding a magnifying glass and a small ruler. He was talking to himself as he measured something. Beside him, there was a small hoe.

Liu Jinding only glanced at the old fellow and didn't take any more notice of him. But then, to his surprise, Xie Zhichang went over to the edge of the field, bowed and said warmly: "Are you busy, Uncle?"

Liu Jinding was taken aback. He looked at Xie Zhichang, then at the old fellow.

The old fellow looked up from where he was kneeling and regarded Xie Zhichang and then Liu Jinding standing next to him, appearing as though he was striving to remember something.

Xie Zhichang was unperturbed and said: "My name is Xie, Uncle, Xie Zhichang from Meiling. Last time I came, we talked about my family tree. My mother–"

To Liu Jinding's surprise, the old fellow slapped his forehead and burst out laughing: "Aiya! Zhichang! It's Zhichang! From my old hometown. You see, I do remember!"

Xie Zhichang indicated Liu Jinding, saying: "This is my nephew on my wife's side, Liu Jinding. I told you about him." Turning to Liu Jinding, he continued: "This is the principal of the university. You should call him 'Great Uncle'."

Once reminded that these were family and fellow townsmen, the principal became most affable. He stood up, dusted himself down, cleared his throat twice and said: "Hurry up now. Let's go inside and sit down." Listening to him, he had a full-on Meiling accent.

When they went inside, carrying their gifts, Xie Zhichang pulled Liu Jinding back and whispered: "Take your shoes off! Take your shoes off!"

The principal heard him, and waved his hand, saying: "No need, no need. There's no need for ceremony with guests from home." Even so, he himself removed the cloth shoes he was wearing. Thereupon, Xie Zhichang and Liu Jinding hastily changed into the sandals laid out by the door.

Once inside, they saw how neat and tidy the home was of this senior officer of the Agricultural University who looked so much like an old peasant farmer. It was astonishingly clean. Everywhere was polished to a shine without a speck of dirt anywhere. It couldn't help but make people ask themselves: What kind of woman runs this household?

When they were sat down on the sofa, the principal – who they later discovered was actually only deputy principal at the time – suddenly turned serious and said: "Zhichang, when friends from home come visiting, they don't bring gifts. You should know that."

"I do know that," Xie Zhichang said hurriedly. "But when a nephew comes to see his uncle, he shouldn't come empty-handed, should he!"

"No, that's not right either," the principal said. "You should take them away."

Treading carefully, Xie Zhichang responded: "It's such a long way and they're here now. It wouldn't be setting any kind of precedent."

But the principal gestured in disagreement, saying: "It can't be done. You must take them away."

At this point, Liu Jinding's heart sank and his face reddened. If the man didn't accept the gifts, he felt that that would be that. By the look of it, Big Mouth Xie had reached a dead end, too. Half hanging his head, Liu Jinding looked timidly at the principal, afraid he was going to say something even worse.

Inspecting him more closely, the principal seemed to be in his forties, although he was going grey at the temples. The rest of his hair was very neat with not a strand out of place. His face was copper-coloured and craggy like the hills, but the edges and corners were clear and distinct. He had three rows of wrinkles like ditches across his forehead that looked as though they had been dried out by the sun. His teeth had many years of dark staining that was undoubtedly caused by excessive smoking. Although he wasn't tall, he had an imposing and impressive appearance, and his eyes had a forbidding look to them. He was wearing a hand-stitched Chinese-style jacket with two rows of knotted thread buttons, jeans and a new pair of cloth shoes with rounded openings (the pair he had taken off at the door were old ones). If you only took him at face value, he was the very image of a regular peasant farmer. In particular, his accent was pure, old-style Meiling, not differentiating between *si* (four) and *shi* (ten), and that is something deep in the bone.

Perhaps it was the sight of Liu Jinding sitting uneasily on the edge of the sofa, squirming his buttocks and looking uncomfortable, that inspired a surge of sympathetic affection in the principal. At any rate, he suddenly pointed at Liu Jinding and said: "He's a fine lad. You mustn't lead a boy from our old hometown astray, Zhichang!"

"We've just come to visit you, Uncle, so he knows his great uncle's circumstances. That's all there is to it."

The principal looked serious and thought for a moment. Then he gestured again, saying: "A drink! We need a midday drink! And a smoke, of course. Remember, there won't always be a next time!"

"Surely we can't have lunch with you here," Xie Zhichang replied. "You must be busy."

"Nonsense!" the principal exclaimed. "If someone comes visiting from the old place, do you think I'm not even going to give them a meal?"

"No, no! You're too busy..." Xie Zhichang replied.

"Didn't you say the lad wants to come to this university? Then you must eat here. If you leave now, don't bother coming back another time!"

As the mood lightened, Liu Jinding breathed a secret sigh of relief.

Although the principal was insistent on inviting his fellow countrymen to lunch, when he checked his watch, he said: "I'm so sorry, but my wife doesn't like to be disturbed. Come on, we'll go out to eat."

On their way to lunch, Xie Zhichang told Liu Jinding: "Don't be fooled by the principal. He really is a top official!" Then he moved a bit closer and whispered in his ear: "He's henpecked! He's scared of his wife."

They went to the small dining hall of the university. It had a number of private rooms, and the principal chose one and told his guests to go in. As host, the principal ordered four dishes and a soup. It was a simple meal: a dish of fried peanuts, five-spice braised pig's trotters, "fish fragrant" pork slivers, flash-fried mutton with onions and hot-and-sour egg-drop soup. For fillers, there were two bowls of rice and one of noodles. The principal said he preferred his noodles chewy like tendons. When the dishes arrived, he raised his chopsticks and said: "Don't hold back, eat up." Then, he went on: "Open the wine, Zhichang, and have a drink. I've got my wife to answer to and I can't drink too much these days. I won't have more than two cups."

But once they started drinking, it certainly wasn't a case of just two cups. Xie Zhichang was an expert toaster with wine, and every toast he proposed was well-founded. The drinking went on, and the principal became expansive. He said: "Do you know what I ate when I was studying at Columbia University in America? A hamburger every day, just one hamburger. I was so hungry, my ribs were sticking to my spine. It was so bad that there was nothing else for it, and every day I began to eat the wheat shoots in the laboratory."

After they had drunk a certain amount, the principal's eyes were a little unfocused when he suddenly pointed at Liu Jinding and said: "I've only got a daughter. It would be better if I could have a son like you."

Not one to miss such an opportunity, Xie Zhichang said: "He is the child of my family and you should consider him your disciple. If you let him spend more time with you, he would do everything you tell him."

At that point, Liu Jinding hurriedly stood up and said: "We shouldn't let the principal drink any more." He went over to the door of the private room, took a towel from the washbasin stand and poured out some hot water from the flask. He wrung out the towel, folded it neatly into a square and offered it to the principal with both hands. He waited for the principal to wipe his face, took back the towel, turned away and then went back to the principal similarly offering him a toothpick. He did all this without saying a word.

"It's Jinding, isn't it?" the principal asked.

"When I was little," Jinding responded, "my father had my fortune told using the 'eight characters' and it showed that, of the five elements, I was deficient in metal (金, *jīn*). So my father gave me the name 金定 (*jīn dìng*, meaning 'settling the metal'). It was me who changed it later to 金鼎 (*jīn dǐng*, meaning 'gold [metal] tripod')."

SEVEN

FROM THEN ON, it took more than just an ordinary sort of person for Liu Jinding to consider them a VVIP.

The first time Liu Jinding met him, he already had some pretty "showy" titles: an American PhD, deputy principal of the University of Agricultural Science and Technology, leading expert in wheat, expert adviser to the Ministry of Agriculture, committee member of the Chinese Government's "863 Programme" to promote the development of advanced technologies, etc. Four years later, when Liu Jinding graduated, he was deputy provincial governor in charge of agriculture at the age of forty-seven.

In fact, based on his popular reputation and his unusual talents that made him a model national expert, some people predicted he would go right to the top.

His name was Li Delin, and he was originally from Meiling. Whenever he used the telephone, he always announced himself as Lao Li.

After Liu Jinding met Lao Li, his luck underwent a significant change. He reckoned that every step he took in life was connected somehow to Li Delin. By the time Liu Jinding was deputy mayor of Huanghuai, he was no longer calling him "Principal", but rather addressed him very respectfully indeed as "Teacher".

He had never actually been taught by this Teacher, whose field was genetic engineering. Liu Jinding himself studied agricultural machinery systems at the university. He had only heard him give one open lecture on the subject of hereditary genetics. He hadn't understood a word.

To tell the truth, Liu Jinding didn't enjoy agricultural machinery, and had never really wanted to attend the University of Agricultural Science and Technology in the first place. But his "school recommendation" gave him no option but to go there. Back then, when he met Li Delin for the second time, Li asked him: "What do you want to major in?" Liu hummed and hawed, not knowing what would be best. Li Delin wagged a finger at him, saying: "Study agricultural machinery. The country needs talent in that field."

Every day of his four years at the University of Agriculture was a struggle. As far as his classwork went, because he was bright, he managed the classwork fine but without enjoying it. He also read a lot of novels during those four years. He particularly liked the mysterious and equivocal character Xiao Bairu in *Tracks in the Snowy Forest*, and for a while she was his fantasy lover. And there was the character

Captain 203 who was being pursued by Xiao Bairu. He liked the nickname "203", it sounded really impressive. He also read *Lady Chatterley's Lover* and even thought he could smell the scent of a woman as he did so. It was still a banned book at the time, and the students had to make do with a single shared copy. The lustful thoughts it filled him with at night necessitated frequent trips to the bathroom. Then there was Victor Hugo's *Ninety-Three* in which a trivial mistake causes a disaster. But right on the brink of that disaster, the old marquis' coolness in the face of calamity as he stands on the deck of the warship with the cannonballs rolling about around him, left a deep impression on Liu Jinding. The man was a true aristocrat of the old school! And what about *Le Destin Secret de Georges Pompidou* in which the protagonist's skill with words turns a middle school teacher into a president...

It was only many years later that Liu realised that what he had studied at university was not "agricultural machinery", but "human life". At the time, he longed for the chance to talk romantic love with someone, but the problem was, there wasn't a single pretty girl in the Department of Agricultural Machinery. Perhaps all those novels he was reading raised his sights too high, but in his eyes, all the female students in his department were hideously ugly. Occasionally, he would think of Wang Xiaomei and those days of exchanging notes at Weichuan Middle School. How wonderful they had been! But he never heard any news of her.

Xie Zhichang visited the department several times, hoping to get the principal to hook him up with flower and plant businesses through his contacts, but every time he was sent packing in no uncertain terms. "What kind of person do you take me for? This is a university!"

Privately, Xie Zhichang moaned to Liu Jinding: "What's he playing at? A big noise like him, and he won't even give me a little help!"

Even so, he still urged Liu Jinding to hang around Lao Li's place as much as possible, keep on the alert and be as attentive possible for anything that might help him after graduation.

But Liu Jinding was just an ordinary university student, and it wasn't easy for him to get to see Lao Li, who was a very busy man. From time to time, he went to the secluded little square courtyard at the rear of the campus, and several times saw the principal's wife. But every time he was very curtly "invited" to leave.

Indeed, the principal's wife never allowed Liu any kind of face, and in his eyes, she really acted like the stony-hearted beauty. The first time he went there was a Sunday. That morning, he bought a basket of fruit and walked to and fro in front of the courtyard gates before finally plucking up courage to knock on the principal's door. When the door opened, standing there was a tall, dignified woman with her hair pinned up on her head. She was wearing a long skirt and on her pretty, pale face, under slightly raised eyebrows, a pair of clear, coldly forbidding eyes gazed out. "Who do you want?" she demanded.

Her look stopped Liu Jinding dead in his tracks. He certainly didn't dare bring up his supposed distant relationship to the principal, and even forgot to say that he was from Lao Li's hometown. All he managed was: "Is... is the principal in?"

Just as coolly as before, the principal's wife replied: "No."

Liu Jinding stood awkwardly, and for a moment he couldn't think what to say next. Lamely, he offered the basket of fruit, saying: "I just came..."

The principal's wife didn't even glance at what he was holding, and just said: "He's not in. Please come back another time." And with that, she shut the door.

The first time he had the door shut in his face, Liu Jinding stood there for a long time. A buzzing started in his head, and it took him a good while to pull himself together. The first thing he thought of was Xie Zhichang. If it had been Big Mouth Xie there, would he still be standing outside the door? Of course not! Big Mouth seemed to have the knack of being able to open any door that got in his way. That was when Liu Jinding realised that if he was going to get anywhere, he would have to grow a thicker skin. The next time he went, he didn't hang around the courtyard gates, but went straight in, picked up a broom and began sweeping the yard. When he had swept up all the fallen leaves, the door of the house opened, and the principal's wife appeared.

She had obviously just washed her hair, as it was hanging loose and smelling fresh and fragrant. Its indescribably subtle perfume filled the yard. She was wearing a snow-white embroidered silk gown and standing elegantly in the doorway. Just as rudely as before, she said: "Who said you could come in?"

He was rather taken aback and stammered out: "My... my uncle."

"And who is your uncle?" she asked.

"Xie... Xie Zhichang."

"And who is Xie Zhichang? I don't know him."

"He's a relative of the principal's from his old home, back in Meiling."

"You think you can just come in here as you please, saying you're a fellow villager? I don't care if you're a seventh cousin or an eighth great aunt, you weren't invited... so just leave."

The way she said "leave" seemed to Liu Jinding to be a little less cutting than the icy "please" of the previous occasion. Nonetheless, he put down the broom and hurried out.

He didn't know why, but secretly, deep down inside, he rather appreciated this kind of rudeness. The principal's wife's indifference somehow enhanced her glamour. To his mind, this was precisely the tone such a beautiful and elegant woman should adopt. He found the sound of her voice and the fragrance of her hair intoxicating. Her "just leave" was far more appealing than any "hello".

It wasn't long before Liu Jinding's musing led to a degree of infatuation. He was possessed by her glamour. Often, when he was on the running track, her image would appear in front of him. She had a mature, lofty, utterly distinctive beauty of the kind that is made all the more alluring by its unintentional provocativeness. The effect of that "just leave" was the same as when he and some of his classmates had eaten some wasabi: both shocking and exhilarating. And it lingered in his imagination, just as the spiciness of the wasabi had done on his tongue. Once, in a dream, he plucked up the courage to caress the breasts of the principal's wife, which were cool and firm and round like peaches. He woke up in a cold sweat.

He even began to feel that the principal and his wife were two completely different sorts of people and entirely unsuited to one another. How unjust heaven was to let an old man who looked more like a peasant than a real peasant, marry a beautiful woman like her. Of course, that was it! If he didn't have an American PhD and all those other flashy qualifications, would she even have spared him a second glance? Hard to be sure, though. Anyway, although he would never dare do anything, there was nothing wrong with thinking about it, was there!

For some time after this, the little demons inside him made him go back every Sunday to sweep the principal's yard, only now he wasn't just hoping to get to see the principal. His head was all over the place. From time to time, he would hear something that gave him pause for thought, the sound of a window blind, the rustling of some kind of activity or even the patter of footsteps. But the principal's wife never came out again, even to tell him to go away. He didn't make a nuisance of himself, but just swept the yard and went away.

Then, on one occasion, the principal's wife suddenly came out of the house, looked at him and said: "I heard Lao Li say you're studying agricultural machinery. Is that right?"

"Yes," Liu Jinding replied hurriedly.

"And you're from Meiling?"

"Yes."

"Stop sweeping. You can go see him in his office."

She was much more polite this time. She had never "invited" him into the house before.

By now, it was shortly after graduation. When Liu Jinding saw Li Delin in his office, the principal was as little on his dignity as before, and just as friendly. "Well, my young friend, sit down," he said. "Do you smoke? Here, take one."

"Thank you, but I don't smoke," Liu Jinding replied.

Li Delin seemed a little on edge. He fiddled with a box, picking it up and putting it down again, then said: "It's good that a youngster like you doesn't smoke." He fell silent for a moment, before asking: "Have you graduated?"

"Yes."

Li Delin shook his head and muttered to himself: "Yes, I suppose I really should do it." He sounded rather distressed. Then he suddenly asked: "What do you think? Should I or shouldn't I?"

Liu Jinding knew that, for a while now, the whole university had been quietly discussing the rumour that the principal had secretly been chosen as the next deputy provincial governor. It must be true then! Liu Jinding replied: "Yes, sure, it must be a good thing!"

"A good thing?"

"Of course! You don't know how happy all of us in Meiling will be to have a top official to our credit. I'm sure you'll go on to be governor."

"Not necessarily." Li Delin sounded doubtful and really rather worried by something. He struck a match with a "whoosh", lit a cigarette and took a few puffs. Perhaps because Liu Jinding was from the same village and didn't have any rank or influence, Li Delin felt he was harmless and it didn't matter if he spoke more openly: "I'll tell you the real truth, young man. I'm just someone who grows plants. I grow some wheat and give a few lectures, and that's all. I'm not interested in doing anything else."

"You're a nationally acclaimed expert. What's in a deputy governor's job you think you can't do? Of course, you'll be governor sooner or later. That's what I reckon."

Li Delin shook his head, smiling, and said: "Well, you're not shy about giving an opinion, are you, young man! And you're very persuasive. But if I take this step, there may be no going back."

Liu Jinding hesitated, not knowing what to say next. If the man became provincial governor, why would he want to "go back"? Surely, no matter how high the target, the only way was up!

Li Delin nipped out his cigarette, and said: "You should know, young man, that my wife is dead set against me being deputy governor." Then he continued, talking to himself: "It's like she wants me to solve Goldbach's Conjecture... it's just some Arabian Nights fantasy isn't it!"

The mention of the principal's wife stopped Liu Jinding in his tracks, but he did say one more very important thing: "Everyone in Meiling really hopes you become provincial governor."

"That's enough talking about me, it's giving me a headache," Li Delin said. "Let's talk about you. Now you've graduated, what do you think you'll do?"

Liu Jinding looked at him eagerly, but didn't reply.

"You want to join the faculty here, is that it?"

Liu Jinding still didn't express an opinion, and just said: "I'll take your advice."

Li Delin walked up and down his office for a bit and said: "It's not impossible for you to join the faculty, but the question is whether you stay with your specialty in agricultural machinery, or go back to basics. I think you'd be better off going back to basics."

That was the last thing Liu Jinding wanted to do, but he repeated: "I'll take your advice."

"Here's what we'll do. I'm going to write a note for you to take back to Meiling. All right?"

When Li Delin said "write a note", he didn't realise he was beginning to talk like a deputy governor.

Liu Jinding was dismayed as he left the principal's office clutching Li Delin's hand-written letter. He really didn't want to return to Meiling. He had been away at university for four years. What was going home now all about? He couldn't help feeling a bit resentful as he thought to himself: You're going to be a provincial governor soon, old man. Why can't you find me a suitable position in the provincial capital? Even so, however he looked at it, he couldn't help believing that there had to be something magical about this "note". After thinking about it for a few days, he came to see that going back to basics was actually a very important step for him.

As he walked along the tree-lined road on the campus, Liu Jinding's thoughts turned again to that "cold beauty", the principal's wife. He knew that he had been in that courtyard, through those doors, for the last time. But he still couldn't help wondering just what kind of a woman she was. She was certainly nothing like the principal; they came from two different worlds. How did they even manage to live under the same roof?

It was only when he was about to leave the university that he found out her name was Luo Qiuyi, and she was the daughter of a professor. That went some way to explaining the situation, as those scholarly types like to keep things neat and stick together. Even so, he was proved right in the end. Not long after Li Delin was made deputy provincial governor, he and his wife got divorced. There was nothing acrimonious about it, no shouting or raging, they just agreed to separate.

Goodbye, University of Agricultural Science and Technology.

Farewell, Qiuyi.

EIGHT

IN JULY THAT YEAR, Liu Jinding rolled up his bedding and went back to Meiling.

43

After arriving home, he slept for three days and felt totally dejected. Four years at university, and there he was dragging his bedroll back home. How could he look anyone in the face?

When Gardener Liu Quanyou saw his son coming home, he was delighted. But his son was sulking and didn't say a word to him. He had been working with plants and flowers all these years, and his back was getting increasingly bent, he himself was getting older and older, and becoming more and more taciturn. When his son returned, all he asked was: "How are things in the big city?" Liu Jinding thought the question too hackneyed to merit an answer, and just grunted. Liu Quanyou was worried when he saw his son go to bed, not eating or drinking anything, and he didn't know what to do. He went into Liu Jinding's bedroom, paced up and down a bit, felt his son's forehead to check he wasn't feverish, and then went out again.

One night, Liu Quanyou sat down at his son's bedside and said quietly: "I've still got a few really good bonsai. You can give them to whoever you want."

Ten days after returning to Meiling, Liu Jinding finally took his Certificate of Dispatch from the university to the Personnel Bureau. He thought to himself: I'm still a university graduate, after all. The least they can do is find me something in the county town. There are a couple of work units that would do there. The best is the Bureau of Agriculture, but the Agricultural Technology Station would do at a pinch. I'd prefer the bureau, but I'll make do if I have to. In any case, he could still get Big Mouth Xie to get to work on his behalf. But he felt he had already asked too many favours, and he didn't really want to do that. As for Lao Li's "note", he hadn't done anything with that yet. He was going to wait and see with that.

To his surprise, a month later, he received a work assignment. He was being sent to the county's most remote Agricultural Technology Station in Miaotai Township. He asked around and discovered that there were only three people at the station: a station head and two technicians. They didn't even get paid a salary but had to get their money from the seeds they were able to sell.

Even then, Liu Jinding still didn't produce the deputy governor's note, and there was a reason for that: he had taken a peek at its contents. What it said, in essence, was that he hoped Liu would get a posting at grassroots level. Well, so much for that! Even without the note, he couldn't get any more "grassroots" than the Miaotai Station.

It was then that Liu Jinding plucked up courage and went to the County Government Office. The director there was called Tang, who seemed to be a kind and well-intentioned sort. When Liu Jinding got to the offices, Director Tang asked him: "Who are you looking for?"

"County Commissioner Xue."

Director Tang laughed. "Do you know how busy the county commissioner is? What's it about?"

"I've got a letter for him."

"If it's a petition, turn right and go to the Petitions Office."

"It's not a petition. I've got a hand-written letter for him from the provincial governor. Governor Li told me to deliver it in person."

Director Tang stood up when he heard this and invited Liu Jinding to sit down. He went and poured him a glass of water which he put down on the table in front of Liu Jinding. Then he hurried out of the room. After a while, he hurried back in and said: "Follow me."

That was how Lao Li's note was finally deployed. And, incredibly, a couple of weeks later a new posting for Liu Jinding arrived: it was to the County Agricultural Technology Station as deputy director.

Liu Jinding couldn't be sure whether this new posting wasn't the result of some kind of mix-up. That day, he had met with County Commissioner Xue and put down his "note" in front of him. The commissioner had looked at his old classmate's letter over and over again, taken in the few lines of bold cursive script and not uttered a word. What made the difference, of course, was his old high-school classmate now being the deputy provincial governor in charge of agriculture.

After Liu Jinding had left, Commissioner Xue called Director Tang into his office. He waved the letter at him and banged the table, asking: "What's this then?"

Director Tang went over to the desk and looked at the letter. "It's asking you to train him up from grassroots level, isn't it?"

"Yes, that's right, but isn't he already a graduate? Where can I send him? And to do what? Eh?"

"Send him to the Miaotai Station."

"Yes, that's grassroots all right. But is that all there is to it?"

"Maybe... maybe it's a bit too 'grassroots'. I don't suppose he'd want to go, would he?"

"Shit no, he's studied it all already, but what else can we do?"

Director Tang suggested cautiously: "I think there a few things you need to give careful consideration to here. One, Li Delin is deputy provincial governor in charge of agriculture and controls twenty million in liquid funds, and he decides who gets what. Two, we are a big agricultural county and he gives final approval to any major project. Three, in my experience, a provincial governor doesn't hand notes like that to people at the drop of a hat. If he has written it, then he–"

"You're right, you're right," said Commissioner Xue, slapping his forehead. "He may be an old classmate, but he is deputy provincial governor now. How about I give him a call and ask him?"

Director Tang said cautiously: "Do you think that would really be appropriate?"

Commissioner Xue had been about to reach for the telephone, but he stopped and said: "You think not?"

"No. Suppose you do ring him? He may well just say: 'I think he shows promise and I want him trained up from grassroots level, that's all.' What would you say then?"

Commissioner Xue scratched his head and said: "Nonsense. He's a straightforward sort, he wouldn't be that devious."

"You think not? You have to be very careful with letters like this."

"Not really. Anything official from the deputy provincial governor has to carry his official stamp. That's the law."

"I checked the date. He wrote this three days before he took up the post..."

"So it's not an official request from the deputy governor, then?"

"It's precisely because it was written before he took up the post that even more..." He didn't finish the sentence.

Finally, Commissioner Xue said: "Here's what we'll do. I'll initial the letter and hand it on to the Personnel Office. They can look at it and decide."

And that's what happened. Once the letter had undergone analysis by Tang Mingsheng, director of the County Government Office, it became something much more complex.

Everyone in Meiling County knew that Tang Mingsheng was a

good man, low-key, humble and prudent, never over-reaching himself. However, he was also shrewd, capable, careful and thoughtful, and he had won the trust of his superiors. Anything that was handed over to Tang Mingsheng was bound to be handled properly.

Liu Jinding hadn't heard of Tang Mingsheng at the time. All he knew was that after he handed over the note, things had changed miraculously. The county had been going to send him to the Agricultural Technology Station in Miaotai Township, but in the blink of an eye, he had become deputy head of the County Agricultural Technology Station. Was it a dream? Whatever the reason, it had to be said that the deputy governor's note had done its work.

Later on, Liu Jinding became good friends with Tang Mingsheng, and later on still, ended up as his boss. His opinion of him always remained the same: that he was "a good man".

For Liu Jinding, the miracles kept on coming. Once he had gone through all the formalities, he reported for duty the day before National Day. When he arrived, the old director of the Agricultural Technology Station complained loudly, saying: "This is balls! I've already got three deputy directors, and they've sent me another!"

"So what are my duties?" Liu Jinding asked him.

Somewhat irrelevantly, the old director replied: "Well to start with, no one gets any fucking favours here. Everyone gets one wicker chair."

Six months later, Liu Jinding began to feel that his wicker chair was a little cold and draughty, so he added a foam cushion. But before his buttocks had even warmed up, a directive came down making him deputy mayor of Guanzhuangxiang. The Agricultural Technology Station had just been a standard posting, and the deputy directorship was indeed only a deputy post. The post as deputy mayor was at associate level. In Meiling, associate level and above made you a proper official, so Liu Jinding had now definitely entered the bureaucratic arena.

When the appointment was announced, Tang Mingsheng, who was already director of the County Party Committee Office, made a point of telling him that when Governor Li had come home to visit his family during the Qingming Festival, he had mentioned Liu Jinding. Just a few words though, Tang Mingsheng said.

Tang Mingsheng was a very cautious individual and never

revealed more than was absolutely necessary. There was, in fact, a lot that he didn't tell. Meiling had an unwritten rule that any high-up who arrived, no matter which faction they represented, if they were at deputy departmental level or above, had to make a "report" at the first available opportunity. What this meant was that they had to report to the secretary of the County Party Committee and the county commissioner as soon as possible, and a reception party had to be held for them at the first convenient opportunity. This came about because of a mistake, some time before. A newly promoted deputy director of the Provincial Finance Department passed through Meiling and was stopped and fined by the traffic police. The Finance Department official was so furious he found an excuse to delay payment of the already allocated local government funding. When the secretary of the County Party Committee got to hear about it, all hell broke loose. The director of the County Party Committee Office was disciplined and transferred. From then on, the rule was applied for any visiting high-up. The problem was, it was very difficult to enforce, because no one knew when a high-up was going to arrive. It was fine if it was an official visit because that would be announced in advance, but if it was a private visit, what then? It was Tang Mingsheng who thought up a way of handling it. He ordered someone to set up hotlines in the offices of the Provincial Party Committee, the Provincial Government and the Provincial Party Committee Logistics Department. He was a sort of "information officer" who visited each office every year to collect a so-called "consulting fee". In this way, everyone got to hear about an upcoming visit by a high-up, no matter whether it was on public business or private.

But when Li Delin came back to Meiling to visit his family that Qingming Festival, at first no one knew about it. He hadn't told anyone he was coming, except for his chauffeur. In order to submit his expenses, the chauffeur told the section chief of the chauffeur team, and the section chief told his deputy department head. So when Li Delin's car came off the expressway and was just crossing into Meiling County, he had a big shock.

On the county boundary between Meiling and Chang, a grand convoy of a dozen or more limousines had pulled up with a row of people standing in front of them. There were also two girls in uniform dresses, standing in the cold wind, holding bouquets in their hands.

In each of the previous Qingming Festivals, he had come back to visit the family graves, but it always involved just a quick trip. He might also greet a few old classmates and have a meal in the county town. This time, however, it was different. This time, he was a deputy provincial governor, and the top brass of all four County Departments had unexpectedly come to the county boundary to welcome him.

As soon as the car stopped, the bigwigs gathered around. They stood in a row in front of the car, some pulling open the door, some holding flowers. An irate Li Delin stepped out of the car and said: "What do you think you are doing, Lao Xue? You're going to get me in trouble, making a fuss of me like this!"

Relying on the fact he was an old classmate, the former county commissioner and new secretary of the County Party Committee, Xue Zhiheng, laughed and said: "You've come back, Your Honour, and didn't breathe a word about it so you could reprimand us. Some people might call that bullying!"

"It's a private visit," Li Delin said. "I'm not stopping long. I'm going home to visit the family graves and see my old father. All this pomp and ceremony is outrageous!" He cupped his hands in salute, and went on: "Thank you, but why don't you all go home and let me get on with my own business?"

"Allow me to explain, first," Xue Zhiheng responded. "We haven't come to greet the provincial governor, we've come to welcome an expert, a national expert in wheat propagation. I seem to remember that you are still a consultant to our County Agricultural Technology Institute, aren't you? You never resigned, did you?"

"Let me stress again," Li Delin said. "I'm on a private visit. If you make this kind of show over me now, do you think I'm ever likely to come back?"

"I know it's a private visit, and I know you are very busy. I don't want to delay you, but you have to take a little time to brush the dust off and have something to eat, surely?"

"I'll just have a quick bowl of noodles and be on my way."

"What about our local wine? You could really help make a name for it! Surely you'll have a glass or two!"

"I've come back to visit my family graves. What would it look like if I went there all red-faced with wine? I'll have some next time."

"Not even a drop?"

"Not even a drop!"

"All right, we'll do things your way, OK?"

They had lunch at the County Party Committee's guest house. It was only supposed to be a simple meal, but it was still very lavish. There was squid, sea cucumbers and imported lobsters.

"What's all this?" Li Delin said. "We agreed I'd have a bowl of noodles, so why did you lay on all this?"

"The noodles will be here soon. Anyway, without wine, it's not a banquet, just a meal," Xue Zhiheng replied.

The two men were old classmates, and Xue Zhiheng didn't want to show off, but equally he didn't want to let the side down and fail to show his old friend sufficient respect. The two of them talked about local affairs and about old classmates and as they were chatting away merrily, Li Delin took the opportunity to ask: "I had a student called Liu Jinding. Did he come and look you up?"

"He did. It's all fixed up."

"What do you make of him?"

"He's all right. He shows some promise."

At this point, Tang Mingsheng, the director of the County Office interjected: "Secretary Xue has fixed him up at the County Agricultural Technology Station."

"He's very young to have a county position, isn't he?" Li Delin said. "Didn't I say he should start at grassroots level?"

"Yes, he is young, but he's very keen," Xue Zhiheng replied.

"Youngsters should start at the bottom, so they get proper training," Li Delin observed with a wave of his hand, sounding quite offhand about it.

After lunch, Li Delin announced emphatically: "You all stay here and we'll say our goodbyes, so I can have some privacy."

"How about this?" Xue Zhiheng replied. "I'll go with you to see your parents. Just me."

"If that's how you want things, I'll go straight back to the city now."

"All right, all right, have it your way. Off you go, all of you, and we'll give Governor Li his privacy."

And that's the way the day went. Li Delin really was just an ordinary person on a visit home and he didn't allow any entourage. When his car was about half a kilometre outside the village, he stopped and got out. Then he walked back into the village on his own. He had six packs of cigarettes stuffed in the various pockets of his jacket and when he reached the entrance to the village, he started calling out to various degrees of relatives, greeting each one individually and offering them cigarettes. When all the cigarettes were gone, he went home.

It wasn't long before word had spread all round the village that Lao Li had come home, and even though he was provincial governor, he was still just the same as before. Of course, this only served to confirm and burnish his reputation as a "people's governor".

The day after Li Delin left, Xue Zhiheng took Tang Mingsheng with him to make a special visit to Li Delin's father. In the car, Xue Zhiheng raised the question of Liu Jinding again. "We fixed things for Lao Li," he said, "so why did he keep talking about starting at the bottom? What's that all about?"

"I know," Tang Mingsheng replied. "We fixed it all up nicely, and he still went back to... Anyway, Governor Li approved ten million for that big project in our county."

"And you think he still might not be happy with us? No way. I'm an old classmate of his, and that's not the way his mind works."

"There's something I need to tell you, Secretary Xue. Recently, there has been a flood of memos from the authorities saying that cadres need to be younger and better informed. All the cadres in our county at the middle level and above are getting on a bit. The average age is fifty-two-and-a-half. Perhaps we should be doing something about it..."

Xue Zhiheng nodded and said: "You're right, that is quite old. Let's discuss it at the next meeting. Maybe we should think about Liu Jinding. He's still a youngster, isn't he?"

Maybe it was all a misunderstanding, but Li Delin had mentioned Liu Jinding at the lunch table, and that was a fact. And it was also a fact that Liu Jinding was very quickly promoted to deputy mayor.

Liu Jinding had no idea that the principal of his university had come home to visit his family. All he knew was that one sentence Tang Mingsheng had said to him, which had got him all excited. It meant that the principal still remembered him. He hadn't even been back in Meiling for a year yet, but he was getting one promotion after another. He wasn't going to forget that kind of favour in a hurry.

Xie Zhichang came dashing over to see him too, saying: "I hear you've been made mayor. The whole county knows about what the provincial governor said. You should go and see Lao Li. He's done you a huge favour."

The next Sunday, Liu Jinding made a special trip to the provincial capital.

Li Delin was still living in the courtyard at the rear of the campus of the University of Agricultural Science and Technology. Liu Jinding looked around him as he went in through the gates, and when he didn't see any slippers at the front door, he asked: "Should I change my shoes?"

Li Delin was wearing a pair of battered old cloth shoes, and he said, as he continued walking: "Change them? No! What's the point?"

Li Delin might have become deputy provincial governor, but the house certainly wasn't as clean as it had been before. The ashtray on the coffee table was almost overflowing and the wastepaper basket beside it was full of old instant noodle pots. There was a crumpled pillow on the sofa. It would have been unimaginable in the past. Then Liu Jinding remembered: the principal had got divorced!

Despite his status as deputy provincial governor, Li Delin was still very normal and matter-of-fact. "Sit down," he said. "Sit where you like."

"You need to hire a cleaner, Mr Principal, sir," Liu Jinding said.

"I have. She works on hourly rates."

Liu Jinding had brought four cartons of Zhonghua cigarettes with him, which he had wrapped in newspaper. He secretly put them down in a corner of the sofa and said: "I've been thinking of you, Principal, so I came to see you. But I'm afraid I didn't bring anything."

"You were quite right not to. If things aren't going too well for you back there, what good is it you rushing up here? Why have you come?"

"No, no, there's nothing wrong. You've always treated me like a son, so I just wanted to come and see you. But I do have one small request."

"Go on."

"I want to take you out for a meal. You choose where."

"A meal, eh? Have you brought any money?"

"I have."

"And I can choose where?"

"Wherever you like, Principal."

Li Delin checked his watch and said: "All right then, follow me."

As it was autumn, Li Delin put on a baseball cap as he led the pair out, pulling the peak down low.

Liu Jinding looked around when they were outside and asked: "Aren't we going by car?"

"No need. Just follow me."

The two of them, one behind the other, went out of a little gate at the rear of the campus and followed the street. From a distance, no one could possibly tell that the man in the baseball cap was a deputy provincial governor. He just looked like a little old man.

Liu Jinding followed him at a leisurely pace down the street. They crossed four road junctions before turning into a narrower street, which Liu saw from the sign was called Shuncheng Street. Li Delin stopped in front of the door of a braised noodle restaurant and said: "Here we are."

Liu Jinding hesitated at the doorway. The restaurant had a double front and looked very dirty and chaotic. He asked hesitantly: "Is this the place. Are you sure–"

"This is the place. The noodles are delicious. They serve them by the ladleful, one ladle per bowl. I'll get some seats, you queue to order."

And that is exactly what the restaurant was: it served noodles by the ladleful, one ladle per bowl. They were served with mutton, and they added so many chillies that sweat would break out all over your body when you ate them. It wasn't a big place so there was always a queue. When Liu Jinding finished queuing and had collected his wooden tokens for two bowls of braised noodles, he looked round and saw that Li Delin had found somewhere to sit. He had also already ordered a couple of side dishes, a bowl of peanuts and some soy-braised beef and added two "Little Ers" – 100ml bottles of the liquor Beijing Erguotou.

When the noodles came, Li Delin said: "Try them, try them. What do you think? Nice and chewy, aren't they!"

Liu Jinding took a mouthful. "Delicious!"

"You mustn't tell anyone about this. It's our secret," Li Delin said.

"I won't, I won't!"

When the noodles were almost finished, Liu Jinding saw how much Li Delin was sweating, so he hurriedly stood up and offered him a paper napkin. Then he handed him a toothpick and said: "If I might give you a little advice, Principal, you should get married again, so you've got someone to look after you."

"Let's talk about it later."

Liu Jinding had actually brought 3,000 yuan with him for his visit to Li Delin, and had been afraid that it wouldn't be enough. But he had only spent ten yuan on the meal, the cost of two bowls of noodles. Li Delin had paid for the side dishes and the Erguotou. Even so, Liu Jinding was feeling very pleased with himself: he now shared a secret with Li Delin.

When Liu Jinding got back to Meiling, he made a special trip to his family home. He ran into the flower shop and told his father: "You must not sell that bonsai with the flowers like little bells, no matter how much anyone offers. You've got to keep it back for me."

Liu Quanyou looked at his son and said: "That tree will choose its owner, and it's not for any Tom, Dick or Harry. Do you know how many people–"

"I don't care who it is, just don't sell it. I'm going to send it to the governor when he gets promoted up to Beijing." From then on, every so often, he would make a special trip to the provincial capital to eat noodles with Li Delin on Shuncheng Street.

NINE

THE RELATIONSHIP BETWEEN LIU JINDING AND LI DELIN developed over bowls of noodles. When the two of them ate together, Li Delin would talk about city and county affairs, mention a few officials and their particular characteristics, chatting away freely and at length. He would tell him which city mayor had come to see him the day before, and what they had talked about; which county secretary had what hobbies, that kind of thing. Liu Jinding mainly just listened, not saying much himself, and handing Lao Li a toothpick when he finished his noodles. Every time he made the trip to spend some time with Li Delin, he said it was just because he had a craving for braised noodles. But as he kept eating his noodles, he got transferred from village level to county level, first as assistant to Tang Mingsheng, then as deputy director of the office. Still he kept eating and moved on from the County Office to Huanghuai City, where, although he was still only deputy office director, he was now at deputy divisional level. So in Liu Jinding's eyes, Li Delin was the most important person in his life and his true benefactor.

Liu Jinding acknowledged to himself that each of his promotions was down to Li Delin, one way or another. Of course, his timing was also fortuitous. Although he always said that he had graduated from the Agricultural Engineering Department, most of what he had read had actually been literature, and his own literary skills were not at all bad. There were two qualities essential for office work: one was to have good literary skills, and the other was to be very observant. Liu Jinding had both. "Advancing youth" and "advancing intelligence" were two of the catchphrases in society at the time, and that's what helped him on his way too. He kept his continuous ascent going for ten years, by which time he was the youngest director-level cadre in the area. He also felt that his benefactor was inexorably on the rise too, and was certain to get promoted up to Beijing, so he stuck to him like glue.

Of course, there were times when his benefactor gave him the cold shoulder, which made him look foolish in front of everyone and he would lose face. But every time that happened, it wasn't long before they ended up even closer than before.

In the year in question, Liu Jinding had just been promoted from deputy secretary-general of the Municipal Government to deputy secretary of the Municipal Legal Committee. As general secretary posts go, the Municipal Government secretary was really just another official, albeit one of the big secretarial posts. But being secretary of the Municipal Legal Committee was a different thing altogether, because it also involved being deputy secretary of the Party Committee. This was a top leadership position with public, inspection and legal responsibilities. Liu Jinding was very smug about his new appointment, or to put it less politely, he became very arrogant.

On 19 May, there was a huge fire in Meiling County. Eight hundred *mu* of land, equivalent to about 130 acres, was burned and all the wheat that was about to be harvested was turned to ashes overnight. It was this sudden disaster that caused him to lose face completely and suffer a public reprimand.

It was windy at the time, and the wind fanned the flames so that the fire burned all night. It was said that by midnight, the flames had turned half the night sky red, and smoke was billowing through the air for several kilometres around the site of the fire like a giant black flag. Fortunately, nearby villagers all rushed out to isolate the fire in time, otherwise, nearly ten thousand *mu* of wheat in the vicinity would have been reduced to ashes.

Liu Jinding got two telephone calls in the small hours of the morning. One was from the top brass and the other from his subordinates. The one from his subordinates was the duty report from the Municipal Public Security Bureau, while the one from above was from Li Delin, the deputy governor in charge of agriculture. When Li Delin had heard the news, he personally called Liu Jinding to learn more about the situation, and said that he was coming over immediately. Liu Jinding naturally did not dare ignore the situation, but after answering the phone, instead of rushing directly to the scene, he had his car drive to the junction with the expressway to welcome Deputy Governor Li.

So it was already daybreak by the time Liu Jinding hurried up to the scene accompanied by Li Delin. By that time, a huge area of wheat fields had been turned to blackened ash, which was filling the air like a cloud of black butterflies, and sporadic flames were flaring up like signal fires warning of the approaching enemy. Fire engines and other assorted vehicles were hurrying along the east-west road that ran round this area of farmland. All the top officials who were standing there solemnly surveying the scene had faces that were so black with ash, it was hard to tell who was who.

After he got out of the car, Li Delin said nothing, but just squatted on the ground, a handful of black ash in his hand.

It so happened that, on this particular day, the municipal secretary of Huanghuai had taken his whole team for a meeting away from the city, and they couldn't get back immediately. Liu Jinding felt that the situation demanded he say something, so he waved his hand and called out in loud, accusatory tones: "Come here, everyone! Come over here! Can't you see the deputy governor has arrived?"

All the municipal, county and village officials turned to stare. They looked at each other, then silently turned away again. Liu Jinding said peremptorily: "Is there anyone from the Municipal Office here?"

Helian Dongshan hurriedly called out from the middle of the group: "I'm here!"

Liu Jinding looked at him and asked irritably: "Where is Director Wan? Why hasn't Director Wan come himself?"

"Director Wan is out of town on business," Helian Dongshan replied. "He ordered me here."

"What about the County Office? Who's here from the County Office?"

Director Ma from the Public Security Bureau, his face black with ash, called out: "I'm here."

All this time, County Party Secretary Xue Zhiheng was standing in the middle of the group, not saying a word.

Liu Jinding pointed at them all and said severely: "Let me tell you lot, we have to find out who is responsible for a huge incident like this. We have to investigate whether it was started on purpose or not. You people from the County Office and the Municipal Office, I want you to break this case within three days. Arrest whoever needs to be arrested and use any means necessary. Lao He! Helian Dongshan, that's your name, isn't it? Your Municipal Office is in charge of this case..."

The whole group of officials remained silent. Standing in the middle of it, Helian Dongshan didn't know how to reply. All this time, Li Delin stayed squatting on the ground, not saying a word.

At this point, Liu Jinding said: "Now I'm going to ask Governor Li to give you your general instructions."

To his surprise, Li Delin got abruptly to his feet, pointed at Liu Jinding and said: "Blah! Blah! Blah! Blah! Blah! Blah! That's all I've heard from you all this time, and what use is that? What precautions are you taking? What steps are you taking to remedy the situation? And what do you mean by 'break the case in three days'? How can that possibly be done? What a load of nonsense! Where's your sympathy and fellow feeling? What about all the people who need this food? Where's your sympathy for them?"

Li Delin looked at the black ash in his hand and continued: "Food, this was all food! It's been turned to ashes overnight! Doesn't that make you feel bad?" His lips trembled as he said these words, and tears formed in his eyes.

In front of them all was a burnt, blackened wheat field. The ash swirled in the breeze, flying into the sky like the ashes of ancestor money. Li Delin scattered the ash he was holding back onto the ground. "Just look!" he said. "This is a whole year's harvest for a farmer. It's not an easy job. The wheat takes up all your time, but you still have to stop any fires. That is a big task on its own, and you can't slack off for a moment..."

The officials continued to stand there in silence, seemingly deeply moved by his words. This was the first time Helian Dongshan from the Municipal Office had heard Li Delin speak in person. He looked at the little deputy governor with an admiration that sprang spontaneously from his heart. He thought to himself that this was a good man, and a good official.

Liu Jinding felt as though he had just been hit over the head with a club. This was the first time he had been on the receiving end of a direct verbal reprimand from Li Delin, and in front of so many people too. His face went a deep purple. He just stood there like an idiot, wishing the ground would open up and swallow him.

Finally, Li Delin said: "Lao Xue, you are the county Party secretary. You speak now."

Xue Zhiheng stepped forward from the middle of the group and said: "What you have said is quite right, Governor Li. Comrades, this is a heavy lesson to have to learn. Every one of us..."

After the affair was over, Li Delin said to Liu Jinding: "I had to be more severe with you precisely because you were my student. From now on, don't go spouting nonsense about things you don't understand but want to pretend you do."

As for Liu Jinding, although he was less than impressed by this, he did understand that a student should never resent his teacher, so naturally he reined in his emotions considerably. Afterwards, he gradually began to get closer and closer to his teacher again... until that day.

CHAPTER TWO

ONE

As for Li Delin, he could never have dreamed of having three women in the course of his life, let alone getting married to a woman like Luo Qiuyi.

Even now, so many years later, that scarf was still hanging in the wardrobe. It was a keepsake from when they got engaged back then.

It was a scarf made from the kind of fine wool that only came from Xinjiang, and Luo Qiuyi had brought it back from there when she went to see the poplar forests.

She had knitted it herself and said it had taken her more than a month. It was very long, very white and very soft, and when you put it on, it looked like a Tibetan welcome scarf. A tiny red maple leaf was embroidered on either end. She said it was her personal symbol.

That was back when Li Delin was a research student. It was early spring when Luo Qiuyi arrived, and he was checking the growth of the young shoots in the "test field". She had made a special trip to Meiling from the provincial city, and when she found Li Delin in his test field, she hung the scarf around his neck.

At the time, the new shoots of the wheat were just turning green, and the winter snow had not yet fully thawed. Luo Qiuyi was wearing a red high-neck sweater under an elegantly cut parka as she walked towards him out of the sun. She looked like an oil painting, standing there in the middle of the fields, noble, slim and extremely beautiful. He just stared at her dumbly until she hung the scarf around his neck. "I've just been reading Xu Chi's *Goldbach Conjecture*," she said. "It's really well written."

At that time, he hadn't read *Goldbach Conjecture* and didn't even know who Xu Chi was, so he just looked blank. It was only later that he found out it was a piece of reportage about a famous mathematician called Cheng Jinrun.

It was as though love had struck him like a bolt from the blue, very abrupt. Li Delin had remained dizzy all day and couldn't remember anything he had said, only that she had brought him a hot water bottle, saying: "I heard your stomach is not good. This will keep it warm at night."

The old director of the County Agricultural Technology Institute took Li Delin to one side and said: "What's the matter with you, lad? The gods of love are favouring you, and a fairy goddess is in your grasp! Aiya! Hold her tight! Hold her tight!"

The first time she came to the institute, Luo Qiuyi only stayed a few hours, and that afternoon, when she was leaving, Lin Delin escorted her to the Meiling Bus Station. The station was heaving, with people milling around like sheep and running for their bus. When he escorted her in, he was afraid they might bump into someone he knew, so he deliberately kept her away from the crowd. To his surprise, Luo Qiuyi deliberately hurried forward a few paces, taking him by the arm so everyone could see. Li Delin said: "Don't! This is the county town. We can't!"

Luo Qiuyi raised her head high and said: "I'm not worried! What are you afraid of?" Then as she was about to get on the bus, in the middle of the crowd of people, she put her mouth close to his ear and said, in English: "I love you."

That evening her perfume was still hot on his ear, so hot that he couldn't sleep. He asked himself, over and over again, whether he was dreaming. He put the scarf neatly beside his pillow and stroked it from time to time.

But seven years later, they parted. When she left, she took everything she owned. And she also took their six-year-old daughter.

The only thing she left was the scarf, and that was because he had worn it. Their marriage had been the work of his mentor, Professor Wu.

TWO

WHEN HE WAS LITTLE, his greatest dream had been to eat steamed white bread. As the son of a farming family, having white bread at every meal was his heart's desire. Later on, when he had developed ambitions and ideals, his dream was to make the folklore of thousands of years come true and discover a mythical type of wheat that bore twelve ears and let people all over the country eat steamed white bread. The truth was that, as a child, he had eaten sweet potato flour bread until he was sick of it. So when the *gaokao* was reinstated, he decided to apply to the Institute of Agriculture.

That year, Li Delin was hardest-working student in the Institute of Agriculture, later known as the University of Agricultural Science and Technology. Other than when he was sleeping or eating, he divided most of the rest of his day between the lecture theatre and the library, and he very seldom went out strolling the streets or dancing like his classmates. A dance craze was sweeping through society at the time and even when they were just walking down the street, many of his fellow students could be seen keeping a "one, two, three, four, one, two, two, three, four, one...." rhythm. Li Delin never even entered a dance hall. Actually, that's not true, he did go once. It was the evening of 4 May, Youth Day, and his classmates dragged him along that one time. His companions danced away to the music, while he was left sitting in the corner all evening with only their leftover melon seeds for company. No one asked him to dance, and he was too embarrassed to ask any of the girls. He held put until nine o'clock and then escaped.

All this wasn't just because he was an introvert. Although he didn't want to admit it, deep down he was ashamed of his appearance. He was short, dark-complexioned with deep lines on his forehead, and had a face shaped like a butternut squash. Compared with others, he always felt like an ugly duckling. He rarely participated in any of the class's group activities.

He was, however, Professor Wu's favourite student. He was the highest achiever in the whole Department of Agriculture. In particular, in his third year, he was the only student in the entire institute to have a paper published in the *Soil Science Society of America Journal*. He also had two articles included in the internationally renowned *Journal Citation Reports*. Because of these achievements, he was regarded as an ornament to the Institute of Agriculture. That year, Professor Wu, who had just become deputy director of the institute, rated him so highly that he let him skip a grade to become his research student. Even Columbia University in New York made overtures to him.

His classmates were astounded. How could someone like him, with no connections, get an article published in a world-renowned periodical? What they didn't know was that he had spent pretty well every vacation at the Meiling County Agricultural Technology Institute. Under the supervision of a distantly related maternal uncle, he had become a temporary intern at the institute where he got his meals but no salary. Of course, this was also down to Professor Wu's patronage. The professor had personally called the institute's director to get him to allocate Li Delin two parcels of land to conduct research into different varieties of wheat.

Professor Wu was quite a character, a straightforward man who spoke his mind. His full name was Wu Tianduo, and he was a nationally acknowledged expert in maize. His pen name was Wu Yong, which was a reference to the old saying *"bai wu yi yong shi shusheng"*, which basically means "intellectuals are no use for anything". During the Cultural Revolution, he was seized and subjected to public criticism by his students because of this pen name, which they said showed he was part of the "capitulationist faction". Later on, when the Agricultural Institute was merged with the Forestry Institute, he was sent down to the countryside in Huaiyang. There, he was put into a "bullpen" with Professor Luo Huaijin of the Forestry Institute, and they ate together, lived together and worked together. After returning to the city, the two men stayed firm friends, meeting up once a week to play three games of Go. Luo Qiuyi was Luo Huaijin's daughter.

During these meetings, Professor Wu would pass on bits of news from the college. Whenever he talked about the current cohort of students, he would shake his head and say: "They're not up to scratch, really not up to scratch at all." But as he went on talking, he would mention his favourite student, Li Delin, and whenever he did, he was always full of praise, saying he was "as rare as a phoenix feather or a unicorn horn".

As he warmed to his subject, he would forget about the Go board and say, in a loud voice: "Search, go on, search all the country's forty-nine agricultural colleges and see how many students you find who are good enough to be published in America! How many get an article published in the *Soil Science Society of America Journal*? That's the journal of a world-class organisation!"

There is a saying that "a casual remark sounds significant to an attentive listener", and Luo Qiuyi, who always served the tea, had heard Professor Wu singing the praises of his student on more than one occasion. So even before she met Li Delin, his name had already wormed its way into her brain. Once, Professor Wu said to her, quite deliberately: "Well, Xiao Qiu [Little Qiu], when you get married, you should marry a scientist like him." Luo Qiuyi blushed furiously.

It was a time when reading was really popular, and girls were all into "romance". If they had grown up in a scholarly family, as Luo Qiuyi had, then the partner they imagined for themselves, or at least the measure by which they gauged his suitability, was to be found in the pages of a book.

That was also the year that Xu Chi's *Goldbach Conjecture* was first published in the inaugural issue of *People's Literature*, and then reprinted by *People's Daily* and *Guangming Daily*. It caused a national sensation. Everybody across the whole country was discussing the mathematical phenomenon of "1+2". The thing was, though, no one was actually very sure what that "1+2" actually meant. Even the people writing articles about it didn't know. It was like a maze, or a riddle, and whoever deciphered it would be deified. As a result, girls everywhere became madly interested in Chen Jingrun, the subject of the essay, and hundreds of thousands of love letters were sent winging their way to Beijing. He really was the man with the golden ticket!

It was at this point that Luo Qiuyi read *Goldbach Conjecture* for herself in *Guangming Daily*. "Conjecture" is a word that sets a woman's heart a-flutter. Luo Qiuyi kept the newspaper on her bed beside the pillow and read it many times over. She couldn't help herself reading it aloud in her bedroom. Every time she read it, she burst into tears... Beijing was too far away and simply as a "conjecture", Chen Jingrun seemed too mysterious and out of reach. But didn't she have her very own scientist, or scientist-to-be at some stage in the future, researching wheat right next to her? So why not?

So it could be said that it was that "conjecture" that brought the two of them together. The second time Luo Qiuyi went to see Li Delin was when the wheat was sprouting. Li Delin was cultivating a wheat hybrid called Meiling Number Seven. He had successively propagated the different varieties called Meiling Number One through to Meiling Number Seven, which had resistance to lodging and disease, and increased grain weight. After that, he began to cultivate Huanghuai Number One, which was a double-eared wheat. It was said that the yield could be more than doubled. But just when he was about to succeed with Huanghuai Number One, something went wrong. But that is a story for another time.

When Luo Qiuyi came to Meiling the second time, she was carrying a bag of fruit and also arrived with a heart that was now settled, after a long period of fluttering uncertainty. She had come in search of a "conjecture" and finally had one of her own. It was unthinkable for any self-respecting female student in a department of Chinese literature not to have her own "conjecture". Truth be told, to begin with, she didn't even fancy Li Delin. She had many suitors that year... and there was Li Delin, short, face like a butternut squash and resembling a knot in a lump of wood. But it was Li Delin's eyes, in combination with the *Goldbach Conjecture* effect, that finally won her round.

It was a Sunday in late April, and the weather was getting hot. Luo Qiuyi was dressed in an outfit that was all the rage at the time: a moon-white, short-sleeved top and sea-blue culottes with black polka dots. Her hair was shoulder length, and altogether she looked modest but animated, lively and sexy like an iris flower.

The director of the Meiling Institute went to find Li Delin and slapped him on the back and said: "Hurry up, that girl from the provincial capital is here again. I've just seen her."

When the two of them met, Lin Delin had just come back from the wheat fields. He was still barefoot and didn't dare look her in the eye. He just said: "You've come then."

Luo Qiuyi replied innocently: "It's Sunday, so I came to see you."

That day, the sun was out and the temperature was just right for pollinating the wheat. All Li Delin could stammer out was: "Then you... I... I must go and pollinate the wheat."

Luo Qiuyi thought this sounded very mysterious. She was intrigued and asked: "Is it all right if I go with you?"

"To be honest, there isn't much to see."

At this, she simpered like a little girl and said: "Can I come too? I want to see it. I could give you a hand."

She looked so cute as she said it, and Lin Delin's heart gave a lurch as he said: "Of course, of course. Let's go."

On the way to the wheat fields, she asked: "How do you pollinate? Can you explain it to me?"

"Wheat is a self-pollinating plant, so the heterozygosity rate is very low. This means we have to cross-pollinate by hand to get the variety of..."

Luo Qiuyi's face was flushed as she asked: "How do you 'cross-pollinate'?"

"First you have to take out the stamen."

"What 'stamen'?"

"It's the male part of the flower," he replied.

Luo Qiuyi flushed an even deeper red and asked: "What do you mean when you say 'take the male part'?" The phrase inevitably made her think of imperial eunuchs.

Li Delin explained: "Each wheat plant has three stamens and one pistil. First you remove the stamens, then you cover the plant with a paper bag, tag it and isolate it. You pollinate it within one to three days, and of course, you have to select the best of the 'male parts'—"

"Can you pollinate any time once the flower has opened?"

"There are only about twenty minutes when the sexual generation is at its height." Li Delin couldn't help glancing at Luo Qiuyi when he said "sexual generation".

Luo Qiuyi hastily changed the subject: "I heard people say that you once commented you wanted the whole country to eat steamed white bread."

A little embarrassed, Li Delin replied: "I can only say that... well, it's a wish, yes a wish. When I was little, we were really poor–"

"It's a great idea! Really great!" Luo Qiuyi said excitedly.

Li Delin continued hurriedly: "When I was little, all I wanted to do was eat white bread. I didn't think about anything else, I didn't dare."

Luo Qiuyi became even more animated as she turned to him and said: "In the south of China, there's a man called Yuan Longping. He's known as the Father of the Rice Paddy. In the future, you could be the Father of Wheat!"

Li Delin blushed furiously and said immediately: "No, no, not at all, I wouldn't dare. I wouldn't dare compare myself to him. He's so far ahead of me."

Luo Qiuyi was carried away in her own fantasy: her boyfriend would become China's Father of Wheat! How great would that be! She looked adoringly at Li Delin and said emphatically: "Why not?

Just get on and do it! Be the Father of Wheat! You *are* China's future Father of Wheat! Why don't you have the guts to admit it?"

Li Delin didn't reply and just lowered his head to look at the ground. Luo Qiuyi thought he was being modest, too modest even. But that was exactly what she liked about him.

When they reached the wheat field, she helped him pollinate the hybrid wheat, and as he handed her first the tweezers and then the pollinator, their hands would occasionally touch and it felt like an electric shock. It was indescribably exciting.

That day, the pair were alone in the field. The sun was shining, long white clouds floated in the sky, the wheat was blooming, and the air was filled with the sweet smell of yin and yang. "Do you like me?" she asked. He just grunted. "Do you think my outfit is pretty?" He just grunted. "It's either pretty or it isn't. What does that grunt mean?"

"Yes," he replied. "Yes, it is pretty."

Luo Qiuyi didn't go home that evening, but stayed at the institute. Of course, Li Delin didn't dare do anything rash, and arranged for her to stay in a dormitory for female workers on leave from jobs elsewhere. He knew that she was a professor's daughter and very sophisticated, so he bought her a new plastic basin, soap, towels and so on. However, at nine o'clock, she came running over, and said, red-faced: "I can't stay there. The bed smells."

Li Delin looked at her in amazement, not knowing what to say. She sat down on a chair and said in a low voice: "Why don't we have a bit of a chat, and I'll just have to make do with your place here for the night."

Li Delin turned his head to look at his narrow single bed. His heart was pounding.

"How quiet the night is," Luo Qiuyi said.

"It is quiet."

"'Listen! The night has a heart. The little insects are chirping, the heart is beating. Count the stars, the stars mark the heartbeat...' Do you know whose poem that is?"

"No."

"Mine"

"It's good."

"Do you really think so?"

"Yes, it's really good."

"Is this your hometown?"

"Yes, we're eighteen miles from the county town."

"Who else is there in your family?"

"My mother's dead, so there's only my father."

"Is he in good health?"

"He's all right, except his legs aren't great."

"Why doesn't he get them looked at? I could find him a doctor to treat them up in the provincial capital."

"It's poor circulation. That's hard to treat in old people."

"What about you? Do you go home often?"

After a bit, Luo Qiuyi seemed to get rather tired, and she leaned across to rest her head on his shoulder, saying softly: "Have you washed yet? Why don't you go and have a wash?"

Later on, as the two of them were sitting on the edge of the bed, Luo Qiuyi snuggled in close to him and said softly: "Hold me. It's all right for you to hold me."

Li Delin held her in a clumsy sort of bear hug, still timidly holding back. In the end it was Luo Qiuyi who made the move to snuggle in even closer so the two of them were hugging each other properly... but they were both still quite timid, and after they had hugged for a moment, they separated. Luo Qiuyi adjusted her dress slightly and said: "Let me recite a poem for you." And with that, she launched into a poem by the Russian writer, Alexander Pushkin:

I remember a wonderful moment,
As before my eyes you appeared,
Like a vision, fleeting, momentary,
Like a spirit of the purest beauty.
And my heart beats with a rapture new,
And for its sake arose again,
A godlike face, an inspiration,
And life, and tears, and love, and you.

"Do you like it?" she asked once she had finished reciting.

"It's nice," he replied. "Really nice."

"You've had a busy day. You go to bed, and I'll stay with you for a while."

"You have the bed," Li Delin replied. "I'll find somewhere else."

"It's late. Don't go disturbing anyone. Let's just... keep each other company."

Later, the two of them leaned into each other, snuggled together askance in the bed...

That night, in the narrow single bed, Li Delin half held Luo Qiuyi, as though she was a piece of fairy fruit. Really nice, he said to himself.

In the second half of the night, all was quiet except for the chirping of the insects. While Luo Qiuyi was pillowed on one of his arms fast asleep, he had not slept a wink. The moonlight shone in through the window, shimmering like a mirror made of water.

In the moonlight, Li Delin gently moved the quilt to one side, smelling the fragrance of her hair, her breath, from top to bottom. Little by little he looked furtively at Luo Qiuyi: her snow-white face, her neck, her gently heaving breasts, her rounded buttocks and slender legs. He could not help but look, over and over again. He felt as if he was drunk or in a dream.

After the two of them got married, Li Delin asked her, unbelievingly, what she saw in him. He was just the son of a farming family. Deep down, did she really like him? She thought for a moment, and said, forthrightly: "It's your eyes, the light in them."

In fact, she really was fond of him, and it wasn't just because of the light in his eyes.

THREE

THE PARADOX OF LUO QIUYI AND LI DELIN began on the day of their wedding.

Although the wedding was a simple one, it was actually held twice: once in the provincial capital and once in the countryside.

At that time, Li Delin had not long gained his Master's degree and was staying on at the institute. Luo Qiuyi had just graduated from university and was assigned to a work unit directly under the provincial government. Neither of them had yet been allocated accommodation. By good fortune, Professor Luo had just been assigned a new, larger house by the Forestry Institute, so he gave the original house a simple make-over and left it to Luo Qiuyi. Everything needed to decorate the new house was paid for by the Luo family.

The wedding party in the city was all arranged by the Luo family too. As it was the wife's family in charge, everything was done according to Luo Qiuyi's wishes – she was their only daughter. It was only a small gathering of friends and family, with Professor Wu as the marriage witness. A simple meal was laid on in a restaurant. The couple moved in together, and that was the marriage done.

But after the wedding in the city, Li Delin was continuously depressed and moody. The house belonged to the Luo family, and they had paid all the wedding expenses too. Although he knew it was all well-intentioned on the part of his wife, it made him feel uncomfortable as a man.

One evening, Luo Qiuyi asked him what the matter was. "Nothing," he replied.

"What do you mean, nothing? Look at the face on you! What is it?"

Li Delin was silent for a moment, then said: "We're married. Shouldn't... shouldn't I tell my family?"

Luo Qiuyi asked him in amazement: "Didn't you ring home and invite your father to the wedding?"

"My father's getting old and his legs are bad. Besides–"

"What are you trying to say?"

Li Delin looked at her anxiously: "Qiuyi, will you come home with me?"

"To the countryside? Do we have to?"

"Yes, we do. I have to tell my father."

"Can't you telephone him?"

"No," Li Delin insisted. "I have to talk to him."

In truth, Luo Qiuyi really didn't understand. Li Delin's "talk to him" didn't mean the same thing to her as it did to him. For no good reason, she suddenly flared up: "Stand up! An educated person like you squatting on the ground! What do you think it looks like?"

As they spent more time together, Luo Qiuyi discovered that he had a really bad habit: he liked to squat down on the ground when he had something to think about.

Li Delin stood up quickly and asked abruptly: "Do you look down on my family because we're poor?"

Luo Qiuyi was stunned into silence, then rushed forward to hug him, saying: "How can you think that, darling? The man I married is the Father of Wheat, isn't he? How could I look down on you for being poor? If you just want to make a trip home, of course I'll go with you."

Li Delin suddenly began to cry. Through his tears, he said: "If you don't come back with me now, I'll never dare show my face there again."

Luo Qiuyi stared at him. "Aiya! Is it that important?"

"You don't understand. I owe it to the villagers. When I went up to university, the village head Uncle Shushan rang the bell and gathered all the village elders together. He told them: 'Delin is the first person from our village to go to university. He's only a little lad and not very strong so we need to support him. The first thing we can do is ensure that all his land stays in his name, and whatever that land makes will be his subsidy from us. Then, one day, if he doesn't make it in the city and comes back, he'll still have the land. The second things is that every household, big or small, will make a contribution.' Now I've got my Master's and got married. If I don't go back and tell them, they might think I am being disrespectful."

"You should have said! Why didn't you say?" Luo Qiuyi exclaimed without hesitation. "Let's go back and take some gifts with us. How's that?"

Li Delin knew how fastidious she was, and said appeasingly: "I was afraid... it wouldn't be quite what you are used to."

"Don't worry, I won't let you lose face!"

And so it was that, not long after New Year, the husband and wife made their way happily to the village, carrying bags full of gifts.

At that time, just as winter turns into spring, the air was dry, cool and clear, and the wheat seedlings in the fields were looking green and shiny after a winter of nurturing. As the pair travelled along the old Huanghuai road, Luo Qiuyi was in a state of high excitement, pointing and asking questions all the way, as if the simple visit home was a holiday full of useful new experiences and information.

"Ai! A European magpie! That is a European magpie, isn't it?"

As soon as they arrived, Li Delin found himself surrounded by villagers. He greeted them one by one, feeling as much at home as a fish returned to its pond, and respectfully according to seniority, offered round cigarettes. Luo Qiuyi too found herself surrounded by the village women, all singing her praises and flattering her until her head spun. Everyone was calling out at once, and she didn't know who to reply to first.

In the midst of all this, a snotty-nosed kid clambered down from his mother's arms, grabbed Luo Qiuyi's waist with one hand and pointed with the other saying: "Granddad! You should be calling me 'Granddad'."

Luo Qiuyi stared at the child blankly until Li Delin came hurrying over and pulled him away, saying: "Stop making a racket, Little Er Ye."

A chubby woman gave him a slap full across the face, then said with a grin: "You little imp! Are you trying to pull village rank on her? If you're her granddad, then where's the red envelope you've got ready for her, eh? Now, fuck off out of the way!"

Everyone burst out laughing.

When the couple reached the gate of the courtyard, with everyone still clustered round them, they saw a hobbling old man with a face streaked like a monster being pushed forward by the crowd. Li Delin hurried towards him with a cry of: "Dad!" He turned to Luo Qiuyi and said: "This is my dad."

Luo Qiuyi's jaw dropped. What she saw was a little old man whose whole face was soot-black, yellow and red, striped and smeared with the remains of food. A rope of garlic, chilli peppers and red dates was hanging from his waist, and he looked for all the world like a clown who had just escaped from the circus. A group of men grabbed his arms and hustled him forward as if he were a criminal being escorted to a police station. In fact, he had a big grin on his face that only served to make him look even more grotesquely clownish. Luo Qiuyi huddled closer to Li Delin and whispered: "Look how they're bullying him! It's awful!"

"We're in the countryside," Li Delin whispered back. "It's just how they do things here, don't worry about it."

The old man turned an almost obsequious gaze on Luo Qiuyi and said: "You've come home! Come in! Come in!"

As they approached, they saw a brazier in the gateway, and some of the women shouted out: "Hurry up now! Step over the brazier, step over the brazier and go in!"

Luo Qiuyi was almost dying with embarrassment. She thought to herself: Are people still doing that in this day and age? She really didn't want to step over the brazier, but by now she was being almost frog-marched forward by the group of middle-aged women who were too strong for her to resist, and they forced her to do it.

A cooking pot had been set up in the courtyard with some stewing meat bubbling away inside. Beside it was a wooden table piled with vegetables, and the yard rang with the sound of a chopping knife. A woman was cutting up some meat and stuffing pieces of it into her mouth as she did so. There were wicker baskets of fried bread on the table too, and a little boy was running to and fro carrying them. It was early spring, and although the temperature was still cool, hot air was swirling round the courtyard and there were people everywhere. The yard was bedecked with red "double happiness" characters, and filled with a variety of square wooden tables and benches. Once she was inside the house, Luo Qiuyi could scarcely catch her breath between hugs and embraces. The hubbub of voices from aunts, great aunts and cousins of all kinds was so loud it made her ears ache. What she didn't know was that the whole village had been hard at it for three days getting ready for the wedding celebration, ever since Li Delin had phoned home from the city.

The wedding banquet began at midday. Uncle Shushan, the village head, made the opening speech and proposed the toast, saying: "Don't worry, I'll keep it short. Our Li Delin is now a... a what do call it? A BA..."

A young lad next to him shouted out to correct him: "An MA, he's an MA."

Uncle Shushan glared at him. "Fuck off, I know what he is, he is a great scholar. He had an essay of his sent to America. How great a scholar is that! Today, he has brought his wife back home. She is the daughter of a professor, from a great university family. How pretty and clever she is! How smooth and glossy her skin is! Now she has married into our little Li Village, we must make sure we treat her well. I just have one more thing to say and that is that even if we can't give her the full three days of feasting, we can keep the food coming all day to celebrate such a great event, and make sure there is enough wine for everyone to have a great time. Now, let's get stuck in!"

From the time she arrived at the village a little after ten that morning right up until the evening, Luo Qiuyi didn't go outside, except for twice when she joined Li Delin in the courtyard to toast the guests there. Otherwise, during that whole period, she didn't even get a mouthful of water to drink. The villagers served her food but, when she saw the houseflies crawling over the rims of the dishes, it turned her stomach, and she couldn't eat. The running party that was going on in the courtyard continued from noon to evening, with guests coming and going in equal numbers and the shouts of the drinking games ringing out. Li Delin was constantly being hailed by one group or another, and he toasted all of them, drinking until his eyes glazed over. Inside and outside, the house was thronged with women and children wanting to see the new bride and generally making a lot of noise.

The celebrations went on until nine o'clock in the evening, when a group of men crowded into the house, reeking of wine, and shouting: "Where's the bride? Where's the bride? Come on! Come on! It's time you went to the wedding chamber! Into the wedding chamber!"

The Li family home was overrun by the ongoing party. Uncle Shushan had offered the upper storey of his own house as the new couple's bridal chamber. The bed was made up with brand new quilts and bedding, all in crimson satin. The group of men bundled Li Delin and Luo Qiuyi over to the house and up the stairs. The couple had only just sat down, when someone shouted up from below: "Hurry up, Delin, there's someone wants to see you!" He was being summoned to have a drink with the village head.

At the same time, the crowd of men surged into the room demanding Luo Qiuyi light their cigarettes for them. She forced herself to keep her temper, stood up and patiently lit their cigarettes one by one... but they kept putting them out again. Three times they did this, until she lost her temper and refused. But the men wouldn't let up, and kept bothering her, pushing and shoving and getting in her way. Suddenly there was a crash and the lamp went out. There was no knowing who started it, or how many were involved, but suddenly the men were all over Luo Qiuyi with their hands. They were groping her breasts, her buttocks, her thighs. Someone was even crawling on the floor grabbing her ankles. Another put his mouth up to her face, almost choking her with his foul breath. Luo Quiyi held out for as long as she could, and then collapsed. The scream she gave as she did so terrified the men, and the filthy hands were all abruptly withdrawn.

"Fuck off! Fuck off the lot of you!" Luo Qiuyi yelled.

In the darkness, the figures scuttled away like rats. For the rest of the night, Luo Qiuyi did not relight the lamp, but just sat there in the darkness until dawn. It was only as the day was breaking that Li Delin was brought back, drunk and incapable, and laid out on the bed. His porters beat a hasty retreat.

The cock crowed and the new day was with them.

Luo Qiuyi's pent-up fury had made her as dangerous as a keg of gunpowder. She suddenly lifted Li Delin up off the bed, snatched off the crimson quilt that stank of wine and vomit, and hurled it out of the upstairs window. Then, with no one to notice, she went downstairs, out of the house and out of the village.

Almost immediately there was a cry of: "The bride's run away! The bride's run away!"

It wasn't until he woke up mid-morning that Li Delin discovered his bride was gone. He was immediately surrounded by a crowd of assorted aunts and other relatives, all wagging their fingers at him and shouting instructions: "You go home and have a word with that wife of yours. The whole village spent three days getting that party ready! How could she be so rude?" Li Delin was crestfallen and humiliated. The only thing he could do was make his excuses and get back to the city as quickly as possible.

It should come as no surprise that the "cold war" between the two of them, once they were back in the city, lasted a good month.

On the evening of the day they returned, Luo Qiuyi hid in the bathroom and stood under the shower, washing herself over and over again. However hard she tried, she couldn't get rid of the smell. In the end, hair loose and draped in a bathrobe, she scampered from the bathroom to the bedroom, where she hunted around for a while, before coming up with a pen and paper. Hastily she scribbled out a divorce contract, slapped it down in front of Li Delin and said: "Sign it! We're getting divorced!"

Li Delin just sat on the sofa, his head in his hands, and didn't say a word.

"What did you call them?" she spat furiously. "Simple folk? Kind-hearted? They're ignorant barbarians! Criminals! Cheap and shameless!" She was so angry she almost choked and threw up. When she had finished her rant, she ran back into the bathroom and started washing herself again.

For a month afterwards, the only sound in their home was the water splashing out of the shower...

After that, it was Li Delin who was the first to wave the white flag. He had seen the pinch marks on Luo Qiuyi's body. Of course, all the washing had done no good, and even several weeks later, she was still black and blue all over with bruises.

FOUR

It was after he had been sleeping on the sofa for three weeks that Li Delin surrendered.

He was, in truth, a stubborn and bigoted man, and he still nursed a sense of grievance, even though he didn't say anything. Instead, he repeatedly apologised to Luo Qiuyi for the villagers' boorish behaviour. From then on, everything between them was apparently fine, but something continued to fester deep down inside them, and things were never quite normal ever again.

After a while, the two of them attempted a reconciliation and, in this respect, it was Luo Qiuyi who seemed more to be the instigator. It was her, one evening, who picked up the pillow from the sofa and took it back into the bedroom. The twin holidays of the Mid-Autumn Festival and National Day were fast approaching when the two of them were walking along a path through the trees after work, admiring the night sky.

"It's soon going to be the holidays," Li Delin said.

"That's right," Luo Qiuyi replied. "The Mid-Autumn Festival..." Then she went on, in a rush: "Why don't we invite Father for a visit?"

Confused, Li Delin asked: "Whose father? Yours or mine?"

"Idiot! Why would we need to invite my father?"

Li Delin's eyes grew moist, and he hesitated for a moment before saying: "No, no, let's leave it. I'll go back for a visit instead."

Luo Qiuyi looked at him in astonishment: "What are you on about?"

"Nothing, nothing," he replied hurriedly.

"Well, stop humming and hawing. That's no use to anyone!"

"I just meant, do you really want to invite him?"

"I'm a reasonable person, aren't I? It's a holiday. We should have our family round us at the Mid-Autumn Festival, so of course I want to invite him."

"That's very generous of you," he said, in hurried agreement.

At the time, they were living in an old apartment. Under Luo Qiuyi's supervision in making preparations for the visit, the couple actually found themselves working closely together for the first time. They cleared out the second bedroom that they had been using as a study, swept it clean and bought a single bed and new bedding especially for the visit. Thoughtfully, Luo Qiuyi even bought a spittoon to put beside the bed.

Li Delin's father arrived. He tottered in through the door. He really had no idea how he should behave towards this sophisticated city girl who was his new daughter-in-law, so he kept a fixed smile on his face and dipped his head and said: "Daughter-in-Law, is your old man well? Are you both well?"

He had brought two bulging bags full of peanuts, red dates, millet and pumpkins. In the end, he only stayed three days.

Perhaps because he had caught a chill on the way to the city, the old man coughed throughout his first night there. And because he had asthma, his coughing was as wheezy as an old pair of bellows. Luo Qiuyi didn't get any sleep. But she put up with it. The next morning, the old man spent more than an hour on the lavatory and Luo Qiuyi was gagging as she cleaned up after him... but still she put up with it. That wasn't all though. At midday, she came back from her classes and saw great piles of peanuts on the coffee table with their shells scattered all over the floor. As she swept them up, she discovered that the old man had been expectorating on the floor as well, and his phlegm seemed to be stuck to every single shell! Gritting her teeth and barely making it through to the next day, when she went through one of the doors of the apartment, she brushed against the door frame and discovered that the old man had blown his nose onto his fingers and wiped the mucus on the doorframe. She got a whole handful of it! This was too much for her. She went completely to pieces and fled to her parents' home.

That afternoon, Li Delin and Luo Qiuyi had a flaming row in Li's office. She enumerated his father's various offences and said bluntly: "What's wrong with him? Is this any way for a person to behave!"

Li too was shaking with fury as he banged his desk and shouted: "Fuck your mother! He's my dad!"

Luo Qiuyi was flabbergasted by his swearing. She didn't think he knew how! She glared at him and yelled back: "What did you say? You just try saying that again!"

Li Delin realised he had mis-spoken. In the countryside, "Fuck your mother!" was just something you said all the time and he had carelessly let it slip out. All he could think to do was repeat: "He is my father."

But Luo Qiuyi wouldn't let the matter drop: "You actually dare curse my mother? You actually... I demand an apology. If you don't apologise, I'll never forgive you!"

After three days, there was nothing for it but for Li Delin to take his father home to the countryside.

Afterwards, the direct result of Li Delin's second "capitulation" was that his household had established its own five-article constitution.

Article One: no country folk allowed through the front door, and no exceptions for relatives, including Li Delin's father. Luo Qiuyi said: "This is not us disrespecting them, it is them not respecting themselves. If it is something urgent, they can see you at your office."

Article Two: No smoking indoors. Luo Qiuyi said: "If you really have to smoke, you can smoke outside."

Article Three: No alcohol. If politeness demands having a drink, no more than 100ml.

Article Four: To ensure success in giving up smoking and drinking, Li Delin's salary is to be handed over to Luo Qiuyi for safekeeping. Luo Qiuyi said: "You can access it any time for any reasonable purpose."

Article Five: Proper hygiene habits must be cultivated, and attention paid to appearance. Change into clean clothes when going out, and put on slippers when coming in to the house. Brush your teeth, and wash your face, hands and feet before going to bed.

Article Five was something of a sticking point for Li Delin. He was firmly entrenched in his daily habits, and this really did not suit him at all. It wasn't long before going home felt like going to prison, and it tormented him. Gradually, he found himself less and less willing to go home after work, and he would stay later and later in his office or in the laboratory before finally trudging back. Sometimes, he would spend half the night sitting outside in the corridor, smoking. What he really wanted was to be sent away on university business, and he looked for any excuse to do so. Eventually, he even began to think of fleeing the family home altogether. Secretly, he started writing to all manner of foreign universities, hoping to be offered a place to study for a PhD.

Luo Qiuyi's view of the situation was completely different. She saw this as an opportunity. She thought she could get him to transform his ways and become – as she saw it – a grown-up intellectual and a proper scientist with some real clout. In pursuit of this, she was very free with their money. She bought him three top-quality Western suits, and the shirts and belts that went with them were all well-known brands. She even went as far as to send him to a specialist hairdresser on Sundays, where she instructed the stylist to sort him out with a new hairstyle. Previously, his hair had been parted to one side and looked rather dishevelled, but after this it was always swept back with hair oil. Every time he went out, she would straighten his collar and cufflinks and say: "There, doesn't that look smart!"

He would always just grunt and say: "It's OK."

Once, Professor Wu had some reason to come and see him. Luo Qiuyi immediately started bustling around offering him cups of tea and glasses of water. Then, one minute she would appear with some fruit she had just sliced, the next minute it was some melon seeds and sweetmeats, and finally she brought in hot towels for his hands. Professor Wu cast an appraising eye over the spotless apartment and said, with feeling: "What a lucky man you are, Delin!"

Once again, Li Delin just said: "Yes, it's OK."

In the winter of the next year, village mayor Uncle Shushan arrived, carrying two cloth bags. One contained a dozen or so sweet potatoes, and the other held a dozen or so freshly hulled ears of sweetcorn. He had come up to town to sort out something about his niece going to university. It was after dark by the time he reached Li Delin's place, as he had had to stop to ask directions about a dozen times. He knocked on the door, and after a short pause, it opened. "It's me, Daughter-in-Law," Uncle Shushan said. "Is Delin in?"

Luo Qiuyi stared at him in amazement. "He's, he's not back yet. Why don't you go and look for him at the university?"

"Here you are," Uncle Shushan said. "It's nothing much, just some sweetcorn and sweet potatoes, but they're this year's crop. I thought you'd like something nice and fresh. What shall I do with them?"

"Put them down outside the door," Luo Qiuyi said.

By the time Uncle Shushan had done as she said, she had already shut the door.

His eyes were full of tears as he made his way downstairs. On reaching the ground floor, he went outside and squatted down in a corner to wait for Li Delin to return home.

Li Delin stopped dead in his tracks when he saw him. "Uncle Shan!" he exclaimed. "What are you doing here?"

"Your wife wouldn't let me in!" Shushan complained loudly.

Li Delin didn't know what to say. Instead, he asked: "Have you eaten? Come on, follow me."

That night, Li Delin stayed with Uncle Shushan in the small university guest house. The two of them had a few drinks and gossiped the night away. Finally, Uncle Shushan put his mouth up to Li Delin's ear and said, resoundingly: "Delin, that wife of yours is no good. Just look what she's done! Look how she came running home! We welcomed her with open arms, and she didn't have a friendly word to say to us, not even a grunt! The way I see it, she thinks she's too big for our little village. What about that bridal quilt she tore up and threw out? Our village put its heart into making that for her. And that bit of fun in the bridal chamber, that's just our country custom. So what if she got groped a bit by the lads? Isn't that just what we do to a winter melon to get rid of the mildew? What did she think we were going to do when she caused all that trouble? Call it a joke? Laugh it off?"

At this, something clicked in Li Delin's brain, and he suddenly remembered that when he and Luo Qiuyi got married, she had put a small box into their big leather trunk. Once, when he was looking for something for her, he came across that box as he was rummaging around, and he couldn't resist the opportunity to open it. What he found was a bundle of twenty or so love letters, tied up with a red silk ribbon. She was married now, so what was she doing

80

still keeping something like that? What did she think she was doing?

After Uncle Shushan left, the cold war broke out again between husband and wife. This time, it was Li Delin who set it off. When he was angry, he never said anything but just sulked all day, and at night he moved out of the bedroom to sleep on the living room sofa.

"What's the matter?" Luo Qiuyi asked.

"Nothing... no, nothing," Li Delin replied.

"I know you. When you say 'nothing', it means something's up. Spit it out!"

"Really, it's nothing. I've just got stuff to think about."

Luo Qiuyi threw a pillow at him. "Well, off you go and think about it, then!"

Gradually, an emotional chasm developed between them. It didn't seem to be any one big thing that caused it, just a whole string of little things. Whatever Luo Qiuyi said, Li Delin never answered back, and on the face of it, he always seemed to listen to her. But in reality, his silence indicated the size of the emotional gap that existed between them. They simply didn't talk about it.

Even though they weren't saying much to each other, Luo Qiuyi was still very solicitous of her husband over the little things. Every morning, a cup of warm milk, an egg, a slice of bread, even some fruit and assorted other little dishes would appear promptly on the breakfast table. Whenever Li Delin needed to change, there were always fresh clothes neatly stacked in the closet. And every month, on payday, she remembered to slip 200 yuan into his jacket pocket so he had some spending money.

In fact, Luo Qiuyi still thought she could covertly influence him, reform him, even. To an outside observer, she seemed to be successful too. In terms of haircut, clothes and general lifestyle, anyone could see the major changes in Li Delin. But no one could see what was going on inside his head.

Of course, one way or another, things had changed between them. Although Li Delin had his suspicions about his wife, he hadn't been able to find out who she was carrying on with. Then, suddenly that summer, the household had two things to celebrate. One was that Luo Qiuyi fell pregnant. The other was that Li Delin had a response to his quest to study for a doctorate abroad when

Columbia University sent him an official notice of admission. Of course, Li Delin was delighted when he learned that Luo Qiuyi was pregnant, but he also had a few qualms that, in the new circumstances, she might stop him from taking up Columbia's offer. But when she saw the letter, Luo Qiuyi was almost childlike in her delight. She hugged him and whispered from the depths of his embrace: "That's wonderful, darling. Now we have two reasons to celebrate!"

Despite this, Li Delin still hesitated. However you looked at it, his wife was pregnant, and if he was to leave now, wouldn't that be a bit unfeeling?

"You think I should still go, even with you in this condition?"

"Go? Of course you should go! It's such a great opportunity, why wouldn't you go?"

"Then you–"

"It's only three years, isn't it? Don't worry about it, it's not a problem. Besides, I've got my mum and dad here. I'll wait for you."

"Then thank you, thank you for your understanding."

"You have to remember that I married a scientist, the Father of Wheat. That's more than worth a little inconvenience! You must remember that I won't be there to look after you, and you mustn't overdo things. There's just one condition: you've got to give up smoking. Then just think how much you are going to learn about Western science..."

That evening, the two of them cuddled together, a little spark running between them. Li Delin put his ear to Luo Qiuyi's belly, and listened for a long time... until she whispered gently: "It's too soon. It's just a little seedling, your little seedling. But by the time you come back, it will be calling you 'Daddy'."

His head resting on his wife's breast, Li Delin was very moved by this: "Then you..."

"Phoning is too expensive, letters are better. You must write to me."

"I'll write, I'll write. I'll write every week."

"Always remember, there'll be two people waiting for you here."

"I know, I know!"

Li Delin couldn't help himself, and his hands strayed to Luo Qiuyi's breasts. She leaned closer into him and said: "So, darling, you're still thinking about 'pollination' are you, Dr Li, my little foreign PhD. Is that what you're thinking about?"

"Do we dare? It's not a problem?"

"What kind of problem could there be between husband and wife?"

Li Delin carefully climbed on top of her and nibbled her earlobe. She gave a little cry and lay back into the bed.

The month before Li Delin left was their happiest time together. Luo Qiuyi started making him nicer things to eat. They often went out together, went shopping together and cooked together. His colleagues threw him a going-away party, and Luo Qiuyi went with him. Even when he was drinking, she didn't really try to stop him, giving him a lot of face in front of the others. When it came to sorting out his luggage, they went window-shopping and picked out what he needed. From head to toe, all the clothes he took with him had been personally chosen by Luo Qiuyi. Even though the final decision always rested with Luo Qiuyi, they jointly discussed every decision and it was all very harmonious.

Then, one day, Luo Qiuyi suddenly exploded again: "So what exactly is it? Don't make me guess, OK!"

"Nothing, there's nothing, really there isn't. Is this... is this because I'm about to go?"

"You've got something on your mind. If it's not me and it's not the child, what is it? Spit it out!"

"There's... there's nothing else. You've... you've thought of everything. I was... I was just thinking about... about going home for a visit."

"I knew there was something. What's the matter with you? Do you think I'd stop you? It's your duty to go and see your old man."

She took an envelope out of her bag and gave it to Li Delin.

"Here's a thousand yuan. Go home and give it to your dad."

He stared at her and asked: "This..." He knew that all the household savings had already been changed into US dollars. This must be from Luo Qiuyi's own personal secret stash. After this, he didn't dare ask for anything else. When he went home on his trip, he discovered that his father had really aged and his legs, which had always been bad, were now making walking difficult. When Li Delin got to the village, he saw his father tottering along, carrying a small bundle of firewood and slumping down to sit underneath the old persimmon tree at the entrance to the village. When Li Delin came up to him, he panted out his son's childhood nickname: "Are you Little Rootstick?"

Li Delin's heart lurched and he said: "Dad, it's me!"

"Is that you, Delin? Where's your wife? Why hasn't she come with you?"

Li Delin didn't reply. And there was the problem. Li Delin's father already had one foot in the grave, but he was in no position to look after him, and even less did he dare suggest taking him back to the city to care for him. That evening, when Uncle Shushan invited him to dinner, he got drunk again. He was so overcome by remorse and resentment that he began to weep and wail: "I'm such a bad son!"

"If you ask me, you should dump her," Uncle Shushan said.

FIVE

THE THREE YEARS HE SPENT IN AMERICA were a very hard time for Li Delin.

Even when he had received his doctorate and was about to leave for home, he still had no idea where to find New York's busiest street, Seventh Avenue. He had spent the whole three years living frugally and struggling to get by. By day he went to classes, and most evenings he was in the laboratory working part-time for his professor. When he was tired and couldn't take any more, he would sit on the steps outside the lab and smoke a cigarette to lift his mood. He got through those three years one day at a time, relying on those cigarettes.

When he first got to the States, he kept to his side of the bargain by writing to Luo Qiuyi once a week, telling her what was going on over there. Her replies were always very long, saying how much she missed him and how much she worried about him; she even wrote a couple of poems. Later on, after their daughter was born, she was so busy that the letters gradually tailed off. If there was anything important, she telephoned.

In the year he received his doctorate, he had the possibility of staying on in America. His supervisor, Professor Weiner, was very supportive and gave him two choices: one, stay on to do post-doctoral research; two, he could give him a recommendation to a large American company. Luo Qiuyi telephoned him to say that if he decided to stay, she would bring their daughter over so they could all be together. In other words, she was encouraging him not to come back. But in the end, he did go back. There were four reasons he insisted on doing so: one, he was worried about his ageing father; two, he wanted to finish his research into Chinese wheat varieties; three, he had been sent abroad at the government's expense, and if he stayed, he would have to pay a lot of money back to the university; four, he had never got used to American food, and endured chronic enteritis. Every time he ate a burger, it came right back up again. What he really craved was braised noodles.

On the evening of his return to China, the couple were very soon squabbling again. Of course, he was delighted when he first met his daughter, but little Jiajia was still only two, and as soon as he picked her up to cuddle her, she started wailing and crying, which really put him off. He forced himself to keep holding her for a while but it wasn't long before he handed her back to the nanny Luo Qiuyi had engaged, saying: "I guess she's still shy with strangers."

"Are you surprised?" Luo Qiuyi said. "She's almost three, and this is the first time you've held her."

"You're right, it is. But wasn't it you who told me to go to America?"

As they argued the toss, Luo Qiuyi suddenly realised that Li Delin had become a stranger. He was no longer that introverted, unsophisticated Li Delin of before. He might not actively have studied Western "culture", but it had undoubtedly brought about a change in him. He talked in a loud voice now, as if he didn't care who heard him.

What she didn't know was that, when Li Delin went to class the first day after his arrival in the States, he had been reprimanded by his supervisor. Professor Weiner had told his students to introduce themselves one by one, so they could all get to know each other. When it was Li Delin's turn, he stood up and said: "I am Li Delin... I'm Ch... I'm Chinese."

To his surprise, Professor Weiner pointed at him and shouted: "What is your name? Say it louder! Louder! Louder still! Don't you have any self-belief? Someone who doesn't believe in himself, doesn't have any place among my students! So, say it again. What is your name? This is no place for anyone without passion and energy either. You're in the United States now! Understand?"

There he was, Professor Weiner, an American of Jewish descent, standing on the podium, eyeballs starting from his head, radiating explosive energy. He told Li Delin: "Remember, America is a country that worships individuality. From the moment God created you, you are always 'I'! You've always got to remember that 'I'! You need to shout it out to everyone: 'I, Li Delin, am from China...'" From then on, day by day, Li Delin grew more assertive.

During his three years in America, Li Delin didn't lose any of his old bad habits. In fact, in some ways, far from them disappearing, they got worse. For instance, his smoking got heavier and heavier. After his return, of course, he was still not allowed to smoke in the apartment, so as soon as he got up in the morning, he went out to squat on the doorstep of the building and smoked three cigarettes before going back indoors. In his jacket pocket, he always carried a miniature ashtray that Professor Weiner had given him, and he took it out whenever he needed it. In the dead of night, he would scramble out of bed, grab a cigarette and miniature ashtray, and then scurry outside to sit on the doorstep. Any neighbours going up or down the stairs would see the glowing tip of the cigarette and call out: "Is that you smoking there, Professor Li?"

And he would reply: "I'm just having a couple of puffs."

While Li Delin was in America, he and Luo Qiuyi kept up their exchange of letters like parted lovers, sharing their thoughts and feelings and hopes for an early reunion. But as soon as he got back to China, relations between them became more strained. To start with, he hadn't discussed his return with Luo Qiuyi. At the time, there was a bit of a fad for going abroad and Luo Qiuyi had been reckoning on going to join him. Because she had never let Li Delin have any say in running their lives, she took the initiative to prepare selling the apartment. She would give his father some of the proceeds and then go and join Li Delin in America. She believed that research conditions were better in America, so Li Delin would be able to continue his work and repay his country for all its support at the same time. As for her, she could take the opportunity to pursue her own studies. But as it turned out, all these hopes were in vain. Naturally, she wasn't best pleased.

The thing she found really intolerable was that, far from giving up cigarettes as she had demanded, he was actually smoking more heavily than before. This just increased her ill temper. What was more, even though he had spent three years in the States, living and studying, he still took no care over his clothes and just threw on any old thing before going out. Luo Qiuyi said: "You're back now and you still don't do your buttons up. What do you think you look like?" But he just stood there and no matter what she said, stayed silent, a disapproving look on his face. Consequently, the atmosphere in the apartment was icy.

As their life returned to a boring normality, Luo Qiuyi no longer regarded Li Delin as the Father of Wheat of her former dreams. Now, he appeared to her as just a farmer in a battered old hat, stinking of tobacco smoke. So what if he has a foreign doctorate? He still drank and smoked too much and was full of other faults. As her disappointment increased, and unable to hold back any longer, she said: "Can we really go on like this? What do you think?"

Li Delin just kept quiet, as he always had. He was fully aware that Luo Qiuyi was the daughter of a professor, that she was very beautiful, had made the running in their getting married and had given him a daughter. But ever since she had been with him, she hadn't enjoyed a day's good fortune, and in his heart, he felt as though he had continually to be apologising to her. But living like this, not in control of anything for himself, that really was... well, what it meant was that, although he had wanted to come back to China, he really hadn't wanted to return home. So now, he spent all his time either teaching or in the laboratory.

But even though his home life was very unhappy, his career was going from strength to strength. In less than three years after returning from America with his foreign doctorate, he had had a string of honours heaped on his head, including: adviser to the Expert Committee of the Ministry of Agriculture; academic leader of the State Council's "863" Programme; and provincial management expert. It wasn't long before he was promoted from deputy director to director of the Department of Agriculture. In the autumn of the third year, the Institute of Agriculture was expanded and renamed, and when the team was appointed, he was promoted to vice-principal of the new University of Agricultural Science and Technology. His ability to leapfrog up the ranks into the vice-principal's post was directly down to his former teacher, Wu Tianduo, the previous vice-principal. Before retiring, this Wu Tianduo had limped, leaning on his cane, one step at a time, right up to the seventh floor of the Provincial Party Committee offices, and when he met with the minister of the Organisational Department of the Provincial Party Committee, he said loudly and directly: "Check it out! Just check it out! Look at all the forty-nine agricultural universities across the country. How many of them can get papers published in the United States? How many people's articles are published in the *Soil Science Society of America Journal*? That is a world-class academic journal! Li Delin is now a PhD in biology from the United States. After he got his PhD, a big American company wanted to hire him with a huge salary, but he refused and returned to China. If you don't make use of someone like that, who are you going to use?"

Then he went on: "In three months, I will reach retirement age. I am taking the initiative to step down in favour of a better candidate so Li Delin can take over as vice-principal of the university. I would ask the committee to give this proposal serious consideration."

The chairman of the committee replied: "Don't worry, Lao Wu. As long as he's got the ability, we will certainly consider him."

"Good!" Wu Tianduo said, thumping the floor with his cane. "Let me leave you, Chairman, with two lines of poetry by Gong Zizhen: 'I urge the Lord of Heaven to constantly rejuvenate, and not overlook talent because it does not fit the normal pattern!'"

A month later, after going through the Organisational Department's investigation and the standard democratic recommendation procedures, Li Delin's appointment as vice-principal of the University of Agricultural Science and Technology came through.

On the evening of the day he was promoted to vice-principal, Li Delin got drunk again. To be honest, he really had no choice in the matter. The deputy minister of the Organisational Department of the Provincial Party Committee came to the announcement ceremony, bringing his entourage with him. After the ceremony was over, the principal and the secretary of the university jointly decided to ask the deputy minister and staff to stay for a "light meal". The reasons for the invitation were unarguable: first, Professor Wu was a highly respected academic, and as he was taking early retirement, the meal could be viewed as Lao Wu's official farewell party; second, Li Delin held a foreign PhD and was a nationally recognised expert on wheat, so his appointment as vice-principal certainly had to be celebrated. The deputy minister and his entourage couldn't possibly refuse the invitation, so they stayed. The banquet took place in the university's small dining hall. It was only natural that, when the toasts began, they were directed at Professor Wu, both because of his seniority in age and also because of his selflessness in stepping down in favour of someone younger. But he held out his hand and pointed, saying: "Thank you everyone, but I have high blood sugar and my doctor says I mustn't drink alcohol. How about this instead? Li Delin is my student, and he has a good head for wine, so he can stand in for me." After that, everyone turned their attention on Li Delin. Whenever the professor was toasted, he had to drink; and whenever he was toasted himself, he had to drink too. On after another, he had to return the toasts of the departmental director, the principal, the secretary and so on and so on. By the time the party broke up, he was in a terrible state.

In the end, it was the staff of the Departmental Office who helped him home. When two of them half-carried him to the door of his apartment, he sobered up just enough to wave them away, and say, grandly: "You can go now. I'm fine." But when the pair had left, he couldn't find his key, so he pounded on the door, shouting: "Open the door! I am Li Delin and I come from China! Open the door! I am Li Delin and I come from China!"

But the door remained firmly shut. After a while, he sloped off lopsidedly to wait in the corridor.

That night, Luo Qiuyi was spitting with anger. She thought it was outrageous of Li Delin to get drunk like that when he had just been made a vice-principal. He had lost face completely.

Next morning, the door opened. Standing there, Luo Qiuyi could see that Li Delin had sobered up and was squatting silently in the corridor, smoking. "You'd better put that cigarette out and come in," she said, unenthusiastically.

After he had gone into the apartment and changed into some slippers, Li Delin saw that there was an already completed divorce contract lying on the coffee table.

Luo Qiuyi said, icily: "After a performance like that, I'm not going to wait a single day more. Sign it!"

Head down, Li Delin sat on the sofa and said nothing.

"Well, what do you mean by all this? Say something!"

Li Delin remained silent. At that moment, a divorce was exactly what he wanted. He didn't want to wait another day either. But the trouble was, he had just been made vice-principal, and if he were to get divorced immediately, he was afraid the story would get out and spread like wildfire, ruining his reputation. Besides, they had a daughter now too, and constantly rowing like this wasn't good for the child at all.

He looked up and said: "I'm really sorry. There was nothing I could do about last night. From now on–"

"There is no 'from now on'," Luo Qiuyi interrupted him. "How many times have you said that? Sign!"

So it goes without saying, cold war hostilities were resumed. Li Delin didn't go home for a whole month and stayed in his newly allocated office suite.

A month later, Li Delin surrendered again. It was the third time he had waved the white flag. Taking the advice of his respected teacher, Professor Wu, he moved back home again. Professor Wu had said: "I've watched Luo Qiuyi grow up. Everyone knows she comes from a wealthy family, she's intelligent, beautiful, kind-hearted. Look how clean and neat she keeps your apartment, how she organises everything for you. What more do you want? She has ambitions for you, and you've got to understand that. What is more, you're a leadership cadre now, and you have to look to your image!" And with that, Professor Wu took him into custody and escorted him home.

After that, Li Delin and Luo Qiuyi's life together proceeded along a pattern of mutual indifference. During this time there did seem to be the opening for a reconciliation, but it was missed because neither of them could see their way to taking it. For Li Delin, the sticking point was his secret pain at his father never being allowed to come to the city again, and for Luo Qiuyi, it was Li Delin's refusal to cut himself off from all those country relatives of his, no matter how much she wanted him to. As time passed, a kind of tacit agreement seemed to have developed. Luo Qiuyi was quietly attending a foreign language class. She had already passed the College English Test Six and was now working towards her IELTS, in preparation for going abroad at some stage in the future. Li Delin was devoting himself, heart and soul, to Huanghuai Number One, and was indeed making some progress.

In a flash, a few years had passed, and neither of them could take it any more. In the summer of the year in question, word spread round the college that Li Delin was going to be made deputy provincial governor. Almost as soon as the news broke, more and more people came looking for him. All these self-proclaimed relatives, fellow villagers, classmates, friends and students practically laid siege to his home. And, of course, as soon as they heard in Meiling that he was about to become deputy provincial governor in charge of agriculture, party secretaries and county commissioners from every county in the area all came to pay their respects, and his telephone never seemed to stop ringing. Luo Qiuyi was beside herself with fury, and one night, she couldn't stand it any more and unplugged the telephone.

Finally, Li Delin and Luo Qiuyi laid their cards on the table. She said: "Let's get divorced. I'm begging you!"

In truth, Li Delin had also long since given up any hope. "If we do, what about the child?"

Luo Qiuyi replied in a tone that brooked no argument: "You don't get to look after the child. I'll take her with me. All you have to do is sign. Once you do, we'll be free of each other."

"Won't you reconsider?"

"I don't want to wait a minute longer. It's for your own good too. You know that if your promotion comes through and you're made deputy provincial governor, you're going to have to think about your reputation. Just get on with it and sign."

Finally, Li Delin said: "All right, I'll sign."

On the day they finalised the divorce, Luo Qiuyi said spontaneously: "That's it, we've separated. Let's go and have one last meal together."

"All right, where do you want to go?" Li Delin said, automatically.

"Somewhere close... and somewhere quiet. How about the UBC coffee shop?"

The two of them sat down in a quiet corner of the UBC and ordered a simple meal. Some Russian piano music was playing in the background, long, slow and melancholic like the vast expanse of a great river. Tears sprang unbidden to Luo Qiuyi's eyes. "Do you remember that year I proposed to you? How I came all by myself to find you at the County Agricultural Technology Station?"

"I remember. Of course I remember! You were so..." He couldn't get the word "beautiful" out.

"Childish? Is that what you were going to say? I was too young back then. I thought life was so pure and straightforward. I really was childish. I also played my part in all this. Try not to blame me too much."

"No, no, it's me who should be apologising. I've got so many faults. It's going to be hard for you looking after our daughter by yourself. It's a two-person job. If you have any problems, you must tell me."

"I know we've separated now, but there are a couple of things I want to say to you. Call them my parting words."

"Go on."

"I said back then that the man I was going to marry was a scientist, China's King of Wheat. Do you remember?"

"You had too high an opinion of me."

"No, even now, I don't regret saying it. It's also why I'm not in favour of you being deputy governor. Anyone can be that, but there's only one King of Wheat. I hope you'll remember those words."

Li Delin looked at her thoughtfully and said: "Don't worry, I won't forget what my profession is."

"If you want to be a real scientist, you have to cut the umbilical cord, not have anything more to do with that home village of yours. Otherwise, they'll destroy you."

Li Delin fell silent for a moment, then said: "You're still prejudiced against countryfolk, aren't you?"

"It's not that I'm prejudiced, I just have a few problems with them. I'm telling you, no matter what modern times we are living in, they still think with their bellies. How many problems is your belly going to solve for you?"

After a while, she spoke again: "So be it. But whether you want to hear it or not, I am going to repeat my second piece of advice: they can destroy you."

SIX

AT FIRST, after the separation, Li Delin felt completely at a loss.

Luo Qiuyi's beauty still haunted him, but at the same time, he felt a sense of relief that he was free. After a day of meetings, it was nice to go home, free and unfettered. If he wanted to squat on the floor, he could squat on the floor; if he wanted to sit on the sofa, he could sit on the sofa. He could lie on the sofa smoking a cigarette, curled up or stretched out, and tapping the ash onto the floor... it was grand not to have anyone nagging him. There were a lot of business meals, too many for him to cope with really. Occasionally, he drank a few too many glasses of wine and no one told him off. If he really didn't want to go home to eat, there was a small cafeteria in the college, or he could go out for braised noodles and spicy pepper soup. There was no longer anyone to say: "Brush your teeth, your breath stinks!"

At the time the couple broke up, the Huanghuai Number One project he had been nurturing so carefully had begun to bear fruit. His most significant achievement was the successful cultivation of a strain of double-eared wheat. Although only one plant survived, it was the dawn of hope, especially because, in his theoretical work, he had progressed even further. His article entitled "The phenomenon of genetic variation in hybrid wheat" was published in an internationally renowned journal and attracted the attention of the foreign academic community. As a result, he became an internationally renowned expert on wheat.

No one had any idea that his theoretical article on wheat had been inspired by the breakdown of his marriage! His research on the combination potential of wheat strains, that is, the research on the advantages and disadvantages of wheat hybridisation, led him to discover that the so-called "strong-strong combination" was a misapprehension.

It was like his marriage. Luo Qiuyi was from a family of high-ranking intellectuals. She was beautiful, generous and high-minded. She would be regarded as an excellent woman and an ideal mother. As for Li Delin, although he came from a poor family, he had an American PhD and was an expert in bioengineering. He too could be regarded as an excellent man and an ideal father. This man and this woman, one male one female, one yin and one yang, should have been an ideal combination. The sum of the two of them was "excellent + excellent", which should have been "one plus one equals three, or four, five, six, seven, even eight". It should have been highly advantageous. However, in real life, their emotional energies, the equivalent of two wheat strains' genetic coding, had never been able to combine. Always ill-matched, they were, in fact, mutually exclusive, and in the end, couldn't survive. Why not? Looked at this way, it was a matter of energy fields. Everyone is a magnetic field, and whether this magnetic field can connect with that magnetic field is not just a matter of fate. Of course you can get married, but it won't be any good. In this regard, a tragedy of a marriage, like a calcium carbide reaction, was ultimately responsible for Li Delin's "wheat theory".

Since becoming deputy provincial governor, he had to attend meetings in three or four different venues a day, not to mention drinks in the bar. There was no time to go to the research station. His laboratory gradually became covered with a layer of dust. "Wheat" was getting left further and further behind, and at the time, there was nothing he could do about it.

After the divorce, Li Delin was very lonely. His student, Liu Jinding, came over every so often, just to go with him to eat noodles. At the time, Liu Jinding was already deputy director of the Huanghuai City Office. He knew his teacher's moods. Every time he came to the provincial capital, Li Delin asked him: "What are you doing here again?" and he would say: "I'm greedy and want to eat those noodles on Shuncheng Street." Li Delin didn't think anything of it. Sure, braised noodles were ordinary people's food, but couldn't he, the deputy governor, be an "ordinary person"? So the two went to eat braised noodles together. For Liu Jinding, however, every time he ate braised noodles, he benefitted in one way or another. Within a year, Liu Jinding became the director of the City Government Office.

The day after Liu Jinding became director of the Huanghuai City Government Office, he came to the provincial capital again. This time, he had a stack of pictures of young women in his pocket. After going into Li Delin's home, he said: "Let me give you some advice, Master."

Li Delin grinned and said: "So you came here specially to give me some advice, did you?"

"Yes, there's something I've been wanting to say to you for a long time."

"Go on."

"You've just become deputy provincial governor. You need

someone to look after to you. If you keep living this bachelor life, people will start to talk."

"Oh, is that all? There's no rush, I'll give it some thought. Has anyone actually said anything?"

"Not yet. It's just that, with you on your own... well, to put it another way, I know that your old dad back in the village needs someone to look after him."

"Yes, it's true, my father's legs are bad and I keep meaning to bring him up here. But I'm so busy every day, I never get round to it."

"I've already been transferred to the city, Master, so I can't keep an eye on him either. Do you want me to find someone?"

Li Delin shook his head. "It would be hard to find someone suitable."

At this point, Liu Jinding took out the stack of photos from his pocket and put them on the coffee table, saying: "Master, these girls have all been carefully selected by me. All of them are young and beautiful, and they all have a bachelor's degree. You choose one, and I'll go and talk to her."

Li Delin glanced at the pictures and shook his head again. "I have to be a bit realistic at my age. Too young is no good, and too beautiful is not good either..."

When Liu Jinding saw that he wasn't going to look at the pictures properly, he said: "To be honest, none of them have the... er... temperament or character to be the wife of a respected teacher like you. Tell me what it is that you are looking for."

Li Delin thought for a moment, then said: "All I need is someone who knows how to look after people and who doesn't mind mucking in with my father. It doesn't matter if she's not educated."

(To tell the truth, in Li Delin's subconscious, the theories he had worked out about combining the qualities of strains of wheat, and his "theory of wheat" regarding the survival of plants, were indefinably influencing his thinking. Later on, when he thought back on this affair, it was too late to have any regrets.)

"All right," Liu Jinding said. "Leave it to me."

That summer, when Li Delin went out on a tour of inspection for the first time, he came across something very exciting. It was something that reinforced his "wheat theory". When out on inspection around Huanghuai, he visited three counties in three days. It may have been that the city's top brass knew about the teacher-student relationship between him and Liu Jinding, but however it was, they sent Liu Jinding, as director of the City Government Office, to look after his needs. On this particular day, Li Delin had been listening to reports all day in the city and by the time he finished dinner, he was really tired. Liu Jinding asked him cautiously: "You must be exhausted after a day of meetings like that. Shall I take you somewhere to relax a bit?"

Li Delin was rather startled by this suggestion: "What do you mean 'relax'? I can't do anything that will get me into trouble."

"Don't worry, Master, I know this is your territory. I wouldn't do anything to cause you any trouble. All I meant was I could take you somewhere to have a bathe."

"I've got a bathroom at home, haven't I?"

"It's not quite the same thing. I'm talking about a spa. Just follow me."

So Liu Jinding left his entourage and took Li Delin to his car alone. They drove out of the grounds of the City Government Guest House and made their way to the front doors of the Flower World Hotel.

The hotel was newly opened and was the most luxurious in Huanghuai. It was a Sino-foreign joint venture and a "five-star" service centre combining accommodation, catering, entertainment and a spa. It had twenty-two floors, and Liu Jinding took Li Delin directly to the seventh floor in a special lift. At the lift door on the seventh floor, a group of people wearing white uniforms and white gloves were waiting respectfully in the corridor.

Xie Zhichang stepped forward wearing a white Chinese-style suit and said: "Uncle! Uncle! I've been hoping you would come!"

Li Delin was very surprised to see him there and said: "Is all this yours, Zhichang?"

"It's a Sino-foreign joint venture. Your past kindnesses and Liu Jinding's contacts helped a lot. Now you're here, treat it as your home."

Li Delin was very touched and said: "I haven't seen you for ages, Zhichang. You've made it big. Didn't you run a flower company? How did you get into real estate?"

"Diversification is the thing now. I'm still selling flowers too..." Xie Zhichang replied rather vaguely

"Ah, very good, very good. Now, you must stop calling me 'Uncle'. There are only a couple of years between us. Call me Lao Li."

"But you're an even more important official now, and we're certainly cousins, at least."

"Even so, just call me Lao Li."

After that, Xie Zhichang walked the two men away from the lift. He waved his hand, and the hotel manager Bai Shouxin trotted forward to greet them, saying respectfully: "Ah, yes, yes! Welcome, welcome! How wonderful to have such an important official as our guest! Mr Xie has already explained who you are, you are..."

Li Delin stretched out his hand and said: "Hello. My name is Li. Just call me Lao Li."

Liu Jinding hurriedly took over the conversation, saying: "Yes, this is the old Comrade Li, up in town from the province. Please go ahead and set things up."

"You just see to yourself, Zhichang," Li Delin said. "I won't be bathing with you."

"All right then," Xie Zhichang said, knowingly. "Liu Jinding can keep you company. Look after him well, Shouxin, I owe him a lot!"

"Don't worry, President Xie, I will," Bai Shouxin replied hurriedly, before barking out some orders: "Get a move on! Open up Number One, Number One VIP Room!"

Number One VIP Room proved to be a huge, luxurious private room that seemed to take up half that floor of the building. It contained a large circular sofa, coffee tables, a sound system, a stage curtain, recording equipment and other such stuff. Li Delin and Liu Jinding had no sooner sat down than a parade of white-uniformed flunkies filed in, each carrying a tray on which there were all manner of fruits, teas and liquors. One by one, they put them down on the coffee tables, then withdrew without anyone saying a word.

After a while, the door opened again and, led by Bai Shouxin himself, twelve women slipped in one after another. They were all wearing the same white gauze dresses that were almost see-through and thin as cicada wings, with red corsages on their chests. There was a dream-like quality to the way the floated in. Each one of them was wearing a small badge at their waist with red numbers on a white background: 1, 2, 3, 4, 5, 6... They lined up and stood in front of the two men.

Bai Shouxin stood to one side respectfully and said: "Honoured Gentlemen, these girls just arrived today. They're all from the north-east and they're college graduates too. Make your choice, Gentlemen."

At this point, Li Delin's face suffused with anger and he turned on Liu Jinding: "I thought you were talking about going for a bath. What do you think you're up to here?"

Liu Jinding hurriedly tried to explain: "Don't get angry, Master. I... I just thought... I just thought you might have a dance first to work up a sweat, and then..."

Li Delin wasn't mollified at all: "Outrageous! Have you forgotten who you are?"

Liu Jinding hastily gestured to Bai Shouxin: "Tell them to go away, Manager Bai."

Bai Shouxin could see that things weren't right, so he gestured to the twelve girls and led them out of the room.

Once they had gone, Li Delin said: "You are my student, Liu Jinding, and there is something I have to say to you. You are working at grassroots level, and you have to deal with all manner of people. I know it's not easy. We are in a market economy now, and I know we have to be a lot more free and active, but one thing remains essential, and that is to maintain propriety in everything we do. If you don't, you're going to get into trouble."

"Yes, Master, I will remember your words. I just thought you might like to relax a bit... I didn't mean anything else by it."

Finally, Li Delin sighed and said: "You know, I spent a long time in America and I never saw anything like this."

That night, the two of them took a bath together and let a Yangzhou master masseur massage their backs. When they got back to the City Government Guest House, Li Delin said with feeling that he was indeed refreshed. Although Li Delin had rebuked his student to his face, deep down inside him, there was still a little bit of his sex drive left that he wasn't going to admit to. He had had to use all his willpower to control himself so that he didn't weaken.

Yes indeed, when those twelve girls were stood in front of him, it had been all he could do not to gawp open-mouthed. What was going on there? All the same size, the same figure, with the same coquettish manner. And all of them looking like they'd stepped out of a fashion magazine, they were so tall and delicate. And highly educated too? How was it possible? Not only that, either: they'd all come to the city to do that job? It was quite incredible!

Leaning back on his bed, he lit a cigarette and exhaled slowly. He wasn't exactly sure why, but he couldn't help asking: "Were those girls really all from the northeast?"

"They could well be," Liu Jinding replied, circumspectly. "They all had northeast accents."

Li Delin sighed again and said: "Did you see how tall they were? Every one of them! They were all so young, and so beautiful too. How could they be up to anything bad?"

"Times have changed, Master. Nowadays young people–"

"Are they really all college graduates?"

"It's possible. According to Lao Xie, this manager Bai is a very capable fellow, and it was him who recruited these girls. I've heard that there are just three requirements when recruiting girls like that."

"Oh yes, and what are they?" Li Delin asked, puzzled.

"Well-put-together, unmarried and university educated. And of course there are the details like looks, vital statistics..."

Li Delin gave a series of sighs as he said: "Aiyayayaya, it's really... really not right."

"You're from the countryside, Master, and you've spent many years in the classroom, so maybe you're not too familiar with the way society is going. Those girls are all in it for money. There's a popular saying about it. Have you heard it?"

"No, what is it?" Li Delin couldn't help asking.

"They're called northeast tigers, and people say they are coming out of the mountains to raid the cities, descendants of the Chinese who collaborated with the Westerners way back, bold and brazen as you please. There are some girls from Hunan too, and they're known as the Hunan Women's Regiment."

Li Delin laughed and said: "What nonsense! How can they be descendants of collaborationists? And you're saying those beautiful girls are all tigresses?" He gestured dismissively. "Enough! Let's not talk about them any more."

Li Delin spent a sleepless night as he let his imagination roam free.

The next morning, as they were having breakfast, he told Liu

Jinding: "I've thought it through, and at my age, I need to be a bit realistic. I'm not going to find love, so I'm better off looking for what I need back in my home village. You can help me find someone a bit more traditional, someone down-to-earth who knows how to look after a man. She doesn't have to be particularly clever. If you find someone suitable, we can try her out looking after my old dad and see how that goes."

"So what you're saying, Master, is that you're looking for a kind of nanny-housekeeper. Is that right?"

"Yes, that's the idea," Li Delin replied rather vaguely. "She shouldn't be too old, but if she can look after old people and can muck in with everybody, then we'll see what comes of it."

"I get the picture."

Three months later, during the Mid-Autumn Festival, a woman from Meiling called Xu Ercai presented herself in front of Li Delin.

SEVEN

OBJECTIVELY SPEAKING, the "June 29th Incident" had a definite impact on Li Delin.

For quite a while, he was not at all comfortable in his new role as deputy provincial governor in charge of agriculture. He had become like a spinning top, spinning from one meeting to the next.

His was an inland province and what was considered a major agricultural producer. As deputy governor in charge of agriculture – actually, it wasn't just agriculture but forestry, animal husbandry, fisheries and auxiliary industries, all under the control of the one department – there were far too many meetings, and he was required to speak at every one of them. Sometimes, he had to go to two or three different conference venues a day, and he would end up taking the wrong speech. Although the texts of his speeches were prepared for him in advance by his secretary or sometimes with the help of other departments, he still made some glaring blunders at first. Once, he rushed to attend a provincial forestry conference, but what he took out of his bag was the speech for the provincial hog slaughterers' conference. When he began to speak, he declared: "Comrades, pig farmers, you..." He suddenly went quiet and stayed that way for a long time before saying: "No, that's wrong. I'm sorry, Comrades, that's wrong!" The hall erupted with laughter. Any other leading cadre wouldn't have been so open about reading the wrong speech. They would just have swapped notes and started again. But he had actually admitted his error.

On another occasion, at a high-level forum, he unexpectedly got the name of fellow important official wrong. This was a real faux pas. After the meeting, the other official was very upset and said: "Can't you even remember my name, Lao Li? We've worked together for years!" He had no choice but to own up and apologise for his absent-mindedness.

What Li Delin was most uncomfortable with was listening to reports. All the prefectures and cities came to "report on progress", but really most were asking for money. As soon as they had delivered their reports, they had to discuss them for an hour or two, without even a break to pee. There were always many things he didn't under-stand, so his mind often wandered. As he listened, all he could think of was being somewhere else. Once, he dozed off while listening to a report. In his reverie, he suddenly remembered that it was time for the wheat to bloom. (Wheat has the smallest flower with the shortest life-span of any plant anywhere. A tiny little bit of a flower, almost invis-ible to the naked eye, pink with a spot of yellow. It is hermaphrodite. There is no second flower, and there will never be a third. Its love story is over in an instant, carried on the wind, like a kiss.) He even blurted out: "That kiss! So amazing!"

The whole room was astonished! When he came back to his senses and saw that everyone was staring at him, he said hurriedly: "It's noth-ing. Go on with your report. Very good. Very good."

Almost immediately, a little saying about him started circulating round the province: "Governor Li heard the report – very good."

It takes time to adapt. But he was a PhD who had studied abroad, and he had been intensively trained by his Jewish tutor, Professor Weiner. Wasn't it all just talking, anyway? Having spent so much time immersed in conference rooms, he quickly adapted. When he found himself in places where he was not familiar with the situation, he also gradually learned to use "macrolinguistics", summarising things "one, two, three, four" according to general policy, and occasionally throwing in a few American jokes: all also "very good"!

In this way, Li Delin established an excellent reputation with the cadres of the provincial agencies. First, he had no pretensions and a very equitable temperament; second, although he was a PhD who had studied abroad, he had a local accent that made people feel comfortable with him. In addition, he was a well-known national expert on wheat and his affinity with his area of responsibility was much greater than that of normal officials. What particularly appealed was that, being in charge of agriculture as he was, he always went to the grassroots level to check on the crops. He wore a straw hat and if he had to squat down, he squatted down. He knew exactly how many stalks of wheat and even how many ears an acre of land could produce. The media called him the People's Governor.

However, this People's Governor was criticised in a briefing during the "June 29th Incident". It started out with a group petition triggered by land acquisition. Improper handling led to the incident known as the Lying Across the Tracks Petition that shocked the whole country.

It began as a land acquisition dispute between Huanghuai City's Flower World Group and rural farmers. Objectively speaking, the land was expropriated four years previously, and the money for it had already been paid. At that time, an amount of one thousand yuan per *mu* had been agreed, and because the price was so low, the purpose of the land acquisition was never made explicit.

Xie Zhichang, who was still a "flower man" back then, took advantage of the reform and opening up of the country, and his first move was to become the boss of the Meiling Flower Company. When he moved the company to Huanghuai, he turned it into a Sino-foreign joint venture and changed its name to Flower World Group. He was chairman of the board. He bought this particular piece of land in the name of Flower World Group. Right at the outset when acquiring the land, Xie Zhichang had made a solemn promise. Hand on his heart, he said: "Friends, young and old, you must believe me when I tell you that, in the future our company will grow plants and flowers on a massive scale and open a huge flower market so you will have a great place to make your living. You old folk will be able to live off your pensions, you youngsters will have work in the flower business, and all of you will be looked after." But he did not specify exactly how they would be looked after.

However, the year after the company got the land requisition, the area earmarked for city centre development in the overall urbanisation plan more than doubled and the suburban areas around Meiling became part of the fully urbanised sector. Construction projects sprang up everywhere, and land prices rocketed. In particular, the agreed land requisition fee of 1,000 yuan per *mu* had various deductions applied to it, so that the villagers eventually got less than 500 per *mu*. That wasn't the worst of it, though. Almost immediately, Xie Zhichang used the large area of land he had promised would be used to grow flowers and build a flower market to enter into an urban development plan with a Hong Kong consortium. The first thing they did was put up a luxury hotel. Although, nominally at least, the flower market did open, none of the local farmers used it. The promised pension had a starting age of eighty and, even then, only amounted to a hundred yuan per month.

As a result, the villagers protested. They mobilised more than a hundred people, old and young, and surrounded the headquarters of Flower World Group to protest about the second phase of the company's violent demolition process, along with their failure to meet the terms of the contract and the unauthorised change of land use. An old man was injured in the protest, but they continued to forcefully demand that the land be returned, and they be compensated for their losses.

The matter was handled by Liu Jinding, who was at the time deputy secretary-general of the Huanghuai City Government Office and deputy director of the Demolition Office. It was the first major case he had handled since being appointed deputy secretary-general. Before setting out, he arranged for Helian Dongshan, a deputy departmental-level detective and a member of the Party Committee of the Municipal Public Security Bureau, to work with him. He called Helian Dongshan into his office, and asked: "Lao He, are all the fifty police officers we requested in place?"

"They are in place, as the city requested."

"Do you have a gun?"

Helian Dongshan hesitated for a moment, before replying: "Is it appropriate to bring weapons?"

"You must bring one. You should be fully equipped."

"Very well." Helian Dongshan had no option.

"Bring some blank arrest warrants... and two sub-machine guns."

Helian Dongshan glanced at him and asked: "Secretary-General Liu, is that appropriate under Public Security regulations?"

"What is the first article of the "Three Rules of Discipline and the Eight Points for Attention'?" Liu Jinding asked bluntly.

"Prompt obedience to orders."

"Well, bring your men and follow me."

As they left his office, Liu Jinding patted Helian Dongshan on the shoulder in a very knowing way, and whispered: "You're experienced, Lao He. Don't load the guns. It is not permitted to carry ammunition."

Helian Dongshan breathed a sigh of relief and immediately replied: "Understood."

By this time, the headquarters of Flower World Group had been surrounded for three days. The glass front of the building had been smashed. A large group of villagers who had lost their land were there wearing white headbands and holding white cloth banners with big black characters that read: "Return my land! Blood payment for a blood debt!" Although only a hundred people were involved in the actual protest, it looked like a much bigger crowd. This was because it wasn't just the protesting villagers gathered in front of the office building; there were a lot of passers-by who had stopped to watch too. In fact, spectators tended to considerably outnumber protestors in those days.

Liu Jinding led the police in through the back door of the Flower World building. After some discussion, fifty policemen lined up outside, put up some red tape and blocked the front entrance. Liu Jinding ordered someone to bring up a table and put it on the steps in front of the building. Then, he jumped up onto the table, holding an electric megaphone in his hand, and shouted: "My fellow villagers, young and old, I am Liu Jinding of the Municipal Government! You should know that I am also a farmer and come from three generations of farmers. So I am in sympathy with you. Please trust the government. If there is a problem, we can solve it. You mustn't make trouble or start looting. I must also remind you that Flower World Group is a Sino-foreign joint venture, and the foreign businessmen were invited in by us. The mayor has said that anyone who harms the investment potential of the city is guilty! So let us sit down and discuss any problems. Any problem can be discussed within the framework of the law, but we can't make trouble or cause damage."

Everyone was taken aback for a moment, but then shouted in unison: "Tell that Xie fellow to fuck off!"

Liu Jinding shouted into the megaphone again: "Listen to me, everyone. I am now going to announce the decision made by the city government working group." He turned his head and looked behind him, saying: "Bring Xie Zhichang out!"

At this point, Xie Zhichang finally came forward. When protestors saw him walking out of the lobby, flanked by two police-men, there was a shout from the crowd: "That's him! That's the bastard who lied to us."

Liu Jinding bent down and took a red printed arrest warrant from Helian Dongshan who was standing next to him. He held it up high, right in front of everyone, and shouted through his megaphone: "According to the investigation carried out, as the general manager of the Chinese side of the consortium, this man is under serious suspi-cion of corruption. Arrest and review are now to be carried out. Take him away!"

Everyone was stunned, as Xie Zhichang was surrounded by several more policemen and led away.

A deep-throated roar exploded from the crowd, and they shouted in unison: "Leave him here. Leave that bastard here!"

Liu Jinding raised the megaphone again and shouted: "Where is the village head of Balizhuang, Laohei, Wu Laohei! Come on forward, please come on out!"

Wu Laohei, the village chief of Balizhuang, had been hiding at the back the crowd, but when he heard the megaphone calling him, and the word "please" being used, he shouted back: "I'm here, I'm here!" With that, he pushed his way through the crowd, and walked trust-ingly out in front.

As Wu Laohei walked over to the table, Liu Jinding asked: "Are you the village head?"

"Yes, I am."

Before the man could say anything else, Liu Jinding winked at Helian Dongshan, who motioned with his hand, and Wu Laohei was immediately held down by the four policemen. Then, Liu Jinding took the second arrest warrant that Helian Dongshan handed him.

He held it up high and said to everyone: "According to our investigation, Wu Laohei, the head of Balizhuang Village, colluded with the developer in private and is suspected of embezzling public funds and accepting huge bribes. Detention and review are now implemented. Take him away!"

There was the click of handcuffs being snapped shut, and Wu Laohei was taken away by the four policemen.

Everyone was stunned into silence for a full ten seconds and no one seemed to know what to do. Then, as they watched their village chief being taken away, the villagers of Balizhuang lost their heads. In an instant, the place was buzzing like a huge beehive as they all started voicing their opinions. Some wondered whether the village head might indeed be greedy – after all, he was dark-skinned and fat, and he'd been headman for twenty years. After a while, the farmers who had lost their lands began to talk among themselves, their voices low, until, with roars and shouts of encouragement from Wu Laohei's family and relatives, they all rushed forward again, causing a great commotion. Someone shouted: "Why should the village head be arrested? You can't take him away!"

Liu Jinding raised his megaphone again and shouted: "Stop! Stop! Be very clear that the police will shoot anyone who crosses the red tape in front of you! Any of you who dares challenge the law, go on and step out in front here! I will tell you one last time, anyone who is found to have embezzled land funds will be dealt with very seriously. Within ten days, according to national regulations, I will give you all an explanation. But now, all of you making trouble here now have three minutes to leave the area!"

Still standing on the table, Liu Jinding looked round at the crowd and saw that some people still seemed to be threatening action. He shouted again: "Municipal Officer Lao He, enforce the law! Break the legs of anyone who dares come forward and crosses the red tape! I take full responsibility for anything that might happen."

There was a gasp from the crowd. A group of middle-aged and older women came rushing to the front, pulling their husbands and sons back, crying: "Let's go, let's go! It's none of our business."

Ordinarily, that should have been the end of the matter. It was certainly the most exciting event so far in Liu Jinding's official life. Moreover, that evening he received a phone call from the secretary of the Municipal Party Committee, praising him and saying: "Good! Correctly handled. Yes, very good!" Those words kept Liu Jinding happy all night.

Three hours later, Flower World Group's president, Xie Zhichang, was quietly released from detention. Naturally, when things died down, he was keen to show his appreciation to Liu Jinding. On the evening of the thank-you, Liu Jinding was feeling very relaxed and pleased with himself, so he drank a few more glasses than normal and got a bit carried away.

Amid the compliments, someone asked: "Would you really have ordered them to open fire, Secretary-General Liu?"

"I'll let you in on a secret," Liu Jinding replied triumphantly. "There were no bullets in the guns. I gave strict orders: no bullets." This garnered more compliments, with everyone saying what a brilliant ploy it was.

Then someone asked: "What about Balizhuang's Laohei, Secretary-General Liu? Is he really under arrest? Is he really a problem?"

Liu Jinding glanced at him, and asked: "What do you think?" With everyone's eyes on him now, Liu Jinding made a remark that was to become very well-known and widely circulated: "Guess how long that old man has been the village head?" He paused and answered himself: "Twenty years. He has been the village head for twenty years... what do you think? What I say is, there is no problem if we don't investigate, but if we do, there certainly will be."

Everyone nodded and said: "That's right, that's right!"

Even for someone nicknamed "Bigmouth Xie", Xie Zhichang felt that Liu Jinding was being a bit too free with his words, and he hurriedly tried to smooth things over for him, exclaiming: "Enough said! Drink up! Drink up!"

Helian Dongshan, who was there at the party, was disgusted with what he had heard. He didn't say anything but just stood up and left quietly.

At the time, no one thought that a bigger storm was brewing. Wu Laohei, who had been the village head of Balizhuang for twenty years, was no pushover. To start with, the Wu family were important in Balizhuang. He had four brothers all with more relatives, and together they exerted a lot of influence in the village. His third son in particular, who owned a gold shop in the city, had an extensive network of contacts there. What Liu Jinding said at the banquet was quickly passed on. Seven days later, the farmers in Balizhuang who had lost land reassembled and, with no warning, stopped a train on the Huanghuai City line. They wore white headbands and carried banners that read, variously: "Support the central government", "Support the constitution", "Petition with tears of blood" and "Give back my land!". More than three hundred of them lay down across the railway tracks.

The situation was now much more serious. If it was not properly handled, the entire national railway system would face paralysis! Consequently, the secretary and mayor of Huanghuai put aside their work and hurried over to the halted train. Because Li Delin happened to be engaged in "research" in Huanghuai at the time, he too was ordered by the Provincial Party Committee and the provincial government to rush to the scene and join in handling the situation. By this time, it didn't look as though persuasion was going to be sufficient. The mayor had talked until he lost his voice, and had agreed to some conditions, but the problem hadn't gone away. It was the first time Li Delin had seen such a battle. He didn't believe that farmers would really make any more trouble and wanted to try to talk them round himself. However, just as he stepped out in front of the crowd and shouted: "Everybody...", an egg came flying out of the crowd towards him. Fortunately for him, Liu Jinding, who was standing behind, rushed forward to shelter him, and took a faceful of raw egg. At this point, the villagers seemed to lose all restraint and their behaviour had to be seen to be believed.

Liu Jinding whispered in Li Delin's ear: "We've got to start arresting people, Governor. Arrest the ones who are making the most noise, and the rest will soon settle down."

"No, nonsense!" Li Delin shouted. "No one is to be arrested yet."

The arterial Beijing-Guangzhou railway line was paralysed for two hours and forty-six minutes. After Li Delin had requested instructions from the Provincial Party Committee and the Ministry of Public Security, armed police arrived to clear the field. The armed police detachment came in from the sides, with four officers to one protester, dragging them away one by one and loading them into police vans. Only once they had cleared the scene did the rail traffic recommence.

Because of the great impact of this incident, the secretary of the Huanghuai City Party Committee and the mayor were both removed from office. Deputy Governor Li Delin and others were also criticised in the report. Li Delin felt that since the secretary of the Municipal Party Committee and the mayor had been removed, as the deputy governor involved in handling the incident, he should resign voluntarily. So, on his own initiative, he wrote a combined report and resignation for the Provincial Party Committee. Perhaps because of his expert status, the Provincial Party Committee did not approve it. The secretary of the committee added five words to the report: "Take this as a warning."

When the new Municipal Party Committee secretary Xue Zhiheng took office, Liu Jinding escaped any form of sanction because he was not directly responsible for the railway incident, even though he instigated the whole affair.

However, as he was about to leave, Li Delin criticised him and said: "Let this be a lesson to you, Jinding. Do you still think it's such a good thing to be an official?"

However, in terms of their personal feelings, the two were even closer than before.

EIGHT

ON THE NIGHT OF 15 AUGUST, it was already dark by the time Li Delin reached his home village.

On this occasion, Li Delin didn't ask for his driver to take him back. Instead, he quietly called Liu Jinding and asked him to take a car to wait at the intersection with the Huanghuai Expressway, and pick him up there to go back to the village. He also made it very clear that Liu Jinding was not allowed to tell anyone he was coming.

So Liu Jinding drove the car himself, waited at the intersection as instructed, met Li Delin and took him directly to Meiling.

Along the way, Liu Jinding didn't say anything except to tell Li Delin: "It's the Mid-Autumn Festival, Master, but I didn't get you anything. I've just brought two boxes of mooncakes."

Li Delin himself always took mooncakes when returning to his hometown to visit relatives, so he felt that the two boxes were not taboo, so he just grunted and said: "Don't do this in future."

"We're at the provincial capital. Shall I stop or not?" Liu Jinding asked.

"No, don't stop. Didn't I say I don't want anyone to know. You can drop me off half a kilometre away from the village, and then go home. Tomorrow morning, meet me at the usual place."

It was already dark when the car left the expressway and was passing through cornfields. Li Delin got out of the car. In the gathering dusk, he found himself surrounded by fields, with a bleak wind blowing and in front of him just an empty greyness. He suddenly felt a little dislocated, and asked: "It's this way, isn't it?"

"That's right. The road has changed a few times," Liu Jinding said.

"All right then. This will do."

Liu Jinding took the four boxes of mooncakes from the boot of the car, including the two that Li Delin himself had brought back from the provincial capital. Handing them over, he said: "I know the way from here, Master. I will park the car here and take you to the entrance of the village."

"That would be good. It's pitch black and I'm really a little disoriented."

The two walked together, and as they reached the entrance of the village, Liu Jinding said: "Here we are, Master."

When Li Delin saw the old persimmon tree at the head of the village, his heart stopped racing. He felt a surge of affection as he turned and looked at Liu Jinding. He took the four boxes of mooncakes Jinding was holding and said: "I'm sorry for dragging you out here during the Mid-Autumn Festival, so hurry back now and rejoin your family."

"Thank you for your consideration, Master, but let's get you home first. Your old father is waiting for you."

At this moment, the moon swam out through a gap in the clouds, its light falling on the ground like water. The village was quiet, except for the occasional bark of a dog. They were rather insipid barks, as though the dogs were reassuring folk that they weren't the least bit fierce. As the two men walked along the bumpy village road, the shadows of the trees whirled in the moonlight and twisted in a silver-grey expanse. In a daze, Li Delin felt as though he had gone back to his childhood... involuntarily, he sighed, tears flowing from the corners of his eyes. "I'm so sorry, Dad," he said to himself.

But when he opened the gate and stood in the yard, he was struck dumb in amazement.

A tableau was silhouetted in the moonlight. In the main room, a woman with a bob haircut was sitting with her back to the door. Opposite her was his ageing father. His legs were stretched out, resting on the rim of the basin, and the woman was about to wash his feet. She put her hand in the basin, and then said: "Try it and see if it's too hot."

The old man put both his feet into the basin. "Hmm, yes, good, just right."

As the woman washed his feet, she said: "Your toenails need cutting. I'll do it when I've finished washing your feet."

Li Delin stood in a daze for a while, then walked in through the door and said: "Father, I'm back."

"Is that you, Delin?" Father said. "It's about time you came back."

"Well, here I am. And this is...?"

"Cai," his father said happily, "this is my son, Delin." Then he turned to Li Delin, saying: "You must thank Director Liu. Director Liu has been really helpful."

At this point, the woman turned her head and said in a low voice: "So there you are!" Then she quickly got up, took the mooncakes he was carrying, put them on the table, and asked: "Have you eaten?"

Li Delin nodded and asked: "Wh... which Director Liu?"

"The one that's your student, what's-his-name. See what's happened to my memory!"

"He's from the city," the woman said. "Liu Jinding, Director Liu. He asked me to come."

Li Delin nodded and said: "Oh, I see. Then I'm afraid it's me who is causing you all this trouble."

The woman glanced at him and said: "It's no trouble to take care of an old man."

That night, when father and son sat down together, his father kept complimenting the woman, whose name was Xu Ercai, saying that she had been here for more than two months, washed his feet at night and made a good square meal every day too. "I get seasonal food every day, and she's very capable. She really knows how to look after an old man," he gushed.

Later, Xu Ercai, who had been busy at the stove, brought Li Delin a bowl of hot-and-sour noodle soup with two poached eggs in it. Xu Ercai put the bowl on the table and said: "You've been running around all day, you need feeding up. I put some vinegar in it. I don't know if you like that or not."

Li Delin immediately felt warm inside. This was a proper home-style meal! Years ago, whenever he had a winter cold, his mother would make this for him. "That's fine, it smells good," Li Delin said. "Thank you, thank you."

"My pleasure," she replied.

Li Delin found himself sweating slightly after eating the noodles, and he felt even warmer inside. "Those noodles you made are really delicious," he said. "I just want to check: it was Liu Jinding who asked you to come, right?"

"Yes, Director Liu drove over and talked to my village head, and the village head talked to me. Then Director Liu drove me over here."

"Then I won't stand on ceremony," Li Delin replied. "You've helped me take care of my old dad and you've looked after me so well too. I am very grateful. But there's something I have to ask about, and that is salary. Did Liu Jinding say anything about it?"

"The money is not important. Director Liu told me the old man is getting on, and you are too busy working. Let me look after the old man first. It's no more than I should be doing, and there's no need–"

"No, no, that's not how–"

"When Director Liu came to my house," Xu Ercai went on, "he gave me ten thousand yuan, saying it was some kind of household resettlement allowance. I didn't want it, so he just gave it to my mother. I told her to give it straight back to him."

Li Delin immediately said: "There is no need to refund the money. That's how things should be. It was me who gave him the money in the first place."

Because it was their first meeting, Xu Ercai was quite cautious in front of Li Delin. She sat there with her hands on her knees, head down, and kept her questions brief and to the point. In terms of appearance, she was of middle height, maybe verging on tall, but still looked a little frail. In the evening light, her face took on an oval appearance and her chin was a little pointed but, overall, she was quite presentable, and she was clearly very capable. Her local accent made Li Delin feel comfortable in her presence, but it also seemed to increase her invisibility. Whenever she stood up, there was something very appealing about the twist of her hips and rump. But there was something in her eyes too: stubbornness, maybe, or tenacity? Li Delin couldn't be sure.

The two of them chatted about household matters for a while and then Li Delin asked: "If you come here, what about your folks–"

"I've got five brothers and sisters," Xu Ercai replied, "two older sisters and three younger brothers. My mum and dad are both in good health, so I've got nothing to worry about."

"You're from Daxuzhuang aren't you? Is it far from here? You'll want to go back and see your folks whenever you have the time."

"About ten kilometres, not far."

Li Delin hesitated and asked: "How old are you?"

"On the household register, twenty-nine, but actually, I'm only twenty-eight. I don't know where the extra year came from."

Li Delin gave a little exclamation of understanding, then smiled and asked: "Have you found anyone for yourself yet?"

Xu Ercai moistened her lips and shook her head.

"Too picky, right?"

Xu Ercai didn't reply.

Later, Xu Ercai told Li Delin that she had taken the university entrance exams twice but had been unlucky and missed out by a few marks each time. The reason why, at the age of twenty-eight, she still hadn't found a husband, was entirely down to her elder sister. Her sister had gone to a teacher training college in Huanghuai, and then pursued her studies elsewhere. She had married one of her classmates and they lived away from the provincial capital. Every year when they came back to visit, they drove a smart car and looked so cool and stylish that everyone was green with envy. Xu Ercai wanted to find a partner too, a good and capable one, at the very least no worse than her sister's... so she kept looking, but so far no one suitable had turned up and she was still unmarried.

When Li Delin got up the next morning, he found that breakfast was already on the table, in the form of a bowl of millet porridge and a small basket full of freshly baked oil buns. There were also boiled eggs and a small dish of pickles. It was all good, hearty food for busy people, and quite delicious.

When Li Delin left, Xu Ercai accompanied him to the entrance of the village. Li Delin thought she must have something to ask him, but she just followed behind him without saying a word. Rather confusedly, Li Delin had the impression of being with a family member.

Just over a kilometre away, Liu Jinding's car was already waiting. Li Delin got in and asked: "Is she the one you found?"

"What do you think of her? I can always find someone else."

"No, she's fine. The old man is very happy. I'll refund you the ten thousand yuan."

"As long as she's OK, the money doesn't matter."

"No, that won't do, I have to give you the money. If you don't take it, I'll send her back immediately."

"OK, OK, I'll take it!" Liu Jinding said hurriedly and then went on: "So what do you think, Master? She may not be a real looker but she's a good, honest sort."

Li Delin gave a non-committal "um" and said: "Didn't we agree we would see how she gets on with the old man first?"

"Yes, that's what I suggested."

"All right then, let's... let's settle for that." But then he went on: "Simple and down-to-earth is fine, I don't have any problem with that, but I'm fifty already, much older than her..."

"If you want her, what can she have to say about it?"

"It's more about my father. If he's got someone to look after him, I can rest easy."

"Let's give it a try then."

That winter, just before the New Year, Li Delin received a call from Liu Jinding, saying that his father was ill with a high fever and had been sent to the county hospital. Li Delin rushed to the hospital and was dumbfounded by what he found. How could they call this a hospital? It was more like a temple fair! The hospital corridor was jammed with a jostling line of people; a policeman had even been stationed to keep order. When Li Delin walked to the front of the queue, the policeman stopped him and said: "Join the queue, Comrade, join the queue. If you're from the province, you'll get preference..."

Li Delin didn't understand what he meant, and said: "I am from the province."

"Are you really from the province? The governor's father is on the second floor... you can go up and visit him."

Li Delin was dumbfounded for a moment and quite taken aback. He hurried up to the second floor, and on a corner of the staircase, he saw the village head, Uncle Shushan, shouting at people to form a queue. Uncle Shushan saw him and greeted him: "You've come, Delin!"

"Uncle Shushan, what are you–"

"There are so many people here and I have to greet them for you. Your father is really very sick this time. Secretary Tang from the county is here. He's on the ward. Hurry up and see him."

Angry as Li Delin was, it wasn't the time to say anything. Up on the second floor, he saw several villagers carrying flowers along the corridor. In fact, both sides were lined with baskets of fruit and flowers. He was about to say hello to some of the villagers, when Tang Mingsheng, the new county Party secretary of Meiling and a group of other people came out of the ward. Li Delin hurried forward and said: "What are you doing here, Xiao Tang?"

"Need you ask, Governor Li? Your father is sick, so of course I've come to see him!"

Li Delin frowned and said: "Why are there so many people? It's chaos! What kind of impression does it give?"

"Governor, you can't blame me for that," Tang Mingsheng said. "I just came as soon as I heard the news. There are other counties in the city district too, and if people want to come, what can I do about it? It's your fault you're so popular, isn't it!"

Li Delin went into the ward which actually turned out to be a suite of rooms. The outer room was full of people, most of whom he didn't know. Ignoring them all, he went straight over to the bed where his father was lying, with an IV drip giving him fluids. Li Delin asked: "Is he still running a fever?"

Xu Ercai, who was standing in front of the bed, said: "He's been dehydrated for a day and is still feverish."

"What on earth happened?"

"That time it snowed, he went to the fields to transplant some cabbages. I told him not to, but he wouldn't have it, even though it was freezing."

At that moment, Liu Jinding walked in, out of breath. As soon as he entered, he said: "Master, Secretary Xue from the city has heard the news, and he will come over as soon as possible."

"Tell them not to come! Just say I've already left and gone back to the city," Li Delin replied anxiously.

"Are you sure that's appropriate?"

But Li Delin had made his decision and said: "Go now, Jinding! Go and ask for an ambulance for me, but be quiet about it. We're leaving right away and taking him back to be looked after in his home village."

"But what about all this stuff?" Xu Ercai broke in. "There's so much of it! What should I do with it?"

"Leave everything, we don't need it," Li Delin said impatiently. "Give it to Uncle Shushan and the others and let them take it back."

Xu Ercai was stunned for a moment, and said forlornly: "And what about me?"

Liu Jinding had arranged everything by this time and had come back into the room when he finished his phone call. "Do you really need to ask? Use your head! You're going back in the ambulance!" he said.

In fact, it was Xu Ercai who was the most distressed by the old man's illness. She had never seen anything like it before. At first, she thought he had just caught a slight chill when out transplanting a few cabbages on a snowy day. All he needed after being out in the cold and wind was a bit of a lie down and a bowl of ginger soup. That's what all countryfolk did. But after the old man had been in bed for a day, he was still running a high fever. She was afraid that something would happen, so she took him to the county hospital on a hand cart. She didn't think of calling anyone until she got to the hospital. But then she phoned Liu Jinding and things began to move. In less than an hour, first the ward was changed, and the four-bed room was replaced with a private suite. Then a group of doctors gathered around, talking away to each other. The way all this happened left her speechless. In just one day, her view of the world was transformed!

NINE

No one could really explain exactly what happened that night.

Li Delin couldn't, and neither could Xu Ercai. Later on, it left them both wondering whether it was Fate taking a hand.

On the night of New Year's Eve, Li Delin's apartment at the University of Agricultural Science and Technology finally had a homely feel to it. His father had at last come to live in the city. There were now three people in the family: the old man who had just been discharged from hospital; Xu Ercai, who was making herself busy round the apartment; and Li Delin himself. A new spring couplet had been pasted up at the door, dumplings made by Xu Ercai were cooking in the pot and a few side dishes were laid out to go with the wine. There was the sound of firecrackers outside, the New Year Gala broadcast by CCTV was about to begin, and everything was warm and cosy.

At that time, as far as Li Delin actually even thought about it, Xu Ercai was still employed as a housekeeper. On the twenty-seventh day of the twelfth lunar month, on the day the old man was discharged from the hospital, Li Delin said in very grateful tones: "You've been kept so busy for so long, Ercai, it has been really hard on you. The New Year is almost with us, so why don't you take this three thousand yuan and go and do some shopping. You can buy yourself some new clothes and get some presents to take back with you and spend the New Year at home with your family." With that, he put the money he had specially got ready in front of Xu Ercai.

Xu Ercai hesitated for a moment, and said: "Your old father's only just got better, and neither of you even know how to cook. Better wait till after New Year. Then I'll take some time off and go back and see my family."

In fact, over the previous few days, Li Delin had already become quite dependent on her. If she really did go back for the New Year holiday, she was right, they wouldn't have anyone to cook for them. He would manage, but what about his dad? "All right then," he said. "But you should still phone your parents so you can hear each other's voices at least."

"The chicken!" Xu Ercai suddenly burst out. "The chicken's still on the stove." She rushed off to the kitchen.

By nine o'clock that night, the old man was dozing on the sofa, snoring from time to time after having drunk two glasses of low-strength wine and watched the New Year Gala. Xu Ercai brought over a basin of hot water and shook him gently. "Wake up, Grandfather. Let's warm up your feet and get you to bed."

The old man blearily opened his eyes and said: "OK, OK! Look at you all, tired and sweaty! You'd better get yourself to bed."

Xu Ercai washed the old man's feet and helped him to his room to get ready for bed. Then she sat down and watched TV with Li Delin. "It's the middle of winter! How come it's so warm?" she said and took off the jacket she was wearing.

Li Delin saw that, now she had taken jacket off, she was only wearing only a pink slip on her top half. "You'd better put your jacket on, or you'll catch cold."

"It's too hot in this room. I'm all sweaty," she replied as she sat, cracking melon seeds with her teeth.

"The heating is turned up for the New Year. You'll get used to it."

As they watched a cross-talk act, Li Delin looked at the pile of melon seed husks on the floor at her feet, but he didn't say anything. Even so, she jumped to her feet, saying: "I'll sweep them up, I'll sweep them up. When it's not so humid, I'll mop the floor again." With that, she went over to the bathroom to get a cloth that she used to gather up all the husks under the coffee table. Then she wetted a mop and began to clean the floor. When she got to the sofa, she said: "No need to move, just lift your feet."

Li Delin lifted his feet and watched her plying the mop. "It feels like there's a humidifier on in here, doesn't it?" he said.

"You've been drinking. Should I make you some cooling soup, to clear your head?"

"No need. You just sit down and have a rest."

"I can't stand being idle. The more I sit, the hotter I get." She put down the mop and went to get a basin of hot water, which she brought over to Li Delin, and said: "Now give your feet a good hot soak, OK?"

With the basin steaming away in front of him, Li Delin had no choice but to take off his shoes and put his feet into the water. Xu

Ercai pulled up a small stool, sat down and matter-of-factly reached out and began to wash his feet for him.

By this time, Li Delin had a rather dazed expression on his face and it was actually his feet that seemed to come back to their senses first. As his toes soaked in the water being massaged by Xu Ercai's gentle hands, a moist, soft, slightly prickly sensation rushed up to his head... what bliss! Then, out of nowhere, he noticed another physiological reaction: he was getting hard. He tried to stop it, but his body down there wasn't listening to him. It was like a sluice gate being opened and there was nothing he could do about it. Totally embarrassed, he sank deeper into the sofa and said: "The central heating is really roasting! It's so hot in here!"

Even as he shrank back, Li Delin took the opportunity to have another look at Xu Ercai. She was still a young woman, and the scent of a young woman is like ripe peaches. Except with her, it wasn't only ripe peaches, there was also a bright, scorching, flame-like smell of meat mixed with damp sweat. There was a smell of wild grass in her hair, too. It was a different scent from the one he remembered from before, but it seemed to be awakening something. Seen from a little distance, her face, although not beautiful, was shining with sweat and full of life. Under her single-fold eyelids, her eyes were shaded by long eyelashes, a little shy, a little hesitant, hiding their true expression, as if they had been startled by something. The whole effect was undeniably endearing. Her ears looked as though they had been pierced, but there were no earrings. Her earlobes were fine and pink, bright with the colour in their tiny blood vessels. It was a physical presence that was unfamiliar but intimately close.

Li Delin was still struggling with his physical reaction, and it was only just in time that the telephone rang. Li Delin put on his slippers and stood up to answer it. Xu Ercai picked up the basin and went to pour the water away.

The calls were all New Year's greetings, most of them from local mayors and secretaries, and were just for form's sake. Li Delin laughed politely and dealt with them one by one.

At close to eleven o'clock, Xu Ercai said: "It's still too hot. I'm going to take a shower."

"The water heater is electric," Li Delin replied. "Do you know

119

how to turn it on?" This was rather a redundant question as Xu Ercai had already been living in the apartment for several days.

"Yes, I know. I'll be quick." And with that, she hurried off to the bathroom.

Li Delin sat on the sofa and smoked two more cigarettes, still in a daze. He pinched out the second cigarette, stood up and took a few steps towards his bedroom. At the same moment, Xu Ercai came running out of the bathroom, wrapped in a towel, and they bumped into each other. Instinctively, Li Delin grabbed hold of her to stop her falling, and the two of them found themselves clinging together. The touch of her young body sent a flame ripping through Li Delin.

It was then that Xu Ercai said something, in a trembling voice, which had an even more explosive effect. The bath towel she had been wearing had fallen to the ground and her two small breasts stood proud, thrusting themselves at him like startled rabbits. Naked, she snuggled into Li Delin's arms, and said in a trembling voice: "It's time you fucked me now."

In fact, the word she used for "fuck" is only heard in the countryside, in the vast sorghum fields, with their slashing blades and flashing green light. It has the primitive urgency of slash and burn farming; it has the nonchalant swagger of outdoor sex; it was the first word that Li Delin learned as a child from the farmers in the fields. It smacks of irreverence and banditry, toughness and brute force; it has a dominating masculinity. It was very provocative.

Without a word, Li Delin picked Xu Ercai in his arms and carried her into his bedroom.

When he woke from his sleep the next morning, Li Delin was astonished to find someone next to him. He lay there stunned for a moment, until the events of the night before came vividly rushing back to him. He rolled over and asked: "Are you still hot?"

Xu Ercai said nothing, bull rolled over too and snuggled into him like a kitten. Then she grabbed Li Delin's hand, pressed it to her breasts, and whispered: "Feel me and see!"

Excitement surged through Li Delin again as he changed position and they did the deed again. "What did you say last night?" he asked.

"Nothing... I didn't say anything," Xu Ercai whispered back

"You did. Now say it again."

Xu Ercai said vaguely: "No, no, I don't remember saying anything."

"Think hard!"

Xu Ercai thought and thought, and suddenly she understood, and shouted at the top of her voice: "Fuck... fuck... fuck! Fuck me hard! Fuck the fuck out of me!" The flood overwhelmed Li Delin.

When they had finished, they lay there, sweaty and exhausted. After a while, Xu Ercai sat up, took a pack of cigarettes from the bedside table, selected one, lit it, then snuggled back into Li Delin and put it between his lips. "We are both the same, you and me," she said, "and you can't do without me."

Li Delin took two slow drags on his cigarette, before responding: "Wait till the New Year's over, then we'll go and register. OK?"

"Sure, that's fine."

" I do have a few conditions," Li Delin said.

"Tell me, I'm listening."

"You know my circumstances, right? So the first condition is that you look after my father and do all the housework."

"Don't worry, that goes without saying."

"Second, you can't use my public position for personal gain or interfere in politics." Then, he added: "That is to say, you are only responsible for managing the home. You're not allowed to interfere in my work."

"Fine, fine. I wouldn't expect to."

"Third, you are not allowed to accept gifts from anyone without my consent, especially red envelopes. You can't take a cent in cash from anyone."

"What about relatives?"

"Not even relatives. Any gift that's given you will be to try and get you to do something. You can't offer to help anyone, so why should you accept any gifts?"

Xu Ercai considered this for a moment and said: "Fine, fine. I agree, OK?"

Feeling he might have come on a bit strong, Li Delin petted her and said: "Those three conditions aren't just for you, they're for me too. Will you remember them?"

"I will. Now, what do you want to eat?"

TEN

THREE MONTHS LATER, Xu Ya'nan fell pregnant.

After becoming the wife of the deputy governor, Xu Ercai went to the Township Police Station quietly to change her household registration and her name. She changed her name to Xu Ya'nan. After moving to the provincial capital and meeting some of the people there, she felt that "Xu Ercai" was too "rustic". She wanted to wash the dust of the countryside off as soon as possible, and from then on, she didn't let anyone call her Xu Ercai.

When the change in her registered permanent residence was going through the normal process, the officer at the local police station tried to make things difficult for her. "Just leave it here. The officer who deals with residence permits isn't in at the moment."

Xu Ercai tried the usual pleas: "Comrade, I've come from the provincial capital and it isn't easy for me to make the trip down here. Can't you handle it?"

The policeman looked at her askance and said: "I don't care if you've come here from heaven. It can't be done in one visit. Go home and wait."

Xu Ercai's temper flared, and she slammed her marriage certificate down on the desk, shouting: "Are you blind? Don't you see who my husband is!"

The officer was not a very intelligent man and sneered at her contemptuously. "Oh yes? So who is your husband then?"

"Li Delin!" Xu Ercai snapped back immediately.

The little policeman didn't recognise the name at once and said: "I don't care what kind of Li he is! He could be anyone!"

Xu Ercai grabbed the telephone and dialled a number as she yelled back: "OK then, if you don't know the governor, maybe you know the county Party secretary? I'll call Lao Tang now. I want to ask him where he finds fucking idiots like you..."

Suddenly, the light dawned on the officer, and he began to understand just what kind of trouble he was in. He grabbed Xu Ercai's hand and said: "Sister-in-Law, I'm sorry, I'm sorry, I was in the wrong. It won't happen again. Please give me a break this time. I'll do it now, I'll do it now!"

Xu Ercai slammed the phone back down and said: "I think you're a regular little bully, who chances his arm to see what he can squeeze out of people. Now, hurry up and change my name. Do it now!"

"I'm sorry, I'm sorry! I remember now! Governor Li comes from our county. Of course, you're from our county too, Sister-in-Law..."

That was when Xu Ercai transformed herself into Xu Ya'nan.

When Xu Ya'nan returned to the provincial capital, she didn't mention a word about what had happened at the police station. Li Delin asked: "Is the *hukou* done?"

"Yes, it's done."

"Remember you're pregnant. Don't keep running around all day long. You could have done the *hukou* any time. Why are you in such a hurry?"

"I'm OK, it's still early days. And our baby's bound to be tough, anyway." Then, she leaned close to Li Delin, put her hand on his shoulder, and said: "Do you think it's a boy or a girl?"

"How should I know?"

"I went back and asked the blind fortune-teller. It's a boy."

"All fortune-tellers are frauds. Don't believe them."

"I'm not kidding. That blind man's the real thing. It really is a boy."

"If you say so. My family has only had one boy in three generations, so if it really is a boy, you'll be a hero in the Li family."

"Is that so?" Xu Ya'nan asked coquettishly.

"That's what I said!"

"Then, tonight, you should pay your 'seed tax'."

"What century do you think we're living in? What 'seed tax'?"

"You know!"

"I don't!"

"Do you really want me to say it out loud?"

Finally, the penny dropped, and Li Delin asked: "In your condition? Do we dare?"

"We do! We do!"

Xu Ya'nan had been feeling a little drunk ever since becoming the wife of the deputy governor and changing her name. Of course she wasn't *drunk* drunk, but how else to explain it? First of all, the people she met were very different from before. These were all educated people and people with titles: mayors and ministers, and the like. They were all of the same type, and all very particular about their behaviour. Second, she was quite unaccustomed to receiving such respect. It was a kind of respect she had not experienced before, but of course she found it very advantageous. There she was, a girl from a poor peasant family, a country girl from Xujiazhuang, and suddenly so many people were showing her respect! How could she not become a bit drunk? But what she didn't know was that sometimes, this kind of "respect" can be a slow-acting poison. When a person gets used to being "respected", that's when she is in danger.

Li Delin was the deputy governor in charge of agriculture. He spent a lot of time in meetings and less time at home. Whenever Li Delin was not at home, she always took his father outside, saying: "It's good for you to get some sun." Then she would stroll from room to room round the house, poking around here and there and then there and here again. All those official documents with the provincial government's seal just lying on the desk! She would lick the tip of her finger and leaf through them, page by page, humming to herself... it was all very cosy.

One day, she took a long, thin cashmere scarf out of a bureau. It was so beautiful, white and soft, like snow. She hung it round her neck and stood in front of the mirror, admiring herself.

Suddenly, she heard the sound of footsteps followed by an abrupt voice shouting: "Put it back! That's not yours!"

Xu Ya'nan was shocked. She turned and saw that Li Delin had come running in, his face red.

"Why are you back?" she asked.

"There's a document I forgot," he said angrily. Then, he stepped forward and unceremoniously tore the scarf from around her neck and hurried into the back room.

Xu Ya'nan was a little dazed and stood there blankly, not knowing quite what to do.

Li Delin took the file he had come for and hurried out of the room to see Xu Ya'nan with tears in her eyes looking very disconsolate. "That's belongs to someone else," he explained. "If you want one of your own, just buy one!" He turned to go.

"Wait a minute. Whose is it?"

"Someone else's. I'll tell you about it when I get back."

"It belongs to your ex-wife, doesn't it?"

"Yes," he said neutrally and left abruptly.

Xu Ya'nan was fuming. She ran into the back room and found the scarf hidden in the cupboard. "Pah! Pah! Pah!" She spat on it three times, then threw it on the ground and stamped on it. She was still not satisfied, so she found a pair of scissors, cut the scarf into strips, shoved them in plastic bag and threw it into the rubbish bin outside the door.

Her bad mood lasted all day, and she was just looking for anyone to vent it on. At ten o'clock that morning, Liu Jinding opened the door and walked in carrying two cartons of cigarettes. As an old friend of the family, he didn't stand on ceremony and said to Xu Ya'nan: "How are you doing, Cai? Are you getting used to things here?"

Much to his surprise, Xu Ya'nan flared up at him: "Cai? Cai? Who are you calling Cai! Who are you, anyway? Are you trying to disrespect me too? Everyone else wants to! Well, dream on!"

Liu Jinding was taken aback, and asked: "Why are you getting on your high horse? Who's got up your nose?"

"How many times have I told you? I've changed my name. My name is Xu Ya'nan!"

Liu Jinding realised what he had done and immediately apologised: "Yes, yes, I know! Ya'nan, yes, Ya'nan is a fine name! I'll make sure I remember in future."

But Xu Ya'nan was in no mood to be mollified and continued to cut up rough. For one thing, she didn't bother to call him "Director", as she always had done in the past: "Lao Liu, Liu Jinding, yes you, I'm asking you, just whose side are you on? Whose side?"

Liu Jinding was dumbfounded and said: "What... what do you mean?"

"You are my matchmaker, right? You brought me here, right?"

"Yes, yes, so what's the matter?"

"I'll ask you again, which side is your arse sitting on? It's got to be one side or the other!"

"What are you trying to say?"

"You think I don't know? You think I don't know the money for his ex is all sent through you? That's right, isn't it?"

Liu Jinding understood now. Li Delin's maintenance and tuition fees for his daughter were indeed passed on through him. He said: "You've misunderstood, Sister-in-Law. Those are just various tuition fees for his daughter..."

"You can keep your fancy explanations! From now on, you'll keep your nose out of all that shit with his ex. They're divorced, but you still keep hanging out with her! What do you think you are up to? From now on, no more contact and not a cent more money. If I hear any more about it, you'll never set foot in this house again!"

Liu Jinding was so angry when he heard this that, without another word, he snatched up his briefcase and marched out. He was the deputy secretary-general of the Huanghuai City Government! He was a senior government official! Why should he put up with such abuse? "What the fuck!" he yelled as he went out. He couldn't help himself.

At noon, when Xu Ya'nan was cooking lunch, the drains backed up. Raw sewage came flooding up into the kitchen sink, and the whole room stank. She had to get someone in to look at it. In a panic, she found a phone book next to the telephone, picked it up and flipped through it. She saw a number for the Provincial Government Office and dialled it. The other end was picked up by a deputy director of the General Office, who said: "Hello, who do you want?"

Xu Ya'nan imitated him mockingly in reply: "Who do you want? Who do you want? How can you be so shameless? What's going on with the sewers? There's shit everywhere and it stinks! It's not fit for human habitation!"

The deputy director of the General Office was taken aback, and said solemnly: "Excuse me, but who are you? This is the Provincial Office."

Xu Ya'nan said what she had quickly learned to say: "This is Li Delin, Governor Li's home!"

The deputy director of the General Office replied immediately: "I see, I see! Yes, I understand. I am so sorry that we did not do our work correctly. I will send someone over right away."

Xu Ya'nan was amazed at the effect of that one impetuous phone call. Twenty minutes later, the chief of the logistics section of the Provincial Government Office had come hurrying over with three maintenance workers. After a while, staff from the Logistics Department of the University of Agricultural Science and Technology also scurried in. Suddenly, two groups of people had assembled and were busy changing all the pipes inside and outside the house. Before leaving, they even tidied up their mess and took all the rubbish out. Xu Ya'nan just stood there, hands spread in stunned amazement.

Xu Ya'nan's mood gradually improved during the afternoon, but then she answered a phone call, and her temper flared up again. The call was from her younger brother, Wangjia, who said: "Older Sister, you have to do something. Dog Egg is in trouble!"

This just made her mad, and she yelled down the phone: "Don't use nicknames with me! Dog Egg, Donkey Egg, I don't care what kind of egg, they're all so crude and ugly! Tell me properly."

"Your brother, Wangcai, is in trouble," Wangjia replied. "He's been arrested and is down at the police station."

"He's normally such a good lad. What are they accusing him of?"

Wangjia explained: "He was driving his flatbed trike and ran into someone. It wasn't a bad crash, but they tried to screw him for twenty thousand yuan. He didn't have the money, so the police arrested him..."

"Well, find someone who cares! I don't!" she snapped and slammed down the receiver.

After a while, Wangjia called back and wailed down the phone: "Sister, the sky is falling in on your family and you really don't care? Your mother cried so hard she fainted, and Second Daughter-in-Law is demanding a divorce–"

"Your brother-in-law has told me to stay out of family affairs, so stop bothering me," Xu Ya'nan replied. "I really don't care!" She hung up on him again.

Xu Ya'nan paced round the house distractedly. She glanced at the phone book from time to time and turned away. After a while, she looked at the phone again. Unable to stop herself any longer, she went over to it. Then she hesitated once more, asking herself: Lord! Who should I call? There were two small notebooks next to the telephone, one for the province and the other for the city. She flipped through them and came to the name of Tang Mingsheng in Meiling, which had a handwritten phone number beside it. "Well, fuck this for a laugh!" she said.

Then she picked up the phone and dialled the number. When the call was connected, Tang Mingsheng said: "Hello, who is this?"

"Secretary Tang?" Xu Ya'nan replied. "Is that Secretary Tang? I'm Delin's–"

"Ha!" Tang Mingsheng laughed down the phone. "Sister-in-Law, why are you calling? Is there something I can do for you?"

"I shouldn't really be calling you, Delin wouldn't have let me, but there's something I hope you can help me with."

"Tell me what's the matter."

"It's my brother. He had an accident driving his trike. It's no big deal, but the police arrested him..."

Tang Mingsheng hesitated and said: "If you had asked me first, Sister-in-Law, I would have said this isn't something you should get involved in. But since you have raised it, tell me, which police station is it?"

"Huazhen, Huazhen Police Station."

At six o'clock that afternoon, Wangjia called again and said: "It's all good, Sister. Wangcai's been released. County Party Committee Secretary Tang himself called—"

"I know. Don't bother me with this kind of thing again."

That night, Xu Ya'nan waited for Li Delin's return with some trepidation, in case he was still upset. During dinner, Li Delin said: "Who said you could call? From now on, don't call the office on a whim. It's bad, very bad!"

"The water was flooding the kitchen, and it stank," Xu Ya'nan replied aggrievedly. "There was nothing I—"

"I have lived here for seven years and the drains have never been blocked before. Why has it happened as soon as you arrive? I bet you've not been paying attention to what goes down there."

"OK, OK, I'll be more careful in future."

After the meal, Xu Ya'nan sank down into a corner of the sofa, head down and frowning, her hand pressed to her belly. Li Delin looked at her and asked: "What's wrong? Are you not feeling well?"

Xu Ya'nan frowned and whispered: "The baby kicked me."

Li Delin hurried over, squatted in front of her, and asked: "Really? Let me listen."

"Listen away and tell me it's not a boy. There he goes, kicking again... and again."

Li Delin put his head on her stomach, listened for a while, and said: "We'll soon have to hire someone."

"What for?"

"To look after you."

ELEVEN

Li Delin and Xu Ya'nan had been married for less than three years, but already he was regretting it. The regret was like a river in spate, crashing through his heart and churning his intestines.

The fact that she did indeed have a boy seemed to bring about a dramatic change in Xu Ya'nan. She was feted everywhere as the heroine of the Li family, and it made her very arrogant. At first, she just yelled at the nanny who had been employed, scowling, scolding and crying at every opportunity: "Was it you who stole the eggs from the refrigerator? How many did you eat? Sick them all up again, every one!" She also became more and more rude to her father-in-law. The old man wanted to hug his grandson, but she snapped at him: "Go away! Old folk are so useless, you'll probably drop him, and then what?" In the end, she even laid down rules for Li Delin in the form of another three-clause charter.

When Xu Ya'nan gave birth, Li Delin was devoted to her in every possible way. Whatever she wanted to eat, she got. When she was in the hospital, she asked Li Delin to wash her feet, and Li Delin rushed off to get the hot water. At the time, he also felt that, now she had given birth to a boy, she was the rightful queen of the Li family. They all rushed to meet her every need. And the baby was so cute too! Li Delin never tired of looking at his little face, his little hands, his little feet and soft plump flesh. Xu Ya'nan liked to lift the baby and let him look at the child's "little willy". Li Delin was always afraid the child might fall, and kept saying: "Slowly does it, slowly does it! It's very risky." During this time, Li Delin looked after her in every possible way, spoiling her even. But all this spoiling did indeed spoil her.

Xu Ya'nan was discharged from hospital seven days after the birth, and on the night of her return home as she was sitting on their bed, breasts exposed ready to feed the baby, she got Li Delin to take a couple of sucks first so as to let the milk down for the baby to consume. Of course, Li Delin was happy to do this. From then on, in fact, he agreed to anything she asked. After a while, Xu Ya'nan changed her approach and asked Li Delin to rub her breasts while the baby was feeding. "When my tits are full," she said, "you have to massage them for me."

Secretly delighted at the idea, Li Delin asked: "How can I massage them when you're feeding the baby?"

"When the little baby is feeding from one, the old man can massage the other – can't you, old man!"

Li Delin reached out his hand to massage the breast, and he actually squirted some milk onto his face. Xu Ya'nan laughed and said: "What an idiot you are!" Li Delin just laughed too. Then she added: "I hope I can rely on you to do everything you have promised!"

"Yes, yes! Of course, you can rely on me."

"You said that if it's a boy, I will be the queen of the family, right? So from now on, what I say goes in this family, OK?"

"OK, OK, whatever it is, what you say goes!"

"Now we've got a son, he is the centre of this household and you're not to think of anyone else."

"Don't worry, there won't be anyone else except for my old dad and my daughter."

"You dad is your dad's concern, and your daughter is your ex-wife's. What I'm talking about is our family, just the three of us."

Li Delin didn't want to argue any more, so he just said: "Yes, you are right. Just the three of us and we'll be really happy living together."

"Speaking of living, I have some rules for you," Xu Ya'nan said as she changed the baby over to the other breast.

Li Delin switched breasts too and replied: "Go on!"

"Rule one, I take care of all our food and drink at home and you give me your salary and allowances every month. Rule two, after the child is a month old, you get to pay your 'seed tax' once every three days. You only pay it to me and if you've got any left over, you're not allowed to pay it to anyone else. Rule three, you are not allowed to have any contact with your ex-wife."

Li Delin listened without saying anything, and his silence was taken as acquiescence.

When the baby was one month old, Xu Ya'nan insisted on having a proper "first month" celebration for the baby and laying on a big banquet for the guests. Li Delin was very unhappy with the idea and said: "It's too ostentatious for a man in my position. People will talk. Let's just have a quiet family meal and leave it at that."

"What are they going to say?" Xu Ya'nan responded. "That we

stole our baby or kidnapped it? That we sodding bought it? I'll rip the fucking face off anyone who gossips about us!"

Li Delin was stunned by her vulgarity, but she held her head up and continued: "I've given the Li family a beautiful, fat baby, so why shouldn't I have a party? I just want all my relatives and friends to know that I have given the Li family a son. What's wrong with that?"

"It's just not on, and that's all there is to it."

"My family won't stand for it if you don't let me have a party. If we can't have it here, I'll have it back in the countryside. How about that?"

Li Delin hesitated for a moment, but still refused.

Without another word, Xu Ya'nan stepped forward and slapped the baby hard on his backside. He started to wail loudly. Then she picked up the child and shouted to the babysitter: "Follow me."

Li Delin only managed one word: "You..."

So Xu Ya'nan ignored Li Delin's opposition and took the baby straight back to their hometown.

The baby's first month party was the most glorious day in Xu Ya'nan's life. Never had she held her head higher nor had her ego so thoroughly massaged. Afterwards, she privately told friends that it made her whole life worthwhile.

The party was laid on by Tang Mingsheng, secretary of the Meiling County Party Committee, and because of his involvement, not only were all the drinks provided for free, there was also a fifty per cent discount on all the other costs. The manager of the hotel knew that the celebration was in honour of the provincial governor's son, and he made sure that he was seen everywhere, nodding and bowing, as he looked after the guests like a dutiful grandson.

The entrance to the Meiling Grand Hotel was full of flower arrangements and the first, second and third floors were completely taken up with a total of sixty-six tables. Xu Ya'nan stood at the right-hand end of the room on the first floor, near the door, and next to her was the little nanny holding the baby. Xu Ya'nan had put on special make-up for the day. Her lips were bright red, her eyebrows had been shaved and neatly drawn back on to look very thick, and her hair was newly permed into wavy curls. She was wearing a sky-blue skirt and jacket – of the type that is effectively the uniform of urban women white-collar workers – appropriately decorated with a red corsage. On her feet were a pair of half-heel, soft-upper kidskin shoes stitched with blue and white stripes over flesh-coloured tights, which made her as eye-catching as a shop window mannequin. She stood by the entrance, hands clasped in front of her chest in a pose she had seen on TV when people were greeting honoured foreign guests. Just behind her was a long table with a green tablecloth on which stood an inkstone and brushes, specially for the guests to write their messages of congratulation. On either side of the long table were two tall "money trees" and behind them sat Xu Ya'nan's two younger brothers, Wangjia and Wangcai, one in charge of receiving red envelopes and the other supervising the signing of the book of congratulations.

Naturally, the local relatives were first to arrive. Members of the families on both sides, along with friends and more distant relations, crowded into the hotel in groups. The people from Xu Ya'nan's native village were led by "Old Donkey Face". Of course, he was the village head and that was only his nickname, but it was what everybody called him. He went up to Xu Ya'nan and said: "Well, then, Cai! I was wrong! Aiyo! You had a boy! Our Ya'nan has given birth to a young dragon! Good work! How wonderful! Has the governor not come back with you?"

Xu Ya'nan looked at him. This was the same Old Donkey Face who had scolded her so many times when she was a little girl, and the very sight of whom had made her quail on so many occasions. Now, suddenly, the tables were turned, and she smiled and said: "My uncle, the branch Party secretary, has come. Delin wanted to too, but I wouldn't let him return, because I was afraid it might be misinterpreted."

Old Donkey Face agreed, saying: "Yes, yes! Such an important official, he's right not to come back." Then he shouted to everyone with him: "Remember, you can't call her Cai any more. She's Ya'nan now. That's right, isn't it? And as for the baby, it's a real little tiger cub..." The other villagers gathered around carrying all sorts of gifts: baskets of eggs, woollen blankets, newly made garlands of lucky tiger-head shoes, red envelopes. Some of them called her "older sister", some "younger sister", some "aunt", some "auntie", some "niece", some "cousin"... but all of them full of praise and admiration.

The father's family, led by Uncle Shushan, also arrived. Li Shushan called out: "Cai! Cai! The first time I saw you, I knew Delin had found the right person. And you're from Meiling too! He scooped the jackpot first try! You had a boy, didn't you! The Li family has an heir! How wonderful! How wonderful! What about Delin? Why hasn't he come back for the big event?"

Xu Ya'nan was very upset when she heard him calling her "Cai" at the top of his voice, but she let it go and said: "Is everyone from the family here, Uncle Shushan?"

"Yes, yes! They're all here, they're all here! Of course we've all come! There's a new baby in the family! No one would miss an important event like that!"

Everyone rushed up, shouting "sister-in-law" or "younger brother" or "younger sister" or "nephew", and carrying sack after sack of walnuts, red dates, peanuts and dried persimmons... red envelopes too, of course.

The third group of people who came to offer their congratulations were businessmen and entrepreneurs. Most were from the county, but a few had made a special trip from further afield. They were all very smart in their Western suits with their mobile phones and leather briefcases, but almost none of them actually knew Xu Ya'nan. Their real reason for coming was to "introduce" themselves to the governor's wife, all with their eye on the main chance for the future. So they surrounded her, talking away, handing her their business cards, claiming to be distant cousins and so on. Each one of them tried to make sure it was them who Xu Ya'nan would particularly remember... so naturally, the red envelopes they handed over were all very well-padded.

At eleven o'clock, officials' cars began rolling up, one after another. The news that Li Delin was holding a first month party for his son leaked out, either by design or accident, from the office of the secretary of the County Party Committee of Meiling, Tang Mingsheng. He had told Xue Zhiheng, secretary of the Municipal Party Committee, about it at a meeting. Xue Zhiheng was dubious at first, saying: "I'm not sure that's the right thing to do. Is Governor Li coming back or not?"

Tang Mingsheng said: "His wife didn't say it, it seems..."

Xue Zhiheng scratched his head and said: "And it's going to be held at the Grand Hotel, is it?"

"Yes, I'm setting it all up."

"I'm really happy my old classmate has got himself a young wife. I really have to go, don't I? But I am the municipal Party secretary, and if I'm seen there, people are bound to start gossiping... it's a bit of problem." Then he asked: "What about other cities? What are they saying?"

"It seems that some people have been calling to ask—"

"All right then, ring around and find out what other places are doing. I will go there for midday, but I won't stay to eat."

"OK, but what about the other offices and committees here? Do we tell them?"

"You'll have to figure it out."

At this point, Tang Mingsheng began phoning around, and it became apparent that the city secretaries and district mayors all knew, as did quite a few county-level officials.

Most officials like to be prompt and this lot were no exception, as they began rolling up around 11.30 am. They split into two groups. One comprised the mayors and secretaries of the Municipal Party Committees from various cities, and some county commissioners and secretaries of County Party Committees too. They all brought their office managers and began to laugh and joke with Xu Ya'nan as soon as they arrived: "Congratulations, Sister-in-Law!" "So young too! Surely no more than eighteen!" "What a beautiful baby!" "Tell the governor he owes me a drink."

Then the office managers went over to the long table at the back, handed over their red envelopes and stepped promptly away, not hanging around for any small talk. The other group comprised "*nongkou*" cadres from the Departments of Agriculture, Forestry, Fishery and so on, most of them local-, city- and county-level bureau chiefs. There were so many people in this group that it took quite some time to get through them all, as each in turn greeted their "little sister-in-law", handed over their red envelopes, and voiced their blessings and good wishes. But after that, they hurried off and didn't stay around for the food. Xu Ya'nan loved being called "little sister-in-law", and she greeted everyone who did so with a flashing smile. "How did you all know?" she said. "I told Delin not to tell anyone. And you're all fellow countrymen too..."

The last to arrive was Xue Zhiheng, the new secretary of the Huanghuai City Party Committee. By that time, the banquet had already begun, and the whole place was full of voices, buzzing like a huge beehive. Xu Ya'nan had just sat down to catch her breath and was breastfeeding the baby when Tang Mingsheng walked in with Xue Zhiheng. Xue Zhiheng said, with a laugh: "Sister-in-Law, what do you think you are doing coming onto my patch without saying hello!"

"I don't know what you mean!" Xu Ya'nan replied. "You're so important I didn't want to bother you, so I told Secretary Xiao Tang."

"He doesn't count, he's not the boss."

"Well, it's not my fault in any case. Delin wouldn't let me tell you."

"And you didn't say anything just because he told you not to? Next time, make sure you let me know!"

"All right, if that's how you want it. Next time something comes up, I'll be sure to tell you, so you're not to be cross with me."

Xue Zhiheng joked away with Xu Ya'nan for a while, then glanced at Tang Mingsheng. Tang immediately said: "Is it time you were going back, Brother?"

Xu Ya'nan said: "Then you must go, but I thank you, Secretary Xiao Tang. Next time you are down in the province, I will invite you for a drink."

"No need for thanks," Tang Mingsheng replied, "we'll just be on our way."

"Yes, make sure you look up Xiao Tang if anything more crops up in the future," Xue Zhiheng said. After a little more light-hearted conversation, he said goodbye. Xue Zhiheng did not give a red envelope on this occasion, but he did quietly instruct Tang Mingsheng to settle the "one-month birthday party" account.

Only Liu Jinding did not attend the party and that was because his master wouldn't have wanted him to. Afterwards, he telephoned Li Delin and told him that Xu Ya'nan had laid on a one-hundred-table banquet at a hotel in Meiling County. People from all over had attended and their cars had blocked the street. "This is very bad, Master," Liu Jinding said. "It's very bad for your reputation."

Li Delin put down the phone, held his head in his hands and squatted down on the floor.

The next day, her child in her arms, Xu Ya'nan returned home like a victorious general, bringing with her several dozen assorted relatives from both sides of the family carrying baskets of brown eggs and other goodies. Although some of these people left that same day, more than a dozen of them remained, so accommodation had to be arranged in the small university guest house. They stayed for three days.

After getting back, Xu Ya'nan was still criticising her husband in front of everyone: "Your student, Liu Jinding, wasn't even there to take a single photo of the party and it was such a big event! What's that about? Let him do his own thing in future!"

Li Delin couldn't really say anything in front of all the relatives, but from then on, he became more and more reluctant to go home. He was also in a permanently bad mood. So, things were in a real mess at home, and not much better when he went to work. In particular, his double-eared wheat trial, which was part of the overall national project, had been unsuccessful. Since he became deputy governor, although he still kept personal control of the project, he had had no time to actually take any part in it, and he passed the entire cultivation process over to his graduate students. But when those students failed over and over again, some people began to question the overall viability of his "wheat theory". This was all very painful to Li Delin. Since marrying this woman from Xujiazhuang in Meiling, he felt like a frog in a pot of warm water: each day was a little worse than the one before, but by the time he realised he was being boiled, it was too late. During this period, it was inevitable that he recalled past pain and regretted ever setting off on his current path. As he turned it all over in his head and tried to apply his wheat theory to human emotions, he suddenly discovered the fundamental difference between people and plants: every person is an individual, and what we call simplicity and kindness are not quantifiable. So how did this apply to Xu Ya'nan?

The memory of that night was devastating. Even a long time afterwards, Li Delin still worried about what happened. He couldn't even think about it. How could she have dared? How could she do such a thing?

That is when he made his decision to divorce.

CHAPTER THREE

三

ONE

WHEN HELIAN DONGSHAN WAS FIFTY-EIGHT and about to retire, he suddenly became confused.

It dawned on him that the world in front of him was totally different from what he had previously thought. He was like someone of great enthusiasm and high ideals, who had survived all the hardships thrown at him and was hurrying on to a chosen spot, only to find it was actually somewhere else entirely.

It was like being sure you had planted an aubergine, but watching a loofah gourd grow in its place; or knowing you had put plain water in the pot, but the food coming out tasting salty; or pruning back the overhanging branches and mending the road a long way ahead but eventually finding it a mass of wolfbane once again. However it was also like raising a flea but harvesting a dragon; like a dung beetle, in a moment of inattention, suddenly finding it was pushing a golden egg; like a toad suddenly turning into a swan. Really, how unfair and unpredictable life was! It was like that Ma Zhiyuan poem in which "an emaciated horse travels the ancient road scoured by the west wind, withered vines tangle round ancient trees, a heartbroken man finds himself at the ends of the earth". Now, finally, he understood what it meant to be filled with conflicting emotions. In the dark night, he often cried out to himself, as if in pain: "How did I give birth to such a son?"

Helian Dongshan was nicknamed "Blade". He also had an enemy: his biological son. It was his son who had given him the nickname.

Helian Dongshan's son was called Helian Xichu. He only had that one son.

When his son was born, he had just solved a major case and been given a third-class merit award by the Ministry of Public Security. At the time of the birth, he was busy finishing off that case. He was deeply ashamed and penitent for not waiting at the hospital for the delivery. When he hurried back to the hospital that evening, his son had already been born. Standing in front of his wife's bed, he stared at his baby son in a daze. He was overjoyed but at a loss how to show it. In the end, he hung the medal that he had just been given round the new-born's neck by way of apology. But his son ignored him and wailed loudly, as if to say his father's medal was nothing in his eyes.

Helian Xichu was not originally called Helian Xichu; his name was Helian Huasheng. Huasheng is the Chinese transliteration of "Watson". Helian Dongshan had long wanted his only son to follow in the footsteps of Sherlock Holmes' partner. Helian Huasheng privately changed the name his father had given him to Helian Xichu. His online domain name was borrowed from the famous Xichu Bawang ("Overlord of the Western Chu", referring to Xiang Yu). Since his father's name was Helian Dongshan (Eastern Mountain), he changed his name to Helian Xichu (Western Chu), and he also called himself the Overlord, the implication being that he was setting himself against his father.

In fact, in terms of size, Helian Dongshan was more like a praying mantis and if that had been his nickname it would have been more accurate. He was thin, tall, lean and long in the arm. As he stalked about on his investigations in his police uniform, he looked like an animated dark blue clothes rack. He had many bad habits, such as smoking, drinking, taciturnity and a very quick temper. In his son's eyes, he was quite simply a tyrant.

It is often said that the eyes are the windows to the soul. But in Helian Dongshan's case, that took on a rather sinister meaning. His "window" was rather too small, and a little bit... it is difficult to find the right word, but Helian Dongshan's eyes had a slight squint. There are very few people whose eyes are so narrow that little of their sclera can be seen, and they are always looked at askance; at first sight their appearance can look quite majestic, but that doesn't last, and a sinister, murderous impression takes over. Dispassionately speaking, he used his eyes for his police work, but his son put it much more cruelly: he said that his father used his eyes to kill, that they were his "murder weapon". Long ago, his colleagues gave Helian Dongshan a nickname, "Laser Eyes". It stemmed from his ability to solve cases and was a mark of respect, of admiration, even.

According to the city's unified regulations, all division-level cadres withdrew to the second rank at the age of fifty-five. Under special circumstances, this could be extended to fifty-eight. Helian Dongshan was a recognised expert crime-solver, solving crimes in the City Bureau, and the director did not want to let him go, but he had reached the upper age limit and had to retire from the bureau. When he did so, all he took away with him was a potted asparagus fern. He liked its small, vulnerable, affectionate appearance. Also, the plant had been given to him by Xie Zhichang, president of the Flower World Group. He had always thought that Xie might be implicated in a case that he had never managed to solve, and he wanted a reminder of him.

When Helian Dongshan took that plant home, he put it on a corner cabinet that he looked at every day. He wanted a permanent reminder that there was a case he had not yet cracked.

However, whenever he looked at the fern, he also saw the set of keys that was kept on top of the cabinet. They were new keys, keys that used new technology and keys that represented his new life. They had been brought back from Beijing by his wife. They were the keys to an apartment.

They were special security keys with a slot only on one side and were a hybrid of Japanese, German, American and Italian technology. The Japanese technology used two curved lines, as attractive as a trim-figured woman going bare-legged; the German technology used chrome plating, like the same woman wearing fine, long, close-fitting riding boots; Americans were the smartest in adding a pendant ring, which was like a wide-brimmed straw hat with a silk fringe; then finally the Italian style, with a touch of the trademark Sicilian mafia. Those were the attributes of the "foreign pattern" key. Rumour had it that the company with a foreign name that made them had infiltrated China, and, with a shake of its tail, transformed into a joint venture.

As a veteran division-level detective, Helian Dongshan was still up-to-date with his knowledge of the kinds of lock in common use, not to mention all the older types. The security door locks popular from the 1980s onwards were divided into three types: A, B and C. To the expert eye, the security level of the lock could be identified from the key, in particular, from the grooves and milling on the key. This particular set of keys was obviously super B grade, with hyperbolic grooves. There was a piece of tape on each of the keys, with the words "Donghu 313" written on one, and "Bedroom 1", "Bedroom 2" and "Bedroom 3" on the others. Clearly, they belonged to an apartment with three bedrooms and one living room. One day, when he came back from work, he had heard his wife say to her cousin in the kitchen: "...two sets. When I bought it, it was 1.6 million, and now it's worth more than five million..." When she saw that her husband was back, she coughed and changed the subject.

Just the sight of those keys set something off in Helian Dongshan, and a burning sensation spread through him. He always had to smoke three cigarettes in a row to quench his anger. At night, when he needed to get up to piss, he would always see the potted fern and the bunch of keys again. The keys gleamed like cats' eyes in the darkness, shimmering and shining. He would stand there, looking at them helplessly.

Going into the bathroom, he would turn on the light and stand in front of the mirror, confronted by the white hairs on his temples. At those times, the loneliness would spiral out of his heart like a plume of smoke in the desert.

TWO

THERE WAS NO REAL CONCEPT OF TIME in Helian Dongshan's work.

He was brought in on cases, and his main task was interrogating the suspects. He had been doing it continuously for thirty years.

Cases would come in, day and night, and their arrival heralded the "attack", just like sounding the charge on a battlefield. If the "attack" failed or was "stalled", to use the technical term used by the detectives, the reasons for that also had to be investigated. After one "attack", he would rest for two days then return to the fray for another. What came next was the business of the Prosecutor's Office and the courts. He was like a cook, slaving away in the kitchen, who never saw the results of his work served up at the table. That was the nature of investigative work.

Perhaps out of professional habit, Helian Dongshan's face was always darker when the weather was overcast. Nor did it brighten up much when the sun came out, so his expression was always dark, and some might even describe it as horrible. The only bright spots on this black face were his eyes. His eyes were like an electrically charged drill. All his energy was focused into two points, which pierced people through to the heart in an instant, like a drill bit. Or like a blade, the nickname his son had given him; a blade that shone with a cold light. It might only be a small point of light reflecting off the blade, but it was transformative and maybe even a little evil, with a cat-like cruelty, like a lion pouncing on a rabbit, or like a burst from a Thompson sub-machine gun. Any ordinary prisoner pissed his pants within three minutes of coming under that gaze.

Helian Dongshan was a smoker and never without a cigarette in his mouth. He could often get through four packs a day, and his lips were scorched and dry, like charred pomegranate peel. It is difficult for a face like that to make a good impression, and even when his wife was still in love with him, she once quoted the saying: "Ugly can be ugly as long as it has personality." Habitually, however, he would hide his eyes behind the smoke and squint through it.

There were two things Helian Dongshan was never afraid of in an interrogation, and four surprise techniques he used. One of things he was not afraid of was the suspect not speaking. If they didn't speak with their mouth, they spoke with their eyes, their hands, their legs and their feet. Even if they just scratched their ear, he would know what it meant. He always knew what to do, even with the hard cases who were absolutely determined to remain silent.

Interrogation is all about atmosphere, and Helian Dongshan mostly carried out his interrogations at night. A 500-watt light bulb would magnify everything within its range. Helian Dongshan would often stand in front of the suspect, his back turned, so he cast a grim and sinister-looking shadow on the wall, which added to the atmosphere of mystery and dread. When he suddenly turned around, his eyes pierced the wreathing smoke like thorns, and he had a habitual gesture of nipping out his cigarette and grinding it into the ashtray. At that moment, when he looked round, a hand seemed to reach out from his eyes and grab the suspect's very soul.

There was one suspect he interrogated for twelve days straight. This man was small in stature, no more than one metre sixty, squat, with a fleshy nose, thin eyebrows and single eyelids. At first sight he seemed dull and stupid but, look again, and you could see that ice water flowed in his veins. Helian Dongshan believed he was a murderer who killed without displaying any emotion, but who was saying nothing. For twelve days he held his silence, not uttering a word. He knew he was a dead man whether he confessed or not, so the bastard didn't even moisten his lips. To get such a suspect to confess would inevitably require some kind of ploy. He was sat on an interrogation chair from which the wooden seat was removed, so only three steel bars supported his buttocks. He was made to sit on the hard steel for seven days, leaving him in severe pain, but he still didn't say a word.

For those twelve days, the two men's eyes were locked in battle. Helian Dongshan realised that the suspect had a habit of licking his lips every three to five seconds. He was not afraid of being stared at, and when you looked at him, his eyes were empty, like two black holes. Helian Dongshan knew that it wasn't the result of being unafraid but that he had reached the extreme of desperation in his fear. A desperate person is the most difficult kind to deal with. With such a suspect, Helian Dongshan always had a sullen look in his eyes. However, it is often at this moment that the white heat of anger meets the chill air of reality and loses much of its vehemence. From this point on, Helian Dongshan didn't need to rely on his anger, but could use dispassionate observation, since indifference can sometimes be a potent, invisible weapon. Now Helian Dongshan asked only a few cold, factual questions each day. If the suspect wasn't talking, Helian Dongshan wasn't asking, and he would just sit there smoking. But his eyes were like flying daggers, dancing in the air of the interrogation room, leaving the suspect no space to breathe. In the small interrogation room, Helian Dongshan's indifference gradually became like a 10,000-ton hydraulic press. He kept pressing, from the top of the head, pressing in all directions. At first it seemed rather majestic, then it was contemptuous, and finally it was like a cat playing with a mouse, an inconsequential scene from a drama. At first, the suspect's nerves were strained but held out, until finally they reached breaking point. For the suspect, his habit of licking his lips was a way to muster his resolve, but now, his lips were too swollen. He stopped licking them, and his eyes became evasive. On the eighth day of this, he could no longer hold himself upright and began to look wildly around, grunting in his throat. He coughed dryly for a while, and spat...

"Take him away!" Helian Dongshan said in a low, icy tone.

Over twelve days, Helian Dongshan witnessed the entire progress of the suspect's gaze ranging from a chilling, hard confrontation to a diffuse and erratic vagueness. A person who keeps staring at someone will see when they no longer have anywhere to hide. In the later stages, the suspect's gaze was like a fly trapped in a glass, flying around constantly, zigzagging across the room, east and west. Helian Dong-shan noted every place it rested. Gradually, he spotted a pattern and a point at a forty-five-degree angle from the chair was a favoured spot, although the suspect himself seemed unaware of it.

The forty-five-degree angle led to where the stenographer sat. Since there was no confession to be taken down, the stenographer was sitting there, fiddling with his pen.

Later, Helian Dongshan led a search, and his men found a gold Parker pen hidden in a hole in the wall of the suspect's home. The gold pen obviously did not belong to the suspect. The Technical Department lifted two fingerprints from the pen: one belonged to the suspect, and the other was unknown. Further investigations revealed this pen was produced in the UK in 1965, and that very few people in China owned one. Helian Dongshan ran some checks and homed in on the provincial capital. Just a month before, a university lecturer had died in his own property in a residential district there. Further investigations were undertaken. Unlikely as it seemed, a grudge had developed between the lecturer and the suspect. The two of them had simply passed each other on the street, and the lecturer had looked at the suspect once too often, and that look had signed his death warrant.

When the evidence was placed in front of the suspect, he cleared his throat and finally spoke: "I want a plate of steamed buns. The ones they wrap in lotus leaves on Koujia Alley in Xuchang."

Helian Dongshan then became very tolerant and forbearing: "All I need from you is a confession, and you can leave the rest to me."

Helian Dongshan sent people to Xuchang by overnight train so they could get to Koujia Alley the next morning and buy two plates of steamed buns wrapped in lotus leaves. Helian Dongshan told his men to take the buns to the interrogation room and give them to the suspect. The suspect took them and ate six, one after the other. Then he said: "They're better hot!"

"Do you want us to heat them up for you?" Helian Dongshan asked.

"No need," the suspect replied as he ate the buns and drank a jug of hot water. He wiped his lips, closed his eyes for a moment, then opened them again and asked: "Can you let me sleep for a while?"

Helian Dongshan was ninety per cent of the way to achieving his objective, and there was no way he was going to let him sleep. "No!" he replied.

"All right, ask away then. I'll answer whatever you ask." What else could the suspect say?

The interrogation continued for a whole day and night, and the suspect confessed all the facts of his crime. Every time he opened his mouth, he started with "Fuck me, but..." Sometimes the phrase was just a verbal tic, but on other occasions it was violent and obscene, and occasionally it was more like a deep sigh. The stenographer started to record accurately, word for word, but after a while, as page after page filled up with expletives, he simply omitted them.

It is almost impossible for anyone to imagine the truth of what was going on there. The man was just small fry, who did not even graduate from elementary school, and the weapon he used was an ordinary, thin-handled domestic hammer. But in under five years, he managed to commit crime after crime and killed a total of thirty-five people in heinous fashion.

What was truly shocking was how cruel and cunning the suspect was; he was like a savage wolf. His usual method was to use other people for cover, then jump out and smash the back of his victim's head with his little hammer, as easy as if he was cracking a walnut. Helian Dongshan found it hard to understand what kind of circumstances created such a demon. He had no compunction about killing, and most of his victims were innocent folk who were just in the wrong place at the wrong time: an old man picking up rubbish, a disabled woman... and especially the lecturer who had just walked past and looked at him. He had secretly followed the lecturer home, waited until he was asleep, climbed in through a window and killed him. After the murder, he sat down in the man's living room, calmly watched two videos, ate a plate of beef and drank two cans of beer.

During the interrogation, Helian Dongshan couldn't help but ask him: "What did you think you were doing, following someone home and killing them, just because they looked at you?"

"There was a nasty look in his eyes," the suspect replied. "He was disrespecting me."

"There's a nasty look in my eyes too!"

"I am a demon and you are one of the judges of Hell. He was nothing, what did he matter?"

Before his sentence was passed, the prisoner asked to see Helian Dongshan one more time. Helian Dongshan could have just ignored the request, but in the end, he went. Facing the shackled murderer, he said coldly: "There are no more buns for you, Hu Shuwen."

"I know. You caught me, and there's no way out."

The prisoner went on to make an extended confession to a whole list of further, unverified crimes. The first person he killed was his stepfather. His stepfather was a pig slaughterman, a big strong man, but he put up no kind of opposition. He killed him when he was drunk. At that time, the County Public Security Bureau determined that he had fallen over when drunk, fractured his skull and died of a cerebral haemorrhage. Hu Shuwen was thirteen years old at the time. The prisoner said: "Do you know what I was called when I was a kid? Kela. My real name is Hu Kela. Do you know how my dad used to greet me? With his feet. Every time we met, from when I was six, he kicked me! And I remembered every single fucking time he did... Do you know what my greatest ambition in this life is?"

Helian Dongshan looked at him and said in a mocking tone: "To lead a revolution?"

The prisoner shook his head and said: "To be the porter at the county government compound and collect all the stuff they throw away. Then I could go and eat lotus-leaf steamed buns in Koujia Alley now and then. Fuck me, that would be so good!"

"What else do you want?"

"To die like a man with my cock facing heaven! Fuck me, what else is there!" He fell silent for a while, looking at the blue sky beyond the iron cell bars, then asked: "Do you think I could come back as a bird in my next life?" Helian Dongshan did not reply, and finally the man said to himself: "Fuck it all!"

Just at that moment, the murderous intent on the prisoner's face disappeared, and there was an absence of light in his eyes. He was just grey and empty, like the deathly hush after a great rock has crashed to the ground.

That case made Helian Dongshan famous in the Huanghuai Plain. As a result, he became the leading figure in the pre-trial investigation community of the area's entire public security system. He was asked to take on those prisoners who could not be broken by anyone else. That was how he got the honorary nickname in the service of Laser Eyes.

Nonetheless, in his son's eyes, he was a complete loser.

THREE

Helian Dongshan's only life experience was in dealing with prisoners.

Almost all of his energy was spent on conducting his cases. His obsession with interrogation work even surpassed his love for his wife and family.

The trouble between Helian Dongshan and his son started with the words: "Squat down!"

That first abrupt command was what caused the alienation between father and son, and what led to all the subsequent hostility. Without thinking, Helian Dongshan tended to use some of his work expressions in daily life, and he was quite oblivious to how much they could scare his son. He had been dealing with prisoners all his working life, and this had affected the way he spoke to everyone. For example, when his son was carefully following him on the way to school, without thinking he would shout: "Stand still!" The son would stop and not dare move an inch. In fact, he wanted to stop to ask if his son had had enough to eat, but the way he shouted "Stand still!" destroyed any intimacy between the two of them. Or there was the time he wanted to have a quiet chat with his son about the dangers of spending too much time playing video games. Without thinking he said: "You — come here." He wasn't shouting and he wasn't aware of doing anything wrong, but his wife said: "Now look what you've done! He's frightened to death of you!"

Helian Dongshan got married late and only had his son at the age of thirty. He doted on the boy and never dreamed that as the child grew up, day by day, the gap between them would become deeper and deeper, until finally it reached the point where they were as incompatible as fire and water. He remembered very clearly that from the age of eight, his son never called him "Dad" again. Don't shout at him, he kept telling himself, but his son started hiding from him during the week, and a look of animosity began to grow in his eyes. On one particular occasion, when the boy was thirteen, he said something that cut Helian Dongshan to the quick. Once again, he had taken his leather belt off to discipline the boy when he faced up to him and asked, in aggrieved tones: "Am I one of your prisoners then?" Helian Dongshan was rocked to his core.

As a big name in the investigative field, Helian Dongshan was not afraid of a suspect telling lies. Once you tell a lie, you have to come up with a hundred things to support it. Once the lie is out there, the bigger the lie, the more loopholes in it that you have to keep fixing. And no matter what you do, the holes keep getting bigger until, finally, the lie is exposed.

There was an unsolved case that had been kept on the back burner for eighteen years, until it was rediscovered by Helian Dongshan in the city's "anti-vice and illegal activity review". One night, Huanghuai City carried out a co-ordinated operation to clean up "pornography, gambling and drugs", in what was called a blitzkrieg. Sometime after midnight, the entire public security system was dispatched, and more than a hundred suspects were brought in. Afterwards, they were interrogated in groups. Helian Dongshan was in charge of the third interrogation team, and as a result, a truly hair-raising case was revealed.

It was a case that humiliated the whole provincial public security system. In the summer of 1976, a bank robbery was staged in the provincial capital. At noon, in the bustling downtown district, the robber shot and killed a female employee of a savings bank and made off with 1.46 million yuan. He stole a bicycle to make his getaway and disappeared into the crowd... The case had remained unsolved.

But that was not all. For the next five consecutive years, on the date of the robbery, the Provincial Public Security Bureau received a letter from the robber. Its main import was: Dear Mr Policeman, I am having such fun. When will you solve the case? I am waiting!

Of course, this was blatantly provocative. The leaders of the Provincial Department were furious and ordered the criminal police headquarters to take the lead in organising a joint task force to solve the case within a given time. However, because the anonymous letters were cut and pasted from old newspapers, the investigation took too long and there were insufficient clues. Moreover, the robber had fled to another province, so in the end, nothing came of it. Because of the importance of the case, a co-operation notice was issued throughout the entire public security system. It made a considerable impression on Helian Dongshan.

That night, his third interrogation team questioned a total of twenty-nine suspects. Depending on the circumstances, routine interrogations usually went through three rounds before providing a result. The first round is the initial investigation and involves asking basic questions about name, address, employment, etc. In the second, you ask in more detail: what were you doing on the night in question? and so on, while the third round is essentially determinative: detain, punish or release.

Of the twenty-nine people brought in, seven were released on the spot, thirteen were fined, six were detained, leaving three whose fates were undecided. These last three could also end up being fined, but Helian Dongshan said that he needed to make further enquiries. He was particularly interested in one of them. This man had been arrested in a hotel spa, and he had clearly been drinking. Several times he staggered forward to explain that he was a guest of the municipal government... and every time he was ordered by the police to squat back down on the ground. He was a decent-looking person, something over forty years old, well-fleshed and full-featured. He wore his hair slicked back and was dressed in casual designer clothes and highly polished leather shoes. Initial police investigations revealed that this "Mr Slick" had quite a colourful background and was inclined to throw his weight around. He should have been the first one to be released, but he put his foot in it with something he said.

Helian Dongshan started by asking him where he was from. Mr Slick hurriedly handed over his business card and explained that he had been invited by the municipal government to invest in the city and set up a business. He said he had been invited to dinner that night by Deputy Secretary-General Liu of the municipal government, and if they didn't believe him, they could ask Hotel Manager Bai, or phone Secretary-General Liu directly. Police Officer Xing Zhibin, who was standing to one side, said: "Be honest! You were with a prostitute, weren't you! Cut the crap and answer the question."

Mr Slick replied: "I'm sorry, I'm sorry, I drank too much, someone knocked on the door and the girl came in... I did wrong, I admit I did wrong!" Xing Zhibin went on: "Tell the truth now, where are you from?" Mr Slick was very voluble with his answer, quoting a line from the Tang dynasty poet, Cui Hao: "Hubei! 'The yellow crane has gone, never to return; banks of white cloud, a thousand years.'" Xing Zhibin rebuked him: "Stop bullshitting and just say where you're from." Mr Slick said: "OK, OK, OK! Wuhan." At this point, Helian Dongshan stopped the questions and simply said: "Take him down!"

From Helian Dongshan's point of view, three things didn't ring true about this individual. First, there was something odd about the smell his body was giving off, and it wasn't just the alcohol. He looked very uptight, his eyes were glassy and he was too cooperative. Second, he was not a local, but his southern accent was mixed up with northern dialect. Third, he had lied. A receipt in his wallet confirmed he came from Ningbo, but he said he was from Wuhan. What was the reason for this mixture of lies and half-truths?

If he was a local government official or a civil servant, he could be nervous of losing face, but he was a businessman from another province, here to invest. Normally, in such circumstances, the unwritten rule was that he wouldn't be investigated. Even if he was, the most he could expect was a fine. But this person was being overly cautious and also too voluble in his answers. He was like a second-rate actor, pretending to be free and easy, but always with the suspicion of something hidden behind his eyes. His real mistake was in quoting the verse about yellow cranes. That triggered a memory at the back of Helian Dongshan's brain, and he quickly searched through the unsolved cases in his mental filing cabinet. There were five words in it that clicked into place: "White clouds and yellow cranes".

These words were included in the first letter sent by the bank robber to the Provincial Public Security Bureau in 1978. He actually imitated the style of a letter written by Mao Zedong: "Three hundred and sixty-five days have passed. I am disporting myself in a place of white clouds and yellow cranes…" Helian Dongshan walked out of the interrogation room and stood in the courtyard, smoking. He chain-smoked half a pack, leaving a pile of cigarette butts at his feet. Then he walked back to the building and focused on Mr Slick.

During the second half of the day, Helian Dongshan focused in on the words "white clouds and yellow cranes". "Are you from Wuhan?" he asked.

Mr Slick replied, with a distinct southern accent: "No. I passed through there and investigated it for a few days. I told you, I'm here to invest." He put a marked emphasis on the word "investigated".

"Have you tried Wuchang fish?" Helian Dongshan asked.

"Wuchang fish is very famous. Chairman Mao said in his poem: 'I only drink Changsha water and eat Wuchang fish.' Yes, I've tried it. The flesh is very tender. Look, as for that prostitute business, yes, I'm sorry about that, I plead guilty."

"Do Wuchang fish have spines?"

"No. Yes, there are... no, no small spines, but there are big spines. Comrade, I have to sign a contract tomorrow morning in the city. All the city top brass will be there, so do you think–"

"I know, I know you are doing great things. There is another famous dish in Wuhan, isn't there?"

"You are talking about Jiujiu duck neck? It's too spicy for me. Comrade Brother, can you be a little accommodating–"

"I'm not talking about duck necks, I'm talking about lotus root stewed pork ribs. Simmered slowly, and only the local Honghu red lotus root will taste right. Have you tried it?"

"Red lotus root stewed short ribs? Yes, I've had them. Delicious! Now, can I make a call?"

"Do you smoke? There is a brand of cigarettes in Hubei called Yellow Crane Tower. Have you ever tried them?"

"I don't smoke."

"So have you climbed the Yellow Crane Tower?"

"Climbed it? Of course I have. I, I... tomorrow, may I make a phone call?"

"Which of the three towns of Wuhan is the Yellow Crane Tower in?"

"It's in Wuchang, isn't it! Chairman Mao wrote: 'The line runs through from north to south, the turtle and the snake lock up the big river.' It looks like a snake... snake mountain... on Snake Mountain... come on, Comrade Brother, it's late, I'm bursting for a piss!"

Helian Dongshan paced around before suddenly asking: "When did you last go there? In the summer?"

"No, no, not summer. It's no good, Comrade, I'm almost peeing my pants."

"It was summer, right?"

"No, no."

"Winter, then?"

"No, not winter... not really winter..."

"Have a good think. When did you last go there?" Then he continued: "During the first interview, you quoted two lines of Cui Hao's poem, do you remember? Can you recite the whole poem? Recite it now for me."

After a moment he barked out an order, emphasising the word: "Recite!"

Mr Slick seemed to have sobered up and was staring at him in alarm, not saying a word.

All through that night, right up to dawn, Mr Slick refused to say the words "white clouds and yellow cranes". He kept his lips sealed, despite all blandishments, and simply didn't say a word. The less he was willing to speak, the more suspicious it looked. Then he really did piss himself, and the urine dripped down from his crotch. "I'm going to sue you!" he said.

Helian Dongshan was under tremendous pressure to crack the case. The following morning, Director Wan called and personally asked: "Has that businessman Wei been released yet, the one who was staying at the Blu-Ray Hotel?"

"Not yet," Helian Dongshan replied.

"Isn't it just about a prostitute? Release him. Secretary-General Liu of the municipal government just rang to ask."

"Director, this person can't be released."

"Release him. We're in an open society now, and the economy is king, so what do you think you are doing?"

"I think he's a suspect in the 'July Seventh Case'."

The director had faith in Helian Dongshan, knowing that he wouldn't say such a thing lightly. He thought about it for a moment and said: "All right, I'll back off for the moment. I'll give you forty-eight hours. If you can't make it stick by then, let him go." Later, after discussion with the Provincial Public Security Bureau, the time was extended to seventy-two hours.

Every second of those seventy-two hours was vital. If the "attack" failed, Helian Dongshan would be in big trouble. When he woke up, Mr Slick was spitting mad, like a rattlesnake that had been trodden on. He put his finger in Helian Dongshan's face and said: "I am a guest of the city government and I'm going to sue you. I'll have your badge! You'd better believe it!"

Helian Dongshan just smiled and retorted: "Don't get yourself in a state. Why are you in such a state? Let's talk."

As a matter of urgency, Helian Dongshan sent a three-man team, first to Ningbo by plane, and then on by car the short distance to Cixi, his place of permanent residence under the household registration system. They were looking for any kind of physical evidence.

In the course of those three days, the man in charge of the case from the provincial criminal police headquarters made a special trip to compare the photo-fit of the robber, put together from eye-witness descriptions, with Helian Dongshan's prisoner. Section Chief Dong, the head of the task force, said to Helian Dongshan: "It doesn't look much like him. The robber had a small, flat head and a thin face. This man had a big, round head and a chubby face. Besides, the eyebrows and eyes are not very similar..." The truth was, the man who was in charge of the task force at the time of the robbery simply did not believe that Helian Dongshan could solve this eighteen-year-old cold case. Before leaving, he suggested: "Just let him go, Lao He."

"We agreed seventy-two hours, Director Dong," replied Helian Dongshan.

It was the search in Cixi that yielded major results.

After contacting the local Public Security Bureau, the three-man team learned that Mr Slick, whose real name was Wei Shaohua, lived in a newly renovated three-storey building on East Street in Cixi County Township. Downstairs was a shop selling tobacco and alcohol, and the residential apartments were upstairs. So, with the cooperation of the local police, they searched the building from top to bottom, principally looking for a gun, but found nothing. The man's wife was a local woman, and very talkative, but she could provide no answers to their questions. When they contacted the bureau by phone, Helian Dongshan said: "Look again, this time more carefully. See if there is any circumstantial evidence."

So the men repeated a painstaking search. On the third floor, in a sandalwood box inside an old-style suitcase, there was a stamp album that they had checked over the first time. When they flipped through it initially, all they saw was page after page of stamps, with nothing to arouse their interest. This time, they went through it more carefully, and found that the last page of the album contained a sheet of the 1967 issue "Sailing the Seas Depends on the Helmsman". There should have been seventy of the eight-cent stamps in the sheet, but one was missing. Helian Dongshan said quietly down the phone: "Bring them back here."

The three men flew back to the provincial capital and rushed straight to the Provincial Public Security Bureau. They took out the page of stamps and compared them with the stamp on the first anonymous letter sent by the robber in 1978. They found that the perforations matched exactly. The stamp on the letter was from the sheet in the sandalwood box. For a while, the phones at the Provincial Public Security Bureau were ringing non-stop.

By then, they were on the third day, and just three hours remained before the 72-hour time limit ran out. But with this preliminary evidence, Mr Slick definitely wasn't going anywhere. When Helian Dongshan got the news, he said: "Everyone has worked very hard, but this is just one piece of evidence. Check again. It may well be that, after so long, the gun is not found, but search again. This time, check his accounts and cashflow over the last eighteen years."

When Mr Slick was being arraigned again, Helian Dongshan deliberately had his hair cut and put on a brand-new police uniform. As Mr Slick was brought up, Helian Dongshan said: "Well, Lao Wei, it looks as though I won't be hanging up my uniform after all!"

They made more discoveries during the third search in Cixi. In the small three-storey building where Wei Shaohua lived, they found a concealed basement. It had been turned into a large wine cellar, filled with all kinds of wine. What caught the detectives' attention was case after case of Maotai, stored separately from everything else. Going by the labels on the cartons, they were all post-1979, and there were fifteen cases from the years 1980, 1981 and 1982. These fifteen boxes of Maotai from different years were all purchased in different provinces. Why?

Later, it was discovered this man with the slicked-back hair who had used the name Wei Genzhu and now went by Wei Shaohua, was indeed a criminal of formidable intelligence. The money he stole from the bank was never redeposited anywhere. Instead, he bought Maotai in instalments from different cities in different years. Judging from the bills, in order not to be conspicuous, he never spent more than 50,000 yuan on a wine purchase. Back then, five-star Maotai was only eight yuan a bottle, but it rose year by year, and it was now extremely valuable. In the end, despite all his precautions, he had still let the cat out of the bag.

He had kept back one case of each of the years of Maotai he had bought and stored them in a corner of the wine cellar. Presumably, he was planning to drink them himself, over time. This one element of the case sent the detectives running all over the country. Working from the labels on the boxes, they went to Guiyang, Kunming, Hangzhou, Chengdu, Wuhan, Guangzhou, Changsha... and checked countless local records of wine sales, to pin down the suspect's expenditures.

Later, they discovered that after the year of the robbery, Wei Shaohua fled to the south and hid in the small county town of Cixi for twelve years, until 1990, living off the profits from the alcohol and tobacco shop. He had registered himself in Cixi, got married and had children. After that, he drifted around Shenzhen for another four years, trading stocks and making a fortune. He was like the wily rabbit with three exits from his burrow, buying real estate in Shenzhen, and taking a mistress. His cover was excellent, and his wife back in Cixi, who was twelve years younger than him, knew nothing about his goings on in Shenzhen.

Wei Shaohua's wanderings took him all the way to Fenghua, the hometown of Chiang Kai-shek and well worth a visit for its beautiful scenery and atmosphere. It is a popular tourist attraction so there were probably too many people and too many prying eyes for him to stay there very long. After that, he went to Ningbo and visited the world-famous Tianyi Pavilion Library. Cixi is only a few dozen kilometres from Ningbo, so he went back there by boat along the canal. Cixi is a little-known area, so he was able to remain invisible there.

In Helian Dongshan's view, the evidence being collected and verified was highly satisfactory and the suspect's guilt was basically established. But what about the gun? The gun had still not been found.

When the two sat down again in the interrogation room, Helian Dongshan took off the man's handcuffs and said: "Let's talk, Lao Wei, let's talk."

"You couldn't catch me to start with."

"Yes, for eighteen years! You've been hiding for eighteen years."

"It's my fault. An idea, just one idea, that's what did for me."

" A bad idea?"

"I am not short of money. I have more than twenty million to hand. I wanted to earn a good round amount, so I stopped being careful about money, and, as a result–"

"How much is a 'good round amount'?"

"One hundred million." Then he continued: "To be honest, it was Secretary-General Liu of your municipal government who really got me going. He went to Shenzhen to drum up investment last year, and we met at the China Merchants' Association. He was very enthusiastic about a coal mine with exceptional reserves. He needed money to get the stuff out of the ground, and that's where I came in..."

Helian Dongshan sighed. "You're a very smart man, Lao Wei. A one-in-a-million talent, maybe. It's a shame."

"Back then, I had read *Das Kapital* and *Anti-Dühring*. I learned 'The Sayings of Chairman Mao' off by heart. Do you know what it says on page 271? 'Chen Yi is a good comrade.' Actually, it was a blank page, and I filled that in in biro."[1]

Helian Dongshan said: "One year before the Cultural Revolution, in all six cities of Yubei, you were the sole student admitted to the key middle school in the provincial capital. You were only fourteen years old at the time."

"How do you know all this?"

"I went to a lot of trouble to check your original household registration. You can't find it in the provincial municipality, and you can't find it in Yubei County District. But you are in the collective household registration of the key provincial middle school, and there is only one name on that household registration. But then you changed your name and became invisible."

"Back then, I was determined to be admitted to Peking University or Tsinghua. But the Cultural Revolution began, and university stopped. Later, we were sent to the mountains and the countryside. I didn't want to go back to my hometown–"

"You were a bystander during the Cultural Revolution, and you never joined in... how did you get hold of a gun?"

Mr Slick closed his eyes and said nothing.

"Look, Lao Wei, this is the main point, so let's talk about it."

"I don't want to implicate anyone."

"It doesn't matter who else was involved. We're not going to start looking into the Cultural Revolution, but you have to tell us about the gun."

Helian Dongshan took out two photos of Mr Slick's daughters. One was born to the wife in Cixi; the other was born to the mistress in Shenzhen. Helian Dongshan put the photos down in front of him and asked: "Are these your daughters? They're very beautiful."

Mr Slick looked at the photos in silence. The two little girls were as pretty as flowers.

"You should know that your woman from Shenzhen has flown up to see you," Helian Dongshan said. "To be honest, I envy you. That is a really good woman. Even though she knows you have committed a crime, she has still made a special trip to see you. She's even brought a pot of soup she made specially, brought it all that way..."

Mr Slick was taken aback for a moment, and asked: "What did she say?"

"She said she will wait for you."

Mr Slick was silent for a long time, then whispered: "Will I... will I get the death sentence?"

"To be honest, that's not down to me, but I can put in a word with the higher authorities. It depends on your attitude."

Finally, Mr Slick said: "The statute of limitations is up on my case, isn't it? As long as there's no death sentence, I am willing to expiate my crime with good deeds. I will donate more than twenty million to the nation. And in addition..."

The Huanghuai City Public Security Bureau won a collective second-class merit award after cracking the "July Seventh Case". The secretary's intention was for Helian Dongshan to be promoted to deputy director of criminal investigation. But after the report was submitted, it was held back and not approved for ages. In the end, only one deputy director-level detective was approved. The director was afraid that Helian Dongshan would be upset, so he tried to console him by saying that his current rank was effectively the same.

Helian Dongshan could read between the lines. Liu Jinding, the deputy secretary-general of the municipal government, had been transferred to be deputy secretary of the political and legal committee a month previously. It was reported that during the interview, Deputy Secretary Liu didn't say much apart from one sentence: "He's got the ability, but his personality is too assertive." There is nothing wrong with this sentence in itself, but it just so happened that Liu Jinding was one of the people on whom Wei Shaohua had blown the whistle as part of his "expiating his crime by good deeds". It was Liu who had brought Mr Slick in on the deal when the city was looking for investors. The two of them had come to a verbal agreement in Shenzhen that Wei Shaohua would fund the investment, and Deputy Secretary-General Liu would smooth the way for the purchase of the coal mine. When it was done, they were going to split the profits sixty-forty. However, it was only a verbal agreement between the two, and no contract was ever signed before Wei Shaohua was arrested. That meant there were no witness statements and no physical evidence. But both still carried the secret inside them, as if they each had a pair of portable scales, and no matter what physical distance separated them, there was a tacit mutual understanding that they held each other's fate in the balance... so that, after some years, when the two sat down face to face, those scales did indeed weigh out something. But that is a story for another time.

Although his colleagues in the bureau thought he had been treated unfairly, Helian Dongshan himself didn't feel wronged. He had been promoted to deputy director and if it was only a nominal promotion, so be it. What mattered was that the case had been solved.

FOUR

THEN THERE WAS THE ARSON CASE that secretly gnawed away at Helian Dongshan's professional pride.

Acting on instinct, Helian Dongshan initially locked up some suspects in this case after the preliminary investigation. But as he delved deeper into it, he seemed to lose the thread because the background to the case was so complex.

That said, the case itself was very simple. One winter, a large fire broke out in a shop selling gold jewellery on Yaqian Street in Huanghuai. Not only was all the gold jewellery in the shop destroyed, at a loss of more than 1.6 million yuan, but the owner and his wife also burned to death. The fire started at three o'clock in the morning and by the time the fire truck arrived, the quintuple-fronted gold shop and the single-storey building bordering its rear courtyard had been consumed by the fire.

On-site investigations revealed no traces of robbery or violence inside the gold shop. Although the door and cabinet locks had been badly scorched, they were still relatively intact. The only significant discovery was a burnt-out jerrycan in what was left of the shop doorway. It contained a small quantity of petrol and a number of cigarette butts.

The shop was in a street in the old part of the city not touched by redevelopment. The street was also the site of a famous local night market, and although it was not much more than 300 metres long, it was narrow and densely populated. Many of the vendors sold their wares in the open air under tarpaulins, and there were electrical wires everywhere like a random tangle of spiderwebs. Inevitably, many of the cables were in a very poor state and the Huanghuai City Public Security Bureau was considering two different possibilities for the cause of the fire. One opinion was that faulty wiring was responsible and the other was that it was arson. However, no relevant evidence had yet been found, so the initial verdict was one of "accidental fire".

Originally, it looked likely that the case was going to be shelved, but the relatives of the victims kept screaming for justice. Moreover, they brought a private case against a particular individual, saying that he had a grudge against the Wu family who owned the gold shop, and it was he who had set the fire. Young and old alike, the whole family stood in front of the Public Security Office carrying a banner protesting the injustice. They stood there for three whole days, crying and wailing and demanding the arrest of the murderer. In view of the seriousness of the case and the fact that people had died, the director decided to carry out a full investigation. That was how the case came to be assigned to Helian Dongshan.

To Helian Dongshan's astonishment, once he started the investigation, he found himself dragged into it personally. The fact was, he was acquainted with the man the Wu family wanted to sue and had even been given flowers by him; the potted fern he took home from the office had been a gift from this person.

His name was Xie Zhichang, nicknamed "Bigmouth Xie". He was now the general manager of the Sino-foreign joint venture Flower World Group in Huanghuai. He was a well-known local billionaire who also had a string of other titles: vice-chairman of the Huanghuai Chinese People's Political Consultative Conference (CPPCC), vice-chairman of Huanghuai Federation of Industry and Commerce, and representative of the Provincial and Municipal People's Congresses.

When Helian Dongshan took over the case, his instinct was that there must be some reason for the Wu family to have brought up Xie Zhichang and sued him by name. So he decided to get to the bottom of Xie's involvement.

Xie Zhichang's office was located in a newly built five-star hotel. The name of the hotel was the Flower World Hotel, and it was the most famous luxury hotel in the area with an "AAAA" international certification. It was also an entertainment venue that integrated various leisure and vacation services. Its construction gave rise to a large-scale group petition that was the trigger for the "June 29th Incident". In order to appease the farmers who had lost their land, after the situation calmed down, the Municipal Party Committee and the municipal government intervened decisively and forced the Flower World Group to stump up a lot of money in compensation... of course, it always had to be borne in mind that the Flower World Group was already a substantial corporate municipal tax-payer.

Helian Dongshan travelled in plain clothes on this occasion, but even so, he had not expected to be challenged three times before getting to see Xie Zhichang. The first time was at the main door, where a young man in a security guard uniform asked: "Are you a guest at the hotel, sir?"

"I'm here to see someone."

The little security guard was immediately suspicious: "Who are you here to see?"

"I'm here to see Mr Xie."

"Do you have an appointment, sir?"

Helian Dongshan hesitated for a moment before saying: "Yes."

The security guard smiled and said: "Thank you. Mr Xie is on the fifth floor."

Helian Dongshan got to the lift entrance where he was questioned again. When the hostess standing in front of the main lift heard him say that he had an appointment, she politely led him to another lift and said: "Please, sir, this is a special list for Mr Xie and his distinguished guests."

On the fifth floor, Helian Dongshan saw two sturdy men standing with their hands behind their backs. As soon as he got out of the lift, one of them came up to him, bowed and asked: "Who are you looking for, sir?"

It was time for Helian Dongshan to make his identity known. "I'm from the City Bureau and I'm here to see Mr Xie," he said. "Please announce me."

A moment later, Xie Zhichang came out to greet him. He hurried over to shake hands, smiled and said: "Even though I had the good fortune to hear magpies singing this morning, I still didn't expect such a distinguished visitor! Why didn't you call in advance, Chief He? Please, follow me." He knew Helian Dongshan was not the chief, as he had been put right on this the last time they met, but he still persisted in using the title.

Helian Dongshan was amazed to see that Xie Zhichang's office took up half an entire floor of the building. At first glance, it looked like a huge formal reception room. On the east wall, there were rows of framed photographs of Xie Zhichang with the leaders of various provinces and cities; on the west wall, there were rows of framed awards and medals for "five-star cultural enterprises" and "model taxpayer enterprises" and so on; to the north was a bookcase. Xie Zhichang had not read many books, and all of the ones he had were in that bookcase. It was a huge, gilded masterpiece of carpentry. In front of the bookcase, there was a desk so large you could lie on it and roll around. On it, along with the normal office desk furniture and three telephones, one red, one black and one white, there were two small flags: one was the national flag, and the other was the flag of a political association depicting ears of white wheat and gear wheels. To the south was the meeting area with sofas arranged in groups, along with a refrigerator and a drinks cabinet. Helian Dongshan couldn't hold back a sigh as he said: "This is not how things used to be, Lao He. Everything is a lot bigger!"

"It's nothing, it's nothing," Xie Zhichang said. "What does it matter, eh? This trifling office is simply the result of the progressive policies of our provincial and municipal leaders."

"I heard you like fishing? A Toyota Prado with a refrigerated truck behind it so you can freeze the fish as soon as you catch them. Your 'carp with braised noodles' here is famous."

"Yeah, yeah, it's not bad. On a Sunday, I take the big bosses for some fun at the reservoir. You should come with us one day if you're interested, Chief He. I'll make sure you get a good rod."

Xie Zhichang went on to talk enthusiastically about fishing: "Fish are like people. You have to let them get to know you. The things is, I have a little den up at the Tawan Reservoir and I spread bait there all year round. The fish have got used to the bait, and in the place where I spread it, you only have to put a rod in, and you can pull out twenty to thirty catties. Once, I found a great spot where I caught three hundred and twenty catties! My bait is different from other people's, it's specially made to a secret recipe. You should never use your hands to mix it because it mustn't carry any human smell. If the fish catch even a whiff of human scent, they won't eat it." Xie Zhichang went on talking about fishing for quite some time, and ended by saying: "Of course, I only take friends up there. If they're not friends, I don't take them."

As he watched Xie Zhichang, Helian Dongshan couldn't help being surprised. This was no longer the guy who sold flowers door-to-door around the government agencies. This was a "someone". It seems that every such successful person has a unique and secret side.

Xie Zhichang said enthusiastically: "I have wanted to invite you to dinner for a long time, you know, but I am always too busy. I know you are a busy person too, so I'm wary of inviting you. Now you happen to be here today, I'm not going to let you leave at noon. I'm going to make up for it today, no matter what you say." Then he shouted an order: "Quick, bring tea! The best."

After a little polite conversation, Helian Dongshan decided to get to the point. He said: "Did you hear that someone is suing you, Lao Xie?"

Xie Zhichang looked nonchalant and said: "Sure. It's not easy to do business these days. There are so many people trying to sue me."

"You know it's a murder case, don't you? Tell the truth, Lao Xie, you're not involved in this, are you?"

Xie Zhichang replied solemnly: "How could I be? I have nothing at all to do with it. If you've got any evidence, Chief He, I'll come with you immediately." Then he went on: "Look, Chief He, I am an important businessman now, and I'm an old man. How could I possibly do anything like that? Why, only the day before yesterday, Governor Li himself came here specifically to inspect my flower and plant business. I am going to build Asia's largest flower market and a flower-production base spanning three counties. Production, supply and sales all in the same flower basket—"

"Understood. So why, then, would the Wu family want to sue you?"

"It's hard to say. It's not because of the land requisition. I even celebrated with Old Man Wu over that... and I haven't thought of that for ages. Hey, but when Third Brother Wu died in that fire, they insisted that I had sent someone to do it. How unjust is that! It's more unjust than the fate endured by that fellow in that play *The Injustice to Dou E*!"

"I heard that Third Brother Wu threatened you once?"

"What can I say? It never happened. He runs a gold shop, and he is not in the same business as me at all. I don't even know him."

"Ah! So that's how it is, then."

"I am not afraid of him suing me. He can sue me to heaven and back and it won't do him any good. The day before yesterday, when Secretary Liu came here with Governor Li, he specifically told me: 'Just ignore him, Lao Xie, and let him sue.'"

"Which governor, did you say?"

"You think I'm lying? The one in charge of agriculture, Li Delin, Governor Li."

"And who is Secretary Liu?"

"Secretary Liu Jinding of the Municipal Legal Committee – I just told you about him. He's your direct boss. You should also know that the two of them have a master-student relationship. Governor Li was Secretary Liu Jinding's teacher."

"Ah yes, Liu Jinding, Secretary Liu. I know him."

When Helian Dongshan left, Xie Zhichang escorted him right to the door of the hotel. Xie Zhichang tried to make him stay for lunch, but he politely declined, saying he was busy and maybe they could do it another day.

Before Helian Dongshan got into his car, Xie Zhichang took some beautifully packaged tea from the hotel manager Bai Shouxin, who was following behind him, and said: "Chief He, this is the best pre-rain Maojian, the highest quality. Only a hundred catties are produced every year. I sent someone to get ten catties, all for the big bosses, but here's a box for you to try."

Helian Dongshan looked at him and, not wanting to rouse his suspicions, didn't refuse. At this point, Bai Shouxin, who was standing behind Xie Zhichang, saw that he had taken the tea, so he leaned forward and whispered in Helian Dongshan's ear: "Chief He, President Xie has instructed me to tell you that I have a new Thai girl here. A massage therapist. I can find a girl to give you a massage any time you like." Helian Dongshan smiled and said nothing.

As Bai Shouxin was whispering to Helian Dongshan, Xie Zhichang turned his back and pretended not to hear. When Helian Dongshan stayed silent, Bai Shouxin understood that he intended to leave, so he hurried to open the door of the police car, and whispered again: "That's OK, Uncle He, I'll wait for your call." When Bai Shouxin was young, he was a notorious tearaway on the streets of Huanghuai. He had been arrested by Helian Dongshan on numerous occasions, so he had started calling him "Uncle He".

As the saying goes: "If you're going to raise your hand, don't hit someone who is smiling at you." Helian Dongshan thought to himself that Xie Zhichang was more than just smiling, he was going overboard with the respect. He wasn't just issuing general flattery, he was going out of his way to put him at his ease. So what would follow if he ate his food and accepted his gifts? Although Helian Dongshan was disgusted by the whole business, he didn't say anything.

His visit to the Flower World Hotel had roused Helian Dongshan's suspicions of Xie Zhichang. First, why would a straightforward businessman need three checkpoints for his visitors and do everything short of actually carrying out a body search? That showed he was afraid, but what was he afraid of? Second, when he talked about the incident, he referred to it as a "fire", but the Internal Public Security Office was still investigating whether it was arson or fire, so what made him so sure? Third, he had celebrated with the Wu family over the "June 29th incident", in the course of which the Flower World Group company paid the heavy price of 120 million yuan extra in land requisition payments. Fourth, when the two of them were chatting, he kept inadvertently fiddling with his pen, constantly picking it up and throwing it back down on his desk. That betrayed a considerable level of anxiety he was trying to keep hidden. In addition, whether intentionally or not, he brought the provincial governor and Secretary Liu Jinding into the conversation. Could it be that Liu Jinding was also involved? Helian Dongshan was conscious of the need to tread carefully.

What kind of person was this Xie Zhichang?

FIVE

IN HUANGHUAI, Xie Zhichang had always been a benchmark figure, a role model for those who dreamed of getting rich, someone to talk about and to emulate. People used to say: "Fuck me, just look at Big Mouth Xie!"

To start with, Xie Zhichang was the manager of a flower company and a "flower man". When he first came to Huanghuai from Meiling County, he opened a small flower shop. The sales office was at the side of the road opposite the city government. A few potted plants were placed in front of the door and two girls were hired to run the office. As for Xie, he was to be seen riding a broken-down bicycle with a pot of flowers on the carrying rack, scrambling for business everywhere in the city government compound and in various other departments, bureaus and committees.

Back then, he was rebuked and chased out of offices, time and time again, with shouts of "No! Get out!" The average person would have been embarrassed by this treatment, but not Xie. He just kept on smiling. If he was not allowed to enter an office, he would stand outside the door, and say: "My name is Xie, I'm Xie." The young men in the office would mock him and laugh, saying: "Yes, Xie! Meiling's 'Big Mouth' Xie isn't it? Are you at your 'matchmaking' again?" Later, as his visits became more frequent, the office staff didn't have the heart to keep chasing him away, especially as he looked so sincere. It took a long time haunting the government compound, but eventually some doors began to open for him. He was very shrewd and quick to react. He stopped selling plants and switched to giving them away. He started by sending plants to cadres at the county and divisional levels, then, as he found out how things stood in the government compound, he started with the Municipal Party Committee and the municipal government, before moving to the bureaus and committees, sending plants to the offices of the officials one by one. There was no charge for any of the plants. He not only gave out plants for free; every time he gave an official a plant, he also brought a gardener to show how to look after it, and even threw in some plant food. Do you think he was doing all this out of the goodness of his heart?

There were some "extraordinary" officials who wouldn't accept a plant. The polite ones would say they didn't know how to look after it and were afraid it would die within a few days. The rude ones would look angry and say sternly: "What do you think you are up to? Get out!" But he never gave up and would come back another day. If you said you didn't know how to look after a plant, he would look after it for you. He would send a gardener to visit every ten days. He would water it for you and feed it for you. What was there left for you to say? If you didn't like the kind of plant he sent, he would replace it with another, as long as you specified your preference. As a result, the offices of those county- and division-level cadres slowly filled up with plants. He extended his reach from divisional level to departmental level. Of course, department-level cadres are not so particular but for the first-level cadres of the department, most of the plants he gave were "money trees".

Over time, Xie Zhichang's strategy of sending plants began to take effect. The Municipal Party Committee and the Municipal Government, including their various bureaus and committees, would exclusively use Lao Xie's company when large-scale events or meetings were held. And when the higher-level leadership needed plants and flowers as gifts, they said: "Go ask Lao Xie."

To all outward appearances, Lao Xie was an open and enthusiastic sort of person. Not only did he hand out plants and flowers, but when he was old enough, he also did favours for people. Although the departmental- and bureau-level cadres in the city were all quite capable, they were limited to their respective fields, and they were useless once they exceeded the scope of their individual responsibilities. This was when Lao Xie began to demonstrate apparently supernatural powers. He particularly liked taking care of things, such as getting children into certain kindergartens, arranging jobs for relatives in the countryside, or just changing a gas bottle, getting a necessary seal or registering a household... all you had to do was ask and he would never let you down. Even if you didn't ask him and he got to hear about it, he would come round to see you off his own bat: "I'll see to it, I'll see to it for you." Those three words "see to it" were beyond price.

The director of the city's land office, Lao Niu, Niu Huanzhang, known as the Bull Demon King, was a man no one went out of their way to help. When his son missed the entrance requirement for a key university by three marks, and there seemed to be nothing they could do, Lao Niu and his wife sat in their home and wept. Lao Xie found out about this, and without a second word, he went to Beijing three times, Wuhan four times, and sorted the matter out! When the admission letter arrived, Lao Niu was so moved that he almost wept. He grasped Xie Zhichang's hand and said: "You're quite something, Lao Xie!"

"Not at all, Chief Niu!" Xie Zhichang said. "Anything to do with our children is important. I just went to see what I could do..."

Lao Niu had no way of repaying Xie Zhichang, so he said: "Well, Lao Xie, let me find a piece of land for you. It's cheap, only eight hundred yuan per *mu*."

Back then, Lao Xie didn't understand the land market. At the time, land prices in the suburbs were not very high, but the approval procedures were complicated. Xie Zhichang said: "No, I've only got a turnover of a couple of million at the moment. What do I want land for?"

"Don't be stupid! It's your loss if you don't take it. You can get a loan from the bank. I'll have a word with the president." And just like that, not knowing what he was doing, Xie Zhichang got the land.

City Cultural Director Su Canguang graduated from Peking University, and adopted a full-on literary and artistic style, wearing spectacles for his myopia and a neatly folded scarf perpetually round his neck no matter what the season. He had worked hard to prise some money out of the city authorities to lay on a local performance. On the day of the dress rehearsal, he wanted to invite a famous expert from the Provincial Federation of Literary and Art Associations to give his advice. The invitation had been agreed some time before. As soon as they heard that an expert from the province was coming to supervise the rehearsal, the top brass of the Municipal Party Committee and city government all also agreed to come and watch. But the weather suddenly changed on the day and heavy snow began to fall. The expert was contacted by phone, and a car was sent to pick him up, but at the last minute he said he was too ill to come. Su Canguang was a man who was very concerned with his image, and it pained him that he had been boasting about this man's attendance and all the top brass knew about it, but now, at the last moment, he wasn't coming. What could he do? He sat by himself in the little theatre, not saying a word. The cadres of the Cultural Bureau were standing behind him but no one knew how to comfort him. Then someone went and told Xie Zhichang, who immediately took up the challenge, saying: "I'll go. I'll go and get him." And by 6.30 that evening, Xie Zhichang delivered the expert. He didn't use any trickery, he just stood at the door of the man's house from 11 am to 4 pm as the snow kept falling. He was like a snowman by the end... Later, when Su Canguang became the vice-chairman of the Huanghuai CPPCC, he jointly proposed Xie Zhichang as a member of the provincial CPPCC, and then nominated him as part-time vice-chairman.

The first contact between Xie Zhichang and Helian Dongshan started with "rescuing" someone. Bai Shouxin, brother-in-law of Xu Xianguo, the city's director of taxes, was "rescued" from the detention centre.

When Bai Shouxin was a young man, he was a wastrel who liked to take things easy. However, he did have two distinguishing traits: he had studied martial arts from a young age, and he played the accordion. He would also wear a pair of white gloves throughout the year, and he often attracted a gaggle of men and women following behind him when he went out. So he was a well-known figure about town and was nicknamed "White Gloves". He thought they made him look suave and sophisticated.

Bai Shouxin saw people making a lot of money in business and wanted to try it for himself. Before he had even thought it through, he plunged in. He started out in the clothing business, but he was cheated by some people down in Guangzhou the first time he went there. He picked out the clothes he wanted, item by item, inspecting them closely... but when he got home, he found all he had was a collection of rags. Having been cheated himself, he then decided to cheat others. He heard that chemical fertilisers were in short supply, so he bought a truckload of phosphate fertiliser from a plant in the northeast. When signing the contract, he deliberately tricked the vendors, and signed for "cash on delivery". But after the goods were delivered, he was nowhere to be found. He was reported to the Public Security Bureau for fraud and arrested.

As soon as Bai Shouxin was arrested, his elder sister panicked. Her name was Bai Fenglan. In her younger days, she was regarded as the school beauty at Huanghuai Number One Middle School, and she had a long line of suitors. Later on, she married her middle school classmate Xu Xianguo. She was very definitely the boss of the family home, and the same was true where her husband was concerned. She was a formidable woman. There was no way she could ignore her brother's situation, so she kept on and on at Xu Xianguo to "rescue" him. Although Xu Xianguo was the director of the Municipal Taxation Bureau, the system made it awkward for him to intervene in person. He was especially reluctant when he learned that the case was in the hands of Helian Dongshan, who he knew to be both honest and single-minded. So he turned to Xie Zhizhang. Xu Xianguo felt that, if Xie Zhichang acted as the middleman, there was a chance of getting something done.

Helian Dongshan was a member of the Party Committee of the Huanghuai City Public Security Bureau at deputy director level. Xie Zhichang had started out sending him flowers, but Helian Dongshan snubbed him. In the autumn of that year, Lao Xie gave him a pot of chrysanthemums. The large white flowers were in full bloom. Helian Dongshan said: "I don't want them. I'm a smoker so the room is full of smoke and these beautiful flowers will be ruined. Take them away." Lao Xie countered: "There's nothing to worry about, Chief He, nothing to worry about!" Helian Dongshan was unmoved and said: "I am not the chief, so don't call me that. And don't call me the director, either. Take them away." There was nothing more for Xie Zhichang to say. He glanced at Helian Dongshan and then hurriedly looked away again, saying: "Yes, yes, Chief He, I can see you are busy, I can see you are busy."

Then Xie Zhichang sent some asparagus ferns. He arrived with three of his hostesses carrying three pots of asparagus ferns, one for the director Wan Haifa, one for the executive deputy director Jiang Baoguo and the third for Helian Dongshan. As he went into Helian Dongshan's office, he said: "Chief He, I understand that there are only three of you chiefs in the bureau who smoke: Chief Wan, Chief

Jiang and you. I have prepared three pots of asparagus ferns, one for each of you. They can absorb the harmful substances in cigarette smoke. Believe me, it's a scientific fact."

Helian Dongshan understood exactly what he was saying: both the director and the deputy director had already accepted the plants, so he was being forced to accept one too. Besides, he saw how thin and graceful the fern was, swaying gently like a swirling green mist. It was very pleasing to the eye, so he said: "All right, leave it here. How much is it?" Lao Xie had invented the phrase "trial care" just for this purpose. He used it now, saying: "I'm giving it to you for trial care. See how you get on looking after it, and I will refund you if it doesn't work out. It's not a lot of money, and you can settle up whenever." Helian Dongshan didn't have much choice but to agree and thank him.

Xie Zhichang had brought the plants in the morning and came back in the afternoon. Entering Helian Dongshan's office, he said: "I'm sorry to bother you again, Chief He."

"All right, tell me what's up."

"It's about Xiao Bai. I've already talked to Chief Jiang, and he said I should come and talk to you."

"Which Xiao Bai?"

"Bai... Bai Shouxin. His sister Bai Fenglan is really upset–"

"You're talking about the fraud case, right?"

"Yes, that's right. Xiao Bai did cheat those people and it is quite unacceptable, but–"

"It is a serious offence. The amount was three hundred thousand yuan, and the law says he could get up to ten years for that."

"Yes, yes, that's true. But we're talking about a young man here, a first offence too... look, his family has already apologised to the vendors and is willing to compensate them for all their losses. As for the vendors, they've promised to withdraw their private lawsuit. Come on, Chief He, why not give him a little face back?"

"Let me repeat, I am not the chief or even deputy chief, so don't call me that. Go and talk to the director if you think you're up to it."

Xie Zhichang made six visits in four days over this affair. In the end, he managed to get a letter of approval from Jiang Baoguo, the deputy director of the Municipal Public Security Bureau. This enabled him to "rescue" Bai Shouxin. In fact, not only did he "rescue" him, he even found him a decent job. Xu Xianguo, the tax commissioner, was naturally very grateful to him, and from then on, Xie Zhichang had no tax worries.

While all this was going on, Liu Jinding was transferred to Huanghuai. He became deputy director of the Municipal Government Office, then director, and concurrently served as executive deputy director of the city's Investment Promotion Office. Xie Zhichang accompanied him to Shenzhen to attract investment, and that was how the Sino-foreign joint venture Flower World Group came into being. There is no need to say anything more about the relationship between Liu Jinding and Xie Zhichang.

That was all more than ten years before. Xie Zhichang's broken bicycle was first replaced by a seven-seater van, and then by a Santana 2000, and then by an Audi. He had seen no need to inform the Municipal Party Committee and the municipal government about the anomaly of his presumably enormously expensive "8888" licence plate limousine.

Thus, for thirteen years, "flower man" Xie Zhichang used his unique personal charm to conquer almost all the bureaus, commissions and offices of Huanghuai, and the two government compounds belonging to the Municipal Party Committee and the municipal government. Everyone knew about Xie Zhichang. His own personal fortune snowballed. It was said that the piece of land he came by so easily ten years previously made him thirty million! That was what had shown him the true value of real estate. It was equally clear that, after the establishment of his flower business, he crossed a line: not only did he become a billionaire, almost without thinking about it, he also became someone who was not greatly concerned with the concepts of legality and illegality.

It was said that one night, he invited a businessman in Hong Kong to dinner, and ordered a deputy city mayor to join them. He telephoned the man in public, for all to hear, and shouted: "Lao Cui, Mayor Cui, our guest has arrived. What's the matter with you? I don't care what you're doing, be here in ten minutes!" To the amazement of everyone present, in less than ten minutes, a breathless Deputy Mayor Cui appeared at the door of a private room in the restaurant, and said: "I'm not late, am I, Lao Xie?"

The story went that one night, he started awake, unable to believe how much money he had. He started to count the "0"s in his bank account, then counted and re-counted them. God, there were so many "0"s... too many of them! He couldn't get back to sleep. When he rose the next morning, he asked Liu Jinding to have breakfast with him. At the table, he suddenly said: "Secretary-General Liu, Jinding, what is it that I am missing?"

Liu Jinding looked at him and said: "Culture, what you lack most is culture."

So Xie began to recreate himself. He set up his office to look like a government official's: he put two small national flags on his desk, added two bookcases to the office furniture and bought a job lot of books.

As the saying goes, money in a man's wallet makes him brave. Since becoming a part-time vice-chairman of the CPPCC, Xie Zhichang had also begun to pay attention to his personal image. He took a lot of time over how he presented himself, taking care with both his clothes and his manners. He always wore one of two sets of clothes: one Western style and one Chinese style. Naturally, they were both famous brands, and he seldom changed out of them, but his tie, white shirt and leather shoes were different every day. Someone had told him this was "aristocratic style". Even so, he remained very humble, but with a different kind of humility from before. In the past, he was a "flower man", and very self-effacing. Now he was the boss, the chairman and the president. His new humility was founded on an inner pride, or maybe that should be "money". Although he kept things deliberately low-key, his self-satisfaction couldn't help spilling out. He would see people reaching out to shake hands and saying: "Ah, Lao Xie! Yes, yes, Lao Xie." It was the respect implicit in the "yes, yes" that was quite different from before.

In another way, Lao Xie's "low-key" was quite confusing, and when the "arson" was investigated for the first time, Helian Dongshan was almost taken in by it.

SIX

ALTHOUGH HELIAN DONGSHAN had a very good reputation within his department, he was still severely reprimanded for his handling of the case. His offence was so serious, in fact, that he almost ended up out of uniform.

It was all because of a cigarette butt.

Helian Dongshan's investigation of the "arson" started with Bai Shouxin. That day, when he met with Xie Zhichang, he noticed there was something not quite right about Bai Shouxin's expression. He had been following behind Xie Zhichang, eyes down and hardly talking. Nor did he seem to dare look directly at Helian Dongshan. There must be a reason for that. If nothing else, Shouxin's hooligan ways had got him into quite a bit of trouble, and Helian Dongshan had had to deal with him on many occasions. He knew Bai Shouxin very well.

Xie Zhichang made Bai Shouxin the manager of the Flower World Hotel for two reasons. First, his brother-in-law was the director of the Municipal Taxation Bureau, and that made tax matters much easier to handle. The second and more important one was that Bai Shouxin was known about town by his nickname White Gloves, and a group of toughs used to hang around him. The best known of these thugs was Wang Xiaoliu (Xiaoliu means "Little Six", and he was called that because he had an extra finger on his right hand). He was a real thug, who was not afraid of making trouble. He was Bai Shouxin's most trusted associate. Out in the marketplace, Wang Xiaoliu called Bai Shouxin "Brother Xin", and the other toughs did the same. You would see Brother Xin walking down the street with Wang Xiaoliu right behind him, looking a bit like the 1920s Shanghai gangster, Du Yuesheng.

First off, Wang Xiaoliu followed Bai Shouxin into the rag trade and lost his money. Afterwards, he drove a taxi but lost his licence when he injured someone in a fight. Then he took to just hanging around Bai Shouxin. Although his official title was security chief of the Flower World Hotel, in fact, he was up for any kind of criminal activity. The word on Yaqian Street was that Wang Xiaoliu had been seen hanging around the gold shop, morning and night, for some time before the fire broke out.

For these reasons, when he started to investigate the "arson" case, and after undertaking an initial external inspection, Helian Dongshan sent Police Officer Xing Zhibin of the pre-trial division to summon Wang Xiaoliu to the City Bureau. The reason given for the summons was that he was suspected of organising prostitution. Of course, this was just a cover. The Flower World Hotel had a spa staffed by a large number of massage women. According to the city regulations, the Flower World Hotel was designated a foreign-investment hotel. In general, random investigations were not allowed, but if someone made a report, it was a different matter. After Helian Dongshan "invited" Wang Xiaoliu in, he let him stew all night before personally interrogating him the next day.

"Let's have a little chat, Xiaoliu," Helian Dongshan began. "What mischief have you been up to recently?"

Wang Xiaoliu had been interviewed by Helian Dongshan many times, and he was quite comfortable in his presence and even called him "Uncle He". He said: "You're making a mistake, Uncle He. What are you saying I've done?"

"Are you claiming you haven't been up to mischief? Would I invite you to see me if you haven't?"

"Truly, I haven't done anything."

"Think about it. Would I call you in just for a general chat?"

Wang Xiaoliu squirmed as if he was trying to relieve an itch. Xiao Xing, the policeman standing to one side, said: "Behave! Stand still! Don't you know where this is?"

"You don't frighten me. Do I look scared? Pah, how long have you been in uniform?"

"That's enough back-chat from you! Stand up straight. Let's talk about how many girls you have recruited."

"What's it got to do with you how many girls I've recruited?" Wang Xiaoliu slammed back.

"You're very full of yourself, Xiaoliu!" Helian Dongshan interjected. "What's going on? Who do you think you're intimidating?"

"No, no, I wasn't talking to you, Uncle He. Whatshisname here is too…" Wang Xiaoliu sounded aggrieved.

"Let's stick to you and your problems. Tell me what you've been up to recently."

"I haven't done anything, really I haven't. Those young ladies are all graduates of Chinese medicine massage schools. They have contracts, and they are all acting properly. Truly! If a single word I've said–"

"Look me in the eye, and tell me you are doing everything properly."

Wang Xiaoliu lowered his head and mumbled: "If you are going to go on about proper or improper, I'm not—"

"I'll give you some more time to think about it, Xiaoliu, so you can get the lies out of your system and give me some straight answers."

"Do you really think I'd lie to you, Uncle He? If I were a hundred times braver than I am, I still wouldn't dare lie to you! I know in the past I used to be... now I'm doing the right thing. I haven't done anything illegal."

"Then I ask you, a month ago, in August that is, were you ever in Yaqian Street?"

Wang Xiaoliu blinked and said: "Yes, I was there. I often go there."

"Why?"

"Surely you know, Uncle He! Lao Sun's mutton soup shop at the west end of Yaqian Street is famous. I'm very fond of—"

At this crucial moment, Helian Dongshan suddenly said: "And you took a jerrycan along to drink your mutton soup with?"

"It was a lunch box," Xiaoliu said quickly. "Lao Sun's wife can confirm I was carrying a lunch box."

Helian Dongshan didn't press the matter because he knew there was no point. Instead, he asked him again if he had been to Yaqian Street. He didn't think Wang Xiaoliu would admit it, but to his surprise he did so straight away without any fuss. Wang Xiaoliu's eyes blinked rapidly, like a bean on a hot plate. These actions showed that he had made preparations. He had already concocted an alibi with someone, and it was useless to ask again. This complicated matters. At this moment, Helian Dongshan's mobile phone rang, and he told Xiao Xing: "I'm going out for a bit. You can get a statement from him."

Helian Dongshan hadn't expected things to move so quickly. It only took an hour and a half from him leaving the interrogation room. By the time the local newspaper came out, Helian Dongshan had already been suspended.

Instinctively, Helian Dongshan knew there was someone behind all this. The frightening thing was that he had been caught off-guard and hadn't made any mental preparation. He had been too careless and had no idea what could have happened during those ninety minutes.

When he left the interrogation, he answered his mobile. The call was from Deputy Director Jiang Baoguo. It was a trivial matter, but he had to see to it. Then he was waylaid in the pre-trial division to sign off on some expenses claims for business trips. He smoked a few cigarettes, thinking about how to handle Wang Xiaoliu... but things moved quickly after that.

It wasn't really a big deal, but according to the newspaper, it was "Rotten to the core!" How could a policeman burn a suspect's face with a cigarette? It's not as though there was any real evidence against him either! The paper used lots of question marks and exclamation marks that were like little bullets of shame slamming into the whole Public Security Bureau.

Seven days later, the paper published a follow-up report calling the two officers "black sheep of the police force". The implication was quite clear: they should be stripped of their uniforms.

The evening of the day when the "black sheep" article appeared, Xiao Xing's mother and father took him to see Helian Dongshan. As soon as the two old people were through Helian Dongshan's door, they fell to their knees in front of him. Xiao Xing's mother said: "Our boy is still young, please save him!" Helian Dongshan hurried to raise the two of them from their knees and guided them to the sofa. All three members of the Xing family burst into tears as they sat in Helian Dongshan's apartment.

There he was, Xiao Xing, the son of two teachers, who had studied hard for fifteen years and just managed to scrape into the police academy. He took all manner of exams after graduating before finally becoming a policeman and getting a job that brought him a degree of respect. And now, after less than four years in the job, here he was about to be expelled. And if things went really badly for him, he would be prosecuted. No wonder the family were beside themselves.

Their bitter laments threw Helian Dongshan's feelings into turmoil. His instincts told him that their desire to get him directly involved wasn't some chance idea, it was an out-and-out conspiracy against him. Nor was it something that could have been concocted by just a couple of people; there had to be a whole chain of interests behind it. His first thought was Bai Shouxin, and then Xie Zhichang, and behind Xie Zhichang, Liu... but Liu Jinding was now their direct boss! How to handle it? Helian Dongshan calmed himself down and listened again to Xiao Xing's account of what happened. According to Xing Zhibin, after Helian Dongshan left, Wang Xiaoliu kept on trying to provoke him, needling him by saying things like: "You little runt! You're still wet behind the ears! What do you know? Why don't you go to Dongsan Street and see what the old man has to say about it all?" Then he whipped his cock and balls out and began to insult Xing Zhibin's parents to his face in the vilest terms. It was then that Xiao Xing lost it and kicked him. After a while, Xiao Xing calmed down and lit a cigarette to steady himself. But Wang Xiaoliu, who had been squatting on the ground for a while, suddenly leapt up and shook his finger in Xiao Xing's face, cursing and saying: "You just try hitting me again, boy..." Xiao Xing blocked Wang Xiaoliu's hand with his arm, but the cigarette in his hand accidently burned Wang Xiaoliu's neck. Wang Xiaoliu immediately grabbed the hand holding the cigarette and pressed it hard into his own face. Then he started to yell...

Xiao Xing's report and Wang Xiaoliu's statement told two completely different stories. On balance, Helian Dongshan believed Xiao Xing. His reasoning was that Xiao Xing was a bit introverted when he first arrived. Both his parents were teachers. He had been with him for more than three years now. He certainly lacked experience, but he would never do anything this bad. As for this Wang Xiaoliu character, he was a professional troublemaker, and if he had the right backing, there was nothing he wouldn't do. Helian Dongshan knew very well that this was all aimed at him, and he couldn't stay out of things any longer.

So very late that night, he went round and hammered on the door of Director Wan's home. The director was already asleep, but he had no choice but to get out of bed and throw on some clothes. When he saw who it was, he didn't say a word, but took out a bottle of spirits, and the two men toasted each other, glass by glass, in silence. Deep into the night, when the bottle was half consumed, Helian Dongshan said: "It's a conspiracy, Director Wan."

"What's your proof?"

Helian Dongshan didn't reply.

They drank again until they reached the bottom of the bottle, when Director Wan said: "Sacrifice your pawn to save your queen!"

"I can't do that. If I sacrifice the pawn, I won't be able to protect the queen. And if the queen goes, the king is even more exposed."

"You'll just have to play blindfold chess then."

"Give me some time, and I'll crack the case."

Director Wan spread his hands. "There's no time to give. The city is pressing me for a result and the media is on the case too. I can't hold off any longer."

"In that case, I'll take all the blame and leave Xiao Xing out of it. His family..."

Director Wan shook his head. "You're going to be disciplined anyway. And if Xiao Xing takes responsibility, there's no protecting him either."

"I can take it. But have you thought things through, Director Wan? What if the truth of the case comes out one day and it turns out that Xiao Xing has been treated unjustly? How would we feel then?"

"So what are you saying we should do?"

"Whatever else we do, we can't fire Xiao Xing. He's still only young, but if he gets a criminal record now, the rest of his life will be ruined. The first thing to do, if we can, is transfer him."

Director Wan didn't say anything. The two of them knew quite well there was more to this case than met the eye. After a while, Helian Dongshan asked: "Are we going to keep investigating the case, Director Wan?"

"What's the point? We'll just end up investigating ourselves. Best stop now."

"So that's it then?"

After a long, long pause, Director Wan said just one word: "Wait."

That wait turned out to last seven years, right up until another case appeared. That other case was the arson affair, and it finally explained everything. In this affair, time was the only witness. But that is a story for another occasion.

The direct result of it all was that Helian Dongshan had a serious disciplinary offence on his record, and he was suspended for three months to reflect on what he had done. Officer Xing Zhibin received a severe reprimand and was transferred from the pre-trial division of the Municipal Bureau to work as an officer in a suburban police station.

During Helian Dongshan's suspension, he taught himself to play blindfold chess. He sat there in silence, with a chessboard in front of him, closed his eyes and began to recite softly: "Cannon sideways eight to nine, horse forward two to three, chariot sideways one to two..."

But he was not a happy man. He had been thinking about the nature of the relationship between Xie Zhichang and Liu Jinding. And about Liu Jinding in particular. He was general secretary of the municipal government! Would he really dare pull that kind of stunt in the full sight of 300 landless farmers? The incident left a deep impression on Helian Dongshan. Yes, he had ordered Helian Dongshan to bring weapons, which was already a violation. He even ordered the shooting, although he knew there were no bullets in the guns. But Helian Dongshan was still very surprised that he would try that kind of trickery in front of the crowd, knowing quite well what the consequences might be.

After his suspension was over, Helian Dongshan still felt very bitter.

At work, he was the officer who had been disciplined, and at home, he faced a hostile atmosphere too. The difference of opinion "indoors" meant that he had to choke back his anger every time he opened his mouth. This was because he was constantly at odds with his son, and most of the time his wife sided with her boy and secretly schemed against him.

Who in this world treated their own son as an enemy?

It was computer games that set everything off between them. Helian Huasheng had been obsessed with computer games and addicted to the internet since the second grade of elementary school. Right from the start, Helian Dongshan was busy with work and didn't spare the time to try being patient with his son and educating him with reason and persuasion. He always adopted the "belt method". He had a violent temper to begin with, and that, coupled with his disappointment at his son's apparent inability to learn, meant that the blows became harder. He fell out with his wife over it.

It was that "squat down" when the boy was eight years old that left a lifelong mark on Helian Xichu. In fact, "squat down" was

Helian Dongshan's favourite command. His son began to attend kindergarten at five and a half, and he was in the second grade in a key elementary school in the city at the age of eight. That was when the war between them began. When the boy was still in kindergarten, his wife told him that the teacher was always praising their son for his intelligence, his ability to process information and his spiritual nature. Helian Dongshan didn't say anything, but he was very happy. However, one evening, at eight o'clock, he suddenly received a panicked phone call from his wife: "Our son has disappeared!"

The nature of his job meant that Helian Dongshan didn't work fixed hours. When he was on a case, it was quite common for him to be away from home for a month. That meant his wife was always the one who picked the boy up from school. When he heard the news of his son's disappearance, he wasn't too worried at first. However, by nine o'clock, when his son still could not be found, he began to panic too, as he was afraid the boy might have been kidnapped for ransom.

At the time, Helian Dongshan was the chief of the pre-investigation section of the City Bureau, and this was the first time he used public influence in a private cause. It was past nine o'clock in the evening, and the officers in the police station were all off duty. He called eleven police station directors in the city one by one. In total, about half of those directors had been his apprentices, and the other half were acquaintances. It is reasonable to say that every one of them knew the name of "Laser Eyes". As a result, the whole downtown area, the railway station, bus station, riverside park, everywhere, was flooded with policemen... and at midnight, the boy was found.

He was found in a video arcade next to the Xiaoximen Cinema. Helian Dongshan was usually unemotional and self-disciplined, rarely asking anyone for anything. So now, he was furious at owing everyone such a big favour, and he really lost it when he heard that his son had been found in a video arcade.

On seeing his son, he said just two words: "Squat down!"

Helian Dongshan said the words almost without thinking. Then, he slid the belt from his waist... Those two words were like a thunderclap in the ears of the young Helian Huasheng. He gave his father a timid look, shivered, went tight-lipped and squatted obediently. No one knows what he saw in his father's eyes, but from the next day on, he became taciturn, especially in front of Helian Dongshan. He looked at his father like a mouse watching a cat. He was furtive, evasive and seemed to be walking on tenterhooks all the time.

When the son first arrived at junior high school, he was constantly receiving warnings and reprimands for skipping lessons to play computer games. It was after he was absent three days running that he was finally expelled. Helian Dongshan and his wife panicked at the news and rushed over to the school that evening to apologise to the head teacher. At first, although she was protective of her son, the boy's mother also disapproved of his obsession with computer games. She was a peace-loving soul by nature, and acted as a buffer between father and son. But then that stopped working. Later on, husband and wife clashed in a big way over the boy's education, and Helian Dongshan became more and more isolated in the family. Every time he spoke, his wife would break in: "What do you think you are doing? Interrogating a prisoner?"

As his son continued to grow up, Helian Dongshan showed signs of making some concessions over his son's education. Despite his violent temper, he acted in a way that he regarded as lenient and forbearing... and it could certainly be said that he pushed himself to his limit of self-restraint.

Helian Dongshan thought about his attitude towards his son. He knew that children liked to play computer games, and as long as it was not taken to extremes, his own child should not be deprived of what was enjoyed by other people's children. So, taking advantage of the opportunity offered by a business trip, Helian Dongshan reluctantly bought a Nintendo Mini game console for his son. On the boy's birthday, he took it out of his briefcase and put it on the table. He even deliberately softened his voice and said in a conciliatory tone: "You are allowed to play with this, but don't get addicted. Once you've shown me that you've done all your homework, you can play for one hour a day–" Before he could finish, the boy looked at him indifferently, and said: "There's a new generation." Helian Dongshan stared at his son uncomprehendingly, and then the fire in his head suddenly flared up: "What? What did you say?" His son turned away, not looking at him. Helian Dongshan stood up, sat down again, made a huge effort to restrain himself and said: "It's just a game, isn't it? Generation? What generation?" Still his son didn't look at him, and

181

just said contemptuously: "Yours is first generation. They're on the third generation now."

That's when things really went downhill fast.

Helian Dongshan's head was exploding. The truth was, he simply didn't understand. This was a game they were talking about, wasn't it? Just a computer game! Do games have "generations"? It was the word "generation" that really seemed to get to him. "Generations" had to do with time, didn't they? And "new"! What did he mean by that? What else was going to be new now? Laozi? Confucius?... What he had no idea at all about was just how many successful campaigns his son had already conducted in this virtual world and just how advanced and all-powerful he was.

He tried to set his son back on the straight and narrow.

He took several measures to prevent his son getting stuck in the video arcade. The first was an economic blockade. Helian Dongshan froze his son's New Year money, all those gifts from elderly friends and relatives given over the Spring Festival, which amounted to several thousand yuan. Originally, the boy had the money in his personal keeping, but now it was temporarily confiscated, and his father told him he would get it back when he acted like a grown-up. Second, the boy's two-yuan daily allowance – one for breakfast and one for miscellaneous use – was also revoked. Back in the mid-1990s, prices were still pretty low, and one yuan could buy a boiled egg, some bread and a carton of milk. His son was a growing lad, so of course he still needed his breakfast, but now it was going to be given to him at home. Third, Helian Dongshan set his son a daily schedule, and he had to sign in after school by putting a tick against the assigned hour and minute. The son kicked back against all this, and the first thing he did was skip breakfast and go on hunger strike. Then, one day, he plucked up courage and said: "I know you are in charge of a jail at work. Is this one of your jails too?" Helian Dongshan said: "These are just the house rules. Let me tell you, if you establish good habits in your daily life, then..." But his son wasn't listening and just turned away.

Helian Dongshan once took to tailing his son, like a private detective. For a while, when things were quiet at work, he surreptitiously followed his son, morning and evening. He always felt a sense of relief when he saw him going into school or coming back home. Once, he saw his son stopped in the street by three older children, and it was only then he discovered the true extent of his son's resolve and unwillingness to give in. The three older boys shoved his son to the ground outside the school gates and gave him a good going-over. Just as Helian Dongshan was about to step in, the school bell rang, and the three older boys dispersed. His son picked himself up, brushed the dirt off his clothes and staggered in through the school gates. Just at that moment, Helian Dongshan felt sorry for him. When his son got back from school that night, he looked at the bruises on his face and asked: "What happened?" The boy turned his face away and said: "Nothing."

At first, Helian Dongshan thought that this period of strict discipline had been successful in curing his son of his internet addiction, but that proved to be just wishful thinking. Eventually, when he arrived back home from a business trip, he caught his son red-handed in the video arcade. To his surprise, his son was sitting in front of a large games console, his hands flashing over the buttons as though he was playing a piano. All that could be heard was the sound of gunfire and explosions on the screen... and there standing behind his son like bodyguards and shouting encouragement, were the three older boys who had beaten him up. Without wasting his breath saying anything, Helian Dongshan twisted his son's ear and dragged him out.

It was probably on this occasion that the hatred first appeared in his son's eyes. After dragging his son home, Helian Dongshan shoved him down onto his bed, yanked off his trousers, drew out his belt and gave him a ferocious beating. At that moment, his wife returned from work. She flung the bicycle she was riding to the ground and rushed into the house, shouting: "If you like beating people so much, why don't you beat the two of us to death and be done with it!"

As the boy grew up, the gulf between father and son just kept getting wider. It was when both of them lost control that they said the most hurtful things.

Although Helian Dongshan repeatedly failed in his attempts to prepare his son for adulthood, he did conduct one successful observation mission while suspended from duty to consider his behaviour. By this time, the boy was in his second year of high school and recently, according to his wife's observation, it appeared that he was no longer going to the video arcade, and his schoolbag was getting heavier. So

Helian Dongshan also began to pay some attention to what was changing. At first, he thought it was his "belt-based education system" that had made the difference, but after a few days of observation, he discovered there was a new problem.

It was a Saturday afternoon. Usually when the boy came home from school, he dropped his schoolbag on the floor and went to the bathroom. That was his normal pattern. But that night, Helian Dongshan felt there was something different, something wrong. That was it! Yes, instead of throwing the bag down in the living room as usual, the boy had taken it into his bedroom before going to the bathroom. So what was in the bag?

Helian Dongshan was already a deputy director-level investigator in the Municipal Public Security Bureau by this time, and not long before, he had been allocated a three-bedroom and one-living room apartment. Since then, his son had his own personal space. Catching his son unawares, Helian Dongshan went into his bedroom and quickly checked his son's schoolbag. The search revealed the problem, and it was a very serious one. Helian Dongshan found three porn CDs in the bag. Helian Dongshan's expression changed immediately, going black and dangerous. He shouted at the boy to come over and said fiercely: "Now you're really asking for it! What are these?"

The boy lowered his head, his face pale and waxy, beads of sweat starting out on his forehead. He knew that his father was a policeman, and this was serious. When she saw the porn discs, his mother said, in a panic: "Son! Are you some kind of gangster? Is that what you want to be? These are illegal!"

This time, Helian Dongshan didn't explode with anger, the way he had in the past. He just said, very calmly: "All right, I can see this school isn't the place for you. If you don't want to go, don't go."

Then he first pulled his wife away to their bedroom, closed the door, and said: "This is a serious matter, but it can still go either way. If it means he has genuinely gone bad, then there's no help for him."

His wife was also terrified, wringing her hands together as she said: "Yes, yes! But what should we do? He's going to take the university exam next year..."

"This time, you have to listen to me."

His wife was afraid he was going to turn nasty and replied: "Just don't beat him. If you beat him again, he'll only get worse."

Helian Dongshan suppressed his anger and said: "Don't worry, I won't beat him. He's older now and beating's no use any more. I'll take him aside and talk to him."

His wife was still worried, and said: "Are you really going to send him–"

"Don't worry, I'm just going to put the fear of God in him!" Helian Dongshan replied quietly. "I'll have a good long talk with him, and I won't raise a finger."

Helian Dongshan came out of the bedroom and said to his son: "Let's go, follow me." With tears in his eyes, the boy looked at him in horror.

"Come on," Helian Dongshan said. "I'm taking you to the police station so you can hand yourself in."

His wife was about to say something, but Helian Dongshan stopped her with a look. He opened the front door and walked out. The son hung his head and followed him silently.

Papa Blade walked in front, and his son followed on behind. The street had never seemed so quiet. Walking along, he could hear nothing, see nothing. The usual car sounds, human voices and colourful neon lights had all receded like an ebbing tide, and there was only one word left in his heart: despair.

Helian Dongshan did not look back. He couldn't see his son's face. If he had turned around, he would have seen that the boy was biting his lip, his face turning from pale to red and then to purple, and the veins on his neck were pulsing. Helian Dongshan's heart was burning, and his face was a mask of bitter disappointment. He had never in his wildest dreams thought that this hedonist, rebellious, adolescent son of his would watch pornography behind his back. This was quite different from playing computer games. What did they really matter? This was naked men and women... He could see his own son starting off down an evil road, and if he couldn't stop him now, that would be the end of him. But what to do about it?

Suddenly, he heard the sound of footsteps behind him. Helian Dongshan looked back and saw his son running into a building on the other side of the street. They had just turned a corner and were about a hundred metres from the People's Park. The building was a seven-storey hotel, and the son dashed up the hotel stairs. Helian Dongshan's blood was pounding in his head and his chest felt as though he had been stabbed with a red-hot needle. He bent over and coughed violently. He suddenly realised that his son was grown up now and wasn't going to listen to him any more.

Helian Dongshan stood there in a daze for a long time. Finally, reluctantly, he followed his son up the stairs.

Every step of those seven flights was agony for Helian Dongshan. Each one of them proclaimed the failure of his "education system". He couldn't figure out what had happened between the two of them, how they had got to this point. When he reached the top of the building, he found his son standing, ashen-faced, on a ledge. "Don't come any closer," he shouted. "If you try and force me, I'll jump!" He continued, hoarsely: "I have had enough! From now on, I am not your son. I'm done with you! Am I a criminal, the way you glare at me every day? Why do you do it? Who gives you the right? You think, just because you're my father, you're free to destroy me?"

It was getting late, and the city lights were glittering in the background. The night sky was full of the smell of cooking smoke and snatches of music: one moment it was "Sister, you sit on the prow..." and then it was "Say you'll be mine..." followed by "There are many stories in this small town..." Only ten metres separated the two of them, but they seemed as distant as the far horizon.

This time, Helian Dongshan calmed down inside. The situation had suddenly changed, and he and his son had become the two parties in a negotiation. Helian Dongshan had been pitting himself against suspects all his life, but this time, he was pitted against his biological son... When his son ranted and raved, Helian Dongshan said nothing. He felt in his pocket and took out his cigarettes. He lit one with shaking hands and smoked in silence. He was waiting, waiting patiently for his son to vent all his rage.

He knew his son was afraid. The boy had no experience of anything like this and although there was still hatred in his eyes, there was even more panic. He was frightened. If Helian Dongshan wasn't careful and didn't pay attention, if even one word was too harsh, the boy really would jump. Helian Dongshan stood there, without saying a word, chain smoking. After about a quarter of an hour, he finally spoke.

"Son, do you really want to jump from here?" he asked.

"Have I supported you for seventeen years, just so you can jump from here?

"You were right when you said you are now grown up. It was my duty as a father to give you life and to raise you. So now, tonight, this is my last duty to you.

"Just remember, you can't deny me as your father and I can't deny you as my son. Now, just take a proper look and tell me if this is really the way to the police station. I said I was taking you there just to frighten you and get your attention. Actually, I simply wanted to take you to the park and have a proper talk with you.

"There is a big wide world out there, and you have a long road to travel. You're about to face your critical university entrance exam. If you are seduced by these horrible, filthy things, your brain will be addled, and your studies will be ruined. Your whole life will be ruined. Like I say, the world is a big place, you could go a long way, meet lots of people, have lots of choices, learn more about life...

"Of course, if you don't pass the exam, it's still OK. There are a lot of people who don't have that much education and they get on all right. There's something I haven't discussed with your mother, son. If you really don't want to go to college, if you don't want to go out and take a look at the world, it's OK. We've got eighty thousand yuan saved up at home and we can put a bit more in if we have to and buy you a Xiali or some other car. You can make a good living as a taxi driver. Then you could find yourself a wife and life would be pretty good.

"Son, no one is forcing you. I just want you to have a better life in the future."

He concluded: "Son, if you really want to jump, I can't stop you. You've got to decide for yourself."

When he had finished, Helian Dongshan turned and trudged back down the stairs. Every step was an effort, and he felt as though he was treading on his own heart, making the blood pulse fiercely through his body. Turning the corner, he squatted under a telephone pole and sighed. Suddenly, he tasted salt in the wind. It was the taste of his own tears.

It was late into the night when he finally saw his son walking out of the hotel.

Later, he learned from his wife that his son had straight away given the three CDs back to the people he had got them from. It was not in his son's nature to betray his friends, whether there was a crime involved or not, and that was why he was ready to die rather than go to the police station. It was an unforgettable experience for Helian Huasheng, and a pivotal moment in his growing up. It was also the eve of his transformation from Helian Huasheng to Helian Xichu, and his incarnation on the internet as "Overlord of Western Chu". It could be said that with this night, he really walked out from his father's shadow. After that night, his father never again lifted a finger against him. His father had "surrendered". At least, that's what he told himself. His hated Papa Blade had actually surrendered.

So now, he had won this precious "freedom" for himself. It was his last year of high school, and he had all to play for. He felt he had to get into university, because only then could he completely escape the surveillance of those flinty eyes. So when filling out his application for the *gaokao*, he filled in all the available options: one in Shanghai, one in Beijing and the last in Shenzhen. He wanted to go as far away as possible. At the time, "flying the coop" became his biggest motivation for study. In the end, he got into a university in Beijing as he wanted, even if it was only second-string.

It was a long time before father and son exchanged another word.

---

1. This is a reference to an old political anecdote from the Cultural Revolution. It is said that when Marshal Chen Yi was being publicly criticised at a meeting, he called out to the crowd "Look at what it says on page two seventy-one of Chairman Mao's Thoughts: Chairman Mao, the great leader, taught us that 'Chen Yi is a good comrade'"! Actually page 271 is a blank end-page. It is not known whether Mao ever heard about this, but at the memorial service for Chen Yi, Chairman Mao did say" 'Chen Yi is a good comrade'."

CHAPTER FOUR

ONE

LI DELIN ALWAYS REMEMBERED what happened that night.

He was eating oil cakes. They were shop-bought, not home-made. After Xu Ya'nan became the wife of the deputy governor, and especially having given birth to a son, she was very conscious of her position and didn't cook much any more. In the past, she used to make delicious small oil cakes. The noodles were always handmade, coiled up on the chopping board, then finally coiled into a round cake shape. Layer after layer, tossed repeatedly in the wok, hot, soft and fragrant. She knew that Li Delin loved to eat them served with millet porridge boiled in an iron pot and a plate of pickles. But now she was too lazy to cook and asked the nanny to buy it all from the college cafeteria. The oil cakes from the cafeteria were greasy and didn't taste right. The nanny made the millet porridge in an aluminium pot, but she didn't allow enough time, so the oil from the grain was not cooked and the porridge was thin, bland and boring to eat.

It wasn't just that he had no appetite for the food at home; there were many other things that meant Li Delin couldn't bear the sight of Xu Ya'nan. Some of her behaviour didn't just make his colleagues laugh, it also made him look bad. It made his brain hurt just to hear her pick up the phone and say: "Li Delin's residence. This is his wife speaking." Moreover, while all this was going on, the Huanghuai Number One experimental double-eared wheat he had cultivated failed repeatedly, and even his graduate students began to question his "wheat theory". This made him very unhappy. In terms of public affairs, several cities and prefectures were engaging in large-scale demolition and construction, selling land at crazy prices. They crossed the "red line" of the State Council's land policy and received severe criticism from above. He had personally led the investigation team to deal with two incidents of illegal "commercialisation of farmland". He was in charge of agricultural affairs after all, so he had a responsibility he couldn't shirk. The governor specifically called him in and said: "Lao Li, you are a wheat expert, don't you understand the importance of land?" Just this sentence made Li Delin feel ashamed. In this way, a whole string of things came together to make him feel more stressed and bad-tempered.

Xu Ya'nan only cared that he carried a leather briefcase, travelled in a special car, and went out looking smart and properly dressed. She had no idea what kind of mood he came back in from the office, so there was nothing she could do to relieve it, and even less was she able to talk about it with him. So when he got home and saw Xu Ya'nan with cucumber slices plastered over her face, prancing around in front of him and stumbling as she walked... it just made him nauseous. All that was needed was for her to be straightforward and honest, but Xu Ya'nan had been studying how city folk behaved and managed to get it quite wrong. Once, she suddenly produced a scrap of paper with a string of English letters written on it, and asked: "Hey, Qiuqiu's Daddy, is this a brand of face-powder?" Li Delin took a look and saw that it said "American Plaster". "Someone's trying to trick you," he said. "This is for walls!"

Another time, as soon as Li Delin walked in, Xu Ya'nan said: "That Lao Xue fellow doesn't answer my calls. It's just something for our boy's uncle, nothing major. Do you think you could..." Li Delin was furious: "Who said you could call Secretary Xue? You're not to go bothering people with phone calls. I don't want you to do it again." He was really not happy about what was going on, but as he didn't talk much at home and didn't easily lose his temper, naturally Xu Ya'nan didn't notice anything was wrong. But Li Delin had had enough.

After dinner, he watched the news on CCTV, then reclined on the sofa to read some documents. As he read, he gradually slid further down the sofa and dozed off. He wasn't really fast asleep, but just let his eyes close. It was his preparatory move to "sleeping apart", as he had done before. That is to say, he didn't want to go to their bedroom and sleep in the same bed as Xu Ya'nan.

To begin with, she just walked round the room, picking up things here and there, hoping that all the movement would attract Li Delin's attention. But he was very dozy and almost asleep, so in the end, she went into the bedroom to get a blanket, which she laid over him, still hoping to catch his attention. But he didn't even stir.

In the middle of the night, Xu Ya'nan came out of the bedroom wearing silk pyjamas. She went over to where Li Delin was lying, unbuckled his belt and started to feel around in his crotch. Li Delin woke up in confusion and asked: "What are you doing?"

Still digging around, Xu Ya'nan said: "Your little dicky-bird, has it flown away?"

Li Delin sat up in alarm and asked again: "What... what are you doing?"

Xu Ya'nan kept hold of his crotch and said: "I'm looking for your little dicky-bird. Hey, why's it so soft and floppy down there? Did the dicky-bird fly away to find some food?"

Li Delin pushed her away. "Stop talking nonsense!"

"Get up! Get up for me now!"

"What for? It's the middle of the night!"

"What for? You're asking me what for? Your seed tax is due!"

"Go back to sleep," Li Delin said angrily. "I'm tired and I'm not in the mood."

"You may not be, but I am. Get up!"

"Here's what we'll do, here's what we'll do. You sit down and we'll have a talk."

"How long is it since you last paid your seed tax? Go on, tell the truth, have you been paying it to someone else? Talk, you say? We'll do any talking there is to be done in bed."

"Sit down, Cai, sit down. We haven't had a proper talk in ages. Sit down and we'll talk now."

Ever since Xu Ya'nan changed her name, she hated being called Cai, and she wasn't going to let anyone disrespect her like that. She froze for a moment, and then exploded in fury: "Proper talk, you say! You've got a woman throwing herself at you and that's all you can think of! Well, if you want to fuck, we'll fuck, if you want to screw, we'll screw. Even if you do want to fuck, you still need someone to shout it at you, don't you! And now you don't want to, you think you can just shove me aside... just what kind of a man are you?"

Li Delin stared at her open-mouthed. "You... you... what?"

Not caring what she said now, Xu Ya'nan went on: "I suppose you've been grazing on someone else's fields and you're full up. It's bad enough you take all my private savings, but when you come home you won't even pay your seed tax. Let's call your father and see what he has to say about it!"

At that, Li Delin glared at her and said furiously: "What? My father's dead! Are you saying you want to dig him up?"

The mention of his father's name felt like a stab in the heart to Li Delin. The old man had died the winter before. His health had been in decline ever since Xu Ya'nan had the baby, and he gradually called on her less and less to look after him. He was fond of his grandson, but he had dropped him once and the child's face had been a little grazed. After that, Xu Ya'nan didn't let the old man even touch him again. She kept on needling him too: "The old fool needs to look where he's going and get out of the way before he knocks the boy over again." The house was full of imported powdered milk that the old man and the child had both been drinking, but now she hid it away and only gave it to her son. Twice, Li Delin came home from work early and found his father sitting in the courtyard staring into space like some kind of village idiot. "What are you doing sitting there, Dad?" Li Delin asked. At first the old man didn't reply, then he said: "I'm sunbathing. If you sunbathe, the bugs won't get you." Li Delin helped him to his feet, saying: "Let's go back inside, it's getting late." Later on, his father started talking about going back to the country. Li Delin kept trying to dissuade him, but with no success; his father was quite determined. Then, after he had been back in the village for six months, the old man suddenly passed away. Right up to the time he died, he never said a bad word about Xu Ya'nan. But later on, Li Delin heard that, whenever he was out of the house, Xu Ya'nan used to hustle his father outside, mockingly calling him "Mr Bugs-Won't-Get-You".

Xu Ya'nan knew that she had let her mouth run away with her, and she looked a little uneasy as she involuntarily took a step backwards. Finally, the words he had been holding back came tumbling out of Li Delin, as he said coldly: "Let's get divorced. We can't go on like this."

Xu Ya'nan stared at him in amazement. "What did you say?"

"Divorced," Li Delin said firmly.

Xu Ya'nan jumped to her feet and said: "So that's the way things are going, is it? Screwed yourself out, have you? Fucked me enough, have you? Want a change, do you? All right then. Divorce it is. I'm finished with you anyway. We'll do it right now!" She turned round blindly in a circle, and her hands seemed to be searching for something. Then she darted into the back room and picked up the child from the bed. The boy was frightened and began to wail. Xu Ya'nan took him into the living room, held him up in front of Li Delin, and shouted: "Divorce then! Yes, divorce! Since you're hell-bent on killing me, I don't want this child any more either. Why don't I just drop him on his head here now in front of you, so there aren't any loose ends? At least it will save him from being tortured by some stepmother..."

There was a buzzing in Li Delin's head as though his brain had short-circuited. He leapt up from the sofa in a panic. Mouth gaping and almost speechless, he stuttered out: "You... you... you... what do you think you're doing?"

"Don't you want a divorce? All right then! We're better off dead anyway. The boy can go first and I'll follow, and then we'll both be out of your way."

Li Delin had no clue what to do and just managed to stammer out: "Put him down! Put the boy down first and then you can have your say properly."

"Listen, Mr Li. I'm telling you, you may want a divorce, but the only way you're going to be rid of me is when I'm dead!"

The little boy was crying so loudly, he cried himself hoarse.

Li Delin suddenly relented. "All right, all right. I give in. Take the child back to bed."

"What? No divorce? Do it! Go ahead and divorce!" Li Delin put his head in his hands and said nothing.

Xu Ya'nan soothed the child, saying: "There's a good boy. There's a good boy. Don't cry. Don't cry. Look at your daddy. See! Does your daddy want to play with you? Your daddy's a useless bastard! Any conscience he had has been eaten by dogs..."

She soothed the child into silence, gave it to the nanny and came back out of the bedroom.

"So no divorce?" she said to Li Delin. "Well then, come and pay your seed tax!"

So that night, Li Delin ended up paying his seed tax, after all. Although some fear was involved, hatred was the driving emotion. At first, he was so frightened by Xu Ya'nan's vicious brutality that he couldn't find the wherewithal to pay the tax. However, outside the home, he was a provincial vice-governor-level cadre and very few people outside intimidated him like this, so there was still some fire in his belly; indeed it was this inextinguishable, devilish fire that reignited his loins. Once she had led Li Delin into the bedroom, Xu Ya'nan lay naked on the bed, her body turned away so she was presenting her buttocks to him. Li Delin got silently into bed, and when he was stretched out, she suddenly rolled over towards him and said: "Go on then, fuck me. Fuck my brains out. Let's see if you still can!"

Her deliberate coarseness almost made him come on the spot. But he closed his eyes, focused his burning rage and pictured this evil woman as his ex-wife Luo Qiuyi. With that, he rolled over and mounted her without a second thought. That night, the two of them seemed to turn into animals, their lust driven by hatred. Xu Ya'nan howled like a she-wolf and as the end neared, she was yelling and yelling and then suddenly lunged and bit him on the arm. She locked her teeth into his flesh until the blood came and then said: "You needed something to remember me by!"

That was the last time Li Delin paid his seed tax.

When it was over, Li Delin lay awake for the rest of the night. Although they had shared a bed and the seed tax had been paid, they were mortal enemies from that moment on. As he listened to Xu Ya'nan's snores, there was just one word surging through him: divorce.

It had to be done. His very being demanded it. But how?

TWO

FROM THEN ON, Li Delin stopped going home for dinner.

In addition to the formal dinners after meetings, he found himself eating out more and more often. There were hundreds of noodle restaurants, large and small, in the provincial capital. Liu Jinding had eaten in twenty-six different ones with Li Delin.

All foods made from wheat, especially noodles, were Li Delin's favourite. Of course, the first place he had visited was the one on Shuncheng Street, called the Majia Braised Noodles Shop. The noodles and soup were both good and the flavour was excellent, but it was a street restaurant, dirty and messy, and always crowded, mainly with working people. There was often a queue, and having to stand in line was annoying. Finally, Liu Jinding said: "Let's try somewhere else, Master."

"All right, you find somewhere good then," Li Delin replied.

After that, every time Liu Jinding came to the provincial capital and saw a decent-looking noodle restaurant, he would make a date to eat there with Li Delin. When they finished, he always asked: "How was it?"

"So-so," Li Delin would reply. "Only average." So next time they would try somewhere else.

There is a saying that "atmosphere can be acquired, but appetite has to be nurtured". Businessmen who open restaurants are always very savvy and one of them got a jump on the others by coming up with the name "Nourishing Braised Noodles". These "nourishing" noodles were made with lamb meat and lamb bones and the soup contained *codonopsis, astragalus, angelica dahurica*, Chinese wolfberry and other traditional Chinese medicine ingredients. It was allowed to steep for a day to get rid of any "fire *qi*" and fishy taste. Finally, a bowl of "rested" egg noodles was added along with coriander, sweet pickled garlic and chilli oil, which served to give extra balance to the flavour. As soon as Nourishing Braised Noodles made its appearance, Liu Jinding took Li Delin along to give it a try. Despite the cold of the winter's day, sweat broke out on the two men's heads. Liu Jinding asked: "What do you think, Master?" "Hmm, not bad," Li Delin replied. Liu Jinding took that as high praise.

But a couple of weeks later, they went back, and the noodles were no good. Most businessmen are looking for instant success and a quick profit. The meat no longer had to be lamb, and the broth didn't have to be made from the leg bones. The smell of Chinese medicine still seemed to be there, but there were only a few wolfberries floating in the soup. The coriander, sweet pickled garlic, chilli oil and so on were no longer fresh, and the taste was much inferior. When the two men had finished, without even waiting for his master to open his mouth, Liu Jinding said: "No, it's no good any more. We'll have to find somewhere else."

In the marketplace, every day is a new business day, and soon someone came up with the brand name "San Xian Braised Noodles". The advertising was very well done. It claimed to use lamb from Hulunbuir in Inner Mongolia, which was fed on prairie grass and water plants. The sea cucumbers and squid they used were all fresh from the deep ocean, so the name "*san xian*", meaning "three fresh", was well-deserved. The soup base was proper clear stock, and a quail egg could be seen floating in every bowl. Its claim was that it represented "sea, land and sky" in its ingredients with creatures that walked on the land, swam in the sea and flew in the sky. It was said that the noodles were made with top-grade, high-gluten Canadian flour, and individually rolled with fine-ground sesame oil, to be eaten straight away. Liu Jinding took Li Delin there twice, and they thought it was OK. On the third occasion, halfway through the meal, some youngsters at the next table started fighting. Soup was being splashed around and beer bottles were flying. Liu Jinding grabbed Li Delin and said: "Let's get out of here before you get all messy." As a consequence, it wasn't long before the two of them stopped eating at roadside restaurants altogether. From then on, they started going to better-class places, the kind of restaurant that has private rooms. Such rooms are quiet and air-conditioned in summer and heated in winter. Waiters are on hand all the time. If you need anything, you just have to ask. Everything was done to Li Delin's liking and he could enjoy some plain vegetable dishes, a few glasses of low-strength wine and then finish off with the noodles. If the two of them had a bit too much to drink, they couldn't be overheard if they were indiscreet. Naturally, the noodles in these high-end restaurants were very good, but they were also more expensive. Liu Jinding was not worried about the cost because he could just sign the bill. When they finished eating, and Liu Jinding was offering the toothpicks, Li Delin would call for the bill. The waiter would just smile, and Liu Jinding would say: "Let's go, Master. It's all looked after." Li Delin would say: "But I should pay. I don't want to set a bad example." However, after a few times, Li Delin didn't say anything any more.

Normally, Li Delin ate very plainly. All he really wanted was noodles, and he wasn't too bothered about other dishes. But now he was going to high-end places, the more he ate the more finicky he became, and he started choosing his restaurants rather than sticking to just one. The big restaurants all had signature dishes, or specialities. Naturally he wanted to try them, and when he did, Liu Jinding would ask: "Any good?" and Li Delin would reply: "Not bad", or sometimes: "OK".

It was Li Delin's habit, no matter how upmarket the restaurant, to order noodles to end the meal. The only concession he made was to have a small bowl rather than a large one. But it was no longer just braised noodles, he tried all different sorts, and of course he always ordered the best. For example, there was a kind of *yifu* noodles that was said once to have been sent to the imperial household by the magistrate in Yangzhou. They are made using the whites from duck eggs, then fried in hot oil and simmered in clear chicken stock. Fresh prawns and other ingredients are added, and the whole dish has a very distinctive flavour. Then there were Sichuan *dandan* noodles offered by the swankiest restaurants. They are simmered in clear water and then have thirty-one different seasonings added, so they are pure and fresh with not an oil drop to be seen, but incomparably invigorating and deliciously spicy. These superior noodles drew a single word of praise from the notoriously picky Li Delin: "Good!"

This was the time when the mood of society as a whole was quietly changing. First, it was food, and it was across the board: flesh, fowl and fish... everything was being eaten in new ways. Of course, there were different levels of this new gastronomy, high and low, but if you just kept on eating, you could eat your way up through them. It also seemed that the streets of the provincial capital were suddenly full of "hair salons" and "foot spas" that sprang up everywhere like bamboo shoots after the rain. It was a very odd phenomenon, as if the whole population was now obsessed with washing their hair and cleaning their feet. The nationwide "washing" craze began under the guise of "healthy living" but then became part of the commercial "hospitality" scene. After that, of course, both "hair salon" and "foot spa" became codewords in the hospitality industry for something else entirely. And of course, the price kept going up, from twenty yuan to sixty, eighty, a hundred... the sky was the limit. Then, when people had been thoroughly "washed" from head to toe, right on cue, along came the karaoke hall. "Karaoke" flashed in neon lights at every corner of every street and alley, and *Say You'll Be Mine* was on everybody's lips. "Tossed on the storm of life, standing in a foolish daze...", the words flowed out of the microphone, and it wasn't long before, as you stood in the neon light outside the karaoke hall, you noticed the girls standing in the large plate glass windows, preening and spraying themselves with perfume. There they were, all in a row, number badges at their waists, waiting for their number to be chosen. You may remember the political catchphrase "opening up and invigorating". Well, this was a complete "opening up", heart and soul, that was on offer. Very nice too!

Of course, officials of Li Delin's status disdained the foot spas and karaoke halls. However, the standard of food he and Liu Jinding ate did keep going up, almost without them noticing. Sometimes, after a few glasses of wine, Li Delin felt a little dizzy and lacking in energy. Liu Jinding always hastened to ask: "Are you tired, Master?" Li Delin would reply: "It's OK. Just a little tired, it's all been a bit too much. Nothing serious though." Nonetheless, being very conscientious, Liu Jinding took note and made sure that the next time they went out to eat, they went to a five-star hotel where he had pre-booked a room. The place being five-star, the service was even more attentive, so when they had eaten and drunk their fill, the hotel opened a room for them to relax in and conduct any more conversations that needed to be kept private. So the eating continued, and with Liu Jinding by then executive deputy mayor of Huanghuai, it was even less a problem for him just to sign away the bill.

One night, the two of them had just had dinner in a five-star hotel, and Liu Jinding said tentatively: "It's been a long and tiring day, Master. Would you like a little massage?" At that time, the term "a little massage" was just beginning to be used, and now, of course, everyone knew what it actually meant. Li Delin, however, was taken by surprise, and said: "Massage? Massage? What do you mean?"

Like all five-star hotels, the service in the hotels in the provincial capital was exceptional. Liu Jinding only had to push the call button in the room, and two girls appeared. Of course, what they provided was a traditional Chinese medicinal all-over massage. Not only were these two girls good-looking, they were also properly qualified from a TCM institute, and five-star service naturally commanded a five-star price too. They were wearing very short dresses and swung their hips as they came into the room. They were polite and respectful when they saw the guests, addressed them very correctly as "sir" and didn't speak out of turn. Later, as they sat close on the edge of the bed, they were just like ordinary girls, but also as attentive as maid servants. Their soft, gentle hands worked their way down from the top of the men's heads to the tips of their toes, finding every acupressure point, alternating soft and heavy as they worked their way down, scratching every itch and warming every part that needed warming with the sureness of touch of a concert pianist. An hour and a half later, the men were relaxed but invigorated.

Room service brought a pot of chrysanthemum tea, hot towels and fruit.

"Everything all right, Master?" Liu Jinding asked.

"Yes, fine, very good. My old back feels wonderful."

When the door shut and it was just the two of them again, Liu Jinding said: "I've got something to say that I can't very well say elsewhere. Now it's just the two of us, I want to get it out."

"Go on, then."

"You are a provincial-level cadre now, Master, but sometimes, if I may say so, I think you need to push things a bit."

The word "push" was well chosen as it could mean a lot of things until it was narrowed down. Li Delin just grunted.

"I have heard you speak many times, Master, and you are able to talk directly to the people, but sometimes you should dress it up a little, maybe bring in some Western style. If you need to put on a bit of a show, that's what you should do."

In the local dialect on the plain, "putting on a show" could mean a lot of things, so Li Delin remained noncommittal.

Liu Jinding continued: "The thing I most admire about you, Master, is your way with numbers and figures. From what I have seen, you have the best head for statistics of all the provincial and ministerial officials. Population, land, acreage, yield, number of grains per plant and all that kind of thing, you are accurate to three decimal places. When you are reporting to the top brass, you come up with a string of figures that leaves them speechless. You make a lasting impression on your audience, so why not beef it up even more?"

Li Delin was confident about his head for numbers, so he grunted again, off-handedly. Liu Jinding went on: "But sometimes, Master, I do think you need to change your tone a bit. You can't always be so conciliatory to your subordinates. You're not having a discussion with them. They are subordinates, you are their boss. If you want to lord it over them, lord it over them. If you have to give them an order, give them an order. You are the governor, after all!"

Li Delin said nothing.

"Take Secretary Xue Zhiheng, for example," Liu Jinding explained. "Even though he is an old classmate of yours, he is still your subordinate. He's always joking with you, and that isn't appropriate. He's just a department-level cadre, so how can he be so off-hand? Don't you agree? Look at me. You can criticise or scold me as much as you like and then come back and do it some more. I am your student, so you can treat me as if I was your child. Of course, there are some people and some things you have to handle differently, so that, when the crunch comes, you still have someone to trust."

Li Delin gave another noncommittal grunt.

As the two men went on talking, they drilled down even further into the subject. Liu Jinding said: "Master, you are part of the provincial top brass now, and you still have further up the ladder to climb. You are an expert in wheat, and you have your own field of expertise, but I know you make light of that. Even so, now you have reached your current level, it is impossible for you not to continue upwards. Don't you agree? And if you are going to go on up, you can't just rely on your current reputation. The *Records of the Grand Historian* says that even a minor 'lord of the plains' in those days had three thousand retainers. To put it simply, Master, you have to build a support team of your own."

Li Delin exclaimed, disapprovingly: "What has become of us? Are we going down the devil's road? Are we really reduced to recruiting henchmen?"

"Well, Master, in the olden days, henchmen weren't necessarily a bad thing, just a useful tool. When the crunch comes, a few crafty heavies among your followers have their uses. We're men of the times, aren't we? Doesn't every American president have his own entourage?"

Li Delin kept listening in silence, wheezing slightly from time to time, and he looked as though he might be asleep. Liu Jinding kept up his straight-talking: "Supposing you rise to deputy national level one day, Master. That would make you part of the national leadership. Who's to say, you might even get into Zhongnanhai. I don't know if you've thought about it or not, but when the time comes, the people beside you–"

"Stop!" Li Delin said severely, his eyes snapping open. "That's not something I even think about. We'll not mention it again."

"Just supposing, that's all I'm saying. Aren't we in an age now when experts are supposed to be running the country? It's not impossible, Master. The way I see it, your qualifications are plenty good enough to get you to deputy national level. You're the kind of person who is going to make it into Zhongnanhai sooner or later, and when that day comes, you're going to need people with you who know their way about a bit. Now I think about it, there are a few things I regret rather."

Li Delin was taken aback and asked: "What do you regret?"

"If I'm really honest, I shouldn't have introduced you to Xu Ercai. Just look at her! I really made you lose face."

This hit Li Delin like a sledgehammer blow to the heart, and he sat there gasping for breath.

Seeing that Li Delin wasn't disagreeing, Liu Jinding went on: "When I first sent her to your place, the idea was for her to look after your old dad, and you as well. I shouldn't be saying this, but she really is just a coarse servant girl only fit to be a nanny. Still, to start with, she had a sort of rough and ready vigour about her, but now, all that's left is the coarseness, and when she goes out and struts down the street, everyone just laughs at her. If you have visitors, she sits on the sofa ordering you to pour the tea when that should be her job. Then, after a while she'll start picking her nose or scratching her feet and people don't know where to look! As wife of the provincial governor, she really does leave quite a bit to be desired... doesn't she?"

At this, Li Delin sat up abruptly, sighed and said: "It's true, Little Brother, the days have seemed like years recently. How can the woman be like that? And how didn't I see it from the start? Ai, to tell the truth, just the sight of her now hurts my eyes. I don't want to spend another day, another hour, another minute in her company."

Liu Jinding decided it was time to add some fuel to the fire: "If you want to know what I really think, if you were still married to Teacher Luo, I wouldn't be suggesting you got divorced. But that woman you're with now, she's so common and lacking in any taste that all she does is bring shame on you. If you want to divorce her, I'm behind you all the way."

"You're right. You couldn't have known because I didn't think I could say it before. That woman has been driving me mad all this time."

"She has? How? I shouldn't really say this, but just give her a bit of cash and tell her to fuck off!"

"Supposing she refuses to divorce me?" Li Delin said with a sigh.

"Her? She wouldn't dare!"

THREE

XU YA'NAN HAD BEEN IN A FOUL MOOD ever since Li Delin mentioned divorce, and each day at home was like walking on broken glass.

She had her own grievances. Previously, when she was just looking after the old man, she could get on with it as she liked. But after she had him sent back to the country, when she should have been able to take a bit of a breather, she found she not only had to attend to her husband, but to their child as well. There is an old saying that a mother's status rises with her son's, and after the birth, her position as wife of the deputy governor was cemented in place. And, of course, since she now carried that title, she was different from before.

In her eyes, the child was number one priority, and she concentrated all her thoughts and emotions on him. But the boy was still little, prone to wailing and crying, and if he didn't have a fever, he had a cold. It was more than enough to try her patience. Of course, she no longer had time to make her husband the oil cakes or noodle sheets in sour soup or boiled millet porridge, and that at least made her life a little easier. Although her husband really liked those dishes, he was out all the time at official meals and banquets, so he got everything he could want to eat anyway. Besides, she really didn't have the time. But what really took her aback was that when her husband said he no longer loved her, he meant it. She could tell from the look in his eyes these days that a crisis was fast approaching.

As the days passed, she found herself living more and more on her nerves. If the doorbell went unexpectedly or a bowl got smashed in the kitchen, or the toilet flushed in the bathroom, she jumped in fright. Once, when she saw the terrified look in the nanny's eyes, she glared at her and snapped: "Have you stepped on a landmine or something? You're going to be the death of me!"

She had already changed nannies twice, and the next to arrive took just one look at Xu Ya'nan and panicked, because her gaze was as piercing as a sharpened awl. Xu Ya'nan told the nanny she could call her "Auntie Xu", but then she thought that made her sound too old, so she changed it to "Older Sister Xu". However, that only lasted a few days before she decided "Older Sister" wasn't respectful enough and she settled on "Teacher Xu". After all, she was named among the university personnel in the library of the University of Agricultural Science and Technology so why shouldn't she be reckoned an educational professional? The nanny was to discover that this "Teacher Xu" was distinctly neurotic, not to say strange. She was moody, walked as though she was being blown along by a gust of wind, often stayed in her nightclothes and would suddenly appear in front of her, saying: "Why are you so on edge?"

"I'm not on edge, Auntie," the nanny said aggrievedly.

Xu Ya'nan glared at her. "What did you call me?"

The nanny hurriedly corrected herself: "I'm really not on edge, Teach... Teacher Xu."

"Nonsense! Not on edge? I've seen you scuttling out several times a night in that red bodice of yours. Who is it you're trying to seduce?"

Genuinely aggrieved this time, the nanny said: "That red bodice is just my underwear. I... I had the runs."

"Don't bandy words with me! You were stealing food, weren't you! Do you think I'm blind? What were you talking about to my old man in the kitchen?"

"I just... I just wanted to tell Grandpa... to tell him about my little brother getting into university."

"Why didn't you tell me about it? Just remember to keep me informed in future."

After a while, Xu Ya'nan suddenly changed her attitude. She fetched a piece of fabric from the back room and said: "Here, take it. You can make some nice clothes out of it. As long as you stay with me, I'll help you with everything."

Every time Li Delin came through the front door and called out, Xu Ya'nan would be in the back room. She hid behind the door, keeping it open a fraction so she could spy on him, figure out the expression on his face, before walking casually out and saying: "So you're back, are you?"

Li Delin would just grunt and go into his study.

Once he was there, she would rush over to the coat rack, remove his suit jacket from the hook, sniff it all over like a police dog and go through the pockets. Once, Li Delin caught her at it, and she just said: "This jacket really needs dry-cleaning!"

When Li Delin went to the bathroom, she ran into the study and quickly checked his briefcase. If she didn't find anything suspicious, she relaxed. If she were to find anything that suggested he might have been in touch with his former wife, there would be big trouble. Ever since Li Delin uttered the word "divorce", Xu Ya'nan had been in top self-protection mode; she had hidden her household registration and marriage certificate quite some time ago. One day, when she felt her hiding-place was not secure enough, she changed it three times. Later on, she went to the university's data storage room and locked her household registration and marriage certificate in the safe there. In fact, the two of them had been effectively separated for a long time, and Li Delin was always looking for reasons to sleep in the study. From his point of view, this was another cold war… whoever got worn down first would lose. In Xu Ya'nan's opinion, her "old man" was having an affair, and was deliberately neglecting her. So late one night, Li Delin was woken from his sleep by a "click, click" noise. He found Xu Ya'nan, naked under a pyjama jacket that was draped over her shoulders, kneeling beside the bed, with a small torch next to her. She was holding a pair of nail clippers in one hand and his toes in the other and was cutting his toenails. Li Delin made to sit up, but she hurriedly grabbed one of his ankles and said: "Keep still, keep still. I might nick you if you move."

"It's the middle of the night! What do you think you are doing?"

"Your toenails are getting too long. It's time to cut them."

Li Delin stared at her in astonishment and said: "Forget it. Get up from there."

Xu Ya'nan didn't say anything, but kept her head down, clicking away. She was clearly trying to win him back with her attentiveness. Once she had finished with Li Delin's toenails, she said: "Can't we forget the divorce, Qiuiu's Daddy? Can't we live happily together?" Through the darkness, her eyes had a pleading expression. As her tears began to flow, it was clear what she really meant was: Qiuqiu's Daddy, if you agree not to divorce, I will work like a slave for you!

In the quiet of the night, Li Delin's heart softened. He sat up silently and reached for his cigarettes on the bedside table. After a while, he said: "Go back to bed and get some sleep."

Xu Ya'nan looked at him blankly and said: "I can't sleep if you're not there." Li Delin smoked in silence and did not reply.

At this point, Xu Ya'nan twisted up and sat on the edge of the single bed. She said: "I'm asking you one more time: can we forget the divorce?"

And because she dared to persist with this, Li Delin's thawing heart hardened again. "Leave it, Cai!" he said. "I'm getting old and have lots of problems. You are still young. Divorce will be good for both of us. Don't worry about the child..."

Xu Ya'nan looked at him, eyes blazing. Her shaved and repainted eyebrows twitched upwards, twisting her face into a hideous expression. She leapt to her feet, hurled the nail clippers to the ground and said furiously: "All right, divorce it is then! Just make sure you have the money ready!"

Li Delin stiffened. "How much?"

Xu Ya'nan knew he didn't have a huge amount of money, but she still went in strong: "A million!"

Li Delin stared at her. "You have my salary account card. You know I don't have that much."

"That's not my problem. One million and not a cent less!" she said, turning to leave as though she had just won a decisive victory.

Li Delin lay coughing in the study, all night.

The next morning, he wanted to talk to Xu Ya'nan again, but she snatched up the child early and went back to her family in his official car. So Li Delin hurriedly called Liu Jinding to talk to him about borrowing money.

After their phone conversation, Liu Jinding hurried over and asked as soon as he walked in: "What's going on, Master?"

Li Delin was pacing round the house. Seeing Liu Jinding come in, he said: "There's a ray of hope. She's not happy about it, but she's agreed to the divorce."

"Wow, OK! As long as she's agreed, things will be easier to handle. We'd better get a move on with it."

Li Delin hesitated for a moment before saying: "But she's being greedy. She's asked for a million!"

"Give it to her. Just give it to her quickly and be done with it."

"The Huanghuai Number One is still being tested, and the other patents haven't yet been granted. She has control of my salary, so where else can I lay my hands on that kind of money quickly?"

"Forget about the money, it's not a problem. I'll talk to a couple of friends in the business world and have someone send it immediately."

Li Delin scratched his head and then shook it, saying: "Isn't that rather inappropriate? Even if I can borrow it, I won't be able to pay it back for ages. No, no, it's definitely not appropriate."

"Master, it's time to make a clean break from this mess and not let it drag on any longer. Take advantage of her agreement, get divorced quickly and we'll talk about the rest later. It's not a big deal. It's only money."

Li Delin paced the room. After a while, he rubbed his head, sighed and said: "I'm backed into a corner and I haven't got any option. I'm... I'm only borrowing it. I will write you an IOU now."

Liu Jinding looked at the back room, lips pursed and whispered: "Where is she?"

"Gone back to her family." Then he sighed again and said: "Oh, the child is still so young–"

"You don't have to worry about your son, Master. Sooner or later, he'll be back with you. The important thing is to get it all done quickly before anything changes."

Li Delin couldn't help but agree and said: "Well, I'll leave the money to you. Make it quite clear, it's only a loan."

"Don't worry about money. I'll send it to you before five o'clock this afternoon."

After he left, Liu Jinding called Xie Zhichang and said: "Uncle, I want you to get together a million in cash. Governor Li needs it urgently."

However, two days later, Xu Ya'nan returned with the baby in her arms, looking very happy. As soon as she came in through the door, she shouted: "Well, Daddy, your boy can recite Tang poetry now. His uncle taught him. Qiuqiu, recite 'The sun beyond the mountain glows' for your father!"

Li Delin opened the door of the study, came out and said gloomily: "Give the child to the nanny for a moment, then come in here. I have something to tell you."

Xu Ya'nan followed Li Delin into the study. When the door was closed, Li Delin said: "Sit down, sit down." Then, he opened a small suitcase on the desk and said: "I've got the money for you. Do you want to count it? Then, tomorrow, we can get the formalities over with."

"What formalities?" Xu Ya'nan asked innocently.

"Didn't we agree to a divorce?"

"Divorce? Did I say I was divorcing you?"

Li Delin looked at her, and his heart sank. Xu Ya'nan glanced at the small suitcase on the table: "How much is in there?"

"One million. I borrowed it. That's what you asked for, isn't it? Well, I've got it for you."

"I was a virgin when I married you and I want to spend the rest of my life with you. When did I ever say I was going to get a divorce?"

Li Delin began to lose his temper: "You..."

Xu Ya'nan looked at the money on the desk and said: "Well, Qiuqiu's father, we should save this money for our son's education. Now, if there is nothing else, I'll go and make some food."

Li Delin was furious. "Stop right there. Our marriage must be dissolved. I don't want to live with you for a minute longer. We must divorce!"

"All right then, we'll get divorced. Just add a zero to the total, and it's done!" Then, she picked up the cash box on the table. "I'll look after this. When you have scraped enough together, that'll be it." So saying, she went back into the bedroom, taking the cash with her.

Li Delin stood there staring blankly. Had Xu Ya'nan really changed her mind? She was certainly making things difficult for him, adding another zero! That meant ten million. Where could he find ten million?

In the middle of the night, Xu Ya'nan burst into the study, wearing white silk pyjamas and with her hair dishevelled. Li Delin was alarmed to see a shadowy, ghost-like figure standing beside his bed. Turning on the light, he raised his eyes to see that Xu Ya'nan had a kitchen knife in her hand!

Li Delin sat bolt upright and said: "Are you crazy!"

Xu Ya'nan said fiercely: "Sooner or later one of us is going to die. Let me test the knife for you first..." Then, she rolled up her sleeve and slashed her wrist. The bright red blood spurted out immediately.

Li Delin leapt out of bed, grabbed her hand and said: "You, you... calm down, calm down. Sit down and let's talk. Think of the boy!" He didn't have time to find his shoes, so he ran out barefoot, found some gauze, and bandaged up her wrist.

Xu Ya'nan was still standing there as she said: "My eyes are closing! It's all over! The child, what about our child? Will you look after him when I'm gone?"

"Sit down, just sit down and then–"

"If you want a divorce, there is still one way open to you."

"Tell me!"

"I have a little notebook here and if I hand it in, you're sure to go to prison."

"What? What little notebook?"

Xu Ya'nan held up the small book in her left hand and said: "Every New Year, your son's one-month celebration, the money people gave when your father was sick and in hospital. I've kept a record of it all for you!"

Li Delin was furious. "Who asked you to accept all that money?"

"You did. Or at least you didn't stop me!"

Li Delin was at his wit's end.

FOUR

THERE IS AN AREA OF ABOUT FIFTY ACRES beside the Yellow River called the Meiling Botanical Garden, also known as Mei Village. It contains an indoor botanical garden called Nature's Restaurant, and is covered by a fibreglass-reinforced plastic dome supported by aluminium alloy pillars. Modern controls mean that the temperature and humidity can be adjusted according to need. A variety of fruit and vegetables surround the small number of European-style white dining tables. The produce is freshly picked, and there are locally-reared chickens, ducks and fish to go with them. It's open to anyone, and does good business. On Sundays, many young couples who have come for a day out along the Yellow River, go there to eat.

Another section is by way of being the clubhouse, which is not generally open to the public. There is an oval-shaped building resembling the White House, which, in fact, it was named after. The building has complete accommodation, catering and bathing facilities, with what they call super five-star service. The third floor and above are all suites, equipped with modern mahjong equipment and hot spa bathing facilities, mainly for "VIP" services. These services are targeted at two kinds of people: one is officials of a certain level, for whom the services are free, with each person being given a VIP card worth 100,000 yuan, which can be renewed when used up; the other is important businessmen, and they have to pay for themselves. The initial limit for them is also 100,000 yuan, and they can buy more once they run out. It is only if there are a number of suites empty that they are made available to the general public.

There is also an area of fifty acres that was originally intended to be an experimental wheat base, but subsequently, twenty of its acres were given over to what was called the Ornamental Flower Garden. As a result, of the three hundred acres of land originally approved for the experimental wheat base, only thirty acres were left. The temporary Ornamental Flower Garden was covered by a fibreglass-reinforced plastic dome supported by aluminium alloy pillars. It was constructed by Xie Zhichang on his own initiative, and he also served as chairman of the board. The flowers there were all identified as "precious treasures", and each pot was worth several tens of thousands of yuan. If any officials saw a plant they wanted, there was always someone to buy it for them.

It could accurately be said that the whole Mei Village was planned by Liu Jinding. Every time he came to the provincial capital, he had to accompany Li Delin to eat noodles. The governor's addiction to noodles never abated, and constantly having to find new venues was getting rather tiresome. Liu Jinding felt there should be one place that was just right for them. Once, he said to Li Delin: "Teacher, we must have a base." Li Delin wasn't really interested at the time but asked: "What do you mean?" Liu Jinding said: "I mean, there must be a place we can always go to eat." Li Delin disagreed, saying: "It's just a bowl of noodles. There are plenty of places we can go." "I mean, there must be a place where we can meet all year round." Li Delin said offhandedly: "I don't think there's any such place." Liu Jinding didn't reply directly, but just said: "Leave this to me." And that is how the Meiling Botanical Garden came into being.

Liu Jinding had always reckoned that he understood his master better than anyone, and he also firmly believed that one day Li Delin would become a national-level leader. He got excited whenever he thought about it. Yes indeed, after becoming a national-level leader, his master must have a team of trusted followers and reliable talents. According to the historical records, even a small "lord of the plain" had three thousand retainers back in the old days, all of them willing to sacrifice their lives for their master. How much more did the future leaders of the country today deserve the same? He knew that such things took a lot of advance preparation. What his master couldn't think of, he had to think of it for him. Although the future no doubt had many unknowable factors in store and he didn't have everything completely mapped out, he was quite clear that he should first establish a "stronghold" and gradually recruit some talent on behalf of his master. In this regard, he was willing to learn from two different types of people: one was the Jews and the other was Shanxi folk.

As executive deputy mayor of Huanghuai, Liu Jinding had led a delegation to Israel. The main purpose was to inspect that country's drip-feed irrigation technology and modern agricultural facilities. In Tel Aviv, Liu Jinding also stopped by to visit the Museum of the Jewish Diaspora. He took away a lot of impressions from the trip, one of which was the shrewdness and resilience of the Jewish people. The Jews had nearly been exterminated twice in their history, and their people had fled and dispersed to all parts of the world. When they fled, they took only two things with them: one was gold, and the other was the knowledge that they carried in their heads. What was even more admirable was that no matter where they went in the world, as long as there were ten of them together, they would immediately elect a spiritual leader. This leader maintained communication with the Jewish groups who fled to other places, and then connected the "dots" into "lines", and then "lines" into "segments"... so a race that had been wiped out was resurrected and a country was restored.

Liu Jinding had stood for a long time in front of the map of the world diaspora with its small flashing lights, and it left a very deep impression on him.

It was after his return from Israel that Liu Jinding had the idea of building a "base", so he had this three hundred-acre Meiling Botanical Garden constructed. Although we have said that Mei Village was created by Liu Jinding alone, he did not actually pay a cent himself. What he contributed were "ideas" and "relationships" – along with the land he appropriated using Li Delin's name under the banner of scientific agricultural research. The initial working capital was put up by Xie Zhichang from the Flower World Group, and several wealthy coal-mine owners also contributed some money. (Later, when additional funds were added during the infrastructure construction process, these mine owners also became shareholders... "VIP" shareholders, of course.) On the registration certificate publicly issued by the Industrial and Commercial Bureau, Xie Zhichang was named as chairman of the board and Liu Jinding had someone in mind for general manager. Quite simply, this was Liu Jinding's "base".

At first, Liu Jinding's "base theory" was revealed only to Xie Zhichang. On one occasion, the two were eating together. Xie Zhichang was playing host because someone had asked him to look up Liu Jinding to get him to do something for them, and Liu Jinding told him to set up the meal at the Flower World Hotel. (Xie Zhichang was originally good to Liu Jinding, and might even be called his patron, but kindness is like a deposit in a bank: the initial deposit is there but it can easily go overdrawn if you are not careful.) After Liu Jinding became executive deputy mayor, Lao Xie deliberately took more of a back seat, and he also started to invite Mayor Liu to dinner. When Mayor Liu arrived on this particular occasion, the hotel manager Bai Shouxin rushed over to join him, so the three of them sat together, eating and chatting. After a few drinks and a bit of gossip, Liu Jinding said: "Be off with you now, Chief Bai, there's something I want to talk to Lao Xie about."

"All right, you guys, go ahead and talk," Bai Shouxin said equably. "Call if you need me."

After Bai Shouxin left, Liu Jinding said: "Uncle, aren't you always asking me what you are lacking?"

"Yes, and you don't have to tell me. I need some 'culture'. And I'm doing it, aren't I? You've seen all the books I bought. So what else do you think I need?"

"Well, Uncle, let me supplement your culture a little. The two most important things are 'vision' and 'boundaries'. I know you have always wanted to go on to bigger things, so let me ask you, do you want to get into the provincial capital?"

"Of course I do! Why wouldn't I? Can you give me some tips?"

"Well, drink down three glasses of wine, and I'll give you an idea."

Without a word, Xie Zhichang picked up the wine and drank three glasses one after the other, then showed the empty glass and said: "Tell me!"

"Do you know how Shanxi merchants built up their business during the Ming and Qing dynasties?"

Although Xie Zhichang didn't read much, he had, at least, watched *The Qiao Family Compound* on CCTV and said: "Everyone knows *The Qiao Family Compound*. I also know that Shanxi merchants are famous. Look at the coal bosses in Shanxi, they're all very bullish in the way they do business."

"Do you know why they are famous all over the country?"

"Go on, tell me."

"The first and most important thing," Liu Jinding explained, "is that they recognise the importance of having a 'base'."

This idea of a base seemed very deep and mysterious to Xie Zhichang, and he was a little baffled, not knowing where to go with it. Liu Jinding continued: "Uncle, you have been to lots of different places, but have you noticed that every big city, in fact not just every big city, medium-size ones too, has a 'Shanxi-Shaanxi Guild Hall'?"

Xie Zhichang nodded repeatedly and said: "Oh, yes, yes, they're everywhere. I've visited some of them myself."

"Yes indeed. Of course, hundreds of years have passed, and the guild halls have become ancient monuments, but most of them are still intact. Do you know what those halls were used for?"

"Yes, you are right. Go on, tell me."

"Those merchants from Shanxi and Shaanxi were really smart. They travelled east, west, north and south to do business all over the country. Wherever they went, the first thing they did was find a place to stay, and that became their 'base'. After that was established, they invited guests to dinner and made contacts with people from all walks of life so they could build their own territory. This was also the main reason they could do business nationwide..."

"That makes sense, and you make sense."

"Well, Uncle, do you want to build one in the provincial capital?"

"Yes, yes, let's do it. It's just a question of money, isn't it? It will be money well spent."

"If we want this base of our own, we should build a high-end club that can attract outside interest, and at the same time, we can use it to build our own network of contacts. We might end up making money out of it, too. The most important things are to invite the top brass to dinner, establish as many contacts as possible and recruit some talent. They'll be happy to come." Then, explaining further, Liu Jinding said: "With a base, you have the foundation for future development in the provincial capital. You have a foot in the door. We're in the information age now and stuff will flood in from all directions. You won't even be able to count the money you'll make."

As he listened, the temptation was too great for Xie Zhichang. He banged his fist on the table and said: "Right! Let's do it! I'll put up fifteen million. How's that?"

Liu Jinding considered the offer and said: "I'll see to the land. It won't cost too much on the shores of the Yellow River. In addition, I'll ask Governor Li if he can find a way to allocate another four or five million from the poverty-alleviation funds. Ostensibly we can be the 'Wheat Research Base', or we could call it a pilot project for the 'New Rural Cooperative Medical Scheme' and that should be worth another twenty or thirty million. And if that's not enough, we can take another look. I know a few mine-owners who are fighting each other to invest..."

At this point, Bai Shouxin, who was eavesdropping outside, realised what a profitable opportunity this was and pushed open the door, saying: "Mr Xie, Mayor Liu, will you let me in on this, even if it's only one share, or a small share at least? My brother-in-law and I can put together three million, so we can ride along with you, and make some money of our own on the back of yours." Bai Shouxin was a close friend of Xie Zhichang, and his brother-in-law was the chief of the City Tax Bureau, so Liu Jinding was loth to object and reluctantly agreed. So the three men settled the matter: it was agreed that Liu Jinding and Xie Zhichang would each hold thirty-five per cent of the shares, Bai Shouxin would take five per cent and the remaining shares would be allocated elsewhere – as it turned out, to several of the coal mine owners. This was a secret arrangement between the three of them, not to be made public.

After the completion of Mei Village, because it was submitted in the guise of Li Delin's "Experimental Wheat Base", the letters of approval were rubber stamped by each layer of bureaucracy, always with the words "Experimental Wheat Base" across the top. Nominally, it was a public enterprise, with special provincial approval, into which the state invested a small amount of research funding every year. Secretly, it also had private capital investment coming in under a shareholding system, so it was actually a public-private enterprise, or, more like, a public-private investment association that was deliberately very vague about some of its aspects. The first woman Liu Jinding chose to join Mei Village was Wang Xiaomei, and she became the first director of the Experimental Wheat Base appointed by the Meiling Institute of Agricultural Sciences, as well as general manager in charge of finance. Any money spent there had to be signed off by Wang Xiaomei.

Getting Wang Xiaomei involved to manage the place was very important to Liu Jinding. The pair were classmates at middle school, where they had shared a desk. In those early years, the two youngsters secretly handed each other "notes", and might be considered childhood sweethearts. Sadly, there had been an incident in Wang Xiaomei's family and she had attempted suicide. She took a year off school as a consequence, and the two were parted. When they met again later, Wang Xiaomei had already been married and divorced. On the evening of their class reunion, Wang Xiaomei had said to Liu Jinding: "You were my rock." These few words made Liu Jinding's heart leap.

Later, Liu Jinding learned that after Wang Xiaomei dropped out of school due to illness, she scraped her way into a local teacher training college. After graduation, because of her father's connections there, she was assigned to the County Agriculture Bureau and later married the director's son. But the chief's son was a drunk, and often beat her when he was in his cups. She found his treatment of her unbearable, so she filed for divorce, but the man just wouldn't agree. It was only quite recently with the help of Liu Jinding that she finally got her divorce, but her drunk husband was still pestering her, so she asked to be transferred out into the province.

It was in these circumstances that Liu Jinding brought Wang Xiaomei to Mei Village. On the surface, he asked her to come out there to relax and escape her ex-husband's attentions. In fact, he had other things in mind: one was to put her firmly in control of Mei Village finances; the other was to find an opportunity to take her to one side and introduce her to his mentor, Li Delin. He believed that

Li Delin would act selflessly, especially as he was looking for suitable candidates among teachers to become future "national leaders".

Wang Xiaomei was nearly forty years old by this time, but she remained petite and very delicate. Even though she was now middle-aged, she still had considerable charm. Although she had been cured of her youthful depression, she was quiet, taciturn and gave little away.

After the class reunion, Liu Jinding had had some contact with Wang Xiaomei when he was director of the County Government Office in Meiling. The emotions of their relationship were quite complex. Wang Xiaomei had approached him because of the divorce. Although Liu Jinding had never forgotten their previous feelings for each other, he was newly married and still had some scruples. Later, Liu Jinding was transferred to the city, but even so, the two of them gradually grew closer. Finally one day, Liu Jinding booked a room in a hotel in the city and invited Wang Xiaomei to come and "remember the old days". Wang Xiaomei seemed amenable to the idea, but when they were lying on the bed, Wang Xiaomei said something that ended any possibility of the two of them actually getting it on. She looked him full in the face and said: "I'm not attracted to you."

Liu Jinding felt a shaft of ice go through him when he heard those words. The flame of passion was extinguished, and he went soft. But after a little while, he found himself unwilling to accept that this could be happening; his ardour mounted again and he tried to force himself on her. Wang Xiaomei lay there stark naked, not trying to stop him, but in the end he didn't enter her. Using a crude local dialect expression, he asked her: "Is there something wrong with you down there? Are you one of those 'stone girls'?"[1] Xiaomei said she didn't have that condition. The two of them lay on the bed talking for a while before silently getting up and putting on their clothes. Just before they left, Liu Jinding asked: "Do you trust me, Xiaomei?" "Yes," she replied. "I will find someone for you," he said.

On the day of the official ribbon-cutting ceremony at Mei Village, Li Delin was not present. Liu Jinding deliberately didn't invite him. He was afraid that this rather murky "public-private" project wouldn't stand up to Li Delin's scrutiny. He waited until the place had been up and running for a while before inviting him for a private visit. Wang Xiaomei accompanied him throughout the occasion on that day. When Li Delin arrived, Liu Jinding asked her to take Deputy Governor Li to see the experimental wheat field. As the three of them stood on the edge of the field, Liu Jinding introduced Wang Xiaomei to Li Delin: "Our project is a joint venture, Master. This is Comrade Wang Xiaomei sent by the Meiling County Agriculture Bureau. She is also director of our test centre." Li Delin looked at Wang Xiaomei, gave a little surprised exclamation and said: "Wow!" Then, he asked casually: "How much wheat does Meiling grow in a year at the moment?"

"378,000,457.6 *mu*."

Li Delin looked at her again and said: "How many seeds are planted per *mu*?"

"In one *mu* it's about thirty-five catties."

"Ah, and what variety do you plant?"

"To the east of the city it's Meiling Number Seven, and to the west it's *Duan Bai*."

"And what is the yield per *mu*?"

"Nine hundred to twelve hundred catties. The highest Meiling Seven reaches is one thousand, three hundred and fifty-seven catties."

Li Delin glanced at her again and said: "How do you have the numbers off pat like that?" Wang Xiaomei smiled gently but didn't explain. Li Delin continued: "Well, it seems you were the right choice for director!"

What he didn't know was that Wang Xiaomei had been a statistician in the County Agriculture Bureau.

Could it have been that Wang Xiaomei had some kind of Electra complex? Maybe it was something else but whatever it was, from the first time they met, Wang Xiaomei had formed a very good impression of this gentle old man who was the deputy governor. Perhaps she was so used to seeing all those low-level Provincial Scientific Bureau chiefs drinking and shouting and gambling, that the sight of this genial governor gave her a warm glow.

When it came to lunch, of course, Liu Jinding had laid on the very best and tastiest dishes, twelve in all, six hot and six cold. Three of the cold ones were fried peanuts, braised pork knuckles and shredded kelp. These were all traditional dishes that Li Delin loved, while the other three came from abroad: sashimi shipped in by air from Japan, pork neck in savoury sauce from Thailand, and bacon and spinach quiche from France. The hot dishes were: Mei Village roasted native chicken, Mei Village duckling – Liu Jinding made it clear that the chickens and ducks were all raised in the botanical gardens, with no drugs or artificial feed – roast venison served with the penises of a dog, a bull and a deer, stir-fried lily with celery, escargots flown in from France and baked carp noodles. Because Li Delin had lived abroad, the dishes were a combination of Chinese and Western cuisine. The last dish, of course, was braised noodles.

Li Delin was in unexpectedly high spirits at lunch. Before the wine had even arrived, he said: "Let's have a couple glasses." When the fine thirty-year-old Wuliangye was served, he took the initiative and poured it himself, saying: "Let me drink your health, Director Wang! I am very happy to know the base will be in your hands." Unexpectedly, although Wang Xiaomei stood up to reply graciously to the toast, she insisted on not drinking herself. As she poured a soft drink into her glass, she explained that she was allergic to alcohol. Li Delin didn't insist and just said: "That's fine. You have your soft drink and I'll drink the wine." So saying, he drained his glass.

Then Liu Jinding picked up the wine bottle and said: "Master, first I will drink three glasses, and then I will toast you in three glasses. Then, after those three glasses, I have three things to say." Liu Jinding finished the three glasses of wine, toasted his master in three more and then said: "Master, from now on, Mei Village will be your base. No matter when you come, Director Wang will be responsible for your welcome and all your meals and accommodation. You now know that Mei Village has a spa and a sauna, and offers the equivalent of five-star service. That is the first thing. The second thing I want to say is that these service facilities have all been invested in and built by businessmen from our hometown. It is what is called 'business supporting farmers' and they are not in it for profit. But I think also that it will generate healthy and profitable outside business. What I mean to say is that Mei Village hasn't spent a cent of state money, so you can rest easy about that. The third thing is something I say on behalf of Wang Xiaomei, Director Wang. Director Wang knows that you are a nationally famous wheat expert and are the pride of our hometown. She really wants to follow you as her teacher and hopes that you will accept her."

Of course, Li Delin was happy: an experimental wheat base like this, on the banks of the Yellow River, near the provincial capital, that hadn't cost the state a cent, and had Wang Xiaomei in residence! He picked up the wine bottle and drank three more glasses, saying: "Good, Jinding! This has all been very well managed."

Liu Jinding hurriedly addressed Wang Xiaomei: "Director Wang, don't you want to pay your respects to your teacher? Won't you toast him with three glasses? Are you not sincere in your wishes?"

Wang Xiaomei stood, picked up her soft drink and walked up to Li Delin. Instead of addressing him as "Governor" like everybody else did, she just said: "Please accept my respects, Lao Li."

Liu Jinding hurriedly said: "Xiaomei, this is the governor... you... you... what do you mean by not toasting him in wine. This is bad... very bad!"

"I have already said, I am allergic to alcohol," Wang Xiaomei replied. "I really can't drink it, but I am quite sincere."

At this point, Li Delin took over the conversation and said in a conciliatory tone: "If you are sincere, that's all I need to know. I will certainly drink."

Wang Xiaomei's next words made quite an impression on Li Delin: "Don't drink too much wine, Lao Li. However, I can see the cold *qi* in your eyes, and it looks like your heart is a little congested, so I think a glass or two would be good to help free you up a bit."

Li Delin stared at her in amazement. "Oh! How do you know?"

"I just have a feeling."

Simply because of those five words, Li Delin drank two more glasses and said: "How well you seem to know me, Director Wang."

By the time the braised noodles were served, Li Delin had drunk so much that he was already tipsy. In fact, he was in a rather emotional state and he hadn't slept properly for many days. He came over dizzy and leaned his head down onto the dinner table. He kept saying: "It's all right, I'm OK, I've just had a few drinks."

Liu Jinding and Wang Xiaomei hurried to help him up and escorted him to a room to rest. To their astonishment, when they reached the door of the room, he straightened up, pushed them away and yelled: "Open the door, I, Li Delin, am from China! Open the door! I, Li Delin..." Then he collapsed in a heap on the floor.

By the time Li Delin woke up, it was already evening. He opened his eyes and saw that the curtains were closed and a small light was turned on in the room so it was in semi-darkness. A glass of soda water stood on the bedside table. His coat had been taken off, and his tie, underwear and the rest of his clothes were neatly piled on a Western-style couch beside the bed. Through a glass partition, he saw a woman sitting on a sofa in the outer room: it was Wang Xiaomei. He vaguely remembered that when he was helped to lie down on the bed, someone had wiped his face and hands with a hot towel, taken off his shoes and removed the tie from around his neck… Had he thrown up? He couldn't remember. All he knew was that he was clean now as he lay on the bed. For some reason he didn't fully understand, he suddenly burst into tears.

When Li Delin got dressed and went into the sitting room, Wang Xiaomei looked up, saw him and said: "So you're awake."

Li Delin didn't reply. He walked silently over to an upholstered armchair, sat down holding his head in both hands like a child and started crying.

Wang Xiaomei was stunned, but then something ignited a tenderness inside her. She stood up, and went over in silence and sat on the arm of the chair, cradling Li Delin's head. After a moment, she said softly: "Are you feeling any better?"

That night, when Li Delin left Mei Village before getting into the car, he couldn't help but look back at the large white building. "Yes," he told Liu Jinding. "How great it would be to have a secretary like Director Wang!"

"All you have to do is transfer her over," Liu Jinding replied.

"That wouldn't be right," Li Delin demurred.

FIVE

AT THIS POINT, Xu Ya'nan raised the possibility of divorce.

After the two of them had been separated for a long time, Xu Ya'nan developed her own ideas. She thought, since that man Li was determined not to live with her and was giving her the cold shoulder, what was the point in going on? She was still young, after all. As long as she got one million, she would agree to the divorce. But before doing so, she had to explain things to her family and sort out some plan with them so they wouldn't come off worst. So she went back to Meiling in the car, taking the baby with her.

But on the way home, as soon as she set foot in Daxuzhuang, Xu Ya'nan began to feel like a humble little girl again. She felt smaller with every step she took. She seemed to be walking herself back to the old Xu Ercai, and she even felt Xu Ercai's pitiful appearance taking her over again. She still remembered being that skinny, unsophisticated little girl. When she was young and walked through the village, her arms wrapped around her chest, no one ever greeted her, or if they did, it was just a snide shout of "Hey, Cai!"

After getting out of the car, Xu Ya'nan stood at the entrance of the village in a daze. It was the villagers who brought her back to her senses. The sunlight seemed to form a halo round her figure, and her beige dress drew admiring exclamations from everyone around.

Xu Ya'nan hadn't expected that when she returned to her family's home this time, she would be feted as never before. As soon as she drove on into Daxuzhuang, the villagers surrounded her, some calling her "Sister", some "Auntie" and some even "Great Aunt". A former best friend exclaimed in tones of the utmost envy: "How lovely you smell, Older Sister!"

In the streets up ahead, the village chief "Old Donkey Face" was running around like a startled rabbit, spraying spittle like raindrops as he kept babbling: "Hey, yeah, you're back! God, Ya'nan is back! Ai! Quick! Let me catch up! Shall we go to the village office and sit down for a while?" Then he said: "Where is the governor? Has the governor not come back too? Ah, he's busy. I know he must be busy. Lots of state business to see to! I heard that there's another war in the Middle East."

The village bookkeeper, who was nicknamed "The Shrew", was a very stand-offish kind of person. When she was a girl, she had had a secret crush on a man in military uniform. But because he had been a soldier for two years, and even been a guard in the Great Hall of the People in Beijing, he had never deigned even to acknowledge her. Anyway, at this point The Shrew came running over, very flustered. "Auntie," she said, referring to the village system of seniority, "when can you ask the governor about getting the roads in the village repaired? It would only take a word from you, wouldn't it?" Being addressed as "Auntie" almost made Xu Ya'nan burst into tears.

Immediately, all the village elders hurried forward, talking nineteen to the dozen: "You're the governor's wife Ya'nan, and you can take advantage of that. A little pillow talk and you can get anything done!"

"Give her some space and stop badgering her," Old Donkey Face said. "Let her go home first and see her old mother. She's just come home to see her parents, but she's sure to stay a bit longer."

Surrounded by the villagers, Xu Ya'nan walked unfazed down the street until she turned in through the courtyard gates, where she was met by her two sisters-in-law who rushed up to meet her and rescued the baby from the arms of the villagers. With cries of "Older Sister, Older Sister", they brought water for her to wash her face and set about cutting up a watermelon, as attentive as if they were greeting a VIP. The younger of her brothers, Wangcai, turned and shouted so as to ensure the villagers could hear: "Older Sister, have you made any arrangements for your driver? Is he going to sleep in the village head's house?"

"No need to worry about that. He's going straight back," she replied

Barely had she sat down inside before her relatives began to stream in, one after the other. Third Aunt arrived with five catties of sesame oil and kept up a barrage of compliments and polite enquiries. Of course, she didn't dare refer to Xu Ya'nan as "Cai" any more, but she didn't know what to call her instead, so she said: "Qiuqiu's mum, your nephew, your younger sister-in-law's eldest, passed the university entrance exam this year and his studies are going well, but do you think you might be able to help him?"

Before Xu Ya'nan could open her mouth, Wangcai hurriedly took over the conversation, saying: "It's just a matter of checking his marks when the time comes. You don't need to bother Older Sister with that, Sister-in-Law, I can see to it. I know the brother-in-law of the County Education director. We're drinking buddies."

When Xu Ya'nan looked at her brother, he went on: "It's true, Older Sister, really! Director Wang of the County Education Bureau wants to move on so he himself has invited me for drinks three times. When you have time, I'll also get you to drop a word in the ear of the County Party Committee secretary, Lao Tang."

Fifth Aunt's family ran a melon farm, so she brought over two sacks of watermelons. "It's nothing special," she explained, "just melons from our farm, but they're really sweet if you make them into cakes. Ya'nan, can you have a word with the people in the Town Tax Office, so they don't keep issuing tax demands all the time? It's not easy growing our melons..."

Sixth Grandpa came in, leaning on his stick, and handed over a red envelope with trembling hands, saying that it was for Qiuqiu. "I wasn't here for the last provincial homecoming party," he explained, "so I'm making up for it now. It's not much, but it is well-meant. Your fellow villager, Dongsheng, has been running a business out of town for several years. He lost his money, went a bit crazy and started taking smack. He got arrested by the Public Security but I heard that Dog Egg [Wangcai] did some bad things in the past only to get let off. Can you have a word with the county authorities, Ya'nan?"

"That's not the same thing at all, Sixth Grandpa!" Wangcai interjected. "Dongsheng is a drug dealer. That's a serious crime!"

As night fell, an old uncle from Xiaochenzhuang, eighteen *li* away, came hurrying in, carrying a large bundle of fine thread noodles. He said: "It's not been easy to get to see you, Cai! Your old aunt was very good to you when you were little. She even made you a tiger-head hat, do you remember? Now you've got somewhere, can't you find a position for your cousin, Jianqiu?"

From the moment Xu Ya'nan walked in, the house seemed to be as busy as a temple fair. The villagers came and went, one after another. Some were asking for a favour, while others had come only to confirm their status by recalling past friendships, just in case of future need. It wasn't all just self-serving sycophancy; there were elements of genuine regard and pride too. They were proud to have a "professor's wife" in the village, and of course they also wanted to keep up to date with goings-on. The countryfolk all felt that after marrying the governor, Xu Ercai had not only changed her name, she had actually become a different person. If someone as ordinary looking as Xu Ercai could marry so well, why couldn't their own daughters do the same?

Later on, the village chief Old Donkey Face brought five or six of the township cadres one at a time over to Xu's house. The cadres were very self-effacing when they went in and they all said that the only reason they had come was to pay their respects to their "sister-in-law". They didn't stay very long and when they went, they each left an envelope saying: "I don't have much to give, it's just a token." That "token" amounted to about 5,000 yuan but there was always also a

CV in the envelope. After putting down their token, they would add: "I've been a hard worker for many years. Please, Sister-in-Law, when it's convenient, pass my greetings on to County Secretary Tang." Old Donkey Face was very keyed up, and at every appropriate moment, he would say: "Don't worry, she's family. I'll keep my eye on things."

By the middle of the night, only family was left in the house, and Xu Ya'nan finally spoke out: "I've come back this time to tell you not to ask me for any more favours. I can't help any more. I have to get a divorce."

The family's faces went pale, and they looked at each other. The silence was vast and overwhelming. They all regarded her as though she was some kind of monster, as if to say: You had it made! What more do you want!

After a while, Wangcai said: "Are you crazy, Sister? Everything's going fine. What are you getting divorced for?"

Second Sister-in-Law followed up: "Sister, the whole family is counting on you. You can't get divorced!"

Her mother sighed, and said: "You've got a child! What's going to happen to him when you divorce?"

"They're right," Wangjia chipped in. "How are you going to manage? Isn't everything perfect for you at the moment?"

Her father, who was a straightforward, honest sort, just cleared his throat and said: "You've got to think this through properly. That's... isn't that so?"

"He says he'll give me a million yuan if I divorce him," Xu Ya'nan responded.

Wangcai's eyes lit up. "A million?" he said. "That's not chicken-feed! Let me think about it, let me think!"

Wangcai's wife also said: "God, one... one million! That's a lot!"

After a while, Wangcai suddenly concluded: "Don't divorce him! Take the million and don't divorce. If he wants it, he'll have to give more. Hey, wait a minute! If he's promising you money, doesn't that mean he's having an affair? That's it, Older Sister! He's got a mistress! You mustn't let him off lightly!"

Wangcai's wife concurred: "He's right! If he's willing to pay that much, there must be another woman. Has he given you the money?"

Wangjia shook his head and said: "I'm just thinking, it's not only about the money, is it?"

"You have to be patient, Sister," his wife said, "and you have to make certain."

"If you do divorce," her mother said, "the whole village is going to be gossiping about it."

"Mother is right, you absolutely mustn't divorce!" said Wangcai. "If you do, there's nothing left. A few years ago, Fifth Aunt always stood in the street outside cursing us, saying that our family stole a field from her. Now we've got some power and influence, she's like a frightened rabbit and doesn't dare say a thing! My advice is to telephone Big Brother-in-Law. He's an official too. Get him to come back here and make some kind of plan for us."

Having lived in the provincial capital for so long, Xu Ya'nan had become accustomed to looking down on people. Now, she suddenly discovered how stupid all her family members were, and how much nonsense they talked. This disappointed her, and she felt quite sure that they would never come up with any good ideas. Looking at them, she felt tears come to her eyes. Blinking them back, she said: "No, let me have another think about it."

That night, Xu Ya'nan stood alone in the courtyard for a long time. Night in the country was just as dark as ever. It was extremely hot in July, and swarms of mosquitoes swirled above. Not far away, someone was peeing copiously at the base of a wall, and the smell of urine floated back to her. Then came the sound of Father's continuous coughing. No, she was no longer accustomed to days like this, days of being bitten to death by mosquitoes.

In the middle of the night, her mother walked out of the house, stood behind her and said: "Go to bed, Cai." Xu Ya'nan said nothing. "You should decide for yourself. Don't listen to them."

After a while, Xu Ya'nan finally responded: "It's been more than six months since he shared a bed with me. He doesn't want me any more."

"Does he hate you?"

"Mother, I don't want to go on living."

"Does he hit you?"

Xu Ya'nan shook her head and said: "Do you think he'd dare?"

"As long as he doesn't hit you, you should just grin and bear it, if you can. Everyone makes their own calculations. Don't listen to anyone else. Make up your own mind. People live to keep face, but if they are not concerned with face, they can still live, just not quite as well. Now it's not easy for you to keep face, and if you lose face and people look down on you, that's going to make life difficult. If you really can't take it, if you really want to divorce, then you must go a long way away and not come back."

Finally, Xu Ya'nan said: "Go to bed, Mother."

As dawn was about to break, Xu Ya'nan quietly picked up the sleeping child and left Daxuzhuang. The night air was slowly dispersing, and the wind was a little chill. The animal heads on the roof tile ends were just visible, no longer looking quite so ferocious. The east was welcoming the dawn light, but no one else was out and about in the village. Xu Ya'nan walked away quickly, feeling very lonely.

She understood that no one could help her. The only way forward was on her own.

SIX

WITHOUT QUITE REALISING WHAT WAS HAPPENING, Li Delin fell in love with Wang Xiaomei.

Objectively speaking, Li Delin was not a greedy person. But working in the world of officialdom is like going into battle every day, just as Liu Jinding had said, and he had to hold his own. In essence, he was not a very assertive person, but on some occasions, he had no option. If you are deputy governor, every word you say may turn into an "order" or a "policy". If there is any inaccuracy or mistake, even in a single word, it may cause misunderstanding or be used as an excuse to attack you. It is a tiring business. After having to hold it all together at work, Li Delin might have hoped to be able to relax and catch his breath at home. But now, it was just like moving from one battlefield to another, as he had to be on his guard and face Xu Ya'nan's various suspicions and interrogations. It really was getting too much for him.

Everybody has an aura, but there is a huge difference between a coherent and a fragmented aura. Two people may never have met nor had any kind of communication but become enemies at first sight. Extraordinarily, when Li Delin and Wang Xiaomei met for the first time, they immediately formed good impressions of each other. When Li Delin left Mei Village on that day in question, whenever he closed his eyes, he saw the figure of a woman flashing past. That woman was small, pale and neat, with a bead of sweat on the tip of her nose and large doe eyes. Those eyes seemed to have taken root in his heart and could not be forgotten.

The love between these two people grew from silence.

To start with, Li Delin was quite content just to sit with Wang Xiaomei. Wang Xiaomei had suffered from depression, and she talked very little. If you asked a question, she would always reply, but if you didn't ask, she wouldn't speak. Even so, there was always a bead of sweat glittering on the tip of her nose, always apparently on the point of falling, but never doing so. It was like a miniature moon, or a tiny mirror, that illuminated his heart. Whenever Li Delin was upset, relaxing at Wang Xiaomei's place gradually calmed him down. What he found there could be summed up in one word: peace. So whenever he had some free time, his heart floated over to Mei Village.

At first, every time Li Delin went to Mei Village, it was at Liu Jinding's invitation. Gradually though, he started to make appointments with Liu Jinding. Later still, when the two of them agreed to meet, Liu Jinding would make some excuse for being held up somewhere, so Li Delin arrived alone. Again, to begin with, Li Delin invented reasons for his visits, such as inspecting the experimental wheat field, or discussing the specific requirements for winter sowing. But after a while, he stopped looking for excuses, and just came when he felt like it.

As general manager of Mei Village, Wang Xiaomei naturally escorted the deputy governor whenever he visited, and in the course of such contacts, the two of them drew closer together. However, they each kept this feeling of closeness to themselves and neither revealed it to the other. For one thing, Wang Xiaomei had an Electra complex, and her original husband was an alcoholic who beat her when he was drunk. She had survived all the years of being beaten, but they had left her angry and humiliated. Now here was a different sort of man: a high-ranking official, a Doctor of Biology who had studied in the United States and a nationally famous wheat expert. With such a refined man, a man with fatherly affection for her, drunk or sober, he was not going to beat or curse her. This knowledge stirred her deeply. And so the two of them just sat in silence, the light of a kind of tacit mutual understanding in their eyes. Wang Xiaomei's warm eyes were limpid as water, soothing like pain medication, and as the ancients said, they had the silent, moist gentleness of young green wheat shoots. It seemed that there was no need to say anything; everything had already been said. Each small movement, such as adding hot water to a teacup or moving an ashtray, was replete with meaning. Between the two of them, there was no need to speak, and it was as if they were communicating in whispers of dreams. How fine those whispers were!

After they had sat like this for a long time, the two finally spoke. Li Delin told her about his studies in the United States. When he mentioned his Jewish mentor and what Professor Weiner looked like as he lectured, Wang Xiaomei added, with a wry smile: "I, Li Delin, am from China."

Li Delin smiled too. "Yes, that's it. Professor Weiner waved both his hands and said: 'Louder, you have to speak louder!' He also said: 'Believe in yourself.'"

"There is a book by an American author, *The Old Man and the Sea*. Have you read it?"

"Oh, Hemingway's novel," Li Delin said. "Yes, of course I have read it."

"An old fisherman went to sea for eighty-four days and caught nothing–"

"Yes, an old man, fighting the sea and the sharks. He remained honourable in defeat."

"Although he was empty-handed, he still came back."

"Yes, he still came back," said Li Delin.

"Like the sea, quiet and sad."

"Everyone experiences failure. It's fate. Failures are like a series of punctuation marks, of commas–"

"Are they commas?"

"Yes, commas."

"Commas are good."

"You are right. They are quiet and a little sad." After a while, he added: "That's how it feels when I sit with you."

"Really?"

"Yes." Then he hurriedly corrected himself: "No, that's not quite right. It's rather that sitting with you is peaceful."

From then on, every time Li Delin finished his meetings, he

couldn't resist the opportunity to hurry over to Wang Xiaomei's place to sit quietly.

Sometimes, after sitting for a long time, Li Delin would try to shake the crick out of his neck. And sometimes his neck bones would click. Once, when she heard this, Wang Xiaomei stood up and said: "You have a problem with your cervical spine. Let me work on it for you." She stood behind him, put her hands on his neck, and started working on the acupressure points starting at the *jianjing*, and then the *dashu*, the *dazhui*, the *fengchi*, moving along them one by one. Her hand was a little bit cool and moist, first flicking, soft like a feather, then slowly getting heavier. "Is that better?" she asked.

"Better," he replied.

"Close your eyes."

Obediently, he closed his eyes, but couldn't help asking: "How do you know how to do this?"

"I studied a bit of Chinese medicine when I was ill. I used to do it for my father."

"It's very nice. You're very good."

There was nothing suggestive between them. They just sat there, and sometimes she would massage his neck. Then, one day, he caught hold of her hand.

"What's wrong?" she asked.

"Xiaomei, Xiaomei, Xiaomei..." he murmured.

She squatted down and asked: "Does it hurt?" When the two of them looked at each other, she saw that he was crying.

Wang Xiaomei sat down on the sofa and put his head between her hands. Li Delin sobbed: "Why didn't I meet you sooner?"

"You are a provincial governor, but you're still a little child at heart."

"Stupid, isn't it!"

"Yes, it is."

"Your hands are so soft, like a soldering iron."

"Is a soldering iron soft?"

"It's hot, like my heart is hot."

"I'm... a bit hot too, and so are your bones."

"Xiaomei, Xiaomei, Xiaomei, Xiaomei..."

"Don't say my name like that. It's confusing me."

"All right, I won't do it any more."

After a while, he said: "Xiao... I can't help it. Xiao, I want to kiss you."

She said nothing.

"I really—"

"What would your Jewish teacher say?"

Impulsively, he hugged her.

"Dad! Daddy, Daddy... my real Dad!"

It was very good. Two people coming together. Really good, incomparably good. This kind of goodness cannot be appreciated by others. Ignition was mutual, then slow, experimental, as little by little it flared up. Their two bodies were like ice in a fire. First they started to melt, and then they slowly came to the boil, bubble by bubble. When the heat reached a certain point, the water turned to steam, and then it finally evolved into fire. It started with a small blue flame, smoking and smouldering, and then became red, flaming red in the mists of steam. The red flame had to build up again before it could explode back into burning fire. But once it did, it was as high as the heavens and as long as the oceans. The flames were scorching and the waves were turbulent. The ancients once called this a state of "water and fire". Fire and water coming together! Despite having been married twice, Li Delin had never imagined that two people could achieve such ecstasy. And he was very surprised that there was so much water in a woman's body!

Later, Xu Ya'nan attempted to catch her husband *in flagrante*. That night, when the police broke in, Li Delin's legs shook with terror, but Wang Xiaomei seemed unusually calm. Before her divorce, she had had countless arguments and fights with her alcoholic husband, and there was virtually no kind of scene she hadn't witnessed. So she did not panic as the police came in. They were sitting together on the sofa at the time, and she just pressed Li Delin's thigh lightly and said: "Remember what your Jewish teacher said. We're not doing anything wrong, so there's no need for you to panic."

Li Delin calmed down under Wang Xiaomei's steady gaze. After the police captain led his two officers into the room, they stopped dead in their tracks and stared at Li Delin. This was a face they knew from television! For a moment, the captain didn't know what to say.

It was Wang Xiaomei who spoke first: "Officer Wu, I am making a report to Governor Li. What are you doing here?"

Captain Wu stood there looking foolish. He had never imagined that the Governor Li he had seen on television would turn out to be a little old man. He looked around in bewilderment for a moment, then hurriedly straightened his back, adjusted his police uniform and saluted Li Delin, saying: "I, er, we received a report... the report... I'm sorry, I'm really sorry... Wang... Director Wang... it's... it's all a misunderstanding. Yes, a misunderstanding."

Li Delin did not say a word. Wang Xiaomei said calmly: "Since it is a misunderstanding, you can leave now."

Captain Wu was like a headless fly. He saluted again and said: "I'm sorry, I'm really sorry. Excuse me... Excuse me." He beat a hasty retreat as he spoke. At this point, Xu Ya'nan's voice could be heard outside the door...

Neither of them spoke. They just looked at the door, waiting for Xu Ya'nan to come rushing in. Right at that moment, they suddenly found themselves in complete unity.

"Xiaomei," Li Delin said. Wang Xiaomei gave a little grunt of acknowledgement.

Li Delin looked up at her and said: "It's out of our hands at the moment."

Wang Xiaomei gazed back at him silently, then said: "It is."

"So we wait."

"Yes, we wait."

Some confused crashing noises sounded outside in the corridor. The room was quiet except for Xu Ya'nan's continuous cursing.

In the end, Xu Ya'nan did not force her way in, and she was manhandled away by Liu Jinding and others. In the middle of the night, when Wang Xiaomei left the room, she found that the corridor was quiet and deserted.

What Li Delin could never understand, however, was that no matter where his "number seven" official car went, Xu Ya'nan would appear soon after, almost as if someone was reporting on his location. He asked people from the Security Bureau to check the car over, but no tracking device was ever found.

After that, Li Delin took extra care every time he went out.

SEVEN

ONE PERSON'S PRIVATE WAR can bring a lot of suffering.

Since the separation, Xu Ya'nan had been as watchful as a cat. At night, when she was alone in the house, confused thoughts would assail her, always involving the vision of a woman in front of her eyes. In her dreams, she saw pretty and flirtatious women throwing themselves at Li Delin. She would charge them, fighting like a she-wolf as she wrestled with them and tore at their hair! When she woke up, she was lying alone on the bed, drained.

Xu Ya'nan had never studied "the art of tracking", but she learned by practical experience, and succeeded in cultivating her own "pair of eyes and ears" in the residential quarter of the University of Agricultural Science and Technology.

Those eyes and ears belonged to a recyclables collector named Zhou, who people called Xiao Zhou. In fact, Xiao Zhou was neither young nor little, being at least forty years old and fat; but he was very shrewd. He relied on a relative who was in charge of logistics at the university. He started doing odd jobs there in his teenage years, and he didn't even have a place to live to start with. At first, he made a bed in the old university air-raid shelter, and only after a while did he move above ground. First, he first built himself a small shed next to the Logistics Office warehouse, and then he became the full-time recyclables collector for the university's residential area. He had been doing this for more than two decades by this time, had brought his parents to the provincial capital, married, bought a house and had two children. Even so, people still called him Xiao Zhou. Despite being just a waste collector, he wasn't an ordinary sort of man. It was said that he practised *qigong*, wore an unlined jacket all through winter and claimed that his body was protected by "the God of Fire". For a time, he kept up a pseudo-mystical babble with his family, claiming that he had opened his "heavenly eye" and could cure disease. Whether this was true or not, it was certainly the case that a number of professors from the university asked him to "cure" them. Many times, he called on heaven to witness that he could see things hidden from ordinary mortals.

Xiao Zhou met Xu Ya'nan when he was collecting old newspapers. He always had bright eyes and a smooth tongue, and addressed everyone he met as "Teacher", no matter what their profession. Xiao Zhou went to collect old newspapers from the resources room where Xu Ya'nan was working. He had called her Teacher Xu from the first time they met. "Teacher Xu," he said, "please let me know if your house needs cleaning, and I will do it for you."

Xu Ya'nan had just sold him a bundle of old newspapers, but seeing that he was so enthusiastic, she asked: "Where do you come from?"

"Southwest of here, not far from Meiling," Xiao Zhou replied.

"Maybe we have the same home village!"

"Yes, or neighbours, at least."

"Everyone says you smell of shredded plastic, so why can't I smell it?"

"It's nonsense! I wash it off every day." It was this exchange that brought the two of them together.

Xu Ya'nan worked in the University of Agricultural Science and Technology resources room, where they kept the newspapers. With all the to-ing and fro-ing, they got to know each other quite well. What was more important was that when two people are both living their lives in the public eye, the more confidential they become with each other. It helped that Xiao Zhou spent a lot of time at the university, running around everywhere collecting what he could lay his hands on, so he was very familiar with everything that was going on, and knew all the gossip. When he saw Xu Ya'nan on one occasion, he burst out: "Teacher Xu, I saw car number seven down by the Yellow River today. Didn't you go too?"

Xu Ya'nan didn't react at first, and only later realised what he meant: the car he referred to was the one Li Delin always used. When she saw Xiao Zhou again, she asked him: "What were you doing down by the Yellow River?" Xiao Zhou said: "The truth is, I have certain powers, and when I open my heavenly eye, I can see everything." She handed him a pile of old newspapers, and said: "Really?" Xiao Zhou replied: "Do you think I'm lying? Do you know who my master is? Master Zhang Hai! The Master held three big classes at the provincial stadium, and I went to all of them. Do you know how godly my master is? He put some dead leaves in his mouth in front of everyone and held them there for less than a minute, and they all turned green. There were tens of thousands of people in the stadium and they all saw it. So that's the one I revere, Master Zhang Hai. I'm not bullshitting, he laid his hand on the top of my head... Two days ago, Vice-Principal Wang's mother-in-law was dying and I told his wife, Teacher Wu, about it. She called home and found out that the old woman was critically ill, and on her last breath. So Teacher Wu was able to get home in time." Xu Ya'nan half-believed him and said: "If you see car number seven again, tell me. I'll give you fifty yuan each time." "Yes. Ma'am."

To begin with, Xu Ya'nan adopted a "telephone tracking" method. In the evening, if Li Delin hadn't come back, she would call his driver or secretary directly and ask where he was. When she was given the address or location, she would take a taxi there and secretly check it out. But after she had done this a few times, even the driver became tight-lipped and stopped giving out the information. So Xu Ya'nan began calling the General Office of the provincial government. The staff in the General Office were always on duty, and the governor had to report when he went out. When Xu Ya'nan called the office, she would say: "I'm calling from Li Delin's home. Where did Governor Li go?" When they heard it was the governor's family, the staff on duty in the office were always very kind and would ask: "What's the matter?" Xu Ya'nan would say: "Our boy is sick, and I can't get through on the phone." The office staff immediately told her Governor Li's programme for that day, and where he was at that particular moment.

Xu Ya'nan spent many nights on the prowl. After countless phone trackings and field reconnaissances, helped by the guidance of Xiao Zhou's heavenly eye (Xu Ya'nan gave him a hundred yuan for this work), there was what they regarded as a successful case of "*in flagrante delicto*".

That night, Xiao Zhou accompanied Xu Ya'nan in a taxi and visited three locations in a row, before finding Li Delin at the Mei Village Clubhouse by the Yellow River. This convinced Xu Ya'nan of the supernatural accuracy of Little Zhou's heavenly eye, but some people said it was no coincidence that there was a large recycling centre close to the banks of the Yellow River.

First, she found car number seven in the car park, and then Xu Ya'nan quietly located luxury suite number 308 where Li Delin was staying, and booked the room opposite. Then she waited patiently.

At ten o'clock that night, Xu Ya'nan crouched beside her slightly opened door and watched a woman enter the room opposite. Then she dialled "110" on her mobile phone and said: "Come quickly, there is prostitution going on in the hotel!" When the police arrived, although they managed to force the door of the room, they were in there less than two minutes before exiting one by one in a state of considerable embarrassment.

Xu Ya'nan had been watching the proceedings, and when saw the police leaving the room and not looking back, she rushed out yelling: "Hey, why don't you arrest them? Why aren't you doing your job? Are you just going to leave it like this and go?"

The policeman in charge turned round and looked at her, asking: "Who called the police? Was it you?"

"Yes, it was," Xu Ya'nan said.

The policeman was so angry that he just glared at her for a while, before saying: "And who are you? Just what do you think you are doing? If you're not careful, I will arrest you on the spot!"

"How dare you! You won't arrest prostitutes, but you will arrest me? What's going on?"

"Who said there were any prostitutes here?" the sheriff said. "Do you know who's staying in this room? The governor!"

"He is my husband!"

The sheriff was dumbfounded: "Is that your husband sitting in there?"

"Do you think I'm faking that too?"

The sheriff stared at her in confusion, and after a long time he said: "Are you out to get someone here, Elder Sister? You can't involve us in your personal affairs. How can there be any question of prostitution going on over there? That's Director Wang making a report to Governor Li. It's just work. They're properly dressed and it's all above board."

"I don't believe it." She rushed over to the other room like a mad woman, kicking the door and shouting: "You bastard! You bitch! Come the fuck out of there!"

The sheriff grabbed her and tried to stop her, saying: "Please think of us, Elder Sister! This isn't easy for us either. We could get into trouble."

But Xu Ya'nan continued to ignore him and stood screaming and cursing in the corridor for more than an hour. Finally, Liu Jinding came hurrying over, called in both Li Delin's secretary and the driver, and forcibly persuaded her to leave.

For the rest of that night, room 308 was quiet, with not a sound coming from it.

Another night, sometime after, Xu Ya'nan dragged Li Delin out of his study and spent the whole night interrogating him: "Tell me then, did you play away that night? Did you sleep with her? How many times?"

She was using the word "sleep" deliberately, and Li Delin knew she wouldn't let him close his eyes unless he answered her. Thus, the whole night became an exercise in self-justification for Li Delin. With repeated interrogation, she succeeded in turning a deputy governor into a "dishonest witness". In the course of Li Delin's tortuous self-justification, she also found herself transformed from a "neurotic" into someone sitting in judgment. It was an extremely important conversation, as it allowed her to take the moral high ground. She kept on and on at him, making him go over the details time and time again, right through to dawn, when Li Delin couldn't stand it any more and finally said: "Yes, I slept with her, I slept with her!"

"You mean you fucked her?"

"Yes," Li Delin whispered despairingly.

During a meeting the next day, Li Delin suddenly fainted on the podium and was taken to hospital. This was the *nongkou* meeting, and Liu Jinding was also there. Later, he went to the hospital to visit Li Delin, who had been rehydrated with several infusions of fluids. Liu Jinding said: "Teacher, you scared me. You have to be more careful!"

Because there were others present, Li Delin said: "It's OK, I'm just a little tired. I haven't been sleeping well."

Unfortunately, Xu Ya'nan's hatred had taken root in her heart and she wouldn't let the matter drop. After that, whenever she had the opportunity, she would "interrogate" him again and again. Over the long nights, she finally completed the leap from "serf" to "feudal lord". In this regard, every interrogation was a part of her spiritual growth. She stood there, with none of her previous cautiousness, none of the psychological humility of the first-time babysitter. From all this she came to understand a basic truth: once a person breaks free, once they grasp the "truth", they no longer have anything to fear.

It is not good for a person to have shortcomings. Once Xu Ya'nan had grasped the nature of Li Delin's shortcomings, she began to feel better, her attitude became calmer and her mouth became more eloquent. Once you have made the discovery, you can use it as many times as you like to discomfort the other party... She would often stand in front of Li Delin, firmly occupying the moral high ground, holding aloft the banner of morality, and sentence by sentence, taking him apart from top to bottom, from inside to out. She ripped him to shreds. In the marital home, her victory was complete. On one particular occasion, she even succeeded in making Li Delin kneel down in front of her.

"I can no longer be considered a man," he said. "I was in the wrong."

EIGHT

ON THE EIGHTEENTH DAY after Xu Ya'nan "caught him in the act", Li Delin asked Liu Jinding to come out to Mei Village.

It was room 308 again. With just the two of them there, Li Delin wept. He said: "Jinding, you know me as well as anyone and I have to tell you that I can't go on like this any more. Every day seems like a whole year. This woman is so evil, she tortures me every night."

Li Delin went straight to the nub of the matter, and asked, in rather formal tones: "So what do you think we should do?" He sounded as though he was chairing a meeting in the governor's office.

"Do you remember the 'dog skin plasters' they used to sell in the countryside in the old days, Master?" Liu Jinding said. "You couldn't take them off without making the wound bleed again. This matter is similar in that it's both easy to handle, and difficult too. It's up to you to make up your mind."

"My mind is made up. Now, explain."

"As long as you are determined, nothing is impossible."

"Be specific."

Liu Jinding looked out the window and said: "If money will work, then it's no problem at all."

Li Delin shook his head and said: "No, she's insatiable as far as money goes. There's no way."

"It seems that this woman has really got above herself. What is she anyway? Just a jumped-up nanny! So we could get Chief Jiang find a couple of men to 'deal' with her."

Li Delin was taken aback: "'Deal with her' how?"

"At the beginning of the year, wasn't there a woman who was abducted and trafficked up in the mountains? If you have her taken up into the mountains, you won't see her again in this lifetime."

Li Delin considered this for a moment, and then said firmly: "No, that won't do."

"Well, there is another way..."

"Go on, spit it out!"

"There's a mental hospital in Linping, and I know a deputy director. Take her there and have them hold her for eighteen months or so. If she isn't crazy to start with, she will be by the end. It's much easier to manage things if she's crazy."

Li Delin fell silent for a while, before saying: "No, I can't do that. It's not seemly."

"Chronic pain is much worse than temporary discomfort, Master! Then there is only one thing for it... see her off."

Li Delin was taken aback again and said: "'See her off' how?"

At this point, both of them fell silent. The words "see her off" hung in the air, making the room feel very sombre. They both knew what was meant here, but they didn't voice it. Finally, Liu Jinding said: "Does she have any hobbies?"

Li Delin was in a state of considerable distress by now. "Well, it's hard to say. I can't think of anything..."

"Does she like swimming, for example?" Liu Jinding asked. "If she likes swimming, we can find a reservoir and take her for a swim. There are a lot of weeds in a reservoir for legs to get tangled in."

Li Belin was looking paler and paler as the conversation went on. He shook his head and said: "That's no good, I'm done with it."

"I heard she wants to go to Hainan for a holiday. There are so many car accidents now... right?"

Li Delin's face changed, and he murmured: "This... this... none of this is appropriate. No matter what. There's the child too. It's not appropriate."

Finally, Liu Jinding said: "Teacher, let's think in the long-term then. As long as you make up your mind, there is always a way."

"My head hurts, it really hurts! Let's talk about this another time."

That evening was the last occasion the two of them ate braised noodles. They ordered four side dishes: cucumber salad, deep-fried peanuts, cold kelp shreds and pork belly slices in chilli oil. This time there was no wine and the noodles were served in small bowls. When the noodles were brought, Li Delin put down his chopsticks and suddenly said: "I don't want to eat any more."

Liu Jinding looked at him and said: "Shall I get them to bring a bowl of millet porridge? It'll be just as quick."

"Forget it, I've got no appetite," Li Delin said, before adding: "I never used to eat lamb. When I was little, just the smell of it made he sick. I even felt like vomiting when I heard the word 'lamb'. I hated the rancid smell. I started eating it in the late seventies, after going to university. I was poor back then and couldn't afford to eat anything else. So when I was hungry, my only option was a bowl of mutton-stewed noodles out on the street. Then I got addicted to them, and I felt that mutton wasn't so bad, after all."

"Yes, I didn't eat mutton before either, but once I tried it, I kept on eating it too."

"People change."

"It's society that is changing."

Finally, Li Delin said quietly: "If there is a way, it can't be too extreme."

"There is always a way. Sometimes, you only find it after you have set out."

They didn't say "see her off" any more, but the words remained in their heads and stuck in their throats so they couldn't eat a mouthful of noodles. Li Delin had been smoking at the dinner table and he coughed repeatedly. Afterwards, he stood up and walked to the window. Outside, in the light of the setting sun, a shapely woman was walking along the edge of the test field. The woman's silhouette swayed gracefully as she walked. He knew it was Wang Xiaomei. She appeared very elegant, glowing red and fairy-like.

Li Delin looked at her blankly for a while, then turned around, pinched out his cigarette, and said: "It has to be done. You must help me figure out how."

That night, when they were together, Wang Xiaomei suddenly announced: "Lao Li, I don't want to work here any more."

Li Delin looked at her and asked: "What's wrong?" Wang Xiaomei didn't reply, so he went on: "Did someone say something?"

"No, not that, but..."

Li Delin embraced her and said: "Xiaomei, this is how we are, what else is there to say?"

"Nothing else. I just want to stay with you. Just the two of us, in peace and quiet... But, don't you feel it? There are always eyes behind us, watching. Even the waiters look at us oddly and it makes me very uncomfortable." After a while, she said: "We can't live with those eyes always watching us." That was it really, women just want to be able to live a normal life.

Li Delin pondered for a moment and said: "There will be a solution."

Two months later, Xu Ya'nan suddenly disappeared.

Subsequently, Li Delin realised that there were some roads that really shouldn't be travelled. Considering them had just been a passing aberration.

---

1. "Stone girl" refers to the medical condition hypoplastic vagina, the formation of a membrane across the entrance that makes intercourse impossible

CHAPTER FIVE

ONE

HELIAN DONGSHAN WAS READY TO RETIRE. But as a division-level investigator who had been both rewarded and disciplined, he hadn't really thought about what to do or where to go after retirement.

The set of keys was still on the cabinet. Even so, he had repeatedly rejected his wife's suggestion. He said that he would never go to see that rebellious son with the internet handle, the "Overlord of Western Chu". His son was now the technical director of an internet company in Beijing, with an annual salary of 300,000 yuan.

"There's nothing wrong with Beijing, or the apartment. You go if you want to." That was what he said, but his wife came back at him: "Then we will be living apart in future." Helian Dongshan responded: "If we live apart, then we live apart. At our age, there's nothing odd about that." "And who is going to cook for you?" "You're not going to get the better of me like that," Helian Dongshan replied. "I can always go out and eat someplace or other." Despite his brave words, he still felt a little empty at the prospect.

Helian Dongshan was approaching his fifty-ninth birthday, according to the lunar calendar, as a "second-tier" member of staff. As he was once more moving out all his stuff and handing back the key to the main office that he shared with other members of the squad, Helian Dongshan received a call. It was from the Provincial Public Security Bureau, and it ordered him to report to the director of the Bureau by three o'clock that afternoon.

Helian Dongshan was a little confused after taking the call. He thought to himself: Would the director really want to talk to a mere local public security cadre who was on the verge of retirement? No, no way!

But in the public security system, an order is an order, and there was no point questioning it. Helian Dongshan arrived at the provincial offices fifteen minutes early. Inside the building of the Provincial Public Security Bureau, he bumped into a few acquaintances as he made his way along the corridors. They greeted him enthusiastically: "What are you doing here, Lao He?" "Following orders!" he replied. "The director wants to see me." His friends just nodded and didn't press him. He looked for any clues in their expressions, but he didn't see anything.

At five past three, a secretary took him straight into the director's office. The director's name was Qiao. He had a square face, was a little on the fat side and had a rather dignified air about him. He had been parachuted into the local area from the Ministry of Public Security a year ago. Helian Dongshan had seen him only once at a conference, when he was sitting on the podium. The director shook hands with him enthusiastically and said: "Comrade Dongshan, right?"

"That's right."

"Sit down."

The two sat down on the sofa, and Director Qiao continued: "How is your health?"

"It's OK."

"I heard you are a heavy smoker, so light up if you want."

Helian Dongshan smiled but was too embarrassed to take up the offer.

"We have met each other before," Director Qiao continued.

Helian Dongshan was taken aback. "Really? I–"

"Have you forgotten? Ten years ago, the Ministry of Public Security invited you to give a lecture about interrogation techniques. I went specifically to hear you and sat in the back row. You said something I have always remembered very clearly. You said: 'A criminal won't meet your gaze, and he hates being stared at. By the time he has lied three times, he is bound to have given himself away.' That was very well said."

Helian Dongshan was a little embarrassed, and just shook his head and smiled.

Director Qiao turned to look at him and asked: "Lao He, this year you–"

"I'm almost sixty, and it's time for me to retire."

"No, I have seen your file. You're fifty-eight."

"That's according to the solar calendar. My birthday on the lunar calendar is–"

"You're an old policeman. You have worked hard for thirty-five years and solved many major cases. For such comrades, there are organisational considerations that come into play." The director stood up, poured him a glass of water, and then continued: "The Departmental Party Committee has looked into this and been in communication with the top-level Organisational Department. The department has work for you, and wants to transfer you over and give you deputy departmental-level rank."

Helian Dongshan was stunned.

"If you don't have any questions, hurry up and report in. There is a case they want to hand over to you."

Helian Dongshan sat bolt upright.

"This case is of great importance," Director Qiao explained. "I won't say much about the specific circumstances. Deputy Director Wan, who is in charge of the criminal investigation, will talk to you."

Ten minutes later, Helian Dongshan left the director's office. At the end of the corridor, he went into the bathroom, took out his cigarettes, looked out of the window and smoked two in a row. His mind was a blank, and he had yet to gather his wits.

Originally, he had thought this was going to be a routine conversation before his retirement. Now, unexpectedly, at this late stage in his life, he was being promoted to deputy departmental level. As the saying goes, there is always an exception to the rule, and this could only be regarded as an unprecedented exception. More important, there was a big case waiting for him to take over. So then, what kind of case was it?

He had already pulled himself together by the time he walked into the office of Deputy Director Wan. The word "case" had got him excited all of a sudden, and every cell in his body tingled. He had previously worked for Deputy Director Wan, who had been transferred to the Provincial Department five years ago and was now executive deputy director of criminal investigation. When people know each other well, they are less inclined to stand on ceremony. As soon as Helian Dongshan was through the door, Deputy Director Wan threw a pack of cigarettes to him and said: "I bet you're gasping. Go ahead. Light up."

Helian Dongshan took a cigarette from the pack, sniffed it and said: "It smells a bit rancid."

"Can't be! You smoke so much, you can't tell the difference any more!"

When the two of them had sat down, Helian Dongshan said: "Well, boss, it was you who sent the orders, wasn't it?"

"That's right."

"I guessed it was your doing."

Deputy Director Wan looked at him, and after a while, he said: "Do you remember the word I left you with six years ago?"

"What word?"

"Surely you haven't forgotten. I said: 'Wait!'"

Helian Dongshan remembered. Yes, in the middle of the night, because of that business with Xiao Xing, he had barged into Wan's house... "Yes, then you announced my punishment the next day."

"You got off lightly. If I hadn't stepped in like that, you could have been stripped of your uniform."

"The boss is always the boss. And you've always had reason for what you say."

"Then let me give you something else to remember. In the great scheme of the things, there's no point in getting cute with the little stuff."

"Yes, good, that I can understand. Now, when can we get together in private?"

Deputy Director Wan frowned and immediately turned serious: "Let's get down to business for now. There is a case on, and you're in charge of forming a capable team to investigate it. Listen carefully and make sure you understand. One-on-one, you answer to me, I answer to Director Qiao, and he answers to the Provincial Party Committee."

Helian Dongshan's nerves tensed immediately, and he asked: "How big is the case?"

Deputy Director Wan handed him a stack of material in a portfolio and said: "It's not clear yet. The only indication so far is that Deputy Governor Li Delin's wife is missing. The size of the case will only become clear once we start investigating."

"Are you having me on, boss? The governor's wife–"

"Do I look like I'm joking?" Deputy Director Wan said. "Any Provincial Public Security Office that couldn't solve a case like this would get shut down in a flash. Now do you understand why I've had you transferred in?"

Their eyes met. Helian Dongshan leaped to his feet and threw Deputy Director Wan a salute, saying: "I understand!"

"Deputy Provincial Governor Li Delin is currently on a course at the Central Party School. You are responsible not just for investigating this case, but also for guaranteeing his personal safety."

"Guaranteeing?"

"That's what I said."

"But what, exactly, do you mean by it?"

"Just what I say."

"By any means available?"

"Subject to formal approval, yes."

Two days later, Helian Dongshan took up his new post. As the person in charge of the task force, he named this case "Project Number One".

TWO

NEVER IN A HUNDRED YEARS could Helian Dongshan have imagined that when his son grew up, he would become an "arms dealer".

After Helian Xichu went to college, he escaped Papa Blade's surveillance. He was a like a bird released from its cage, soaring freely amid the clouds, or like a fish that has shaken free of the angler's hook and swum off into the wide blue sea. In the virtual world, he was free to become the "Overlord".

Helian Xichu had been selling "arms" since he was in his second year of college. To begin with, he didn't want to sell anything; indeed, he hadn't even given it a thought. In the virtual world, "equipment" could be sold for real money but it was only when he became acquainted with "Old Cat" on the internet, that he was catapulted into the international scene. It was also then that he discovered the vast scale of the global internet.

There is an invisible thread that connects hundreds of millions or even billions of young people in cyberspace. Old Cat was a big name in the world of computer gaming, but at this stage, he/she and the Overlord of Western Chu did not know each other; they were just two domain names in virtual space. Old Cat had met with stubborn resistance when he/she took on the *Devil's Realm*. For five days in a row, they used all the equipment available but could not get past the

Xuantian Gate level. So Old Cat posted an urgent request for help on the internet: "Hi everybody. I am offering a seven-day holiday in Phuket to anyone who can help me get past the fifth level of *Devil's Realm!*"

Old Cat's post generated thousands of "likes", but few dared take it on. This was when the Overlord of Western Chu took up the challenge. He broke through the barrier at three in the morning, and sent the information on how to get the necessary equipment to Old Cat in a QQ message the same night. However, even after receiving the offer, the Overlord of Western Chu refused the reward of the holiday in Phuket. He knew that even though they were nine hundred kilometres apart, the eyes of Papa Blade were still on him.

Partly thanks to Old Cat's endorsement, the Overlord of Western Chu became famous in the gaming world, and he gained a fan-base of his own. From all across the world, his followers gathered like clouds, and he began to acquire an international sphere of influence. It is also because of Old Cat's recommendation that further requests for help flooded in. As a result, he began to sell weapons for all sorts of computer games to his followers. In a short period of time, he sold everything: "electron gun", "laser cannon", "immortal-tethering rope", "heaven-and-earth pouch" and "the seventy-two mystical transformations". When he was in his fourth year at university, a gaming software development company approached him with the offer of a job as technical director.

What is even more extraordinary is that, with that one encounter, Old Cat actually fell obsessively in love with the Overlord of Western Chu. Every day, early in the morning, she would send a message on QQ: "Hey, Ace, are you asleep? Miss you." The Overlord of Western Chu would reply: "Me2." The to-and-fro between them had developed across cyberspace, starting with conversations about "equipment" until, finally, the talk turned to love. By this time, the Overlord of Western Chu had discovered that Old Cat was, in fact, a great beauty living in Hong Kong. She sent the Overlord of Western Chu glamour shots of herself in various poses by email, and she asked him from time to time: "Are my tits big enough? Do you want to touch them?" So, on the initiative of Old Cat, the two of them began to communicate every night by private message.

The online love affair between the Overlord of Western Chu and Old Cat lasted for 279 days. They talked about everything over QQ...

Cat: GG, I miss you. Kiss me, come on and kiss me!

Wang: Me2, me2.

Cat: My dad introduced me to some stick-in-the-mud the day before yesterday and wanted me to see him. I said No!

Wang: Who is your father?

Cat: My dad sells pharmaceuticals. I call him "Old Poison". What about you?

Wang: Me? My old man is a detective. I call him "Blade".

Cat: Haha, Blade! Did he hurt you?

Wang: Has Old Poison hurt you?

Cat: Bah! Old Poison sells quack cures. Nowadays, all medicines that say they cure cancer are fake. He's got lots of money and been married three times. My mother got pissed off with him... Sometimes, I can't wait to kill him. What about you?

Wang: Q.

Cat: Wow, does he still hit you? Does he use a belt?

Wang: QQ.

Cat: Wow, let's double up and hit back! I'm so sad for you. According to international law, you can sue him. You should sue him!

Wang: Some time...

Cat: Me2.

Wang: They don't have any idea of "self", and they never had any "self" of their own. They are screws, and he wants to turn me into one himself.

Cat: Screw? What's a screw?

Wang: Screws are things that are fixed to the machine. A screw doesn't have any self.

Cat: Too right. What age are we living in? We want to live our own lives. So I don't see him any more. As long as he pays off the credit card, I treat him like a petty tyrant.

Wang: Yes, I haven't gone home the last four vacations.

Cat: What does "Blade" mean?

Wang: Pure poison. He interrogates prisoners.

Cat: A cop, right? Treats everyone like a criminal?

Wang: To a cop, everyone's a criminal. We were in the park once, the first time he took me to the park, and he suddenly ran over and handcuffed someone.

Cat: That's so scary. He's an old monster. Sounds like we're the same, GG. Do you hate him?

Wang: I hate him. But I got away in the end. His generation think people are born to endure hardship. This is no longer the age of screws, so why should we? Why can't people just live happily?

Cat: Too right! I'm with you. If you're not happy, you might as well be dead!

That last sentence from Old Cat turned out to be prophetic. Old Cat and the Overlord of Western Chu agreed on the internet to meet in Beijing at noon on Valentine's Day that year. However, on 11 February, there was a lot of snow in Beijing, and on the same day, three days before Valentine's Day, Old Cat died in front of a computer desk in a rented property in Kowloon, Hong Kong. Her cramped accommodation was stuffed with piles of goods purchased online, including 371 items of clothing and 176 pairs of shoes, none of which had ever been worn. When her family found her, she was emaciated, severely dehydrated and in a semi-comatose state. It was reported that Old Cat's last words before she died, were: "It's really interesting."

Three days after the Overlord of Western Chu and Old Cat lost contact, he saw a news item published on the internet in a Hong Kong newspaper: "The daughter of a pharmaceutical factory owner, whose online name was Old Cat, died suddenly at her computer. She was only twenty-three years old when she died." He was shocked and saddened when he saw the news. He spent a thousand game coins to buy Old Cat a wreath on the internet, then he went to bed and slept for three days.

When Helian Xichu woke up, he turned on the computer and found that from New York to the Caribbean, from Tokyo to Beijing, there were thousands of fan posts pouring in, and loads of "likes", all talking about a new version of *Farewell My Concubine*. At that moment, Helian Xichu felt incredibly sad. Sitting at his computer desk, he suddenly felt lonelier than ever before. Something he did not understand prompted him to call home. He had not been home for three years. His mother answered and greeted him happily: "Son, you finally called. Is something wrong? Are you short of money?" Helian

Xichu replied: "No, no, nothing's wrong. Are you OK? He..." "Your father isn't here," his mother said. "If he ever dares to sever ties with you, I will sever ties with him. So tell me, are you short of money? I'll send you some right away." Helian Xichu said: "It's OK, it's just that... I miss you." Han Shufang's eyes filled with tears.

That word "he" was the first time Helian Xichu had mentioned his father to his mother in years. After the death of Old Cat, he suddenly remembered a lot of things from the past about Papa Blade, and the hatred in his heart dissolved. His father was getting older by the day, and he wanted to talk to him on the phone, but he simply couldn't say it... just the word "he" that he did manage could have been the start of so many different things that, inevitably, his mother misunderstood.

Han Shufang missed her son so much. The next day, she bought a train ticket and made her way to Beijing to see him. They were together for two days. Han Shufang didn't know about her son's shattered love. When she saw him, she found that he had grown into an adult. She was so happy every day, she found herself jogging everywhere rather than walking.

Helian Xichu took his mother to see the Forbidden City, the Summer Palace, Tiananmen Gate, the Great Hall of the People... he even took her to eat at the Moscow Restaurant. The magnificence of the Russian-style restaurant frightened Han Shufang, and she kept asking: "Son, isn't this too expensive? Shouldn't we go somewhere else?" Helian Xichu said: "You may not get another chance and the Western food here is famous. Let's eat. It's OK." Han Shufang countered: "Then don't order anything expensive. Let's just try a couple of dishes." Her son tried to set her mind at ease: "Really, it's not expensive."

He arranged everything, so Han Shufang got to taste the foie gras, caviar, borscht, steak and Western desserts that her son ordered... and finally a bottle of red wine. Han Shufang was apprehensive about everything, and asked: "What's this black stuff that looks like millet?" "Caviar. Try it!" Han Shufang took a bite and almost spat it out, saying: "This Western food is awful. It just tastes fishy." She had heard that the bread was free, so she dipped some slices in honey and ate them instead. When they had finished, as she was going to the toilet, she took the opportunity to secretly buttonhole a waitress wearing a red cap and a white dress and asked: "What is the bill for table number seven?" The waitress said: "Table number seven? Two thousand eight hundred." Han Shufang was astounded and muttered: "Two thousand eight hundred for a few slices of bread!"

Han Shufang brought six thousand yuan with her to Beijing to give to her son. To her, this was a large sum of money, but here he was spending nearly half that amount on a single meal! It was really a bit... a bit... but then, what could she really say, when her son's heart was broken?

Han Shufang was a simple, kind-hearted woman, and usually not much of a thinker. But after she got back from Beijing, she gradually began to remember things. In the course of the two days she spent in the capital, she had gone into her son's bedroom and found that he had a brand-new computer, complete with headphones, a camera and stereo speakers. It all looked very advanced. Her son's bed and computer desk were covered in all sorts of food and drink, including coffee, nuts and sweet snacks. All the packaging was in different foreign languages... and the prices were astronomical. The money they sent him for tuition, accommodation, food and miscellaneous expenses was quite limited, so where was all this extra money coming from?

Naturally she didn't share her suspicions with Helian Dongshan. Only once, when the two of them were chatting before going to bed, she couldn't help but ask: "Did you secretly send money to your son?"

Helian Dongshan froze and said: "No, you control all the household money, don't you?"

Han Shufang didn't sleep well that night. She was really worried that her son was up to something illegal. Later, while Helian Dongshan was on a business trip, she quietly went back to Beijing. When she asked him about the money, and he told her the explanation, all her worries were put to rest, and she went back home very happy.

When Helian Dongshan came back from his business trip, Han Shufang said: "You need to change your attitude, old man!"

"What do you mean?"

"You should stop looking down on your son. He's only in his senior year, and he hasn't even graduated yet, but he's already got a job in a software company. Guess what the salary is!"

Helian Dongshan grunted and asked off-handedly: "How much, then?"

"Three hundred thousand yuan," she replied angrily.

"How much?"

"Didn't you hear me clearly? One, two, three, three hundred thousand."

"Nonsense! You must have gone mad!"

"I've read the contract. It's an annual salary of three hundred thousand yuan, plus housing subsidies, travel expenses..."

Helian Dongshan's ears hummed, and he felt a tingling pain in his chest, as if something had broken inside him. He had worked all his life to reach his current position, with a monthly salary of only three thousand five hundred, plus subsidies. His son had been an unrepentant gamer since he was little and had been beaten for it countless times. Now here he was, "playing" for 300,000 yuan a year!

Who could tell him what that was all about!

THREE

As soon as the "Number One Project Task Force" was established, a suspicious mobile phone message was discovered.

Using certain specialised criminal investigation methods, Helian Dongshan discovered the existence of an unusual mobile phone message near Dayouzhuang, in the Haidian District of Beijing, about thirty metres from the residential compound where Deputy Governor Li Delin was staying. After investigation, it was found to have come from an unregistered one-off SIM card, obviously not belonging to Li Delin. After Li Delin reported his wife's disappearance, the same signal appeared twice in the vicinity of the Central Party School where Li Delin was on a course. So if it was a kidnapping case, what else was going on behind the scenes? Was Li Delin also in danger?

Following his superiors' instructions, and because the safety of a deputy governor was at stake, Helian Dongshan flew to Beijing overnight with two detectives from the Criminal Police Corps. He wanted to personally check the location for any suspicious characters.

After Helian Dongshan took his men to book into a hotel near the Central Party School, the three of them went to check out the place. They discovered that it was set amid beautiful scenery: the

Summer Palace to the north, the Old Summer Palace to the east and Yuquan Mountain to the rear. Although it was close to those tourist attractions, with a lot of people coming and going, the campus itself was spacious, elegant and quiet. The buildings were antique, and there was a solemn, peaceful, cultured atmosphere. The site management was very strict, keeping it isolated from the public outside the campus. After looking at the lie of the land and getting a feel for the surroundings, Helian Dongshan got in touch with the local public security, and ascertained that it was a joint public security operation that was relaxed on the outside and tight on the inside. Helian Dongshan understood that there would be no security issues there. But what was going on with that abnormal mobile phone signal?

Helian Dongshan hesitated about whether to meet Li Delin in person. As the deputy governor of an inland province, Li Delin insisted on continuing with his course at the Central Party School after he had reported the case. The three-month training course was coming to an end, and Helian Dongshan was uncertain if this was an appropriate time to seek him out.

Helian Dongshan had always harboured some doubts about this case. He had met Li Delin twice and had formed a favourable impression of him. It was said that he had a good reputation in official circles, regardless of affiliation, and received unanimous praise. He was also an acknowledged wheat expert, and his affinity with ordinary people was incomparably greater than that of most other officials, to the extent that he was known in the media as the "governor in the straw hat". Such a person has few enemies. Who was he going to offend? If this was a question of ransom, there were many much richer targets; any entrepreneur had more money than him. Who would kidnap the wife of a deputy governor? Unless it was by mistake, or...

After giving it some thought, Helian Dongshan decided to take the opportunity when in Beijing to see Li Delin. If he could get a feel for him and understand some of his wife's situation, it would not be time wasted. But when, with enormous difficulty and taking advantage of the lunch hour, they finally managed to arrange an appointment with him, Li Delin suddenly took offence. As soon as Li Delin walked into the hotel room, he was clearly livid. His eyes were staring, his lips trembled and he shouted: "Do you know where you are? Beijing, our capital city! Do you know where I am studying? The Central Party School! This is outrageous! Imagine bringing your shame to Beijing like this! It is not just me you are embarrassing, it is our whole province! What are you doing here? What do you want?"

The officer standing beside him whispered: "Governor Li, I er... we are... that is, we want to understand the situation."

Li Delin really didn't want to answer, so he banged the table and said: "What situation? I've been here for the last three months, what do I know about any situation? I should be asking you! So go on, you tell me! Just what, exactly, have you achieved? Have you found her?"

It was all very embarrassing, and looking extremely uncomfortable, Helian Dongshan gestured at his companions and said: "You two can leave now."

The two policemen put away their notebooks and quietly left the room.

Helian Dongshan took out a pack of cigarettes from his pocket, handed one to Li Delin and lit it. After that, he lit one for himself and inhaled. Neither of them spoke.

Li Delin was sitting in a chair. He took a few drags on his cigarette, then let it burn down. When it was almost out, he took another one and lit it.

Helian Dongshan looked at Li Delin in silence. As he did so, there was a trace of pity in his heart, and even a touch of self-recrimination for his failure to fulfil his duty. This was, after all, a ministerial cadre and a deputy governor. His wife had disappeared and her whereabouts were still unknown. No matter who was responsible, this was a serious business. He had to be absolutely sure of any accusations he levelled at anyone.

As a consequence, he sat there, almost paralysed. It was his emotions that froze him. He could just imagine what these last few days had been like for Li Delin. Although the governor's hair was neatly combed, it was white at the temples. The wrinkles on his forehead were deeply grooved like earthworm trails, and dark spots marked his forehead, indicating some serious endocrine disorder. It was obvious how tormented he was. He was sitting there listlessly, like an empty clothes rack. Also, the insides of his first two fingers were stained dark brown with nicotine. Helian Dongshan's experience told him the man must be smoking at least three packs a day. The man sat there, staring blankly, moist-eyed and looking very depressed.

Suddenly, Helian Dongshan heard Li Delin start to mutter to himself, but to begin with, he couldn't understand what he was saying. After a while, he could just make out a few words. He seemed to be saying to himself: "When the wheat is yellow, there is no sound, and when the hair is grey, there is no sound either. Why should I believe it?"

Helian Dongshan couldn't make sense of this. He didn't know where the man's thoughts had taken him, and it certainly wasn't the right time to try to follow him there. But what he did know was that, just for the moment, Deputy Governor Li's mood had become more settled. So Helian Dongshan simply said: "Governor Li, the main reason we are here now is for your own safety..."

Li Delin quickly seemed to have returned to normal. "I'm sorry, I was a little irritable just now, and spoke rather harshly. Please forgive me."

"I understand," Helian Dongshan replied, before continuing tentatively: "We discovered an unknown mobile phone signal in your vicinity, so we are worried about your safety."

"Is that so? Surely it can't be anything to do with me. There are mobile phone signals flying around all over the place. Are you sure you are not mistaken?"

"We are looking into it."

Li Delin made a little "Oh" sound, looked at his watch, stood up and walked away, saying: "I'll be going home soon. If there is anything to talk about, we can do it when I get back. I've got classes this afternoon." On reaching the door, he suddenly turned around and said: "How you investigate is your business. But I'll leave you with the old saying: let the living see to the living and the dead see to the dead."

Helian Dongshan stood to attention and said: "Yes, sir."

Li Delin walked away. Helian Dongshan stood at the window and watched his retreating figure. His gait was firm enough, but the path he took was a little erratic. Helian Dongshan saw a man in his fifties, with his grey hair being blown about by the wind. He tried to smooth it down with his hands from time to time, but couldn't get it to stay. Altogether he cut a rather sorry figure. He walked along in the sun, alone, looking rather forlorn. As he was about to go in through the door of the Central Party School, he stood, hesitating for a couple of seconds, gazing at something... and then quickly walked in.

Helian Dongshan's doubts were not resolved after meeting Li Delin. He still felt that there was something he didn't understand. At that moment, a call came from the Provincial Office. There was news from the family task force: after contacting China Mobile and China Unicom as part of a blanket telecommunications check, they had found the place where the single-use unregistered SIM card was purchased. It was Huanghuai City. It was then that Helian Dongshan understood why he had been given the case.

That evening, after the three policemen had analysed the information together, Helian Dongshan ordered the others: "We're going back now. Immediately! Back to Huanghuai."

One of the policemen who came with him said: "If we go now, there are no flights to Huanghuai, and train number two-three-three is sold out. We'll have to take the one-seven-nine."

"We'll take the one-seven-nine then." He looked at his watch and said: "You go and get something to eat. We've still got four of five hours in hand. I've got some private business to see to."

FOUR

HELIAN DONGSHAN HAD A SUDDEN DESIRE to see his son.

The pair hadn't exchanged a word for six or seven years and they were like strangers to each other. His son was really nothing to him, and in the eyes of his son, he was an old blade that had long ago been discarded.

In fact, what was making him most uncomfortable was that his son had now become a big player in the gaming industry. What was this Overlord of Western Chu business and what did it mean? Still, a son is a son in the end, and as a father, he was responsible. And now he was in Beijing, especially after that meeting with Li Delin, somehow, he wanted to see his son.

His son had graduated a long time ago, and his company was on a street in the Zhongguancun area. He had also bought an apartment in a prime location nearby. He had learned from his wife that the boy was in pain and broken-hearted after a doomed love affair. Apparently, it was a Hong Kong girl he had met on the internet. He also heard his wife say that these days lots of girls were chasing after their son. His wife added that the boy was still bewildered and unsettled. He really couldn't understand that this prodigal son who played games had actually become a hero of the age and that girls were fighting over him. It was all really strange and he wanted to see it for himself.

Helian Dongshan hailed a taxi at the intersection and travelled to Zhongguancun. He got out of the car nearby and called the number of his son that he had found in his wife's notebook on the table. He sounded a bit unsure of himself as he said: "Do you live near Zhongguancun? I'm here on a business trip. Let's meet up if we can." His son seemed more expansive than him, as he replied: "Yes, very close. I'm behind a big hotel. Turn the corner and it's Xiangheyuan Compound, Building Eight, Unit Three. I'll meet you at the door." "No, I've got a train to catch," Helian Dongshan said. "You'd better come down and meet me." There was a brief silence at the other end of the line, before his son replied: "OK, I'll be right down."

Helian Dongshan waited and waited at the entrance to the Xiangheyuan Compound. He began to get angry but kept on waiting all the same. Then he saw in the distance someone who looked like his son, but not like his son. The boy was walking awkwardly, leaning to one side as if there was something wrong with one of his legs. At first glance, it looked as though he had a large vase of flowers slung over one shoulder, but as he got closer, the "vase" resolved itself into a girl. She was eighteen or nineteen years old, with heavy make-up, and had draped herself off one of his shoulders. It was autumn, and she wasn't wearing very much, so Helian Dongshan didn't dare look too closely. Just as the two of them were about to reach the compound gates, his son pushed the girl away, and the "vase" detached itself from his shoulder.

It was a spur of the moment meeting, and their expectations differed. After so many years, Helian Dongshan just wanted to meet and talk with his son. But he hadn't given any thought to what to say or how to say it. So how to start after so long a separation? Especially since the father and son had been hostile for many years, how could they find an opening?

When they met, it was Helian Xichu who spoke first: "What's this about?"

Helian Dongshan looked at his son. He hadn't seen him for so many years. His son's torso looked thicker and stronger, his face was rounder, and a moustache could be detected at the corners of his mouth. He was casually dressed and stood about 1.8 metres tall. He was grown-up.

"You're almost at my door, but you won't come into my home. What do you mean by that?" Helian Xichu said angrily.

As soon as they met, Helian Dongshan felt that he was at a clear disadvantage. He understood that time was on his son's side; after all, his son had been in Beijing for so long already. Although a note of accusation remained in his voice, there was an element of "intimacy" in his words, as if he no longer held on to the hostility of the past. It had to be said that this was the first time that his son had talked to Helian Dongshan like that. Helian Dongshan said: "Time is getting on. I have something to say, and I want to talk to you."

"Talk about what? What is there to talk about? What can you have to say, standing out in the road like this?"

Helian Dongshan's anger surged again. Barely suppressing it, he checked his watch and said: "All right, let's have something to eat."

Helian Xichu looked at him silently, with a hint of pity in his eyes. "OK, what do you fancy?"

"Let's not go too far. We can find somewhere nearby."

He didn't answer and nor did he introduce the person standing next to him, but the young woman took the initiative and said: "We're not far from that new Russian restaurant. Shall we invite Uncle for some Western food."

Helian Xichu didn't answer, but took a car key from his trouser pocket, pursed his lips and handed the key to her. It was the key to a BMW. The girl took the key, swinging her hips and shaking her waist, as she sashayed off to get the car.

Helian Dongshan looked at the girl's retreating figure and asked: "That... she... is she your girlfriend?"

"She's a fan."

"What... what do you mean?"

"You wouldn't understand if I told you. A fan is just a fan."

"Just... just... just... I don't understand. Does she live with you? Does her family mind?"

"What is there to understand?" Helian Xichu said impatiently.

"We're both adults. She came of her own accord and she can leave when she wants. What's it got to do with her family?"

Helian Dongshan frowned and said: "But, it's wrong, isn't it?"

At this moment, the fan drove up in the car. She poked her head out of the window and said: "Get in, Uncle."

Helian Dongshan wanted to say something, but reluctantly held it back. Now he was in his son's territory, he had lost the initiative. His son opened the car door, and Helian Dongshan sat in the back. Helian Xichu sat next to the fan and said: "Let's go."

The car turned this way and that, and after a few blocks, it stopped in front of a door labelled "Kiev Restaurant". This so-called Russian restaurant was hidden in a back street. It had a small frontage, and was situated down some stairs in a room with something of a basement smell. But it was different once Helian Dongshan entered. Inside, he just stopped and stared. There was a wave of voices, and he was assaulted by a strong smell of mutton, sweet and slightly rancid. It wasn't just that. It was a world of young people, or rather a world of "young professionals": men and women sitting at the neatly arranged tables, amid the flowing melodies of Russian music, drinking red wine, holding a knife and fork, eating steak, big loaves of rye bread. The men had their arms round the women's shoulders, and the women nestled in the men's arms, laughing and giggling. There was a constant sound of kissing, murmuring and cheering. A man and a woman stood up, danced to the music, gyrating a few times, then sat down and went back to their knives and forks. Someone shouted: "Cheers!"

At that moment, a tall, plump Russian woman slipped out from behind a screen that hid the kitchen. Holding a tray in her hand, she glided around the densely packed dining tables like a swimmer, murmuring a constant stream of "*spasiba, spasiba*". The music changed, and all of a sudden it was playing a march tune. Four huge Russians appeared wearing the uniforms of the Soviet Red Army. They marched in front of the dining tables and sang a chorus of "Katyusha". The whole restaurant erupted, and everyone joined in to the accompaniment of a knife and fork percussion section. The young professionals stood up one after another and took group photos with the singers.

It all made Helian Dongshan so dizzy, he almost fainted. He had liked to listen to Russian songs when he was young. Those songs were like a lover in a dream, nourishing his soul. But in Helian Dongshan's eyes, the uniforms of the Soviet Red Army, with their collar flashes and cap badges, represented an era dyed with blood and death. But, right or wrong, they did represent a time in history and should at least be given a minimum of respect. Here, they had just become something else to give flavour to the meal. Laugh, laugh, how the kids laughed! But what did they understand?

But there in that semi-underground restaurant, they still had to wait. Too many people wanted to eat the Western food, and there was a queue. Nor were those young professionals in any hurry as they fiddled with their mobile phones, looking at their screens. Helian Dongshan lost patience. Twice he left the queue to go outside and take calls about the case. When he came back in the second time, the fan said: "Don't worry, Uncle, it will be our turn soon. Only two more tables."

But Helian Dongshan was about to fall apart. He really couldn't wait any longer. He said to his son: "Come outside, I've got something to say to you." With that, he turned on his heel and walked out of the restaurant.

Helian Xichu didn't say anything but followed him out.

As the two stood on the side of the road, Helian Dongshan said: "You're an adult now, and I have no more influence over you, but I hope you will think carefully about changing jobs. You can't keep playing games forever, right?"

Helian Xichu pursed his lips and looked at him coldly. There was a touch of ridicule in his eyes, some pity, and something else too, but it wasn't clear quite what. He seemed to disdain to answer, as if anything he said would be like playing the harp to a cow.

Just at this moment, the fan appeared out of nowhere. She hurled herself in front of Helian Xichu, her black-varnished fingernails flashing as she almost poked Helian Dongshan in the eye with them. She yelled at Helian Dongshan, her voice like a machine gun: "We're not in the 1950s any more! I bet you grew up playing with a hoop and stick and whipping tops! I'm not going to waste my breath on you. You sound just like my old grandma! What do you mean by 'playing games'? You give it a try and see how you get on! Let me tell you, Older Brother is a god! He is a great god who brings people happiness.

He is a one-person happiness factory! Do you know what happiness is? You don't, do you! You're just an old tortoise! All you've done is work your whole life and you don't even know that happiness exists! Do you know how many fans your son has? 17.6 million! Who do you think you are to talk to Older Brother like that? Try it again and see what I do to you!"

Helian Dongshan was astounded. A girl like her had skinned him alive, flayed him to the bone, like an expert slaughterman. The phrase "not in the 1950s" had hit him particularly hard. Yes, he had grown up in that decade, and in front of this girl that gave him no dignity or worth at all. It was so shaming! He shook his head and sighed deeply. At this point, Helian Xichu finally spoke: "That's enough, leave it!"

"He's a stubborn old tortoise and I have to finish him off–"

"Fuck off! Who said you could shoot your mouth off?"

Helian Dongshan turned and left. He was telling himself: Go! Get out of here quick! Leave yourself a little face. You're in a different age now, and it's not yours!

FIVE

HELIAN DONGSHAN HURRIED BACK TO HUANGHUAI, and he did have a good reason for doing so. He had received a clue when he was on the phone. It was an extremely important clue.

This too began with Xie Zhichang from the Flower World Group. As the saying goes, the collapse of an ants' nest can cause the collapse of an embankment of a thousand *li*. Recently, the billionaire of Huanghuai, Chairman of the Board Xie Zhichang, Vice-President Xie, had encountered a little trouble. The trouble came from his wife, a middle-aged woman called Liang Yufen.

In this world of the super-rich, one of the most expensive things is divorce. After Xie Zhichang had been living his rich man's life for a while, he began to feel that he desperately needed some "culture". The need was urgent so he began planning his divorce.

But the divorce brought certain things to light.

Xie Zhichang's wife Liang Yufen was eight years younger than him, and she was a flower girl in the Meiling Flower Market. In her youth, she was very famous in the flower town of Meiling. Not only was she beautiful, but she was also the daughter of the local village

Party secretary. Precisely because she was the daughter of the Party secretary, she quite reasonably became the administrator and toll collector for the local flower market. At that time, all the vendors who went to the market to sell their flowers paid a daily fee. She would strut along the lanes of flowers, combing her hair in the fashionable hairstyle known as twin blades. She wore a red armband bearing the words "Market Administrator", and fluttered and flounced around the market, looking heroic. At that time, vendors of all ages would address her respectfully as "Older Sister Fen".

Back then as a flower man, Xie Zhichang relied on his smooth talking not only to sell flowers around town without paying the management fees, but also to win over Liang Yufen, the flower of the flower market. At first, the village Party secretary saw that Xie Zhichang was only a flower man, and a poor one at that, so naturally he would not agree to the marriage. In fact, he not only refused, but even sent some relatives to beat up Xie Zhichang. To everyone's astonishment, Liang Yufen eloped with Xie Zhichang. A year later, the two returned with their baby. By this time, the old village Party secretary had to acknowledge him, however unwillingly.

Now, at a time when Xie Zhichang was prospering, Liang Yufen was forty-five years old and had become a frigid misery of a woman. Although she also moved to Huanghuai with her husband and lived in a large villa, deep down, she was not happy. As their child grew up and spent more time away from home, she often found herself alone in the big, empty rooms. Moreover, after Xie Zhichang became a celebrity and president of the chamber of commerce, he rarely went home any more. He just returned to show his face and eat a meal every so often. After that, in Older Sister Fen's own words, he began to "fool around". Sister Fen once told Xie Zhichang: "You are chairman of the board, and run a hotel and a spa. You can fool around if you want, but you cannot take a mistress." Xie Zhichang gave his complete agreement to these conditions, saying: "We are a couple, Fen'er, you have no need to worry."

But Liang Yufen just couldn't let go of her suspicions, so she secretly hired someone to follow Xie Zhichang. Three months later, she finally caught him red-handed. It turned out that Xie Zhichang had set up a secret love nest in the Rose Garden compound, and the "bird" in that love nest was one of the northeastern girls from the spa centre. Although Older Sister Fen contemptuously referred to her as "that tiger girl", in fact she was not a typical "northeast tiger", but a tall, slender college student with a Beijing accent who was studying finance and accounting. But just because she originally came from the northeast, Older Sister Fen called her a tiger girl. And it was this tiger girl from the spa centre who now became Xie Zhichang's chief financial officer.

Liang Yufen was a fiery woman who had been left alone in her empty bed for many years, so naturally she was furious. For so many years, the two had quarrelled incessantly and she had no illusions about Xie Zhichang. It takes many years for a person to see another person clearly, but when it happens, it is always too late. Liang Yufen was the daughter of a Party secretary, so how could she be expected to take this? Her anger surged and her heart filled with hate. As soon as she had the real evidence, she went straight to talk to Xie Zhichang about a divorce. But Xie Zhichang was no longer the simple flower man of the past.

"What do you want?" he asked.

"I just want two things: a divorce and for you to fuck off!"

"Well, you've said it. If we're going to divorce, we'll do it now and fuck the one who delays."

"Right then, let's see. I'm not going to be greedy over our common property, we'll split it fifty-fifty."

Even though Xie Zhichang was running a second household, he really hadn't wanted a divorce. He just wanted to give her a fright, get her attention and stop her being so irritating all the time. So he was stunned at this turn of events and said: "Are you for real?"

"The marriage is over. Now let's draw up the bill."

Negotiations went on for a day and a night. Xie Zhichang originally wanted to rely on his silver tongue to win her over again and get her to accept the fait accompli of two households, one major one minor, with no connection between the two. He was hoping to use his promise not to give the tiger girl any kind of official status, and the fact that he and Liang Yufen already had a son and a daughter, to dissuade her from divorce. But she had been alone in the empty house for too long, and felt wronged, so nothing Xie Zhichang might do or say could change her determination. In the end, she said: "I also know that you can't lay your hands on too much cash at the moment, so

just give me ten million, and we can agree to go our separate ways."
Xie Zhichang saw that he had been boxed into a corner and said: "The
money is all invested in projects. I can't raise that much. How about I
give you eight million." Liang Yufen decided to be generous: "Eight
million is eight million. Give me a note for it now, payable in one
month."

The promissory note was issued and the divorce was settled, but a
month later, the note remained unpaid. When Liang Yufen went to
find him, Xie Zhichang pulled a fast one. He said: "I acknowledge the
note, but there's no money. You've got the house and the savings
account, isn't that enough? Do you want to bankrupt me? Do you
want me dead? Look, on my side of things, the project is still under-
way, and I can't come up with a single cent. In any case, you'll get
shares in this thing, and sooner or later they're bound to increase in
value." "You lousy old fart!" Liang Yufen retorted. "If you're talking
shares now, I want at least half!" Later on, she tried to see him again,
but he was nowhere to be found.

Liang Yufen knew that Xie Zhichang had such an extensive
network of connections in Huanghuai, both political and criminal,
that she could never win her lawsuit. For a woman like Liang Yufen,
once she fell in love with a man, she would love him to the end, with
no regard for herself. But once that love turned to hate, she became a
ruthless enemy who would destroy anything in her path. So she went
straight to Beijing and handed over an incriminating letter written by
Xie Zhichang to the Central Commission for Discipline Inspection
and the Ministry of Public Security. The main body of that letter was
only ten words long: "Burn the gold shop and kill him for his money."
She knew very well that once this seven-year-old case was dug up
again, Xie Zhichang, and the hotel manager Bai Shouxin, would be
finished.

A month passed after the accusation was laid, and there was no
movement at all. On Xie Zhichang's part, as Liang Yufen described it,
he and the "little slut" were openly carrying on together. They even
held a joint celebratory banquet at the Flower World Hotel, where
they arrived as though they were a real married couple, showing that
the little slut really had set herself up in pride of place. Liang Yufen
was beside herself with rage. She decided to go to Beijing again, determined to risk everything to make that bastard suffer.

That night, she took train number 188 and arrived in Beijing at dawn. She had just left Beijing Railway Station, when her phone rang and a voice said: "Excuse me, is that Liang Yufen?"

"Yes, it is. Who are you?" she asked.

"I am from the Provincial Public Security Bureau," the voice said. "My name is Helian."

Alarmed and excited, she said: "Who did you say? From the Public Security Bureau?"

"That's right. I am Helian Dongshan from the municipal government."

With tears in her eyes, Liang Yufen said: "You have to act for me in this, Comrade Helian."

"Your letter has been received by the municipal government. Where are you now? Are you in Beijing?"

"Yes, I just got out of the station."

"Stay where you are and have something to eat. I will send someone to pick you up right away."

According to the police who went to collect her, they had just picked up Liang Yufen when some of Bai Shouxin's men arrived. It had been less than half an hour since the phone call, which clearly showed that someone had leaked the information.

Twelve hours later, Liang Yufen was taken into a red-coloured building near the provincial capital. It was hidden by trees and, on the surface, looked quiet and tranquil. However, an armed police guard was stationed at the door. Known as the Red Mansion, it was a Communist Party "*shuanggui*" base for detaining and interrogating cadres under the direct jurisdiction of the provincial political and legal system. Inside the building, Liang Yufen told the team members in detail about the whole story of Xie Zhichang instructing Bai Shouxin and Wang Xiaoliu to set fire to the gold shop. Later, Helian Dongshan made a special trip to interrogate Liang Yufen.

"So tell me, Liang Yufen, were you also involved?" he asked.

"That Bai fellow talked to Lao Xie about it in our house. They didn't try to hide it from me."

"What did your husband say?"

"The Bai fellow asked my husband to give him the nod, and he did. I don't know what they discussed after that."

"Have you thought this through properly? Do you understand what is at stake here?"

Liang Yufen had been in a state of torment for many days. Her face was drained of blood, but she bit her lower lip and said: "I know. It could mean several years in prison, but I'm willing to risk everything."

"Whatever else, you are reporting and exposing a crime, and the court will use its discretion when the time comes. Who else is involved?"

Liang Yufen was silent.

Helian Dongshan continued: "Yufen, this is it now, you can no longer hold anything back. You know that some after I had sent someone to pick you up, Xie Zhichang's people arrived at the station. Think about it. What do you think they were going to do? You almost..."

Liang Yufen was silent for a while longer, before saying: "When you were investigating the case, Lao Jiang and Captain Sun both telephoned Xie Zhichang, and they also had a meal with Bai Shouxin and his men, several times."

The "Lao Jiang" Liang Yufen referred to was Jiang Baoguo, executive deputy director of the Huanghuai Judicial Bureau, while Sun Dehe was deputy captain of the Criminal Police Brigade. The two had a close friendship with Xie Zhichang. Helian Dongshan asked who else was involved but Liang Yufen shook her head. She felt that she couldn't reveal anything without proof. Suddenly, her eyes filled with tears, and she wept bitterly. "How did things come to this?" she whimpered.

On the third day after Liang Yufen was picked up, Wang Xiaoliu, the security captain of the Flower World Hotel in Huanghuai, was also quietly "invited in". Wang had just finished his night shift at the hotel and was picked up early in the morning on his way home. Obviously, his treatment was rather different from Liang Yufen's. He was blindfolded after getting into the car and the black cloth over his head was only removed after he was taken into the Red Mansion, so he didn't even know where he was.

Although Wang Xiaoliu was a professional hardman, he had never seen anything like this. Once inside the Red Mansion, he was taken into a room, his head spinning. He was given no time to catch his breath before four armed police officers walked in, one holding a folder, one holding some clothes and the other two watching him tigerishly. The one holding the folder shouted: "Wang Xiaoliu!" Without thinking, Wang Xiaoliu said: "Here." The man went on: "Take off your clothes, take them all off!" Wang Xiaoliu was so shocked and frightened he pissed himself. He looked at the four stony-faced armed policemen, and wanted to ask what crime he had committed. But he knew that this was not Huanghuai, and he was not on his own territory. He blinked twice and stayed silent. Then, in front of the four armed policemen, he took off his clothes. When only his underpants were left, he cleared his throat and said: "Do you still–" The armed policeman said: "Take them off! Don't leave a thread!" When he had stripped completely, he put his hands behind his head and stood naked in front of the four policemen, his white flesh looking like a plucked chicken. The four policemen searched him all over, before giving him a set of blue-and-white striped clothes. Then the door closed silently behind them as they left.

Now alone, Wang Xiaoliu walked around the room, looking, touching and even banging the walls with his head. He discovered that they were lined with rubber. He told himself: Behave yourself. This is something big.

Near noon, Wang Xiaoliu was brought out. Just as he was about to be taken into the interrogation room, his gaze fell on Liang Yufen in the corridor. He saw Older Sister Fen being led into another room. Yes, it really was her! Shit! They'd even brought in Older Sister Fen!

Of course, this was all deliberately arranged by Helian Dongshan. He just wanted to let Wang Xiaoliu know that Liang Yufen was there, and whether he talked or not was up to him.

In the interrogation room, Wang Xiaoliu discovered that the person questioning him was Helian Dongshan. If it had been anyone else, he wouldn't have been worried yet, but this Helian Dongshan knew him far too well. He had been pulled in and released three times before, and each time he had managed to frame someone else... but this time was different. First, the location had changed and he didn't even know where he was being held. But the most frightening thing was that Older Sister Fen was there too. And she wasn't wearing a striped suit. What did that mean? He knew a little about the divorce between her and Mr Xie. But even so, Older Sister Fen... Wang Xiaoliu was worried.

Helian Dongshan sat there without saying a word, just staring at him.

For more than twenty minutes, the two men looked at each other in silence. Helian Dongshan kept his eyes fixed on Wang Xiaoliu. Wang tried to be evasive at first, his eyes flitting round the room, but there was no escape. Helian Dongshan's gaze was like an awl boring into him, and the expression in those eyes was unforgiving and murderous.

Wang Xiaoliu began to sweat. He knew that the arson of the gold shop was probably out in the open now, and he was best placed to know what had happened that night. Once it all came out, it was a capital offence. But if he did nothing himself, and Older Sister Fen testified, would he be able to handle it? At that moment, Wang Xiaoliu's thoughts were whirling round in flames, and those flames burned his heart and scorched his organs. He kept wondering how he could lie his way out of this. Could it still be done? He had to hold out as if his life depended on it. He had to hold out and hold out until he couldn't hold out any longer, and then see.

Suddenly, Helian Dongshan shouted: "Wang Xiaoliu!"

"Here."

"How many SIM cards did you buy?"

Wang Xiaoliu was confused. "What? What cards?"

"The sixteenth of August. How many SIM cards did you buy?"

"August... August..."

Helian Dongshan's questioning became more intense: "Speak! The sixteenth of August, at the Madao Street mobile phone store. How many cards did you buy?"

Wang Xiaoliu's teeth chattered, like an out-of-control machine gun, and a single word emerged from his throat: "Three."

Wang Xiaoliu originally thought he would be asked about the Huoshao Gold Shop. He had been thinking about what lie to invent and he had one ready. But Helian Dongshan didn't go there. He asked instead about phone cards. Wang wasn't mentally prepared for this, and just spat out the word "three" in his local dialect. But after that, he had no idea at all why Helian Dongshan was going on about phone cards. The more he didn't understand, the more flustered he became.

In fact, that "three" was also a lie. Lying was second nature to him. Actually, on that occasion, following Bai Shouxin's instructions, he bought twenty single-use SIM cards.

Helian Dongshan asked again: "Tell me. Who told you to buy them, and who did you give them to?"

"Bai... Mr Bai. They've all... they've all been given away."

Although Wang Xiaoliu hadn't attended school for very long, he was street-smart and tricky. Whenever he was puzzling over a problem, he used to twist his extra finger in his ear, but just at this moment, his hands were cuffed and he couldn't reach his ears. He scratched the arm of the chair continuously, like a telegraph operator. But as he scratched, he realised that this time, his "telegraph" had let him down. Why had he brought Bai Shouxin's name into it? Aiya! He'd been tricked.

But Helian Dongshan didn't ask anything else. All he said was: "Lock him up!"

Wang Xiaoliu stared at Helian Dongshan in astonishment. As he was taken away, he kept looking back. He was expecting Helian Dongshan to ask something more. If he asked again, he would at least know which way the wind was blowing. But Lao He didn't ask anything else.

That night, as he pulled together all the various strands of information, Helian Dongshan fell into deep thought. The gold shop arson was all settled now, of course, but he hadn't expected that the kidnapping case was tied in with it. So he smoked a succession of cigarettes one after the other, and when he pinched out the last one, he had a bad feeling about things. He didn't dare to think about this hunch until there was some evidence to corroborate it. But at any rate, judging by the current situation, Xie Zhichang and Bai Shouxin were likely to have also been involved in the kidnapping.

But why on earth?

SIX

IN THIS WORLD, there are many ways to make a person remember something.

But for Helian Dongshan, this was the first time he remembered something after being bawled out.

That little girl, the girl who might one day become his daughter-in-law, had made him instantly remember her. It wasn't just a passing memory; she had been burned indelibly on his brain.

Yes indeed, it was the first time he had let a girl put her finger in his face and curse him. It really hurt his self-esteem. In the dead of night, the girl's words were like a pendulum swinging on the wall and jolting him. His son had said she was a "fan" but she had a mouth full of knives that had cut him to the quick, and it was all too much.

It had been ugly listening, especially that crack about the 1950s, which had really hit home. Yes, he did grow up playing with a hoop and stick and whipping tops. At that time, as a child from an ordinary worker's family, there were few toys, but there were as many sweet memories as bitter ones.

This girl had not only savaged him with her words, she had also raised some veiled criticisms and prompted some vivid thoughts. So what was happiness? To be honest, Helian Dongshan had never seriously considered this before. But at his age, with the sun lowering in the west, he already found himself looking at the sunset. And now, here was this slip of a girl forcing him to think about the nature of happiness.

Yes, what is happiness? When he was very young, as a child of the fifties, he knew what happiness was: happiness was sacrifice, happiness was dedication. "Number one, do not fear hardship. Number two, do not fear death" was the slogan of that era. At the time, almost everyone thought that way. After so many years, he still remembered that when he was young, he had a much-cherished diary and the first sentence he wrote in it was the famous saying of the Soviet writer Alexander Ostrovsky: "Man's most precious gift, life, is only experienced once. When you recall the past..." But now? Now, to be honest, he had no idea what happiness was.

So this girl named Yu Zhenzhen: was she happy?

He only found out her name later. Things had changed dramatically. That evening, when Helian Dongshan was scolded by the girl and ran away in embarrassment, he hurriedly hailed a taxi and took it to catch the train. However, when he rushed to the waiting room of the West Railway Station less than ten minutes later and was talking to a colleague, he suddenly felt someone tugging at his jacket from behind. He turned around and saw that it was the "vase".

The girl now stood in front of him, her eyes bright with tears. She bowed deeply, and said: "I'm sorry, Uncle, I formally apologise to you."

Helian Dongshan still hadn't recovered from his surprise, when he saw that all the people in the waiting room had suddenly surrounded him. He panicked and said: "Stop! Don't! What do you think you are doing?"

Now he could see quite clearly that this was indeed the girl with the dyed red hair and big earrings, the same fan who had scolded him at the entrance to the restaurant. The heavy make-up on the girl's face was already streaking, and two black lines of tears were running down her cheeks. She wailed and said: "I, Yu Zhenzhen, have never begged anyone in my life before. Uncle, I am begging you now, please forgive me."

Helian Dongshan still didn't understand. "Don't cry, don't cry! Forgive you for what?"

Yu Zhenzhen wailed again and said: "Big Brother sent me away! He doesn't want me."

Helian Dongshan looked at her blankly, with no idea what to do for the best.

"Uncle, I apologise to you again. I am young and ignorant. Please forgive me."

By now, everyone in the waiting room was looking at him, and even his colleagues were eyeing him suspiciously. Helian Dongshan's face was on fire with embarrassment. He said: "OK, OK, I forgive you, I forgive you."

"Do you really forgive me, Uncle?"

Helian Dongshan was sweating cobs as he said: "Go away! Go away now! I forgive you."

"If Uncle really forgives me," Yu Zhenzhen said, "please call Older Brother and tell him. You won't let him send me away, will you?"

Helian Dongshan was stupefied. He didn't know what to do. The whole thing was ridiculous. These two young people didn't really know each other at all. They had just chatted online and then lived together without any real idea what they were doing. This was not something that Helian Dongshan could accept. Besides, it was out of the question for him to call that unfilial son of his and get mixed up in this affair!

To his astonishment, in front of everyone, Yu Zhenzhen fell to her knees with a thud, facing him.

"Uncle, you must save me! Please save me! I'll die if I have to leave Older Brother! He may be a god, but you are his elder and he will listen to you! Please..."

Helian Dongshan was getting worried. "Get up, girl. Get up now! Listen to me. You two young people have to solve your own problems, OK?"

Even more people were now watching the excitement. A would-be Samaritan rushed over and said to Yu Zhenzhen: "Girl, is this old gangster bullying you? Just say the word and we'll help you!"

Everyone else joined in: "Just say the word, girl, just say the word!"

Helian Dongshan looked at the angry eyes all around him. The crowd looked ready to jump on him at any moment. He was so stunned by the situation he couldn't even get his words out properly. He waved his hands and tried to explain: "No, no! You've got it all wrong! It's not like that... it's not like that."

It was a really tricky situation.

Because Helian Dongshan was out of uniform, someone shouted: "You look like you're up to no good! You're a trafficker, right?"

To everyone's surprise, Yu Zhenzhen suddenly exploded. With a flick of her red hair, she said to the onlookers: "You want to kick up a fuss, do you? You're going to make something of this, are you? Honking away like a flock of geese, you can't wait to stick your beaks in can you! What a joke! Are you all sick? Go and queue up at the Anding Hospital. Why are you wasting time jabbering away here? What's the matter with you?"

Everyone fell silent under her steely gaze.

Helian Dongshan looked at her. Whose daughter was she, this girl called Yu Zhenzhen? She had dyed red hair, two big earrings, two big eyes and black tears streaking her face. She was wearing next to nothing: a little pink waistcoat on her top half, and a short leather skirt and high-heeled boots. In the autumn weather, she still had her shoulders and belly button exposed, and she was kneeling on the tiled floor. Her stockings were torn, and her knees were about to start bleeding. All in all, she looked like a turkey with its feathers singed off...

Helian Dongshan stepped forward and pulled her to her feet. "Get up! Get up now! Get up and say something!"

But Yu Zhenzhen's body was limp like a rag doll. She kept slipping back down and just couldn't get up. "Uncle, look at the state I'm in! Can I still not move you? Are all you children of the fifties so cold-blooded? I'm just asking you to call him. You can save an undying love! I'm begging you."

"You—"

At this moment, the loudspeaker in the waiting room announced that the 179 train had entered the station. The passengers in the waiting room surged forward, and the ticket check began.

Helian Dongshan was helpless, and finally said: "I'll call him. I'll call him now. Just get up."

Yu Zhenzhen's eyes were still filled with tears, but suddenly the tears turned to laughter and she said: "Thank you, Uncle! Thank you, Uncle!"

Helian Dongshan picked up his phone, dialled his son's number, and said angrily: "Be at the number nine waiting room of the West Railway Station in thirty minutes. Yu Zhenzhen is kneeling on the floor here. Come and get her." Right at the end, he added: "You can clean up your own mess!"

To his surprise, Yu Zhenzhen said: "What did I say about you oldies, Uncle? Why can't you lighten up a bit? How can you talk to Older Brother like that? Can't you be a bit nicer?"

Helian Dongshan could barely contain his anger and he wanted to slap her. But instead, he turned to his colleagues and said quietly: "Let's get away from here. Now!"

But Yu Zhenzhen followed him, saying: "Have a safe trip, Uncle. Next time you visit, I'll cook a Western meal for you."

Even after Helian Dongshan boarded the train, he was still on edge. He felt that this meeting between the two generations of the 1950s and 1980s had been a disaster. Time was such a huge gulf! The "clang" of the train was the sound of separation as the distance between the two generations, and it grew wider and wider.

Helian Dongshan couldn't shake off his worry. When he got back to Huanghuai, he briefly took time off from the investigation to go home. When he saw his wife, Han Shufang, he asked: "What's going on up there?"

His wife was taken by surprise and said: "Up where?"

"In Beijing."

"I don't know. What's going on? Did the sun suddenly rise in the west?"

He frowned and said: "All right, don't tell me if you don't want to."

"Why don't you tell me about what you're going on about instead of talking in riddles!"

Helian Dongshan had to come clean: "I heard that your precious son is shacked up with some girl. They're living together! Is that clear enough? It's not on, is it!"

"Which girl are you talking about?"

He was taken aback: "You mean... there's more than one?"

"Didn't I already tell you? There's lots of them chasing after him..."

"I mean the red-head. What's her name... Yu Zhenzhen."

"Oh, you mean one of his fans has walked out on him!"

"What are 'fans'? What do you know about all this anyway?"

"It's internet talk. She's a hardcore fan of our son. He threw her out."

Helian Dongshan was incredulous: "Really?"

"I have seen her... the red-head. Yes, he's sent her packing... You need to do something about your son."

Helian Dongshan shook his head, puzzled by the whole affair. The image of this girl called Yu Zhenzhen seemed to be imprinted on his brain. If she hadn't dyed her hair and applied heavy make-up, she would be a delicate, fresh-looking girl, but she had turned herself into a turkey! Somehow, he found this Yu Zhenzhen, this child of the eighties, very upsetting. And whose child was she? Why didn't her family care? But then again, what could they do? He remembered her sticking her finger in his face and calling him a child of the fifties and an old tortoise!

"Hardcore fans?" Helian Dongshan muttered to himself.

SEVEN

BAI SHOUXIN was also arrested.

On the outside, he was sitting there quietly, but inside he was in turmoil.

Outside the window was the blue sky, white clouds and green trees. The birds were hopping about and singing. From time to time, planes flew overhead. What was this place?

Bai Shouxin was "invited in" on the seventh day after Wang Xiaoliu was arrested. Because he was a deputy to the Municipal People's Congress for the city and there were certain formalities to observe, he was not handcuffed.

His body was still, but his hands were not. By force of habit, he kept trying to take off those white gloves of his, but he wasn't wearing them any more, so instead, he kept rubbing his hands together as if he was trying to peel off a layer of skin.

In fact, he knew very well in his heart that Liang Yufen had turned informer and Wang Xiaoliu was arrested. It was clear that the gold shop arson case had been blown wide open. The only way out now was to save Chairman Xie, come what may. By saving Xie Zhichang, they would save themselves. How could he put a stop to things? Well, it wasn't he who had lit the fire. As for anything Xie Zhichang had told him in private, there wasn't any recording, was there? Of course, Wang Xiaoliu had received his orders from him. But what had he actually said to Wang Xiaoliu? "Teach him a lesson" and "Let him know the score". Yes, that's what he had said. No matter how many times he was asked, that would be what he had said.

Bai Shouxin had always been a hard case. When he was young, he did some stupid things, and he was always making a nuisance of himself with young girls. But he had also got blood on his hands fighting in the marketplace. Of course, since working for Xie Zhichang, he also wanted to be a proper stand-up guy. It was Xie Zhichang who took him in when he was really down on his luck, and now he had earned some money over the years, he had followed Xie Zhichang along the "culture" road and wanted to go straight. Yes indeed, Director Xie had put up the money, and he had represented Director Xie, once actually sponsoring a poetry recital in the city. Director Xie had also sent him to Tsinghua University for three months to study for an MBA, at considerable expense. Now he knew how to conduct himself and how to talk properly. He was very grand and fastidious, but he was also measured and self-effacing, with the word "sorry" often on his lips. Subsequently, he had been reading some of the books that now adorned Director Xie's office.

Over the years, following Director Xie, he had also taken up fishing as a hobby, cultivating many of his own special little places at the fishponds. Fishing is a very "elegant" hobby, mostly enjoyed by the upper-classes, and Director Xie had made friends with a lot of important people through it. He drove up to go fishing with them on Sundays and hung around with them, so he could always be talking about business. Which was great.

In fact, he very much wanted to be an aristocrat, and he genuinely thought he had true nobility in him. But it takes time to nourish the spirit of an aristocrat. Perhaps, if he had been able to live for five hundred years, he might really become a new "spiritual aristocrat", but he had made his money too quickly and had not set out in the right direction. For the time being, he was still at the formative, construction stage. The money was there, but the essence, energy and spirit were works in progress and still at the packaging stage. "Packaging" was a buzzword of the age and one that he had adopted. It could be said that, in material terms, he lacked nothing, but he had lost his freedom... and that caused him heartache.

What he regretted most was having let Director Xie divorce Liang Yufen. Thinking of it now, his guts twisted inside him. He also felt aggrieved with Director Xie. That was it, wasn't it! You said yourself you were playing away but Sister Fen wasn't stopping you having your fun. What did you think you were doing divorcing her? You must have been crazy to want to marry your bit on the side!

Having said that, he knew there was logic behind Xie Zhichang marrying the tiger girl. She was a university graduate and a finance and accounting professional. Although Xie Zhichang was chairman of the board, he wasn't well educated. For a large enterprise with billions in assets, financial acumen was the most important skill and it had to be handled by someone reliable. And what kind of person is the most reliable? From a crook's point of view, just sleeping with someone didn't make them reliable; that only came if you married them. Marriage was by far the best way to tie someone to you. Besides, his tiger girl was still young and beautiful, and very good in bed. This was what he had told Xie Zhichang. But it was too late for regrets now.

That night, when he had been discussing things in private with Xie Zhichang, he hadn't made any effort to keep it secret from Liang Yufen. At that time, Liang Yufen and Director Xie were still together and of one mind. It had, indeed, all been his idea and Director Xie had just gone along with it, but...

Bai Shouxin sat alone in the room for two days and two nights, turning things over in his head, but he couldn't see a way through it. He thought himself stupid and, in the end, only one word emerged: regret.

By the third day, he was going crazy. Every few minutes, he shouted: "Tell Uncle He I want to see him!" The armed officer outside the door opened the little hatch window on the door and shouted: "Wait."

After a while, he shouted again: "Tell Lao He I've got something to say to him. It's urgent!" The officer outside still told him to wait. After a while, he shouted again: "Tell him! I want to confess!" But no one took any notice.

Helian Dongshan knew Bai Shouxin very well, so he had been leaving him to sweat. The case of the gold shop arson was already nailed down without him. What Helian Dongshan most wanted to know was, what was the connection between Bai Shouxin and the kidnapping, and who else might he implicate?

On the morning of the fourth day, Helian Dongshan finally appeared. With him were two armed policemen and an arrest warrant. In the interrogation room, Bai Shouxin blanched when the officer showed him the warrant. He shouted at Helian Dongshan: "Uncle He, I'm being falsely accused."

"Well, you would know best about that," Helian Dongshan said. "What else have you got for me?"

At this point, one of the armed officers put a pen into Bai Shouxin's hand and said: "Sign!"

"I'm not signing anything. I'm being falsely accused. There's no evidence–"

"It doesn't matter whether you sign or not," Helian Dongshan replied. "The law is going to take its course."

There was a sharp click as the other officer neatly put a pair of handcuffs on Bai Shouxin's wrists.

Bai Shouxin held up his handcuffed hands and shouted: "I protest! You can't arrest me. I'm a representative of the Municipal People's Congress. Does the congress know you are arresting me?"

"What do you think?" Helian Dongshan said.

Bai Shouxin was stunned and sat down dejectedly.

But it only lasted a moment and Bai Shouxin jumped up again, quick as a monkey. He said: "I'll confess! I'll make a statement. I'll inform on..."

Helian Dongshan sorted through the papers he was holding and said casually: "Well, let's talk about it then."

"Every time there's some VIP, I give them a gift when they leave. A case of Maotai each. They come from the city, the province, central government..."

Helian Dongshan looked at him and said: "Go on, give me some names."

Bai Shouxin rattled off a series of names of provincial and city government leaders, all of whom appeared frequently in the newspapers. At the end, he said: "There are also some big names from the central government. Do you dare investigate them too?"

Helian Dongshan's face darkened, and he said: "Do you think we're playing a kid's game, Shouxin? All you have to do is talk. Who we investigate is none of your business."

Bai Shouxin had been trying to put the wind up Helian Dongshan. Effectively, he had been saying: Listen to all the big names I know! Do you really dare investigate them? But he fell silent on hearing Helian Dongshan's reply.

"Go on then," Helian Dongshan continued. "Why have you gone quiet? Have you forgotten? You and Lao Xie gave me a box of tea too... the best, you said. Actually, I don't think it's any different from what I can buy on the street, and I've still got it in my office. Would you like a cup?"

Bai Shouxin's tone changed, and he said despondently: "All right, I confess. A bunch of girls from the northeast did come to my spa centre. It wasn't me who recruited them, but I did turn a blind eye. I openly confess that I have used prostitutes, more than once–"

"Is that what you call a confession? Avoiding the serious stuff and admitting to something trivial? Well, let me jog your memory. Six words: three, six, nine, gold, wood, fire. Think about it."

Bai Shouxin's brain started working overtime. What did he mean? Yes, that was it: protection money! Over the years, he had given Lao Jiang 300,000 and Captain Sun 600,000. As for that nine, could it be...

"Let me give you something you can take to the bank, Shouxin. I have recorded statements from Liang Yufen and Wang Xiaoliu, as well as corroborating evidence from Lao Huang at the City Bureau and from Sun Dehe. Do you want to listen to them?"

Bai Shouxin hated Liang Yufen so much he wished she was dead. He felt that he had fallen, alive and kicking, right into the hands of this awful woman! Regret overwhelmed him in a great wave. He felt like he was reaching for a handhold just as the water swirled over his head and all hope was gone. He slumped to the ground with a thud, and said: "This is really unjust, Uncle He. Yes, I said something. I admit that I said 'teach him a lesson' and 'let that Wu fellow know the score' but I never told him to set anyone on fire..."

Helian Dongshan looked at his watch and said: "I've already told you the bottom line, Shouxin. I don't want to waste any more time on you. Now, I will give you one more chance, a chance to do the right thing and confess. You've got five minutes. Whether you talk or not, and whether you tell the truth if you do, is up to you."

"I'll talk. You ask and I'll talk."

"On the sixteenth of August, you asked Wang Xiaoliu to buy three SIM cards. He gave them to you, so who did you give them to?"

Bai Shouxin stared into space, as if caught up in his memory.

Helian Dongshan gave him ten seconds, and then said: "So you won't talk. That's fine. Take him away!"

Bai Shouxin leapt to his feet and said: "I'll talk! I'll talk! It was Mayor Liu wanted them."

"Be precise! Which Mayor Liu?"

"Executive Deputy Mayor Liu Jinding. He came to the hotel for a massage once and said that he found it very inconvenient that his mobile phone number was public knowledge. He asked me to get him anonymous cards."

"What for?"

"He didn't say. I swear to God, I really don't know."

"Does Xie Zhichang know about this?"

"I don't know."

"Really?"

"I really don't know. It was just a casual request. I don't need to ask the chairman about little things like that."

"Take him away!"

After Bai Shouxin was taken away, Helian Dongshan looked out of the window and smoked another cigarette in silence. His instinct wasn't wrong, he thought: just as he'd expected, it came down to Liu Jinding. This showed him that the mobile phone signal detected in Beijing came from Liu Jinding. The fact that that single word was sent by Liu Jinding meant that the problem was serious.

Liu Jinding was a deputy departmental-level cadre, and when things reached that level, Helian Dongshan had to ask for instructions. However, before he had time to consult his superiors, Liu Jinding sought him out.

EIGHT

HELIAN DONGSHAN FELT VERY UPSET after his return from Beijing.

The whole affair was like an invisible burden that had been thrust on him. Although it was invisible and intangible, it still made him stressed. Even when he entered an official government office building, he could still feel eyes watching him.

But when he turned around, he couldn't see anyone. Maybe he was too tired; he was certainly a little dazed from so many sleepless nights. Certainly, the "eyes" on the back of his neck felt very similar to those of his son. The look in his son's eyes was no longer challenging, it was condescending, full of mockery and, perhaps, pity. His son was now the Overlord of Western Chu on the internet, and his eyes were very piercing. His son was a winner in the great scheme of time, and was looking at him through the eyes of a winner, and his subtext read: you are old.

He was fifty-nine years old, and in the eyes of his son, he was a shrivelled old butterfly lying on the railway tracks.

His son was 1.8 metres tall, and he already had a moustache at the corners of his mouth. His son used to have a small round face, but now it was rectangular with pronounced cheekbones and angles. His son wore casual clothes, his expression was contemptuous and rather cool. His son was growing up, but he himself was shrinking. He was originally 1.8 metres tall, but now, when he was measured at his annual physical examination, he was only about 1.78 metres. His son stood tall in front of him, and it made him a little uncomfortable. Needless to say, his son had already escaped from his discipline and had established himself on his own. Moreover, his own current annual salary was less than 50,000 yuan, while his son's annual salary was ten times that amount. The last time he went to Beijing to see his son, he had felt very deflated. Standing in front of him, he could sense the huge gulf between them.

There was, however, one thing he still didn't understand. How had his son got rid of that troublesome red-haired girl, that arrogant Yu Zhenzhen? His wife just said: "She's gone." At Beijing West Railway Station, in front of all those people, she had been uncompromising. She had wept, she had knelt, she had been utterly determined. She had said she would rather die than leave his son. So why did she leave? What magic had his son used? He had been a detective all his life, but this was one mystery he could not solve.

There were many things Helian Dongshan did not understand about the world, let alone just his son. For example, wasn't his son just a gamer? How could he have so many fans? More than ten million, for God's sake! Could it be that thousands of young people across the world were all playing games? What was the world like, in that case? Had everyone gone mad? Or was it, truly, he himself who was now the mad one?

It was his son's eyes that told him: do you think really think "games" are just games? They are a challenge, a challenge about limits, a challenge about imagination and a challenge about your ability to react intuitively. Is it not a good thing to find some happiness in the virtual world amid the extreme cruelty of life's challenges? However you look at it, it's got to be better than playing with a hoop and stick and whipping tops when you were young, hasn't it?

The expression in his son's eyes had said to him: Do you think computer games are just games? They are a personal challenge. They contain good and evil, right and wrong; there are levels and gateways; there are as many challenges as Xuanzang encountered in *Journey to the West*! You have to have the heart of a warrior; they set your blood racing. There is always a price to be paid to obtain anything, and there are winners and losers. Even if you are defeated a thousand times, you can always get up again... what is not good about that?

The expression in his son's eyes had said to him: Do you think "games" are just games? They represent the thought processes of different countries and different nationalities. If you play games from all over the world, you can understand the different ways of thinking and different lifestyles in different nations. How can it be bad to broaden your horizons and travel the world while having fun?

The expression in his son's eyes had said to him: Do you think "games" are just games? The childhood of a nation is the future of a nation. In the online world, gaming is a new way to open up the mind. Do you really think that a childhood of playing with a hoop and stick and whipping tops can be compared to a childhood happily cruising the online world and fighting all-comers!

Helian Dongshan did not know how to counter all this, but he did know that it was all a fallacy. He was unshakeable in his belief that it was fanciful and utter nonsense.

However, his son did work in a large, upright, state-recognised company. It was located in the capital, Beijing, in a magnificent high-rise building in Zhongguancun. It had lifts to take you up and down, and the building was secure against the wind and rain. His son was also a director of the company. Although he did not know exactly what that meant, the annual salary showed its importance. He learned from his wife that the company was strongly supported by the state, with an investment of 10 million yuan every year. How extraordinary to think that the state paid them to "play" like this!

Helian Dongshan understood that the world had changed and soon it would no longer belong to him. It would be a world of young people. As a defender of law and order, a detective, he would soon be too old. The sunset was infinitely fine, but it was almost dusk. So in the future, once the world was in the hands of the "players", what would it look like? He didn't dare to think about it, and he couldn't understand it.

As he neared the top of the steps leading up to the Huanghuai City Government office building, Helian Dongshan stood in a daze for a while, then realised that his wandering mind had run away with him, and he had to reel it back in. He took the lift to the fifth floor to meet Liu Jinding, member of the Municipal Party Committee and executive deputy mayor.

The night before, Helian Dongshan had unexpectedly received a call from the Huanghuai City Government.

"Is that Comrade Helian Dongshan?"

"Yes"

"My name is Ding and I am the secretary of the Government Office. Mayor Liu invites you to come to the City Office at nine o'clock tomorrow morning." Secretary Ding's tone was brusque and authoritative. He hung up without giving Helian Dongshan a chance to reply.

So, Liu Jinding suddenly wanted to see him tomorrow morning! That was interesting. Perhaps he had felt something in the wind and wanted to know which way that wind was blowing.

NINE

THE DIFFERENCE BETWEEN "seeing" and "having a meeting with" was a nice matter of status.

Helian Dongshan was kept a full twenty minutes in the waiting room next to the secretarial section before Secretary Ding took him into the office of Executive Deputy Mayor Liu Jinding.

Helian Dongshan understood that this was intentional. The twenty minutes was to remind him to remember his place.

As soon as Helian Dongshan entered the office, Liu Jinding walked over and shook hands with him warmly. As he did so, he said: "Comrade Dongshan, sit down, sit down."

There were two sets of sofas in Liu Jinding's office. One set comprised large, leather sofas, where you could sit down and enjoy a tea ceremony, as the low table in front was laid out with top quality tea ceremony utensils. The other set was smaller, upholstered in fabric and intended for coffee drinkers, since there was a high-end coffee maker next to it. Computers, telephones and file folders were arranged on Mayor Liu's huge desk. In fact, there were two telephones, one black and one red, and two computers, one desktop and one notebook, both switched on. Behind the desk was a leather swivel chair with a headrest. Behind the chair was a row of tall bookcases, full of books. On the left side of the leather swivel chair, in front of the bookcases, were two red flags as tall as a man: one was the national flag and the other was the Communist Party flag. They lent the office an air of solemnity.

Helian Dongshan looked around, not sure where to sit.

He saw Liu Jinding sit down on the front-facing leather sofa, beckon, and say: "Sit down! I often have foreign guests here, so why don't you enjoy the same treatment I give them? Would you like tea or coffee?"

Helian Dongshan sat down and said: "Tea."

Liu Jinding immediately called out: "Xiao Ding, make a cup of Maojian." Then he went on: "I heard that you're joining the Provincial Public Security Bureau. Congratulations, you'll be provincial director soon."

Helian Dongshan smiled and said nothing.

Liu Jinding continued in an authoritative tone: "Lao He, if you are about to be transferred to the province, there are a few books I should recommend."

"Good, yes, I've heard people say that Mayor Liu is very well read. Go on."

"The ancients said that if you use history as your mirror, you can be sure to be dressed correctly. The first book I would recommend to you is *Records of the Grand Historian*. Have you read it?"

Helian Dongshan wasn't sure where this was leading and said off-handedly: "I leafed through it a few years ago."

"Reading history benefits our work, don't you agree?"

"Yes, Mayor Liu is right. Certainly the *Twenty-Four Histories* is worth reading."

"I think Sima Qian's *Records of the Grand Historian* is the most literary," Liu Jinding said. "In particular, his biographies of the principal figures are all very lifelike, and full of insights. Just think, in ancient times, a lord of the plains had a retinue of three thousand! Even outlaws and bandits were taken into service. What does that mean? It means that our ancestors have always valued true talent. The way the ancients nurtured scholars is just the same as us cultivating talents today. We have to learn from the ancients. They had chariots to travel in, fish to eat, they had horses with 'five-flower' manes, furs worth a thousand gold coins… but no matter how much you spend

284

cultivating people, the most essential thing comes down to one word: loyalty. Nothing is possible without loyalty." Liu Jinding coughed, and quickly went on: "Of course, what I am talking about is loyalty to the country."

Helian Dongshan sat there, looking in silence at Liu Jinding, the deputy mayor. What was he hoping to achieve? Was he trying to establish his dominance? Was he trying to overawe him with his scholarship and cultural accomplishments? Or was he implying something else?

Liu Jinding continued: "The second book I want to recommend is the *Communist Manifesto*. It's a thin little book. I'm sure you must have read it. There are many people who will talk you through it, section by section, but they either have not read it from cover to cover, or if they have, they have not understood it properly. I have read it, and I am not sure that I have necessarily understood it. Just look at its opening sentence: 'A spectre is haunting Europe — the spectre of communism.' What does that tell us? It tells us that, no matter how great the theory is, its doctrine will not be recognised until it has been proved in practice. So it can only be a 'spectre'. Only after it is proven does it become doctrine. Right? So what does that mean for us? It means that some of the things we do may be misunderstood, but we cannot stop doing them because we are afraid of misunderstanding. Reform and opening up are cases in point.

"The third book I want to recommend is William Manchester's *The Glory and the Dream*. It is about the economic revolution in America and Roosevelt's so-called 'New Deal'. I won't elaborate too much on it, but the president of the United States during the Great Depression, Franklin Roosevelt, used many aspects of communism under the mantle of capitalism to revive the collapsed American economy. He met with a lot of opposition at the time, but he succeeded. What does this tell us? It's called being flexible, and if you are willing to change, you can get things done. From that perspective, there are many things it is good to be flexible about."

Helian Dongshan sat silently as if listening to a lecture. He decided this was a smart and capable man. He had shown he was widely read, but what else was behind all this? He was currently executive deputy mayor, and under normal circumstances, he was likely to take over as mayor. But if he was involved in the case Helian Dongshan was investigating, would he really be sitting there and talking in this manner? What did it all mean? If nothing else, it showed that his psychological and mental qualities were certainly not run-of-the mill.

The two men sat looking at each other. While Liu Jinding was talking so freely, Helian Dongshan's mind was wandering, and he thought of the mobile phone signal that had been detected and intercepted sending the single word: success. What exactly did "success" mean?

Liu Jinding was still talking. He seemed to be almost intoxicated by his exalted peroration. However, just at this moment, when his eyes met Helian Dongshan's, Mayor Liu changed tone. It was like a phoenix spreading its colourful wings only to discover its feathers were falling out... Liu Jinding swallowed as if he was choking, and said: "Have some tea, have some tea. This is just idle talk. Comrade Dongshan, first, I want to apologise to you, because we haven't been doing our job very well."

Helian Dongshan came back to his senses and looked at Secretary Liu blankly. What does he mean by that? he asked himself.

"You are an expert and have given outstanding service," Liu Jinding continued. "Huanghuai should be finding prestigious posts for comrades like you who have solved so many big cases and won awards. But we haven't done our job well here, and we always seem to be one step behind. I am very sorry. The day before yesterday, I talked to Number One [the secretary of the Municipal Party Committee] to see if we could keep you–"

"Thank you for your concern, but I'm fifty-nine and it's time to retire," Helian Dongshan said.

Liu Jinding, who still seemed to have his head in the clouds, suddenly returned to earth. He said: "Yes, yes, here in the City Bureau, you should have been rewarded long ago, and it's held you back. I have urged them many times and criticised them for dragging their feet..."

Then, Liu Jinding pointed again to the tea that Xiao Ding had made, and said: "Try it, it's pre-rain first flush." Then he asked casually: "So is your move making its way through the system? Is it still in the works?"

"I don't know. It may be done by now," Helian Dongshan replied.

"That would be quick!" Then Liu Jinding sat up straight and looked directly at Helian Dongshan, who immediately realised that he had something to say. It was necessary for the executive deputy mayor to sign off on the transfer of a cadre. If he found some reason or other not to sign, his promotion to the Public Security Bureau might be delayed.

Helian Dongshan smiled. What could he say? Nothing. He also sat up and said: "Mayor Liu, why did you ask me to come today? What instructions do you have for me?"

"Well, to cut a long story short, have you heard that people from the soy products company near the Flower World Hotel are out protesting again with a big banner that says 'We want to eat!'? The news has even spread abroad and there are international repercussions, which is very bad."

"So what is it you are saying?"

"There is pressure on the city, and on me. That Xie Zhichang isn't exactly snowy white in his business dealings, but if the workers continue to kick up a stink, they are going to cause trouble. I heard that you arrested the general manager of the Flower World Hotel, Bai Shouxin. Is it a serious charge?"

Helian Dongshan straightened up and said: "Yes, it is serious and the evidence is solid."

Liu Jinding sighed and shook his head. "Oh, that makes things difficult. This... this... this Flower World is a major taxpayer in the city. If it collapses, our local economy will be affected. Do you think this would work? Bai Shouxin is a hotel manager, and if he is arrested, he is arrested. Xie Zhichang won't try to get him out. Let Xie Zhichang pay the wages owed to the workers first. He can pacify them and stop their trouble-making, and then we can talk about the investigation again."

Helian Dongshan understood now. He could see which way the wind was blowing. He said: "I can't do that, Mayor Liu. I would have to ask the provincial government."

"Is there a problem with Xie Zhichang?"

"I am looking into him," Helian Dongshan said vaguely.

"I heard that his ex-wife is accusing him?"

"Yes."

"When a couple divorce, there is always bad feeling, and all sorts of nasty things get said. If there is no conclusive evidence, leave him alone. Xie Zhichang is very influential both in the province and the city, and he is a major taxpayer. He has a direct effect on the economic development of Huanghuai City. Some companies that are still finding their feet could find themselves in serious debt."

"I'll have to consult the provincial government about this matter."

"Well, please call them for instructions and then call me."

"I'm not sure that would be right."

Liu Jinding's expression changed. He suddenly lowered his head and said: "What's wrong? I've already explained it to you. You didn't give the city any kind of warning, and just went ahead and arrested him. Do you want to bring down a star company?"

"That wasn't my intention."

"Then what did you mean by it?" Liu Jinding said aggressively. "I'm telling you now, this is not my decision alone. Successful mediation is something determined by the standing committee of the Municipal Party Committee."

"If it is authorised by the Municipal Party Committee, then I can execute it. But I am a subordinate, so I can't make the call. You represent the first-level government, so you will have to do it, please."

Liu Jinding was stunned and said nothing for a long time.

Finally, he smiled dryly and said: "What you say makes sense. The government can't intervene in handling the case, so let's forget it. However, the workers are shouting that they will go to Beijing if the matter isn't resolved. Now, if you could do what you did last time..." Then, he shook his head regretfully and said: "Forget it, let them make trouble. Let's drink some tea."

Helian Dongshan knew in his heart that someone was playing a dangerous game and had encouraged the workers to make trouble. If it was not handled carefully, things would undoubtedly kick off. And if there were international repercussions, and things weren't dealt with, the top brass were bound to send down their own "opinion" which would severely limit his active participation in the case. It would seem that Xie Zhichang was stuck for the time being. He decided to give Liu Jinding a bit of a "jolt" to see how he reacted.

Helian Dongshan straightened up again and said: "I know that certain things are going on in the city, and Bai Shouxin has explained them to me. Murder and arson are not everyday problems. He also told me about a few other things, which are all under investigation."

"Ah, so that's how it stands."

Helian Dongshan decided to cut to the chase: "Recently, we've become aware of a mobile phone number starting with 'one-three-five'. It has been very active. The provincial government is investigating."

At that moment, the phone rang. Liu Jinding jumped to his feet and stood a little anxiously, almost knocking over the teacup on the sofa table. Then he hurried over to his desk and answered the call. He spoke into the receiver: "Uh-huh, uh-huh! I see. Let's leave it at that." Then, he looked at the computer on the desk, walked over to the sofa and sat down again. He said to Helian Dongshan: "Lao He, I gather your son's domain name is the Overlord of Western Chu. He's very famous on the internet."

Helian Dongshan looked at him in surprise, not knowing what to say.

"I go online a lot myself. Your son is amazing. He has a lot of fans. By the way, I heard he is working for a video games developer in Beijing and earning a lot of money. I also heard he has bought an apartment... actually, not just one, so you've got somewhere to go in your old age."

Helian Dongshan was quite taken aback.

At this point, Liu Jinding made it clear it was time for Helian Dongshan to go. "So let's leave it there," he said. "You are right. As the saying goes, 'Heaven's net has wide meshes, but nothing escapes it'. But there are some things... no, I won't mention them now. I'll report all this to Number One and let him decide."

Once out of the City Government Office building, Helian Dongshan's brain was in turmoil. He knew that releasing Xie Zhichang was just the same as giving him more time to fabricate his alibi. He didn't yet know if he should admit defeat in this battle. Why did Liu Jinding mention his son? He hasn't asked about him for years. What was the problem with his son?

TEN

THAT NIGHT, Liu Jinding drove Xie Zhichang to a secluded club-house, where they went into a private room for a tea ceremony.

This was not a place that was open to just anyone. The water was Evian and the chosen tea was Dahong Pao "Big Red Robe" picked from old trees high up in the mountains. The two sat face to face on sandalwood drum chairs with golden cushions, in a neat, clean room with Buddha statues. The purplish-brown teacups they used were made from Yixing clay. They drank small cup after small cup until beads of sweat started out on their heads.

"How is the tea, Uncle?" asked Liu Jinding.

"Good, it's good tea," said Xie Zhichang. "Pure and rich, with a penetrating flavour. The sweat came out with the first cup."

"Are you sure it isn't a cold sweat?"

"No, it's a hot sweat. Look at it pouring off me. Now, as to that affair—"

"I'm not going to talk about that. Do you know what the difference is between us, Uncle?"

"How can I not be aware of it, Mayor Liu?" Xie Zhichang replied. "Nephew, you are an official and I am just an ordinary citizen. No matter where you go, you are always going to be above me."

"I didn't mean that. The way things are in society today, money is not a problem for you. From that point of view, you are a real winner. And in any case, however you look at it, you are my superior. It was you who raised me. The difference between us is that in terms of practicality, I cannot match you, and in terms of knowledge and understanding, you cannot match me."

"No, no," Xie Zhichang said hurriedly. "From the start I was just a flower man, small fry. And now... now it's just... oh, that is to say, you're so well-read."

"Uncle, if you want to make it in the big league, you have to raise your thinking, raise your consciousness. You know a place called Amsterdam? It controls the price of flowers all over the world. The flowers there are all sold in bunches at so many US dollars per bunch..."

"Wow! Good Lord, what kind of profit are we talking about here—"

"Haven't you got that tiger girl working for you? Tell her to look it up on the internet."

"Are you making fun of me, Nephew? There are no tiger girls for me! I'm just a slow old ox that everyone looks down on–"

"That's not what I meant. What's the point of earning money if you're not going to have some fun with it? What I mean is that having a pretty woman dancing attendance on you is all well and good, but you need to keep up your literacy skills, and there are some books you really have to read."

"You're having a laugh, Nephew! It was fine while she was my bit on the side, but now I've actually married her, she's got a real temper on her, and she gives me a lot of attitude!"

"There is one book that all businessmen should read. Have you read it?"

"Culture is expensive," Xie Zhichang replied. "I took your advice and bought a bookcase full of books, but I don't have time to read them. So what is this book you are talking about?"

"It's the American author Dale Carnegie's *How to Win Friends and Influence People*. It would be very advantageous to you to get that tiger girl to read you a section every night before you go to sleep."

"What did you say his name was? Let me make a note of it so I can remember it: *How to Win Friends and Influence People*. Is that right? But, now, what about the matter of–"

"Don't worry, that matter has already been buried," said Liu Jinding. "That's not just my decision. The city government agrees too. In today's society, economic development comes first, and no one is going to let a city's economy crash. And in particular, no one is going to let the same thing happen again. If anyone starts investigating the 'June Twenty-Ninth Railway Incident' too closely, a whole load of people will be implicated, and that is something that no one wants to see. Do you understand?"

"You mean that, with all you lot behind me, no one will dare touch me? Besides, however you look at it, all I did was nod my head, and no one even saw me do that. As long as they don't start going through the accounts, I'm not worried about their investigation."

"So all you did was nod?"

"Yes, but to tell the truth, I did it in front of her."

"As long as you've covered your arse, no one will dare check up on you," said Liu Jinding. "Financially, you've got nothing to be afraid of. You head a private company, and he doesn't have the authority. Even if they do start investigating, I know you have two sets of books... But even so, you don't want to go troubling my master again so soon. Governor Li has his own problems. A bellyful of them."

"I understand, I understand this. I won't go looking for him."

"We've manged to grow a big tree at last and we can't just think about the cool shade it gives."

"Absolutely, absolutely."

Liu Jinding finished his tea and shook himself. He leaned back and said: "I feel a little dizzy. Can you get drunk on tea? Why do I feel drunk?"

"This Dahong Pao comes from an old tree," explained Xie Zhichang. "It's powerful stuff. Are you feeling tired?"

"Yes, I am rather. It really is strong stuff. I am a bit drunk."

"I heard people talk about getting drunk on tea."

They were both silent for a while, before Liu Jinding suddenly said: "Supposing something happened to me one day, Uncle. I mean, just suppose."

"What could possibly happen to you? No, no, absolutely not. Look where you are now! You'll be the mayor soon. What's going to happen to you?"

"I don't know why, but just at the moment, I don't feel so good about things."

"What are you afraid of? We have someone protecting us."

Liu Jinding shook his head, hesitated for a moment, and said: "If something does happen to me, I want your word, Uncle."

"Don't worry, Nephew, even if I lose my family fortune–"

"Your word is enough. It's nothing definite, but... even if you plan ahead, you still have to leave yourself room to manoeuvre."

The two men fell silent.

ELEVEN

After leaving the municipal government building, Helian Dongshan had no time to stop and think.

In order to stir things up in his meeting with Liu Jinding, he had already revealed that he knew about the phone cards. Now, he must act.

At eight o'clock that evening, he called Deputy Director Wan, and said: "Director Wan, has that matter been approved?"

"The Provincial Party Committee has approved it," Director Wan replied. "You and the comrades from the Commission for Discipline Inspection should act together. Take him to the *shuanggui* base first, and the approval documents will be sent over immediately."

Twelve hours later, the approval documents arrived and Liu Jinding disappeared.

CHAPTER SIX
六

ONE

THE PHONE CALL CAME in the early hours of the morning.

Liu Jinding was asleep when his mobile rang. In his dreams, he was trying on a new suit. This suit had been specially customised for him by a Hong Kong boss. The lining was embroidered with the gold monogram "LJD", which was the abbreviation of his name. He stood proudly in front of a full-length mirror, admiring himself. Who was this person? Could it be Liu Jinding? He appeared a little too portly. The Liu Jinding in the mirror was about to take up his new post. Yes, he was going to be the new minister of transportation. For so many years, his goal had always been the Transportation Department. He knew how many people coveted that position. But there was a white thread on the sleeve of the jacket. How could that happen on a custom-made Hong Kong suit? That was very bad. He frowned and pulled at the end of the thread, but it just got longer and longer... at that moment, his mobile rang.

The sound of the phone was particularly harsh in the early hours of the morning. Liu Jinding was startled out of his dream. He answered the phone, then gasped in a jolt of cold air and his hair stood on end. He stood there stunned for a few seconds, as his brain seemed to have stopped working. After a while, he came back to his senses, dashed over to the window, opened a corner of the curtains and looked outside. It was still dark. The light from the streetlamps was cold and unfriendly, and the surroundings were deserted. No one else was on the move. He was motionless too, but his feet were twitching, urging him to get going.

He had been separated from his wife for many years. When his son was very young, he was sent to Canada. As the years passed, his wife went to join her son to study in Toronto and then obtained a green card. Some of his money was deposited at home but some was also in accounts in Canadian banks. To be honest, if he wanted to leave, he could do so at any time. But he had no intention of emigrating to join his wife in Canada. As the saying goes, a clever rabbit has three burrows, and Canada was just a spare burrow. He had become accustomed to the life of an official in his home country, and he wanted to preserve that existence. But now... he walked quickly into the study next door, opened the safe and packed some things. After that, he went quietly downstairs carrying a leather bag.

On leaving his compound, he found himself standing at the side of the street, still in something of a daze. It had all happened so suddenly, he didn't know where to go. Where in this whole wide world could he find his hiding place? At that moment, he was startled by a taxi driver who pulled up beside him and called out: "Hi". Turning around, he heard the driver say: "Did you order a cab?"

Without thinking, he got into the taxi. "Where are you going?" the driver asked.

"The... the station."

Once in the taxi, his brain still felt as if it was wading through glue. He didn't know where the trouble lay. Had Lao Xie informed on him, or was it something else? After what had happened to Bai Shouxin, he had been confused. There were so many things he didn't understand, but he knew for sure he was in trouble. The phone message had only contained a total of fourteen words: "Meiling: the Transportation Department has brought a load of peaches. Be on your guard!"

This call was a hard-won prize. It came from a contact he had been nurturing for six years. This person was a member of the Confidential Department of the Provincial Party Committee, and his home was in Meiling. He had learned this trick from Tang Mingsheng, the former director of the County Party Committee Office. When he was director, Tang Mingsheng had cultivated informants in the three key departments of the Provincial Party Committee. In the beginning, all Tang wanted was to keep abreast of the movements of his superiors and be able to make preparations to welcome them in advance. This tactic had been praised by Xue Zhiheng, then secretary of the County Party Committee. Liu Jinding learned the same trick but used it for himself. For the past six years, whenever he gave gifts to the provincial leaders during holidays and festivals, he told his driver to give an additional gift to whoever was in charge of security. This particular informant liked to grow flowers, and most of the flowers he raised at his home were gifts from Liu Jinding. He also had a younger brother, for whom Liu Jinding had found a job. This man couldn't report in person on this critical occasion, so he had telephoned.

It was not yet daybreak, but National Day was approaching, and the station was bustling with people. He found himself alone in the crowd, feeling a little awkward. He had not bought a ticket at the station for many years. From the day when he became deputy director of the County Party Committee Office, he hadn't needed to. And later on, whenever he got on a train, he went directly through the VIP channel. More often than not, he actually took a plane and went through the VIP channel there too. As someone accustomed to special treatment, finding himself alone among the ordinary folk at the station was a rather uncomfortable experience. In the ebb and flow of people coming and going, he looked and felt as lonely as if he was walking through virgin forest.

Liu Jinding circled the station square twice and walked past the entrance of the ticket hall twice. He looked inside and saw that there weren't too many queueing to buy tickets, but he still did not dare to walk in. He couldn't help worrying about which pair of eyes might recognise him.

So after making two circuits of the station square, he headed west and stopped a taxi. He got in it and said: "Take me to the Friendship Hotel."

He got out of the cab in front of the hotel, but did not go in. After much thought, he decided he had no option but to call his driver. He reasoned that the man had been with him for many years, they were used to each other, and he would be more reliable than anyone else he could think of. Of course, there was another reason to call his driver, and that was to see if the driver was under someone else's control. He thought about it. If the phone rang seven times and no one answered it, he would hang up.

As it turned out, the driver, Xiao Ma, picked up after five rings. He sounded as though he had been roused from sleep, as he yawned and said: "Where to, Boss?"

"Come off at the interchange and wait for me at the end of the bridge," Liu Jinding said. Xiao Ma acknowledged the order and hung up the phone. He was such a conscientious driver, he would go wherever he was told and not ask any questions.

At dawn, there were few cars on the road and Xiao Ma pulled up twenty minutes later. The Shanghai Passat had been allocated to Liu Jinding by the city when he was deputy mayor. This car was in excellent condition and had a spacious interior. However, the seats had not been designed with comfort in mind and did not have proper lumbar support. This made it unsuitable for long journeys and the passenger inevitably ended up with a sore back, so Liu Jinding had asked Xiao Ma to provide some extra cushions. Xiao Ma cherished his car, and he was forever polishing it. The car was part of Liu Jinding's "look" as an official and he was so used to riding in it that he really didn't know how to get anywhere without it. Xiao Ma pulled up next to him, and once Liu Jinding was safely inside asked him: "Where to?"

"Beijing. I've got a meeting."

They drove along Xinxing Avenue. The shops on both sides of the road were still closed, but the roadside breakfast stalls were already steaming away. After crossing Jiefang Road, they turned onto the approach road that led them to the expressway. As the car approached the toll booth, Liu Jinding automatically sank deeper into his seat. Fortunately, no one detained them. He heard the female toll collector sitting in the window hand Xiao Ma a card, saying: "Have a good trip."

Liu Jinding closed his eyes as the car picked up speed. He told himself that he needed a good hard think about the situation.

At eleven o'clock that morning, when the car was approaching Shijiazhuang, Liu Jinding's phone rang. He looked at it. The call was from Secretary-General Zhao of the Municipal Party Committee. His heart skipped a beat as he realised that what he was expecting to happen, was indeed happening. Lao Zhao was an opera fan and the ringtone was set to a phrase sung by the famous Yue Opera performer Shen Fengmei. The line "after four thousand years, you have no need to be ashamed..." repeated several times. He hesitated for a moment but then took the call. As if nothing was wrong, he asked: "Hello, Old Opera Bones, what instructions do you have for me?"

"You outrank me, Older Brother," Secretary-General Zhao replied. "How could I dare give you orders? The City Standing Committee has a meeting. Number One issued the notice. It's in the small meeting room at half past ten."

"Oh, why didn't you tell me sooner? I'm out of town and can't get back. Please give my apologies."

There was no sound from the other end, as if Old Opera Bones was waiting for someone else's instructions. After a moment, Secretary-General Zhao said: "Number One has only just announced it. So you... where are you?"

"I'll be in Beijing soon," said Liu Jinding. "An old classmate is sick and I've come to see him."

"Male classmate or female classmate? Just relax, Older Brother." Liu Jinding laughed dryly and before he could reply, Old Opera Bones said: "That's fine, we'll wait for you to get back."

By this time, the car had reached the Shijiazhuang exit. "Let's take a breather," Liu Jinding said.

"Are you going into the city?" Xiao Ma asked.

"Yes."

Once in Shijiazhuang, they checked in, as usual, to the five-star Hilton Hotel. In the past, every time he went to Beijing, Liu Jinding would break the trip here, relax, take a bath, have a foot massage and so on. In the lobby, Xiao Ma booked Liu Jinding into a luxurious suite with his official business card and took a standard room for himself. When he handed the room card to Deputy Mayor Liu, Liu Jinding said: "Now, just leave me alone, as I am meeting a friend. The Western buffet here is very good. You can have something to eat, take a bath and rest, OK?"

With that, he took five hundred yuan from his wallet and gave it to Xiao Ma, who wouldn't take it, saying: "No need, no need. Shall I see you up to your room first?"

Liu Jinding pressed the money firmly into his hand and said: "Take it, Brother." This was the first time he had called him Brother, and it rather pleased Xiao Ma.

He went to get something from the car, and saw Liu Jinding get into the lift. After that, they didn't see each other again.

Nine hours later, at 8.16 pm, the doorbell rang in room 512, where Xiao Ma was staying. He was in the bath at the time and scrambled out. He wrapped himself in a towel, calling out: "I'm coming, Boss!"

He stood there in astonishment when he opened the door. It was not Deputy Mayor Liu who had rung the bell, but two people he didn't know. "Did you guys knock on the wrong door?" Xiao Ma asked.

One of the men was fat and the other thin, and they were both complete strangers. The thin man said: "Are you Xiao Ma, Ma Yongxiang?"

"Yes, and you–"

"Where is Mayor Liu?" the thin man demanded.

Xiao Ma was startled and said: "What do want with Mayor Liu?"

The fat man took over the conversation: "It was Mayor Liu who called us to come. Where is he?"

"Oh!" Xiao Ma said. "Mayor Liu is in a suite on the eighth floor, number eight-one-eight."

"It's urgent, so please take us to see him," the thin man said. His tone brooked no argument.

However, when Xiao Ma led them to the eighth floor and knocked for a long time, the door did not open. Finally, they asked an attendant to open it. They found that the beds were neatly made, and none of the toiletries in the bathroom had been disturbed. Only the TV was on, but there was no one in the room.

"Where is he?" the fat man asked.

"I don't know," said a stunned Xiao Ma.

The thin man took his phone out of his pocket and walked quickly out of the room, making a call as he went: "Boss, the target is missing. He's run away."

Before long, a group of men rushed into room 818. Seeing this commotion, Xiao Ma went white with shock.

TWO

WHAT SURPRISED HELIAN DONGSHAN was that Liu Jinding, the dignified deputy mayor of Huanghuai, would actually use surveillance-avoidance methods. In the twelve hours after the *shuanggui* order was issued, the slippery eel had made his escape and disappeared into the vast, anonymous crowd. This was getting personal!

When Helian Dongshan received the report of Liu Jinding's sudden disappearance, he asked his superiors to give him the authority to have his mobile phone monitored. It was discovered that he had arrived in Beijing.

As team leader, Helian Dongshan personally led his men to

Beijing overnight. The next morning, they could scarcely believe that the signal appeared in the bustle of Wangfujing Street. One of the task force exclaimed: "He's got some nerve to go shopping at a time like this!"

Helian Dongshan ordered his men to investigate immediately.

As a result, the twelve plainclothes officers stationed themselves within a radius of a hundred metres of Wangfujing Street. Holding photographs of Liu Jinding, they book-ended the street and unobtrusively scanned the pedestrians who flowed past like a tide of lice. But they saw no sign of the missing mayor.

In the afternoon, the mobile phone signal was picked up again in Beihai Park. The officers hurried over there, but once again came away empty-handed. Within ten metres of the location where the signal appeared, there was only a man in his sixties who was leaning on a rock in the rockery, squinting as he sunned himself. He had a rolled-up quilt beside him and was found to be in possession of a mobile phone. He told the officers that he had found it, but, three hours later, he changed his story.

When the officers brought the old beggar in front of Helian Dongshan, he took fright and said: "I have never done anything bad. I swear by Chairman Mao that I have never done anything bad. I was out trying to earn some money for my son's education."

"Where did you get your phone?" Helian Dongshan asked.

"I've already told you, he gave it to me," the old man replied.

"Who gave it to you? Where did he give it to you?"

"A man gave it to me in Shijiazhuang."

"Who was he? What did he look like?"

"Like an official, handsome, in a suit and tie, with a shiny watch."

"Let me ask you again, where in Shijiazhuang did he give you the phone?"

"I'm a beggar, so I was at the intersection. Where else would I be?"

"Which intersection?" one of the officers asked. "Be precise!"

"On the street, there is an intersection with lots of cars. All the people who ride in cars are rich, aren't they? When there is a red light, I will go up to a car at the intersection and ask for money... some people give, some don't, that's just the way it is. All of a sudden, a very decent-looking person threaded his way through the traffic and beck-

oned to me. 'Come on over here,' he said. 'I'll give you some money.'
So I went over to him."

"How much did he give you?" Helian Dongshan asked.

"What can I say? It was a lot, a thousand. He also asked me where
I came from. By his accent, he sounded like a fellow villager. 'Why did
you come to Hebei?' he asked. I told him that I'd come to earn some
money for my child's education. I had to get a bit away from home so
my son wouldn't be ashamed of me and lose face. He asked if I'd ever
been to Beijing, and I said no. He said: 'Do you want to go and have a
look around?' I said, yes, of course I did. He said: 'I'll give you five
hundred yuan for travelling expenses and a train ticket. Go and have
some fun in Beijing.' I thought I had met a real gentleman. Then he
said: 'I'll give you another five hundred yuan in cash. That's for you to
do just one thing.' I thought that whatever it was it was certainly
worth five hundred yuan. He said: 'Take this mobile phone. Consider
it as a gift. But there is one thing: for three days you mustn't turn it
off, answer it or call anyone. Just hold onto it.' I've told you everything. Will you let me go now?"

Helian Dongshan listened, his fury mounting. "Bastard!" he
exclaimed.

What was making Helian Dongshan so angry was the existence of
an "inside man" on the Provincial Party Committee. When the
shuanggui order was issued, only five people knew about it, and three
were leaders of the committee. Of the other two, one was the executive deputy director assigned the task (concurrently serving as a
member of the Standing Committee of the Commission for Discipline Inspection), and the other was Helian Dongshan himself. These
five people weren't going to be able to run away. If one of them was
responsible, there would be no question of a *shuanggui* order. So
which joint had sprung a leak?

The task force returned to Shijiazhuang, and by checking the
surveillance video of the hotel, it was confirmed that Liu Jinding had
not contacted anyone there. He had left alone, carrying a leather suitcase. However, there was one detail that caught Helian Dongshan's
attention. It had been reported that when his men broke into room
818 of the Hilton Hotel, the television was on, and it was showing
programmes from Pingyuan TV. Helian Dongshan obtained the relevant programme schedule for that channel from the provincial

government, and he found the problem. Liu Jinding hadn't touched anything after he had gone into the room. He just turned on the television and tuned it to Pingyuan TV. He had seen a news item on that channel... Helian Dongshan only said one word: "Fuck!"

Before the task force left Shijiazhuang, Helian Dongshan took to the streets alone and made his way to the place where Liu Jinding suddenly disappeared. The intersection was about 700 metres from the Hilton Hotel where Liu Jinding had checked in. Because it was close to the downtown area, there was a lot of traffic. Helian Dongshan saw that when the traffic light was red, people walked in the gaps between the densely packed vehicles, knocking on the windows of the cars begging for money. He saw a fifty-year-old country woman wearing a purple turban. There was no sorrow on the woman's face, just a casual cunning. She tapped on the car windows so boldly, and then reached out to beg for... Yes, someone was bound to give her money. Helian Dongshan saw that a few people handed money out of their car window, while some just ignored her and let her tap away. The cars started to move when the light turned green, but the woman was still standing in the traffic, quite unfazed. Yes, this society was a hostile environment all right! Helian Dongshan shook his head, lamenting out loud that honest workers were no longer respected, and everyone wanted to speculate.

So Liu Jinding, executive deputy mayor of Huanghuai, might have stood in the same position, watching the bustling traffic. What did he see, and what was he thinking? It was from this very spot that he disappeared.

Helian Dongshan stood at the intersection for a long while, until a light rain began to fall. At that moment, a small number of scooters crowded across the intersection. They appeared suddenly, all dressed in rain capes, like mushrooms emerging in the rain. The scooter riders made straight for the gaps wherever they appeared, shouting at pedestrians: "Scooter! Scooter! Who wants a ride?" One middle-aged man slid silently over to Helian Dongshan on his scooter, feet trailing on the ground on either side of his machine. "It's going to rain," he said. "Do you want to go to the Zhengshi Expressway?" Helian Dongshan was taken aback and asked: "Where?" The man said: "You don't look like a local. You can pick up a coach at the Zhengshi Expressway. Do you want to go there?" Helian Dongshan's heart skipped a beat and he asked: "How much?" The man said: "Fifty, take it or leave it." Helian Dongshan shook his head. The man looked at him and rode away.

Yes, west from this crossroads led to the airport; south, to the expressway; east, to the railway station... all roads lead to Beijing. However, when he was in Beijing, Helian Dongshan had already sent a notice to every customs station via the Ministry of Public Security, and Liu Jinding could not have got out that way. If you are on the run, the only way is to the southwest, and you have to be smuggled out, which is a difficult proposition. Since he couldn't get out, where could he go?

After the task force returned to Huanghuai, all their lines of enquiry came to an end. On the surface, it seemed that Liu Jinding was no longer being investigated, and Liu Jinding's family were not called in. Nor did the Provincial Party Committee or the Municipal Party Committee take any disciplinary action against him. On the city government's public website, the name of Executive Deputy Mayor Liu Jinding was still on display in the directory of posts. It seemed that the matter had been put on hold for the time being. In reality, however, Helian Dongshan was adopting the policy of "loosening outside and tightening inside", and the investigation did not stop for a moment. After two vain attempts, the members of the task force checked Liu Jinding's recent phone records and found that a call had been made from the provincial capital at 1.17 am. The existence of an "inside man" infuriated Helian Dongshan. He was so angry that he banged his desk and said: "You must find the traitor!" Through internal investigation and external enquiry, he found that there were two people on duty in the confidential room of the Provincial Party Committee that night, a man and a woman. The man's name was Sun Jianshe, thirty-two years old. The woman's name was twenty-seven-year-old Lin Huan. Under the strict orders of Helian Dongshan, the task force was ordered to transfer the files and recent photos of these two people. Helian Dongshan took the photos and looked at them with a magnifying glass for a quarter of an hour. Finally, he said: "Bring this man in."

When Sun Jianshe was brought to him, Helian Dongshan discovered that he was a standard scholar-type. He was chubby and wore glasses for short sight. His file revealed that he was born in Meiling and studied at the Law Department of Hunan University. After graduating, he drifted around Guangzhou for two years before returning to take the civil service examination. Judging from the resumé, he had no helpful background at home, but he did well in the exams and written aptitude tests, so he was hired by the Provincial Party Committee and became a confidential officer.

When he was angry, Helian Dongshan's voice got deeper. Yet the angrier he was, the calmer he became. He fixed Sun Jianshe with an icy stare and said: "I'm only going to ask you one thing: why would you do such a thing?"

Although Sun Jianshe was still carrying that dark secret, a long time had passed since he had contacted Liu Jinding. He froze for an instant and said: "What... what is it? What do you mean? I... I don't understand."

Helian Dongshan only asked that one question but he kept asking it every few minutes for more than an hour. On each occasion, Helian Dongshan asked Sun Jianshe to raise his head, then he looked at him and said: "Just tell me, why would you do such a thing?"

Sun Jianshe didn't dare look at him but he had no choice. He had drifted around the south for a while after graduating from university and wasn't completely green. At first, he thought Helian Dongshan was trying to con him, and he felt sure that it was impossible for him to be found out. An "approval document" passed through more hands than just his. How could this man be sure he was the mole?

But Helian Dongshan's eyes were terrifying. They were deep dark pools with icy whirlpools and clumps of glistening ice needles in the whirlpools. Sun Jianshe seemed to be pinned down by them. No matter how hard he struggled, he couldn't escape. He could have had no idea of the depth of contempt for the "inside man" contained in Helian Dongshan's interrogation. With the confidence that came from more than thirty years of experience as a policeman in pre-trial investigation, he had seen right through to Sun Jianshe's soul from the photograph long before the interrogation even started. He had already decided that it was him. He repeated his question time and time again, as if he was branding his soul over and over. Helian Dongshan's eyes told him: young man, don't hope for some kind of fluke. Don't insult my judgment, my patience is limited.

Helian Dongshan increased the pressure each time he asked, and at the end of the questioning, Sun Jianshe burst into tears. It was Helian Dongshan's eyes that broke him down. He squatted on the ground and started to cry. His head was shaking involuntarily, and his eyes were full of tears.

"Stand up," Helian Dongshan said softly. "Come on, stand up."

He looked at his watch and said severely: "You young people should cherish a job like yours. But if you want to know the truth, once you are in the Provincial Party Committee machine, no matter how or when you leave it, it will always be watching you. Now, I'm giving you one last chance. If you make a full confession, the whole thing can be handled internally without a report being submitted. As a confidential member of the Provincial Party Committee, you have to know the confidentiality regulations, right? So tell me, why did you do it?"

Finally, Sun Jianshe confessed. He sobbed and said: "No... no one respects me. He's the only one. I... owe him my love."

Yes, the call had been made by Sun Jianshe, a confidential member of the Provincial Party Committee. He had hesitated for a long time before making it. He did so after leaving the Provincial Party Committee compound at midnight and walked three streets away to the phone booth of a cigarette shop on one side of the street.

Sun Jianshe was no fool. The call he made was perfectly judged. He didn't use a code word, it was something better than a code word. More than a month ago, a director of the Communications Department had invited Liu Jinding to dinner at Meizhuang. The reason for the treat was that there were rumours that Liu Jinding would soon be made head of the Communications Department. The director wanted to flatter him in advance. So he asked around, and in the end got a confidential member of the Provincial Party Committee, who had been his university classmate, to invite Mayor Liu to dinner along with Sun Jianshe and some of his friends. That night, the principal guest, Liu Jinding, was in high spirits and he got everyone to play a sophisticated drinking game known as linked idioms. One person thinks of a four-character idiom, and the next person has to come up with another one that uses the end word of the previous one as its beginning (homophones are permitted). If he fails, he is fined. Sun Jianshe, a humble villager, was fined many cups of wine because he didn't have much experience of that sort of thing. Halfway through the game, someone came up with the four-character phrase "*cāng huáng chū táo*", which means "to flee in a panic". When it was Sun Jianshe's turn, he was already tipsy and became suddenly tongue-tied. At that point, Liu Jinding came to his rescue, picking up the wine cup and saying: "I'll drink this cup for the poor lad, but I would like to explain that the word '*táo*' can have two readings. One is '桃' 'peach' as in '桃之夭夭', 'the peach trees are in full bloom' and the other is '逃' 'escape' as in '逃之夭夭', 'to make good your escape', which is completely different. One is something dazzling and beautiful, and the other is about fleeing without leaving a trace." He patted Sun Jianshe on the shoulder condescendingly, and said: "So my little comrade from Meiling, always remember to 'make good your escape'!" Everyone laughed and said what an erudite fellow Mayor Liu was. Later on, this was why only Liu Jinding knew the real meaning of the telephone call he received.

After a morning of interrogation supervised by Helian Dongshan, Sun Jianshe finally provided a very important clue: the existence of a club called Mei Village on the banks of the Yellow River not far from the provincial capital. In this clubhouse, there were occasional gatherings of fellow villagers, known as a dinner club. Mostly, the people who went were "big brains" at registrar level and above in Meiling. Sun Jianshe was very junior, so he had only attended once or twice.

It was the discovery of this Mei Village club that gradually brought a character previously regarded as irrelevant to the forefront of the investigation. This fellow's name was Jiang Baoguo, and he was executive deputy director of the Huanghuai City Justice Bureau.

THREE

THE DINNER CLUB IN MEI VILLAGE had been initiated by Liu Jinding, who believed that this was all part of his strategic vision.

In the beginning, the dinner club was limited to a few villagers from Meiling, most of whom were cadres at or above the county and division level, known to Liu Jinding. They always said they were getting together in the name of "community benefit". After they had met a few times, people came to appreciate Mei Village for its location near the Yellow River dykes, its beautiful scenery and excellent food. Someone suggested that, since they were all fellow villagers and shared a kind of brotherhood, why shouldn't they have a dinner club every month or so, taking it in turns to take the chair, and see how they could help each other out. "Taking the chair" involved that person footing the bill, and the others were all his guests. This proposal was unanimously approved. Liu Jinding was elected, unopposed, as the convener of the dinner club, and also given the title of general secretary.

Later, intentionally or unintentionally, the club evolved into a larger social circle. No longer restricted to people from Meiling, there were also officials who had good relationships with Liu Jinding, and others who had some kind of connection with Meiling. Initially, the dinner club was limited to one table, with only a dozen or so regulars, all of whom were hard-core members from Meiling. Later, officials and a few entrepreneurs joined in, and the addition of a commercial element greatly enlivened the occasions. Most important, someone always took the initiative to foot the bill. Of course, small businessmen weren't allowed in, and Liu Jinding, as general secretary, controlled this aspect very strictly. Those who were allowed were big businessmen, billionaires at least. Finally, it evolved into three levels. At VIP level, everyone was a member of the inner circle; second-level members were all from Meiling; the third level was for businessmen, and they were given temporary membership. One year, when things were at their busiest, the members filled five tables. Everyone in the inner circle had a VIP card, a private room all year round and a beautifully printed little address book containing the phone numbers of useful contacts.

Everyone knew that "Number One" was the central figure of the dinner club.

Number One was the code name used for Li Delin, and it was regarded as a mark of respect. Li Delin was a PhD who had studied in the United States and was also the deputy governor in charge of agriculture. He was the pride of Meiling, and the highest-ranking of all the Meiling officials. Everyone knew that, in the prevailing environment, being a recognised expert meant that the sky was the limit for him in his official career.

Of course, Liu Jinding understood that the long-term members of the dinner club had their own ideas and objectives. The person they all most wanted to meet was not Liu Jinding, but Number One.

Although a healthy tradition of friendship and fellowship existed within the club, that was not the most important thing. So every so often, Liu Jinding would invite Li Delin along, and of course, they all wanted to meet the deputy governor. Originally, dinner club members only drank Maotai, and whoever was in the chair always brought a case of it. Later, because Li Delin only drank Wuliangye, that became the official club drink. Undoubtedly, it was he who gave the club its distinguishing characteristics.

Under normal circumstances, Li Delin rarely participated in the dinner club meetings, only going when Liu Jinding thought it necessary. So every time he did show up, it was rather like the image of a god being placed on the ancestral altar. As soon as he appeared, everyone flocked to worship him. The more people sang his praises, the higher his reputation seemed to rise, in something of a pyramid effect. To help Li Delin remember just who he was, some officials took it in turn to heap outrageous flattery on him. They would propose toasts such as: "Governor Li, in the south they have Yuan Longping, who is known as the Father of Rice. In the north, we have you, and you should be the Father of Wheat or, even better, the Venerable Father of Wheat! Today, I toast you on behalf of the 1.2 million people in this county!" Another would stand up and say: "Governor Li, when I was young, my only wish was, yes you guessed it, to eat white buns every day. You are a wheat expert recognised by the State Council. The Meiling Number Seven that you cultivated has doubled the yield of wheat. Thanks to you, tens of thousands of peasant children can eat white buns! I represent those thousands of tens of thousands. The farmers' children all toast you!" Then again, someone would say: "Governor Li, when I left home today, my wife told me to toast you in a glass of wine on behalf of all the people of the world! Why? Because she read about your achievements in the newspaper. It said that you are still working tirelessly on your 'double-eared wheat' project. This is your huge contribution to all mankind! From now on, no one will ever be short of food!" Of course, these words were not all pure flattery, as there was some element of genuine admiration in them. However, it has to be said that, as the wine kept flowing, it was like people collecting more and more firewood to feed the bonfire of flattery so the flames almost touched the sky. When speech gets taken to this extreme, it really is just like workers stoking a furnace. On another occasion, Jiang Baoguo, the executive deputy director of the Bureau of Justice, staggered drunkenly to his feet and shouted out in front of everyone: "Long live Number One!"

When Li Delin first heard this kind of talk, he would immediately put a stop to it, saying, with a very serious expression: "That's all nonsense! I'm no such thing. Stop it now." After he had heard it a few times, he just began to feel embarrassed and would still try to put a stop to it, saying: "That's enough! It's too much. Don't talk like that any more. I didn't do it alone, and anyone who repeats it will be fined a cup of wine!" In the end, he heard it all so many times that his ears became hardened to it, even though he still disapproved. It really was a kind of brainwashing. If something gets repeated that often, it gives rise to a kind of inflated self-grandeur, verging on the tyrannical, a surging passion and a sense of one's own supremacy. Once a person reaches that state, he becomes set in it for life. Whenever he enters a room, people rush over to help him out of his coat, and when he leaves everyone hurries over to see him off. As a result, Li Delin gradually stopped feeling the need to remain polite in their company. After the wine had been round a few times, he would stand up, clasping his hands gently, and say: "You go on drinking. Don't worry about seeing me out." When he left, everyone watched, but no one dared stop him, and Liu Jinding himself would see him out.

Although it was called a dinner club, whenever officials gather together, they naturally want to talk politics. In reality, talking politics principally involved gossip: who was being promoted, who was on whose side, who said what on the Standing Committee, who made a phone call to Beijing, who did they want to see promoted but because of some misunderstanding by their underlings, the wrong person got investigated and was about to be put onto the Standing Committee, and who got furious about the mistake when it was discovered! Or, who had been grinding away trying to get someone promoted, and had gone to work on the cadres three times in a single year to get it done; or who had tried to bribe the wrong people; or who had got a phone call in the middle of the night when he was secretary of the County Party Committee and been reprimanded like a naughty grandchild... Of course, all these "whos" referred to other officials they were familiar with, and usually different ones in each instance.

At the club, they also privately discussed the fact that, in the current circumstances, an expert senior cadre like Number One, who was still comparatively young and vigorous, was bound to make it to the top sooner or later. Some were bold enough to predict that he was a likely future candidate for deputy prime minister and might also serve in the National People's Congress. It was all like buying stocks and shares: the earlier you invest in a likely prospect, the greater your profit. And emotional investment is a kind of investment too. Participating in the activities of the dinner club was just another means of investment, so when it came to the prospects for Number One, everyone was very excited, and they all wanted to make every effort themselves on his behalf. As a result, one deputy director said impulsively that he was willing to found a corporation and invest thirty million yuan in getting Number One up to Beijing. On the back of that, others said that if they were talking money, it should be a hundred million! Some other people objected, saying that with someone like Number One it was better not to risk messing things up, but spend the money buying public opinion and getting the newspapers to promote a "people's governor" with the tag "the governor in the straw hat". That way they would also be representing public opinion. Of course, that set everyone off arguing incessantly.

For a time, the dinner club met very frequently and everyone was always on the telephone to each other. Businessmen from all walks of life started to hear about the club on the banks of the Yellow River, and they flocked over there, trying to use their connections to get them in. There were also businessmen who scurried over to offer their services: they came in order to pick up the tab. Often before the diners had even finished eating, someone would burst in to pay the bill, hoping to become a VIP member. There were also some officials who wanted to bring a matter to Li Delin's attention, and they would tag along with Liu Jinding, hoping for a chance meeting with the deputy governor.

Of course, every member of the dinner club had their own opinions. Among the officials who actually came from Meiling, Tang Mingsheng was the one with the greatest popular support. He had been director of the County Party Committee Office for fourteen years and had been very hard-working. But he was transferred to a very unfashionable county and made a deputy secretary of its Party Committee. He felt he had been badly wronged, very badly wronged indeed. He didn't understand how someone as steady and conscientious as himself could be left in such a backwater. He had been left stewing for too long and had been depressed for too long, so it was inevitable that his mind began to work along certain lines. He thought to himself that, since everyone else was getting busy, he would get busy too. Although he secretly looked down on Liu Jinding, and had given him his first position after graduating, now, because Liu had an extra diploma, he was two levels above him. Although he was only at the deputy departmental level, the man was an "executive" and was about to be promoted to full departmental level, so Tang Mingsheng had no option but to accept the situation. That was why he was so keen to join the dinner club. He hoped it might give him the opportunity he wanted. But then, that night, fuelled by wine, he had picked a big fight with Jiang Baoguo.

Jiang Baoguo, executive deputy director of the Bureau of Justice, had joined the dinner club entirely out of hatred. He was originally the top deputy director of the Huanghuai City Public Security Bureau, and he was regarded as a reliable veteran. He was transferred into the locality from the army, where he had reached the rank of regimental commander, but the transfer amounted to a demotion. After eighteen years in the Huanghuai City Public Security Bureau, he was finally able to become deputy director. But just as he was about to take over as director, he was transferred out and over to the Justice Bureau. The bureau was a small organisation with few employees, and in no way comparable to the Public Security Bureau. He hated what had been done to him, hated it so much the blood almost spurted from his eyes. In Huanghuai, he hated two people in particular: one was the public security chief Lao Wan, Wan Haifa; the other was the current secretary of the Huanghuai City Party Committee, Xue Zhiheng. So when he drank, he would get to a point when the tears of anger and self-pity began to flow, and he would start cursing: "Dammit! That miserable son-of-a-bitch! He's not even a man!" Everyone could work out who he was cursing. They all knew where things were heading, and no one was going to pick him up on it.

The first time Tang Mingsheng took part in the dinner club, he had very mixed emotions, but he needed to make his mark, so he piped up: "I know all about Secretary Xue. I was his office manager in Meiling for nine years—"

But before he could finish, Jiang Baoguo glared at him, took a swallow of wine and said: "What the fuck do you understand? What did you do for him? Carry out his piss-pot!"

Tang Mingsheng was infuriated by this and said: "You can't talk to me like that, Director Jiang..."

Jiang Baoguo threw a sideways look at him, picked up the wine jug, put twelve wine cups in a row and filled them. Then he yelled: "Drink them! Come on, drink up! Once you've drunk all twelve, I'll tell you what a clown that man is!"

Although both men were deputies, Jiang Baoguo had the edge over him because of his mainstream post, and he definitely felt he was a cut above. But his post, mainstream as it was, was in the Justice Bureau, which was a small ministry that did not occupy a prominent position in the bureaucratic world. Besides, he was still only a deputy, so Tang Mingsheng was not really willing to accept his authority. He said: "I'm not going to drink. What makes you think you can make me?"

"Look, Lao Tang, these drinks are the rite of passage to get into the dinner club. Haven't you heard the saying 'you can judge a man's worth by the way he drinks'? If you don't drink these, do you think you'll ever get promoted? No way! So go on, drink!"

Tang Mingsheng looked at Liu Jinding, hoping that he might say something. But Liu Jinding just smiled and stayed silent. Tang Mingsheng knew that Jiang Baoguo was trying to trick him since there was no such thing as this "rite of passage". So he said: "Director Jiang, do you think I have to drink those just because you tell me to? I refuse!"

Jiang Baoguo had already drunk too much, and his tongue was running away with him. When he saw Tang Mingsheng trying to face him down, he jumped to his feet, banged the table and said: "You have to drink this wine! I'm telling you, I've been in the city's Public Security Bureau for eighteen years, and the executive deputy director has only been there for eight. If that Xue fellow hadn't elbowed me out, I would have been the director. But those eighteen years haven't been for nothing. Just answer me this: do you want to be able to drive your car into Huanghuai in the future? You'd better believe that all it will take is one phone call from me, and the police will stop your car every time!"

Tang Mingsheng was trapped, and he knew it. He went red in the face and said: "You... you wouldn't dare."

It was then that Liu Jinding spoke: "Drink up, Lao Tang. If you can't, I'll drink them for you."

Everyone else joined in: "It's only a few glasses of wine, Lao Tang. Go on, have a drink!"

Still flown with alcohol, Jiang Baoguo said: "This is a rite of passage, Mayor Liu. You can't help him."

Finally, with everyone getting on his case, Tang Mingsheng reluctantly drank the wine. When he had finished, he burst into tears.

At the end of the meal, Liu Jinding was left alone with Jiang Baoguo. With everyone gone, the two of them drank another catty of liquor. When they had finished, they embraced, calling each other older brother and younger brother, and saying it was as if they had known each other all their lives. Jiang Baoguo said with tears in his eyes: "Mayor Liu, I know you're an honest man and I am happy to follow you. Just tell me where to fight and I will fight–"

"No, no, don't call me mayor," said Liu Jinding. "You are older than me. You are the older brother and I am the younger."

"All right then, I won't acknowledge anyone else as my brother, only you! Younger Brother Mayor, just hearing that from you is enough for me. If there is anything in future, all you have... all you have to do is say... just say. I will swim through boiling water... and... and jump through fire!"

Tang Mingsheng had wanted to have a proper talk with Liu Jinding alone, but he got drunk and threw up. He sat in his car and waited and waited until he fell asleep. When he woke up and went to look for Mayor Liu, he found that he had already left. He was so angry that he wept.

Later on, Liu Jinding did indeed help him. He took him to the head of the cadre section of the Organisation Department who was in the process of reallocating the cadres. After Xue Zhiheng became secretary of the Huanghuai City Party Committee, Tang Mingsheng returned to Meiling and became county party secretary. He naturally put this down to Liu Jinding's influence.

FOUR

THIRTY-NINE YEARS after he last slept with the plum blossoms, Liu Jinding slept with them again.

He had sneaked back to Meiling and was living quietly in his father's greenhouse. It was situated in the fields leased by his father, Liu Quanyou, which covered more than twenty acres. Next to the greenhouse was a little wooden shack that was rarely visited by anyone. When he first fled back home, that was where Liu Jinding hid out. From the moment Liu Jinding went in, he felt as though he had returned to his childhood, back to the days when he slept in a wheelbarrow.

Inside the greenhouse, the old flowering plum tree called The King of the Chinese Plum Trees and Butterfly Transformation was still there, and by now it was half as tall as a man. It hid there all alone and was never displayed. On a few occasions, Liu Quanyou had planned to sell it because someone was offering a very high price, but for the sake of his son's future, he held off. Liu Jinding had originally planned to give it as a birthday present to Li Delin but changed his mind. He decided that later on he could send the Butterfly Transformation directly to Beijing when his mentor finally got there. Perhaps it might get sent straight into Zhongnanhai. That really would be something. But now, this turn of events had delayed its eventual progress.

However, if the plant hadn't been sent out yet, at least Liu Jinding had returned.

Liu Jinding could never have imagined that, overnight, he would go from being executive deputy mayor of a prefecture-level city to a wanted criminal. He was nobody's fool and knew that there was no going back now. At the outset, he could have gone abroad; his wife and son were both in Canada, and he had his two passports with him. But he was scared to leave, afraid that someone would stop him at the airport. So after some hesitation, he sneaked back home. He had read a few books, and he reckoned it was just as it said in one of them: the most dangerous place was also the safest.

He slept soundly that first night after sneaking into the greenhouse. Yes, he seemed to have returned to his childhood, smelling the fragrance of the flowers and listening to the sound of the wind in the field, as if he had returned to the days when he slept in a wheelbarrow. He was so tired. He slept soundly and dreamlessly on the hard wooden bed.

At dawn, the wind in the fields surged like the tide on a beach. It was the wind that woke him. He opened his eyes, and everything in front of him was strange: no sofa, no leather swivel chair and his body was very stiff... it certainly wasn't his Simmons bed that he was used to sleeping on. Almost without thinking, there was a stifled sound in his throat as the two words he was about to call out – "Xiao Ding", the name of his secretary – stuck there. In an instant, he felt tears seep from the corners of his eyes. He couldn't bring himself to think about how he had come to this.

Not far from the house was a field of ripe corn, its leaves rustling, and the astringent smell of corn drifting in with the wind, reminding him of his childhood. A scorpion crawled up the wall, as tenaciously as his own ascent in life. Then it rained, and the rain was pelting down. The only sound left in the world was the patter-patter of the drops hitting the leaves of the maize, carrying the dampness in with it.

Liu Jinding went hungry for three days in the greenhouse, and it was the only thing he could think about. During those three days, Liu Jinding, who had eaten all the delicacies of land and sea, only consumed two half-baked sweet potatoes and two ears of tender maize. It really felt like he had returned to his childhood. The sweet potatoes and the corn were picked in the field. He dug a small earth oven in the greenhouse floor, gathered a few plants and twigs, and lit them with a cigarette lighter. He cooked the sweet potatoes and the corn in the oven, devouring them when they were only half-done. It was only after he had gone hungry for three days that he rediscovered the greedy delight of the roasted sweet potatoes of his childhood. They were so delicious!

Liu Jinding was frightened throughout those three days. There was a chord in his brain, stretched to breaking point, and every time the wind blew, he rushed to a crack in the door and looked out, afraid that someone had tracked him down. Fleetingly, he imagined he was invisible. If he could become invisible, the world would allow him to come and go freely. How good would that be! Of course, it was only a moment of imagination, but it lingered in his mind for a long time.

Afterwards, he fell asleep again in the dark. In his sleep, he dreamed he was sitting in his father's wheelbarrow, the wheels rumbling as they made their way along the road to Kaifeng. He seemed to hear his father say: "Here we are in Weichuan." That was the place where he ate white bread for the first time in his life.

Opening his eyes, he found his father Liu Quanyou squatting in front of him.

His father was old. He squatted there hunched over, rubbing his hand on the quilt, and his hand was as rough as a metal file. Seeing him open his eyes, his father looked at him silently for a long time and said: "Is that you? Have you committed a crime?"

"Who told you that?" asked a startled Liu Jinding.

"The chief of the police station has come looking three times, but he didn't say anything. He just asked if you'd come back and when did I expect you."

"What did you say?" His father just shook his head.

Liu Jinding had never sent a cent home in all the years since he graduated from university and started working. Of course, his father was a famous gardener in the county, a "master gardener", and he didn't need his money. However, he was old, and he might soon get dragged into the affair. Liu Jinding couldn't bear the thought of it.

His father was silent for a while, then said: "If you know anyone who wants the Butterfly Transformation, please send it to them quickly. Otherwise, I'll have to sell it. That flower is too evil."

The Butterfly Transformation had always been his father's "darling". It could have been sold for a lot of money. He had told his father not to sell it, so his father didn't. He had said he wanted to give it to someone, so his father had tended it carefully, waiting for him to give it away. Later, he had changed his mind again. He said he would send it to Beijing when they were able to tell when it was going to blossom. So his father had experimented to see if he could control the flowering period. There were a few times when his father called him excitedly and said: "Success! I've done it! I've extended the flowering period by a month!" Then, he kept asking for it to be extended further, and even, unreasonably, asked for regular flowering periods. His father had no choice and tried again and again. Finally, he came up with an idea, and the result of his experiments was that he could put the bole in the freezer and freeze it, then thaw it and wake the flower up again... just like that. But this bole was hundreds of years old. How much of this treatment could it take? His father had told him: "Hurry up. We can't keep doing this. If you keep torturing it, it will die... Even humans can't take this kind of treatment."

Now, father and son were looking at each other silently, as if they had nothing to say, but yet there seemed to be a lot that should be said. For so many years, it had not been easy for the father. He could have remarried, but for his son's sake, he never had. Liu Jinding wanted to say something, but he didn't know how to begin. He rarely smoked, but now he asked: "Have you got a cigarette?" His father took out a cigarette, handed it to him and lit one for himself. The two of them smoked in silence. His father coughed, and he coughed along with him.

"Maybe it was the plant that made all this happen to you."

"Nonsense! How could that be?" Liu Jinding said disapprovingly.

"I tortured it for too long when I was trying to control the flowering period. It hates me. It's... it's an omen."

"What omen?" Liu Jinding said impatiently.

His father fell silent. Hadn't he already told Liu Jinding that the ancient Chinese plum tree had blossomed that June? Never before had the winter plum blossom showed snowy white on the tree at that time of year. White flowers in summer! The tree was showing its resentment. It was a bad omen!

His father could only say: "If anything's up, just... just hand yourself in."

Liu Jinding's anger flared: "Who said anything was up? What could be wrong? There's nothing going on."

"If it's something money can fix, I've still got–"

"I've already told you, nothing's up! I just came back to see this tree. I'm going tomorrow."

His father fell silent for a while, then nipped out his cigarette and said: "Is it a question of money? If it can be solved by spending money, I still have–"

"I said nothing happened. I came back just to see this pot of plum blossoms. I will leave tomorrow."

The father was silent for a while, then said: "It's not about money then?"

"No! Now go! Just go!"

Liu Quanyou arched his back and walked slowly towards the

door. When he got there, he looked back and said: "Go, go quickly. And if you do, don't come back again."

FIVE

LIU JINDING HID OUT IN THE GREENHOUSE for several more days before leaving.

As he stepped out, he hesitated, but then went on. In the dark country night he could just make out the stars. They shone like new nails, distant and comforting. After so many years in the city, he saw the stars as if for the first time. It had been so long.

As he set off down the path across the fields, he was still timid, listening carefully for any movement in the four fields, but the thick night air was as good as an invisibility cloak, and it gave him a feeling of safety. Although the dirt road was bumpy underfoot, the earth was soft from autumn, and he might almost have been walking along a red carpet. The corn all around him was close to the height of a man, and the field was as silent as a forest in the night. In the quiet, the groves of tall corn felt like his army, and he was reviewing his troops. Inside his head, he greeted them all. As he walked along, he tripped over a sweet potato vine, staggered and fell into the mud of one of the ridges. Lying on the ground, his mouth full of wet earth, he couldn't help but smile.

He walked more and more boldly through the dark, brushing the dry corn blades with his hand as he went. The corn leaves were astringent and sweet, and he could just taste that sweetness. At this moment, he felt like a child going home after school. It was nice to be invisible in the country night. This kind of familiarity comes from childhood and is embedded in the bones. Suddenly, his eyes were full of tears, and he wept. Stepping across the cornfield, he entered the nursery forest. It contained Chinese locust trees, and the large, thorny trees gave off a bitter fragrance in the dark night. Then there was the boxwood forest, the short trees like an ink-coloured ocean, with bright points on the waves and the leaves forming an oily black swell that emitted a bitter medicinal fragrance. Next was another sweet potato field studded with oriental plane trees. The planes grew straight and tall, like young girls, slim and graceful with shiny black hair. A winding dirt track led around the plantation of plane saplings, which sloped gradually downwards. As he followed the track, Liu Jinding walked straight into a deep ditch.

He was dazed, and a thick, black fog filled the night sky. The starlight disappeared, and the sky became as dark as the bottom of a cauldron. For a while, he couldn't even see his hand in front of his face. It suddenly hit him that he had no idea where he was. He felt as though he was entangled in a huge black net. It was so dark all around him that he couldn't see a thing. He was panicked for a while, then he said to himself: Calm down, you know this place. What's so scary about walking at night in your home village? He thought about the local geography for a moment as he went downhill, and decided that he had lost his way. He had just made a long, slow turn but had lost his bearings on the way. He remembered vaguely that he had been going south, so he should keep going. Ahead of him was the village of Xiao Zhuang or perhaps Da Xu... he couldn't be wrong about that. Perhaps if he walked on for a while, he would get back on course. But the night was too dark, and there was no sound anywhere. He felt that he was still walking in the ditch, and the farther he went, the deeper it got and the more panicky he became. It was so strange to have been walking for ages, so why couldn't he get out of this ditch?

He decided to retrace his steps. However, after another quarter of an hour, it was still pitch black in front of him. It was then that fear of ghosts set in, and his skin began to crawl. He suddenly thought: Oh shit! I bet I've hit the "ghost wall"[1] and it's making me walk round in circles! He began to shout and yell: "Help! Is there anyone there? Is anyone there?" He felt his hair stand on end as soon as he saw the "ghost fire". The green flames were flickering more than ten metres away, as if they were beckoning to him. For a while, ghosts and shadows appeared all around him, and he felt a swish of cold, as if something had been thrown in his face. He was terrified. With only the boundless night ahead of him, fear crushed him like a mountain. The next instant, he collapsed. Terrified, he faced the endless darkness and fell to his knees with a thud, shouting: "God, please take me! I am guilty, I am a sinner!"

When the green ghost fire attacked him again, he stayed on his knees and screamed: "Lord, no matter which god you are, if you are an earth god, or a demon, or a judge from Hell, please get me out of here! In this life or the next, I will remember your great benevolence. I will give thanks every year and regild your statue..." Maybe it was just a trick of the mind, but when he knelt down and prostrated himself on the ground imploring the gods, the darkness in front of him didn't seem so dense, and the night air that had felt so thick seemed slowly to dissipate. In a daze, he saw some grave markers ahead of him fluttering with paper ghost money. Facing the boundless night, and the grave markers, he muttered to himself as if conducting an internal interrogation. At this moment, he recalled that he was the child of a peasant family, and although he had taken food and drink and other things from people, deep down, he was not a bad person. If he ever made his way back, he would be a good man, and he wouldn't steal even a cent from anyone... By now, he was hurting right through to his marrow. But it was too late, and he knew it was too late. And as for that one, all-important thing, he neither dared nor wanted to plumb its depths.

In the face of the inquisition by the night demons, he crawled along the ground, muttering to himself, and knelt down. Then, when he had calmed down a little, he slowly stood up. Liu Jinding reran the direction he had travelled in his head. He felt that he had indeed taken a wrong turn, and that he should retrace his steps as soon as possible. He could no longer allow himself to be at the mercy of the ghosts being tossed back and forth like this. So he made his heart slow down, gritted his teeth and said: "I don't fucking believe it. Just keep going in one direction, even if you go on till dawn, and see where it takes you. If God really wants to take you, so be it."

Thereupon, he turned around and walked back the way he had come, having emptied all thoughts from his head. The night was still dark, and fear was on his heels. There always seemed to be a ghost behind him. With every step he speeded up, the ghost matched his pace. If he slowed down, the ghost slowed down too. He just had to grin and bear it and move forward. He walked, he ran, he ran faster and faster still, hearing only the whine of the wind in his ears. As he ran, he suddenly felt that there was no sound behind him. At that moment, he looked up and finally saw a light in the distance. He almost collapsed when he saw it and he let out a long sigh of relief. The light seemed so kind and well-intentioned. He said to himself: "Thank you, Mother. I've finally made it." After so many years, it was the first time he had ever called out the word "mother". Yes, it was only then that he remembered that he used to have one. As he walked on, getting closer to the light, he stopped and stood for a while. He now realised that he had reached the entrance to Wanggezhuang Village.

Wanggezhuang is twenty-eight *li* from Yakou Village. Could he have walked that far in his daze? As he recovered from the shock, he began to find himself rather laughable. Had it really been a ghost? How could there be any such thing? Best not to go walking at night, as you just end up frightening yourself. Fuck it!

As Liu Jinding stood there thoughtfully, his feet seemed to want to move forward, but his body was pushing him back. He had been to Wanggezhuang many times. Back then, when he was director of the County Party Committee Office, he did two good things for the village. One was to build a biogas digester so that the whole village could use biogas for cooking. The other was to surface the main street so that 200 metres of concrete road connected the village with the provincial highway. Both of these initiatives were funded with money allocated from on high.

Back then, the Party secretary of this village, a man called Wang Mahu but widely known as Sloppy Wang, came to his office with two bottles of sesame oil. Sloppy Wang was not a tall man. He had been selling bean curd since he was young. His old waist was twisted from pushing a trolley and it was as stiff as a pole, so he had a bandy-legged, swaying gait, rather like Liu Jinding's father. In fact, despite his nickname, Sloppy Wang was a very shrewd man. He came in, bent over, nodding good-humouredly, and said nothing. He put the bottles of sesame oil on the corner of the sofa, then squatted down on the ground, looking up at Liu Jinding. Liu Jinding said: "Secretary Wang, what brings you here? Is something up?" Sloppy Wang looked at the sesame oil he had brought, and said: "I'm sure you are busy, Director, you must be busy... I have come to see you, but there's nothing wrong." Liu Jinding said: "If anything's up, just tell me." Sloppy Wang said: "I heard that the high-ups are allocating funds. Can you give my village a share? Just a little share." He wasn't demanding anything, just asking for a share. Liu Jinding said: "How did you know about that?" Sloppy Wang said: "I also heard that they're going to build some kind of pool, or whatever it's called. Why not build it in my village?" At that time, the construction of biogas digesters in rural areas was still a new thing. It was a policy advocated from the very top, and the pilot villages all got subsidies. So when Liu Jinding put together the proposal, he included Wanggezhuang as one of the pilot villages for a biogas digester. Wanggezhuang's digester was built with money from the province, and every family there now used biogas.

Later on, Sloppy Wang came back to the county twice more to see him, each time carrying a cloth bag. Once he brought "wheat fragrant" apricots, and another time it was tender sweetcorn. He walked in on his bandy legs and, just as before, squatted on the ground and said: "Well, Director, there's nothing in particular." Liu Jinding was familiar with his ways now and said casually: "Let's roll the dice anyway, and see where they land." Sloppy Wang was squinting up at him and said: "I heard there's some more money coming through. How about a share? Just a little share." "You're a canny one, Lao Wang," Liu Jinding replied. "What have you heard?" Sloppy Wang said: "It's state money, so anyone can be given it. Why not give us a share? Just a little share." In the end, his softly-softly wheedling and cajoling meant he walked away with 283,000 yuan. He used it to resurface the concrete road connecting the village street with the provincial highway. This was why Sloppy Wang was held in such high regard in the village.

Liu Jinding mustered his courage and limped over to Sloppy Wang's house. By then, Sloppy Wang had built himself a small three-storey building. There was an electric light at the large red iron gate. The walls on either side of the courtyard were inlaid with two large characters: one was "福" (good fortune) and the other was "寿" (long life), the characters picked out in vermilion tiles, making them look very grand. Before Liu Jinding could knock on the gate, he heard a squeak, as a small door in the iron gate opened, and the man himself walked out, coughing. As soon as he looked up, he saw someone standing at the gate.

After a few seconds, Sloppy Wang cried out in surprise, then said: "My God! Good God! What are you doing here? Hey! Gui's mother, hurry up, hurry up, get a move on! His Honour is here!"

Before Liu Jinding could speak, Sloppy Wang looked around and exclaimed: "Where is your car, where is your driver? Why don't you let him have some water? Look now, look now..."

Liu Jinding was exhausted after his long walk, but he forced himself to stand up straight and say, solemnly: "You still make a lot of noise for someone your age, Lao Wang! I have important things to talk to you about, and I've let the driver go."

"Oh, oh!" Sloppy Wang exclaimed. "Hey, the road was changed a few years ago. Did you go the wrong way? Come in! Come in! I didn't expect you to be visiting my home…"

When they went into the courtyard, Sloppy Wang introduced his wife: "Gui's mother, this is a high official! He is our benefactor! I've told you…" Then he changed the subject and said: "Gui's mother, kill a chicken! Steam some buns! Get a move on!"

A woman in her fifties came scurrying out of the house. She was so panicked that she had put on mismatched footwear, one slipper and one leather shoe. "Come in, come in, come in," she babbled.

After entering the courtyard, Liu Jinding looked around and said: "This is a well-built house, Lao Wang. Is it only you two oldies living here now?"

"Yes, of course," Wang Mahu said. "Our children are up in the city now. One is a national teacher, the other is…"

After they went inside, Sloppy Wang set about pouring water as he pointed to the sofa. "I bought it for one of the children last year," he said. "It's leather. Sit down, sit down. Oh, I really wasn't expecting you. It's quite some time since you transferred to the city, isn't it."

Liu Jinding didn't sit down, but said: "I'm sorry, Lao Wang, but where is the bathroom? I need to use the bathroom first."

"On the left, first on the left. Go, go!"

In the bathroom, after he had relived himself, Liu Jinding grabbed a towel and carefully wiped the dust off his trousers and leather shoes. Then he walked out and sat calmly on the sofa, picked up the tea Sloppy Wang had made for him and took a sip. "Is it Maojian?"

"You have a true leader's sense of taste!" Wang Mahu replied. "One sip and you can identify it! I have coffee too, if you would prefer. My daughter brought it back from the provincial capital."

Liu Jinding shook his head and said: "Maojian will do fine."

"You're right. That coffee stuff tastes like chicken shit. I can't get used to it."

"So what are up to these days, Lao Wang?" Liu Jinding asked.

"I'm not very busy. You know, we are a long way from the county seat, not on the main road, and outside the development zone. We make a loss on everything except selling flowers. No one earns anything much apart from growing flowers."

Liu Jinding went on, seriously: "Lao Wang, the reason I came through the night to see you is because there is a new project, and I want to know if you're interested in–"

Before he had even finished speaking, Sloppy Wang was rubbing his hands and said excitedly: "What project? Is there another poverty-alleviation fund coming down the line? I know you'll have something good for me. Go on, go on."

"To tell the truth, it is not a poverty-alleviation fund but it's almost the same. But I've got to warn you, it's all very confidential. Are you a long-standing Party member?"

"Yes, I am. I've been in the Party for thirty-seven years. Is that OK?"

Liu Jinding pondered for a moment and said solemnly: "First of all, let me tell you that this project is huge, worth more than a billion yuan. There is no problem with the funding, but this project is my baby and I've personally brought it up here from Shenzhen. You can't tell anyone else. That is to say, before it's launched, only you and I can know about it, no one else."

Sloppy Wang looked out the door, widened his eyes and said: "I understand, I understand. What is this... what is this project?"

"If you want a project that you can be sure not to lose money on, you need to clear the land and get the people out. You've got to keep what I'm about to tell you locked up inside. You can't talk about it even if it kills you."

"Don't worry, you don't have to tell me. I have a padlock on my mouth."

"This is a cutting-edge international technology project coming in from abroad. Although it is a chemical project, it is harmless. This is my hometown, and I'm not going to hurt anyone here. People are investing 1.2 billion yuan in one go, mainly for ceramics production. Simply put, this technology was invented by a professor at Duke University in the United States, and now countries all around the world are rushing to develop it. The principle is based on a mixture of ceramics, metals and optical fibres... you won't understand if I go into specifics."

Sloppy Wang's eyes widened and he said: "I understand, I understand. Fantastic! 1.2 billion! You're a real benefactor!"

"No, don't say that. I just want to do something for my hometown."

"Such generosity! I really want to kowtow to you. You are such an important official, but you still remember the common folk!"

"I can't guarantee that this project can be implemented here. I'll just take a good look around and make a proper inspection. A few days later, I'll sign the contract."

Sloppy Wang became worried and said: "Benefactor! Mayor Liu! It would be better off here than anywhere else. If you can bring it here, I will lead the whole village in raising a stele to you! We will burn incense to you for generations to come!"

"Please don't talk like that, Lao Wang. I can't guarantee you will benefit. Let's talk about it again when things are settled."

Sloppy Wang immediately grew excited and said: "Look, we don't have anything rare or special here, but tomorrow, I'll find a place for you, a secret place, where you can try the 'four rare delicacies'! I'm sure you won't have eaten them before..."

The two of them gossiped away for a while, before Liu Jinding grew serious again: "Do you trust me?"

"Trust you?" Sloppy Wang exclaimed. "If I can't trust you, who can I trust?"

"Do you have a bank card? Tell me the card number."

Sloppy Wang was startled and his lips trembled. "What... what's the matter? Bank card... my daughter looks after the bank card, and there's... there's not much money."

"You misunderstand me. In three days' time, I'm going to Hong Kong for negotiations and I'll ask them to send you the first tranche of funding. Whatever happens with the project, that money won't be recouped. It won't be that much, probably around three hundred thousand and certainly no more than five hundred thousand. So you'll be fine..."

Sloppy Wang grew excited again and said: "Yay, yay! You... you... my benefactor! How can I thank you?" As he spoke, he was busy looking for the card.

A short while later, some hot dishes were brought in. There was chicken stewed with mushrooms and pork with vermicelli. Then there was grilled lamb, and scrambled egg with fat hen. The four dishes, brimming over their serving plates, looked fragrant and hearty.

"Shall we eat together, Sister-in-Law?" Liu Jinding suggested.

"Sit down, sit down!" Sloppy Wang said. "It's nothing special. Don't worry about her. We have rules here, and women don't sit down at the table." After that, he pulled back a curtain, rummaged around inside and brought out two bottles of his best wine. "I've kept back these two bottles. It's twenty-year-old Baofeng Daqu. Now a benefactor like you is here, we have to drink it."

In Sloppy Wang's opinion, Liu Jinding was a very reserved kind of person, but on this occasion, he really opened up. He ate the food and drank the wine when he was toasted, never refusing... first three cups, then five cups and then another seven. Drinking along with him, Sloppy Wang said: "Dear Benefactor, I am so happy that you have come to my house for a meal. What does it mean to me? It means that you do not despise me, despite your high office. You take me as I am. Whatever you tell me to do, I will do it. You can rely on that."

"Do I have your word, Lao Wang?"

Sloppy Wang slapped his chest. "You do!"

"One day, I may get into trouble, and I will come to you then."

Flown with wine, Sloppy Wang said: "Benefactor, who are the people? We are the people! Just you come back to the people, and you will be safe as houses!"

"I was only joking, Lao Wang! Drink up! Let me toast you."

Later that night, after countless rounds of wine, Liu Jinding laid his head on the table and stopped talking. Sloppy Wang shouted at him a few times but got no response. Urgently, he called out to his wife again: "Hurry up, Gui's mother, I need your help!"

His wife came out from the inner room and scolded him: "Why did you let him drink so much?"

"This is a VIP. How could I let him come here and not give him a decent drink?"

"Well, this is—"

"This is what? Just hurry up and give me a hand to get him to bed."

"Which room?" his wife asked.

"The girl's room. It'll be cleaner. This is a VIP."

With considerable effort, the old couple carried Liu Jinding into their daughter's room and put him to bed. They undressed him and covered him with a quilt before tiptoeing away.

After the two of them withdrew, Liu Jinding slowly opened his eyes. Although he was a bit dizzy from the wine, he still had some of his wits about him. He looked round the peasant bedroom in something of a daze. He saw the posters of popular female celebrities on the walls, and there was a *wuxia* novel by the pillow, some Da Bao brand cosmetics on the bedside cabinet and several other make-up items. The bed was soft. So it seems that even country girls slept on Simmons mattresses these days!

I'm sorry, Lao Wang, he said to himself.

SIX

THE SECRET ARREST OF JIANG BAOGUO began at midnight.

Initially, Jiang Baoguo was not in Helian Dongshan's sights. He could even be said to be his former boss, as he had been executive deputy director of the Huanghuai City Public Security Bureau before being transferred to the Bureau of Justice. Jiang Baoguo came from a military family, and it was said of him that he was a mighty presence on the battlefield. In normal circumstances, he would have been above suspicion.

Although Sun Jianshe, that confidential member of the Provincial Party Committee, mentioned Jiang Baoguo's name when he explained about the dinner club, he was still not under any suspicion at that time. The key was still that single word: "success".

It was discovered that that one-word message had been forwarded by Liu Jinding through a disposable SIM card. Helian Dongshan had ordered someone to check the original source of the message. Unexpectedly, the investigation led to Jiang Baoguo. It then turned out that Jiang Baoguo, too, was only forwarding it. When it was checked further, it was finally traced back to a prisoner who had just been released from a reform-through-labour camp. Thus the clues to the case were revealed little by little.

The discovery of Jiang Baoguo only came about by chance. He had forwarded the message "success" using a disposable SIM card. If he had thrown the card away and turned off the phone, it would have been very difficult to trace. But he was careless. He had received the message when he was out drinking. He was carrying two mobile phones at the time: one for work and one private. The private phone was using the disposable SIM card. When he received the word "success", he was sitting at the bar. He fished out his phone, took a look and then forwarded the message to Liu Jinding. After that, he continued to drink, and got drunk, so the SIM card was not disposed of in time.

Helian Dongshan was very surprised when the message was traced back to Jiang Baoguo.

After further investigation, it was discovered that Jiang Baoguo had close connections with a prisoner released from reform through labour some time ago. The two had exchanged multiple phone calls.

On the night when Jiang Baoguo was arrested, he was playing mahjong in a hotel room in Huanghuai. His luck was in that night: two-five-eight, triplets, full flushes, he won with whatever he played and he won twelve games in a row. So come midnight, he should have walked away with sixty to seventy thousand yuan. But he still didn't have enough, so he said: "Come on, let's play again." No one dared refuse, so they had to return to the table.

At that moment, the door of the hotel room was forced open, and the chief of the local police station walked in with three plainclothes officers. The business bosses who were playing with Jiang Baoguo all looked shocked, and the mahjong game stopped dead. Only Jiang Baoguo kept playing his tiles, unfazed. "It's all right," he said, "pick up your tiles. Keep playing, keep playing!" Jiang Baoguo's square, fleshy face appeared neither angry nor affronted. He looked over at the police chief and said: "What's up, Xiao Wu?"

Faced by his old boss, Commander Wu looked more than a little unsure of himself as he said: "Don't get the wrong idea, Director Jiang, it's not me who is looking for you. No, it's our comrade from the Provincial Commission for Discipline Inspection."

Jiang Baoguo was taken aback for a moment but didn't show it as he said: "Fuck it, it's just a game of mahjong! Why would the Commission for Discipline Inspection be bothered with that?" Then, he picked up a random tile and played it. "There!" he said. "It's a pair. Another pair!"

At that moment, several of the businessmen who were playing

looked at each other, and one said: "This is nothing to do with us, Commander Wu. We're just playing mahjong..."

All of those businessmen were known to Commander Wu and he just waved his hand and said: "Off you go! You're right, it's nothing to do with you."

The men jumped to their feet and left, not even bothering with the money they had left on the mahjong table.

Jiang Baoguo was taken to the *shuanggui* base in the early hours of the morning. He didn't say a single word for seven days in a row.

Jiang Baoguo had worked in the Huanghuai City Public Security Bureau for eighteen years and was executive deputy director for eight years. He had been in charge of criminal investigation, pre-trial investigation and internal security. He was very familiar with the nature of interrogation and knew full well that, if he did open his mouth, no matter what he said, some flaw would be found in it. So he said nothing at all.

All through those seven days, Jiang Baoguo watched his interrogators with narrowed eyes and an arrogant expression. He watched them in silence, and whenever he looked sidelong at one of them, his eyebrows were always slightly raised, as if he was saying: You've still got a lot to learn, little boy! Sometimes, he would close his eyes and rest for a while, letting his taut nerves relax. At these times, the corners of his mouth would droop, and a long trickle of saliva would drool out of the corner of his mouth and hang there. Then he would wake up with a jerk, shift his posture and continue his silence.

Jiang Baoguo knew that, behind the one-way glass in the interrogation room, a pair of eyes was looking at him. Those eyes were not particularly big and were always narrowed, but they were like scalpels that could dissect evidence from the wings of a fly. As long as he was staring at you, almost nothing could escape his magic eyes. Jiang Baoguo could even smell his scent through the glass, because he knew the man was addicted to cigarettes. Oh yes! He had worked with this person for many years and knew him all too well. From the direction the interrogation was taking, he knew that the person pulling the strings behind the scenes was Helian Dongshan.

Helian Dongshan did not meet his old leader once during those seven days. He knew that Jiang Baoguo had a bad temper and a strong personality and cared a lot about face. If Helian Dongshan, a former subordinate, were to be the one interrogating him, he would never lose face by uttering even a single word.

So Helian Dongshan simply set Jiang Baoguo to one side and mobilised all the police officers to search for the prisoner who had sent the word "success" on his mobile phone and thereby sent Jiang to prison. Helian Dongshan had learned Hua Luogeng's "optimisation method" when he was young, and finally put it to use on this occasion. He started by tracing the single-word message "success". The signal was first sent from Luyang City in Dongxia County, so presumably the word related to something that had happened in Dongxia. Later, it emerged from investigations in Dongxia that the signal had passed through Dongxia, then to the provincial capital, and on to Beijing. By checking all the original phone messages sent over a three-day period, it was found that the source of the relevant message was the provincial capital... Taking the expressway, the distance between Dongxia and the provincial capital was at least 400 kilometres. So transportation seemed to be the problem.

But tens of thousands of cars were travelling on the highway every day, and there were more than 200 intersections, large and small, along the way. It was like looking for a needle in a haystack. How to do it then? Helian Dongshan adopted Hua Luogeng's "exclusion method" and ordered staff to check the surveillance videos at each of the toll gates of the expressway intersections in the provincial capital, Luyang, and Dongxia. As the checking of cars proceeded, Helian Dongshan did not close his eyes for three days and three nights, and kept in touch with the other two places by telephone. Finally, he got his result. After repeated checks in time order, the search was narrowed down to nine cars that appeared on the same day in the three places. After repeated comparisons day and night, they fixed on a white, nine-seater Jinbei minivan with the Shaanxi licence plate A7563.

The entire task force was in a state of high excitement when the minivan was found, because the mystery was about to be solved. What particularly excited them was that, judging from the results of a reverse trace, this Jinbei's last stop before it departed the provincial capital was actually in front of the library of the Provincial University of Agricultural Science and Technology. The camera in front of the library building clearly showed that a minivan with the licence plate

A7563 had parked out front. And that was the vehicle which the deputy governor's wife, Xu Ya'nan, got into before she went missing!

Next, they used the minivan to investigate the people involved. It was found in an oak wood next to a reservoir in Laoyeling, Dongxia. The minivan was burnt out and unrecognisable, with only an empty shell remaining, which provided almost no clues. The policemen who searched only found some messed-up footprints and one or two Golden Monkey cigarette butts nearby. There was also a torn scrap of paper the size of a fingertip, with no decipherable markings. It was this small piece of paper that roused Helian Dongshan's interest. After the provincial government had authorised it with the local area, Helian Dongshan ordered the collection of all discarded scrap paper. The local public security sent seventy officers, who lined up one metre apart and searched the mountains and forests in a radius of five kilometres. In five hours, they collected a total of one hundred and seven pieces of the same document. After technicians had collated them and pasted them back together, it proved to be a two-page invoice for the purchase of a second-hand Jinbei minivan. Acting immediately on this information, the task force tracked down a copy of the purchaser's ID card in the records of second-hand car market and locked onto their target.

Helian Dongshan had spent those seven days standing in front of a telephone, directing operations from three separate maps. Over seven days and seven nights, he smoked two and a half cartons of Gold Leaf cigarettes, ate twelve boxed meals and took fitful night-time naps in a reclining chair, leaving him more annoyed than rested. It was only when the suspect was arrested that he secretly breathed a deep sigh of relief.

The suspect, whose name was Hong Xiaohe, was interrogated by Helian Dongshan himself. Hong was arrested in a car repair shop in Xi'an. He was thirty-one years old, with a small, flat head, an upturned nose and toad-like eyes. He was wearing a car mechanic's overalls with the name of a car dealership printed on the back. He was a native of Xihe County, Luyang, and four months before the incident he was released after serving six years in prison for raping an underage girl. Helian Dongshan went on the offensive as soon as they met, saying: "Take off your clothes!"

The policeman standing to one side took up the order, shouting: "Take them off!"

Hong Xiaohe hesitated before slowly removing the overalls, revealing a pair of red underpants.

This time, before Helian Dongshan could open his mouth, the policeman continued: "Take them off! Go on, take them off!"

When the pants were off, Hong Xiaohe stood there naked, his hands automatically going to cover his groin.

Helian Dongshan used a short baton to lift his hands away and said: "A tiny cock like that, and you still think you have the balls for a crime like this? I'm telling you now, I even know where you pissed with that little cock of yours! At the Tongcheng service area on the Shanghai-Shaanxi Expressway, you pissed in the third urinal, didn't you?"

Hong Xiaohe just stared at him blankly, in dazed astonishment.

Helian Dongshan suddenly shouted: "Zero-two-five-three!"

That was his prison number. Hong Xiaohe automatically straightened up and said: "Here!"

Helian Dongshan picked up the red underpants with his baton, shook them in front of Hong Xiaohe's eyes, and said: "Your mother sewed these for you, didn't she? Six pairs in all, to keep you out of trouble, isn't that right? And have they worked, then?"

Hong Xiaohe said nothing.

Helian Dongshan continued: "Put them back on!"

Trembling, Hong Xiaohe put his pants back on.

"I don't suppose for a minute you're the main culprit in a big case like this. At most, you were just the driver. So tell me, do you want to live or die?"

"Live, I want to live," Hong Xiaohe blurted out.

"Sit down, sit down. That will depend on your attitude."

Helian Dongshan deliberately looked at his watch and said: "This case is too big. I don't have any more time to waste talking to you. It's up to you whether you explain your part in it all or not. I know you are a dutiful son. Your mother is being treated for uraemia in the Provincial People's Hospital. You had to pay a hundred thousand yuan—"

"I didn't kill anyone," said a shocked Hong Xiaohe, jumping to his feet.

"Who did then?" Helian Dongshan leapt in.

Hong Xiaohe spilled the story of the murder, and the atmosphere in the interrogation room suddenly became very tense.

But he didn't say anything more. He seemed to have recovered some of his spirit, and however much he trembled with fear, he didn't elaborate.

Six hours later, Helian Dongshan found a witness. His name was Zhou Shen, and he was the same Xiao Zhou who had been collecting recyclables at the University of Agricultural Science and Technology for more than twenty years. Helian Dongshan had ordered his men to go back over all the surveillance material from the entire campus of the university on the day of the incident. They had discovered that the same burnt-out minivan had stopped at the corner of a flower bed on the campus, where Hong Xiaohe had got out and talked to a tatty-looking man riding a trike, apparently asking for directions. So Helian Dongshan had sent someone to find the old man. Xiao Zhou was well known to everyone at the university and was quickly located. But he did not want to go and only agreed after he was given a hundred yuan as compensation for lost earnings.

When Zhou Shen was taken into the interrogation room, he identified Hong Xiaohe face to face. "It was him," he said. "He was the one who asked for directions on campus that day. He was wearing a grey jacket and a pair of jeans worth seventy yuan. I know that because a student once asked me to go to the wholesale market to buy him the same ones. He asked me how to get to the library, and I told him to drive along the avenue and take the first turn."

Zhou Shen went on: "When I rode back from behind the library building, I saw Teacher Xu in the distance getting into his minivan..."

Hong Xiaohe looked at him dully, regretting not having mentioned all this himself. He had taken Xiao Zhou for some fellow up from the country to collect rubbish and hadn't thought that he might be someone who had been out and about round the campus for more than twenty years and knew the university better than anyone.

After Zhou Shen recorded his testimony, it was already late as he walked out of the task force headquarters, but his head was beaded with sweat and his heart was pounding like a trip hammer. He had kept one thing back: Xu Ya'nan had come looking for him the night before she disappeared. Xu Ya'nan had had particular faith in him, believing that he was a Daoist master who could open his "heavenly eye". She had consulted him about good and bad luck and she had asked him: "Master Zhou, what will happen tomorrow?" Zhou Shen said: "What's the matter, Teacher Xu?" Xu Ya'nan said: "The old man bought me a car, and I can pick it up tomorrow." Zhou Shen asked if she could drive, and Xu Ya'nan said: "I learned a long time ago, and it has been a few years since–" "Which direction is the car?" Xu Ya'nan said: "South... it's south. Not far." Zhou Shen checked it off on his fingers and said: "South? South should be OK. South is your auspicious direction." Maybe it was that very sentence that killed her. Zhou Shen had buried this information deep inside him and not dared tell a soul.

(Ever since then, although he still collected rubbish on the campus every day, Zhou Shen always walked with his head down, and no longer told people about his heavenly eye. Many years later, he is still depressed and mutters to himself as he walks along. It is as if he feels he owes a debt. Whenever someone approaches him for a fortune-telling, he refuses. People ask him about his heavenly eye and want to see it, but he always says: "The world is too murky. I can't see anything any more.")

Interrogating Hong Xiaohe again, Helian Dongshan said: "Look up, Hong Xiaohe!" Hong Xiaohe slowly raised his head, but he didn't dare meet Helian Dongshan's gaze.

"Look me in the eye!" Helian Dongshan ordered.

Hong Xiaohe gave Helian Dongshan a shifty look.

"I have seen your mother, and she asked me to tell you something," Helian Dongshan said. "Your mother said: 'Shuan'er, God is watching. Don't cause your mother any more trouble!'"

When Hong Xiaohe was at home, his nickname was Men Shuan'er, but no one outside the family knew that. He raised his head again and looked at Helian Dongshan. The two of them just gazed at each other for a long time until Hong Xiaohe burst into tears. Through those tears, he muttered: "I didn't kill her, truly I didn't."

Three hours later, Hong Xiaohe capitulated. He finally gave up his accomplice, and the prime offender: "Number 1572". Number 1572 was a prisoner released from the labour camp with him, whose name was Huang Bingyan. Huang Bingyan had helped him out when they were locked up and was his benefactor. He had heard Huang Bingyan say that he had committed this crime to repay an official who was his own benefactor.

Five days later, Helian Dongshan led the task force to arrest Huang Bingyan in a rental house in Shenzhen. Jiang Baoguo knew nothing about this. He was still sitting in the interrogation room in the *shuanggui* building, blindfolded but still glowering, defiant to the end.

SEVEN

Two days after the arrest of Jiang Baoguo, Liu Jinding secretly went to Kaoshan'ao with Sloppy Wang.

The village head of Kaoshan'ao was called Ma Heshun. He and Sloppy Wang had been friends for many years, and were, in fact, brothers-in-law. As well as being the village head, Ma Heshun was also famous as a cook. His speciality was the "four rare delicacies". Sloppy Wang had done his utmost to persuade Liu Jinding to go to Kaoshan'ao to try Mayor Ma's cooking. These four rare delicacies are very famous in the area, and not many people get the chance to try them. This was a way for Sloppy Wang to express his gratitude.

At first, Liu Jinding wouldn't agree. What did he care about food at a time like this? Later, he only decided to go because he chanced to ask: "Lao Wang, is Potou near here?" Sloppy Wang replied: "Potou? Why didn't you say so before? Potou Township is only ten or twenty *li* from Kaoshan'ao, very close." Liu Jinding asked: "Is there a temple in Potou?" Wang Mahu said: "Yes, there is a temple, the Guanye Temple. A lot of people go there to burn incense. Do you want to have a look?" Making sure not to make too much of it, Liu Jinding said he did. In fact, he had already checked out the maps and knew that, in Potou Township, he could join the national expressway to Wuhan in Hubei.

Before they set out, Liu Jinding repeatedly warned Sloppy Wang not to tell anyone about his affairs and projects. He said that if too many people wanted a share, there was bound to be trouble. Sloppy Wang promised that he wouldn't breathe a word.

Kaoshan'ao is a very special village. It is located on the edge of a large ravine (*gouzi*) near a mountain, so it is also called Gouzi Village.

This ravine has flowing water all year round, according to the season. When the mountain torrents come down in summer, the waters are huge and turbulent and it looks spectacular. After autumn, the ravine turns into a narrow, one-foot-wide creek and a jumble of rocks. There is little cultivable land in Kaoshan'ao and a lot of stony ground, so the villagers are not rich. In the early days, the men here were too poor to marry, and most of them bought women from Yunnan, Guizhou or Sichuan. These women were of mixed ethnicity, and with some of them it was impossible to disentangle their origins. They were frequently rescued by the "trafficking police", but such operations were very hazardous. The village men had bought the women with their own money and they weren't going to give them up lightly. The police were surrounded by hostile villagers as soon as word got round that they were in the area.

The village was at the junction of three counties and originally consisted of only about thirty households. After the reform and opening up, a constant stream of villagers from small mountain hamlets moved in, and the population became larger and more diverse. By now, it was quite a big village, but because of its remote mountainous location, it only really grew crowded and lively during the New Year period. After the New Year passed, the middle-aged and youngsters all went off to work in other places, and most of those remaining were the elderly and children, so it became an empty village.

When the two men arrived in Kaoshan'ao, the village was very quiet and they met only a handful of old people leaning against walls, sunning themselves with eyes narrowed against the glare. Liu Jinding began to relax slightly from his state of high alert. As they reached the house of Ma Heshun, the village head, they saw that the courtyard gate was wide open, but Ma Heshun was not at home. Sloppy Wang said: "The bastard is bound to be off playing mahjong somewhere. I'll look for him." He walked off towards a nearby commission store.

After a while, he dragged Ma Heshun away from the mahjong table. When the village head saw that Sloppy Wang had brought someone with him, he was not very enthusiastic. All he said was: "What are you doing here, you old fool? Are you out to swindle me again?"

"Why do you always have such a low opinion of people?" Wang

Mahu retorted. "Hurry up and get your boys together to put on a bit of a show. This is a distinguished guest who has come to eat your four rare delicacies."

But Ma Heshun didn't buy this and said: "You can eat your own farts!"

Sloppy Wang dragged Ma Heshun out of the door and put his mouth to his ear, whispering urgently. A moment later, the two men walked into the house with their arms around each other's shoulders, indulging in mutual congratulations. To their surprise, as soon as the two of them came through the door, they saw Liu Jinding's expression suddenly change. He said calmly: "What's going on? Anyway, I'm not interested any more. Let's go!" He stood up and walked towards the door.

Ma Heshun hurried forward to stop him, smiling and apologising: "You are my guest, my guest! My most distinguished guest! I'm not trying to get rid of you. Sloppy Ma and me are brothers-in-law, close as a pair of chopsticks. We're just joking with you. Don't mind us. Let's get on with it, let's get on with it." So saying, he got moving and ordered his family to pour some tea, then sent someone to pick apples in the orchard. He seemed very enthusiastic.

Even though Liu Jinding wasn't very happy about it all, he really didn't have much choice in the matter. Fortunately, he could leave after the meal and there were worse places to be for the moment. However, he still glared at Sloppy Wang, who patted him on the shoulder and made placatory gestures, saying: "Don't worry, don't worry."

At noon that day, Ma Heshun took charge of the kitchen and summoned some of the village women to help him as he set about making the four rare delicacies for Liu Jinding. These dishes had to be prepared and eaten immediately to get the full effect of their deliciousness. The women were hard at work, stoking fires, cutting up fish, rolling noodles and peeling garlic. They rarely got together like this, so they laughed and chatted as they worked.

At noon, a round table was set up in a room next to the village office, and the dishes were served one by one. The main dish was the most famous of Kaoshan'ao's four rare delicacies and a speciality of the village: the fathead fish that lives in the crevices of rocks in the mountain streams. The fish is stewed, and the soup is as fragrant and white as milk, with the heads of the fish poking out, just as if they were alive. The second delicacy was "five-fried eggs with mountain leek". Leeks are picked from the mountains in the morning before the sun comes up, and wild bird eggs are collected from the nests in the trees on the slopes. The eggs can be laid by magpies, golden eagles, pigeons, thrushes and golden pheasants. The eggs are of different types, colours and sizes, and there are a lot of them. The third was "five-benevolences pumpkin pot". A large, round pumpkin has its top cut off and seeds scooped out before being filled with ginkgo nuts in wild honey. The ginkgo nuts are covered with walnut kernels, almonds are put on top of the walnuts, and raisins on top of the almonds. The whole thing is then steamed in a basket and comes out sweet and delicious. The fourth dish was "mountain delicacy roast wild boar". "Mountain delicacy" needs no explanation, but hunting was forbidden in the mountains, and the wild boar had to be killed secretly. The other dishes included chicken with mushrooms, lamb testicles, eyes and kidneys, stone-ground bean curd, small oil buns and hand-rolled noodles... the table was groaning.

After three rounds of wine and five different types of dish, Ma Heshun, as mayor of Kaoshan'ao, couldn't help probing things a bit further: "Go on, go on! Try them all! We don't often get a great leader in our village! You can see, we don't have much to offer... but can't you give me the inside track, Great Leader? Come on and tell me a bit about this project."

Liu Jinding glared at Sloppy Wang, who was sitting next to him, and said severely: "Mr Wang has told you about it, has he? We certainly didn't talk about it at the lunch table!"

Sloppy Wang knew he was in the wrong, and clapped his hand to his mouth.

Ma Heshun hurriedly said: "It's all right, it's all right, I know how to keep a secret. Don't worry, I won't breathe a word." Then he held up the wine flask: "Come on, drink up, drink up! Let's drink!"

Liu Jinding drank a few cups of wine, and said: "This wine is quite strong."

"Sure, it's strong enough," Ma Heshun conceded, "but it doesn't go to your head. It's home-brew. This is the first run. I've kept back the best. Let me tell you, Great Leader, it's as good as Maotai! Truly!"

Ma Heshun had secretly arranged for some of the village women to come in, one by one, and toast Liu Jinding. The wine began to go to his head. Perhaps because he'd been in hiding for more than a month, Liu Jinding suddenly had the desire to give a speech. He hadn't had a chance for a long time, and as public speaking is a kind of power, he really couldn't help himself. He said: "Lao Ma, Village Chief Ma, you want to get rich, right? Do you know what you need first? Ideas! First of all, change your ideas. In today's society, you can never get rich if your ideas don't change. So how can you change your ideas? What do you need to do? Just one word: read! Do you know why? Understanding! Life is like an endless night. Books are lights and reading them can illuminate your life. Learn to absorb the most advanced ideas in the world. What are they?"

Ma Heshun looked at him, wide-eyed and said: "Aiyaya! Yes! That's so right! No wonder you're such an important man! You're so wise! I'll do it, I'll do it. You're teaching me so much. I have to toast you in two more glasses."

Liu Jinding still had his wits about him, but the wine was beginning to make him a bit wobbly, mentally and physically. He pointed at Ma Heshun and said: "Tell me what you believe. What do you really believe? Don't lie to me. I don't listen to lies. Tell me the truth. Tell me what you believe."

Ma Heshun had also drunk too much. He banged the table and said: "I... I tell you, in this world of ours, God is the boss and I am Number Two! I've never obeyed anyone in my life. Forget about Sloppy Wang there! He may be my little brother-in-law and a village head too, but he's nothing! Nothing compared to me! What do I believe in? I believe in, I believe in... fuck it, I believe in you. Great Leader, I believe in you!"

"Do you really believe in me?"

"Yes, yes, I do. I really believe in you."

"Let's drink to those words," Liu Jinding said. "Drink up!"

Ma Heshun followed suit, exclaiming: "Drink up!"

Liu Jinding was talking expansively, drinking as he went, and now he certainly was drunk. He hadn't spoken at any kind of meeting for ages, but he was back in the swing of it now. What he said was true, but in fact, he himself had never actually asked what he believed in before.

At this point, he was really drunk, and his body felt as though it was floating. Perhaps he felt that so many days had passed that people had forgotten him and would no longer pay any attention to him. Whatever the case, he should leave after the meal. Twenty miles away, right by the national expressway, an Audi car was waiting for him. Whatever it was that kept his brain taut and alert was slowly but surely being numbed by the alcohol. He even forgot what he had said.

EIGHT

County Party Secretary Tang Mingsheng's mobile phone rang at 2.47 in the afternoon.

After it rang three times, Tang Mingsheng pressed the answer button and said: "Hello, who's that?" The voice down the line was loud: "Is that Tang Mingsheng... Tang, Tang... Secretary Tang, right? You..." Tang Mingsheng didn't recognise the voice, and cut the call. But after a while, the phone rang again. Tang Mingsheng answered angrily: "Are you drunk? Who is this?" The voice on the other end said: "Me, it's me! Ma Heshun from Kaoshan'ao! Can you hear me? I, I, no, not me... It's the general secretary, he wants you to come... to come and eat the four rare delicacies! They're our speciality in Kaoshan'ao! It's urgent. Come now!" Tang Mingsheng was a serious-minded man and he tried to get things straight: "Tell me, which official is it? When? Where?" The drunk on the other end of the phone said: "Who is this... who's talking all this nonsense? Get a fucking move on and get over here! It's urgent. You know the dinner club? It's the club's general secretary wants you here. Get over here!" Someone standing next to the phone at the other end said loudly: "Tell him it's me, Liu Jinding!" Tang Mingsheng hesitated for a moment, then said: "OK, I understand."

After the phone call, Tang Mingsheng stood in the office for a while, and asked himself whether he was going to go. The reason he hesitated was because, just two days previously, he had participated in the enlarged meeting of the Municipal Party Committee hosted by the committee secretary, Xue Zhiheng. Eight of the nine members of the standing committee were there, and only the executive deputy mayor, Liu Jinding, did not attend. What made him particularly sensitive to the situation was that, at the meeting, Xue Zhiheng mentioned, without naming anyone in particular: "Some leading cadres have violated organisational principles and left their posts without authorisation. This is a very serious problem." These words made the delegates think. There were even people who talked privately about Mayor Liu "having an accident". After the meeting, Tang Mingsheng specifically asked the secretary-general of the Municipal Party Committee, but Secretary-General Zhao just looked at him, spread his hands and said nothing.

As a fellow Meiling villager, Liu Jinding had promised at the dinner club to help him, and before he was promoted to the county, he took him to visit a director of the Organisation Department of the Provincial Party Committee. That meant he owed him a favour. He thought that he'd better go, but his heart gave a leap and he hesitated. So before setting off, he dialled the number of the old commander, Xue Zhiheng. He said: "Secretary Xue, I've given it a lot of thought, and there is something I need to talk to you about... Mayor Liu has arranged a meal. Do you think I should go?" Xue Zhiheng asked: "Who did you say?" Tang Mingsheng said: "Liu Jinding, Mayor Liu. He has arranged it. He said it was in Kaoshan'ao." Xue Zhiheng was silent for a moment at the other end of the phone, then said: "I don't care what kind of a pissing meal it is, if you dare leave your post without authorisation, I will sack you!" Then he slammed the phone down.

In Huanghuai, only Xue Zhiheng, secretary of the Municipal Party Committee, knew that Liu Jinding was included on the *shuanggui* list, that he had left his post without authorisation and had absconded in fear of arrest. It was a heavy responsibility. He immediately called both the Provincial Party Committee and the man in charge of the task force.

Helian Dongshan rushed over to Kaoshan'ao two hours later. Although the strategy of "external looseness and internal tightening" was being adopted, news of Liu Jinding's *shuanggui* detention had not been released. But over the period of one month and four days, Helian Dongshan's search for Liu Jinding had never stopped. In fact, he had reckoned that Liu might sneak back to his hometown. He had sent someone to carry out long-term surveillance from the house opposite Liu Quanyou's home in Yakou Village in Meiling, but no trace of Liu Jinding had been found. Now he believed that Liu had not gone home after sneaking back to Meiling.

However, Helian Dongshan's arrest force was blocked at Kaoshan'ao, and the two police cars he brought were surrounded on the village street. As soon as the cars entered the village, it was reported to Ma Heshun. At first, the messenger misinterpreted what was going on and said it was the "trafficking police" going after abducted women again. In response, urged on by Sloppy Wang, a tipsy Ma Heshun yelled: "They dare try that again, do they? It'll take more than a few police on my land!" So he hurriedly gathered together two groups, one of old men who surrounded the police cars, and the other of women who formed a protective ring round the village committee, willing to risk their lives to stop anyone being taken away. He himself sheltered behind the mob, secretly issuing commands, without ever letting himself be seen.

Helian Dongshan had just got out of his car in front of the village committee courtyard, and before he could even open his mouth, his legs were being hugged tightly by two elderly women. The police officers he brought were also separated and surrounded by the villagers. People kept yelling: "Gouzi! Dalu! Mangkuai! Call the others! The trafficking police are here again! Block the road so they can't take anyone away!"

Reluctantly, Helian Dongshan contacted the relevant departments via mobile phone. After a while, the secretary of the Township Party Committee came hurrying over. Kaoshan'ao was under the jurisdiction of Tanghe Township. The secretary of the Party Committee of Tanghe stood in the village street and shouted: "Come out here, Ma Heshun!" Still unsteady on his feet, Ma Heshun swayed out from behind the crowd.

Helian Dongshan looked at Ma Heshun and said: "You are Ma Heshun, Village Head Ma?"

Ma Heshun smiled and giggled. "Yes, I am. I thought you were kidnappers."

Helian Dongshan took a piece of paper out of his wallet, held it up to the light in front of Ma Heshun's eyes and said: "Take a good look. This is the great seal of the Provincial Commission for Discipline Inspection. We are not trafficking police, we are here to arrest someone and take him away. If anything goes wrong, you will be held responsible!"

Ma Heshun blinked in surprise and said: "What... what about... the project?"

Helian Dongshan was taken aback and said: "What project?"

"That large project worth 1.2 billion yuan."

"Nonsense!" Helian Dongshan said. "What project? He is running away because he committed a crime! How can there be a 'project'?"

"It's true, it's true! There's a Hong Kong businessman coming over to invest in it. It's all official, signed and sealed..."

The secretary of the Township Party Committee said: "Son of a bitch! All signed and sealed? Have you seen it?"

"I haven't, but Branch Secretary Wang, Sloppy Wang has, with his own eyes!" Ma Heshun said.

"Where is Sloppy Wang?" asked the secretary of the Township Party Committee. "I will ask him." But Sloppy Wang was nowhere to be found.

The secretary shouted: "Get rid of these people, Ma Heshun! This is the leader of the Provincial Public Security Bureau! Where are your brains?"

Ma Heshun said aggrievedly: "Secretary Xu, we are a poor village, and it's not been easy to get a piece of a project like this. I had to give them the four rare delicacies. Now, I... I won't be able to show my face at home!"

Helian Dongshan looked up at the approaching dusk, fearing something unexpected might happen again. He said to Ma Heshun: "Come on, Lao Ma, let's go. I'll go in alone and see Liu Jinding, Mayor Liu, and see what he has to say."

"What do you mean, the mayor? No? God! Is it really the mayor? I... I'll do whatever you want! Of course you can see him. He won't get away!"

So under Ma Heshun's instruction, the women gave way for Helian Dongshan to go into the village committee alone.

Inside the room, Liu Jinding was half awake. He was reclining on a sofa, his head still a little fuzzy. When Ma Heshun led Helian Dongshan in through the door, he realised immediately what was going on, and said to himself: What's the matter with you? What was all that shit with the four rare delicacies? You're only twenty miles from

Potou Township, and there's a car there waiting for you! How he regretted his actions.

When he saw him, Helian Dongshan showed the sealed paper again and said: "Mayor Liu, according to the instructions of the Provincial Party Committee, please come with me. At the specified time and at the specified place, you will be asked to clarify some questions."

Liu Jinding took a sip of the tea on the sofa table, his hands shaking, and said nothing.

After finding some mental balance, he said: "You're an old comrade, Lao He. Look outside and see how many people are protecting me."

Helian Dongshan looked at him and shook his head.

"Do you know why this is?" Liu Jinding said. "I'll tell you! For more than twenty years, I have done a lot of good things for the people around here. I've repaired roads, organised biogas supplies, got medical insurance, repaired school buildings... The people are behind me. All I have to do is shout, and they will throw you out. Do you believe me?"

"I believe you, Mayor Liu," Helian Dongshan replied. "The people don't understand the law, but you are a leading cadre. Don't you understand it either? You know what you have done. You said yourself, people have to have a bottom line. Do you have one?"

Liu Jinding was silent for a while before saying: "There is a problem, Lao He. Do you know what it is?"

Helian Dongshan looked at him and thought to himself: This man's really quite something! He's got a real inner quality! "Go on," he said. "Tell me."

Liu Jinding looked straight at Helian Dongshan and said: "Today it's me, and tomorrow it could be you."

"Maybe. It's the same for anyone who breaks the law."

"So let me offer you some advice. Don't go to extremes and leave yourself no room for manoeuvre. The day may come..." There was a yearning in his eyes. It said: Only twenty miles to go!

At that moment, there were a lot of people, old and young, pale and dark alike in the village streets, hemming him in in the village committee compound.

Helian Dongshan looked outside, then looked back at Liu Jinding. He took out his mobile phone, dialled a number, and said: "Let's do it this way, Mayor Liu. Secretary Xue Zhiheng wants to talk to you." He handed the phone to Liu Jinding.

Liu Jinding took the phone and heard Xue Zhiheng say at the other end: "What are you going to do, Liu Jinding? Don't forget, you are a leading city-level cadre. You know the organisational rules, don't you? Get back here to me at once!" Then, his tone softened: "Jinding, this is all Lao Bai's doing, isn't it? Just come back and clear it all up. I have responsibility with regard to Lao Bai too, and I will make it clear to the Party organisation. Come on back."

Liu Jinding said defensively: "Secretary Xue, Boss, I've been falsely accused. I am in charge of industry and commerce, and I have a purely working relationship with Lao Bai... All right then, yes, OK, I'll do what you say."

Despite uttering those words, Liu Jinding remained hesitant. He was still waiting for someone, but that someone was very slow in coming...

Helian Dongshan looked at his watch again and said decisively: "Mayor Liu, let me remind you that there are armed police outside the village and the whole place is surrounded. I don't think you want to make a big deal of this, right?"

After Liu Jinding had taken the call from the secretary of the Municipal Party Committee, he felt a little chink of hope. He thought to himself that if it was just a matter of Bai Shouxin, there might be a way back. He knew that he had to go anyway. Given the desperate circumstances, he said: "In that case, I will go with you."

Ma Heshun was panicking by now. "You can't go," he pleaded. "What about the... project? The project... is the deal off?"

Liu Jinding's expression didn't change: "The project is still on, Lao Ma. Don't worry, I'll be back."

As he was getting into the police car, a woman ran up and handed Liu Jinding a bag of freshly picked apples. "Here you are, sir," she said. "You didn't drink any tea at the meal, so take these to stop you getting thirsty on the road." This woman had been chosen by Ma Heshun for her good looks to serve the dishes at lunch. Liu Jinding was pretty tipsy and hadn't been able to resist pinching her cheeks as she did so, commenting that they were as rosy as apples. She had been very excited by it and had remembered to look after him.

Finally, the two police cars slowly drove Liu Jinding out of the village under the watchful eyes of the villagers. As soon as they were clear, Helian Dongshan ordered them to speed up. He knew that there was only one squad of armed police at the entrance to the village and if the villagers had really decided to make trouble, he was not at all sure he could get Liu Jinding away. They were not living in the past now, and the so-called "great mass of the people" was only an approximation of what it had been. The sorghum fields were no longer the sorghum fields of yesterday; the corn fields were no longer the corn fields of the yesterday; the "green curtain of tall crops" was not the "green curtain of tall crops" of yesterday.

Sure enough, less than ten minutes after Liu Jinding was driven away, Xie Zhichang finally arrived in an Audi. Following the original plan, his car had been waiting for four hours at the expressway junction, twenty miles away, but no one had come, so he came tearing over to the village. Ostensibly, he was responding to Ma Heshun's invitation to come and sample the four rare delicacies, but this was a code they had worked out between them. It meant he should change plans and come over to collect Liu Jinding.

(At 2.47 pm, when Liu Jinding was drunk, he had asked Ma Heshun to make three calls. One was to Tang Mingsheng, one to Jiang Baoguo and one to Xie Zhichang, inviting them to Kaoshan'ao to try the special meal. Even though he was drunk, Liu Jinding still knew exactly what he was doing in making the calls. Of the three of them, only Jiang Baoguo had his phone switched off and didn't answer.)

When Xie Zhichang walked into the yard, he saw the village committee sitting quietly, with Ma Heshun squatting alone under a tree. Xie Zhichang yelled at him: "Where is everybody? Where have they all gone?"

Ma Heshun stood up and asked who he was you looking for.

"Are you Ma Heshun?" Xie Zhichang asked.

"I am."

"What's all this fucking nonsense about four rare delicacies? Where is everyone? Where is Mayor Liu?"

Ma Heshun said grimly: "He just left."

"Where did he go? You don't mean—"

"He might as well have eaten my farts as the four rare delicacies! Armed police surrounded the village and took him away."

"Who? Mayor Liu asked someone to take him away? No way!"

"This is a huge loss! There were people coming from all over the province!"

Xie Zhichang just grunted a couple of times, then turned and left. Ma Heshun shouted after him: "Hey, hey, don't go. Who are you?"

When night fell, Sloppy Wang also came hurrying back to the village with a hundred or so men he had finally managed to scrape together. As soon as he entered the village, he yelled: "Where is he? What about the project?"

"Where did you get to?" said Ma Heshun. "You're too late!"

In fact, Liu Jinding had carefully calculated the time to escape. After hiding for a month and four days, he felt that the spotlight would no longer be on him and he could make his move. Xie Zhichang's wallet contained a plane ticket from Wuhan to Guangzhou. He originally planned that after eating this meal with Sloppy Wang at noon that day, Xie Zhichang's car would take him directly to Wuhan along the expressway from Potou Township. After that, he would fly from Wuhan to Guangzhou, and then leave the country on his fake passport.

However, he made the wrong call.

---

1. A folk belief that ghosts throw up walls in front of lost travellers, forcing them to walk round in circles

CHAPTER SEVEN

七

ONE

Li Delin was "invited" into the Red Mansion three months after the incident.

He was invited in under the pretext of just having a talk. The word "invited" is enough to show that, as a provincial vice-governor and national wheat expert, Li Delin was being treated with extreme courtesy.

It was at this time that Xu Ya'nan's body was found. It was fished from a reservoir in Dongxia, having been put in a sack, tied with a rock and sunk into the water. It was seriously decomposed by the time it was brought up. The Dongxia Reservoir went down to twenty-four metres at its deepest point, and a team of twelve skilled divers were hired to retrieve the body. It took them three days, and the operation cost a total of 16,000 yuan.

When Li Delin was invited into the Red Mansion, most of the suspects who were directly or indirectly implicated in the case were now brought to justice. At this moment, the files of Project Number One were already piled up as high as a man, but the main protagonist of the case had not yet been definitely identified. However, based on the current situation, all the indirect evidence was pointing to Li Delin.

It was Jiang Baoguo's account that finally connected the entire chain of evidence. There were two links, which had not yet been confirmed. One was Liu Jinding. Liu repeated his story many times. At first, he explained that his master was the driving force, and he himself was just a messenger, but then he stopped saying that and changed his version of events. The other link was Jiang Baoguo, who didn't say anything at first. He waited until all the evidence had him nailed down before he spilled the beans and confessed about Liu Jinding. He said that the only person in direct contact with him was Liu Jinding. Although he had eaten with Li Delin several times, Li Delin had always held back and had never directly discussed this matter with him. In addition, the cost of the killing – 300,000 yuan – was paid by the Flower World Hotel, of which Bai Shouxin was general manager. But Bai Shouxin only signed it and didn't know what it was for. According to Jiang Baoguo, all of this was instigated by Li Delin. However, there was Liu Jinding in the middle, and an absence of direct evidence. Only one word could directly prove Li Delin's involvement in this case: "success". That word was sent to him by Liu Jinding using his mobile phone at the time the crime occurred, while he was still in Beijing.

For as long as Jiang Baoguo decided not to open his mouth, he didn't open it even a crack. But once he did open it, he confessed an amazing secret. He confessed that the person he actually most wanted to kill was Xue Zhiheng, because he had found Jiang Baoguo's personal stash of explosives and detonators in his home. He said that this Xue person was a bad man and a bully. He had been deputy director of the Huanghuai City Public Security Bureau for twelve years, with eight years as executive, and he was on the point of becoming director. When Lao Wan was making the provincial appointment, it was Jiang Baoguo's turn; it should have been his turn. But in order to install his cronies, this Xue fellow not only failed to promote him, he actually transferred him to the Bureau of Justice. He was relegated from the big league to a minor league with fewer than a hundred people, and still as a deputy director. That was real bullying, if ever there was!

In a private room of the Municipal Party Committee guest house, Jiang Baoguo finally had a chance to approach the Municipal Party Committee secretary, so he hurried over to toast him. But Xue Zhiheng showed him no respect at all. He responded to the toast without saying anything, and asked in front of everyone: "Who are you? How about a bit of decorum!"

"Jiang Baoguo from the Public Security Bureau of our city, reporting, sir!"

Xue Zhiheng looked him over and said: "From the City Bureau, eh? Stand to attention! About turn! March!"

Of course, there was no longer any chance of Jiang Baoguo approaching the top table, so he raised his wine glass in both hands and dropped to his knees with a thud. He knelt there with his back very straight and raised the wine glass over his head, hoping that Xue Zhiheng would give him a little face. But Xue Zhiheng just turned away and continued to talk and laugh with others, not giving him a second glance. If Xue Zhiheng had been alone in a private room, being scolded and disrespected by a superior in this manner would have ended there and not mattered, but for it to happen in front of so many provincial and city leaders of all ranks! That that amounted to a public humiliation, didn't it?

In fact, Xue Zhiheng was not normally like that, and had always been very fair with his subordinates. But that day was different. On that day, the Organisation Department of the Provincial Party Committee had made a special trip to inspect cadres in the city. It was not a normal situation and, in addition, Xue Zhiheng had drunk a few more glasses of wine than usual that night. When someone came in, obviously drunk, and toasted him in a manner that ignored their difference in status, it was natural that Xue Zhiheng was very annoyed. What he, the secretary of the Municipal Party Committee, could not possibly have imagined was that a single glass of wine could bring disaster down on his head.

People crave face and this incident became a great source of shame in Jiang Baoguo's life. Real men do not kneel lightly, so how could he have been expected to kneel in public like that? When he woke up the next morning, he sat on the edge of his bed, wept briefly, then slapped himself around the face several times and told himself: Fuck it!

Nevertheless, from then on, he felt as though the shame had been nailed to his heart. It looked like he had no future in Huanghuai so, from then on, he would do as he pleased. Once hatred takes root in someone, it becomes a source of nourishment, and that glass of wine had been the trigger. When a hard-working, diligent person, who has been toiling away for years in the hope of promotion, thinks he has been humiliated, he becomes like a keg of gunpowder laced with poison. All this develops slowly over time. For a man with no light in his heart, only darkness remains. It is like soaking bean sprouts without providing any light: they soak and they soak, and turn into poisonous sprouts from which the venom gradually seeps out. Jiang Baoguo's character changed. His eyes hardened and clouded over whenever he saw anyone. He was bored all day long, and he spoke less.

At first, Jiang Baoguo wanted to move away from Huanghuai and live somewhere else. He wanted to be transferred to the province, but however hard he tried, he was disappointed. For a while, his hatred had nowhere to vent itself, and he was itching to get his revenge. By chance, he learned that the Mine Police had seized some illegal detonators and explosives. Under cover of going to the reservoir to eat fried fish, the chief of the Mine Police Station brought him some in the form of one kilogram of explosives and four detonators. Deep down, in a hidden place in his heart, Jiang Baoguo wanted to blow up the son-of-a-bitch who had humiliated him.

He was in charge of criminal investigation, so he knew the stakes. He told only one person about his intentions, and that was his cousin, Huang Bingyan. He had acted kindly towards Huang Bingyan many times after he had committed crime after crime, and twice had got his sentence commuted. Moreover, when he was released from prison, he maintained a very low profile and kept his nose clean, so Jiang Baoguo nurtured him as his own secret "ninja". When the two were drinking privately together, he had several times instructed Huang Bingyan to follow Xue Zhiheng, and Huang had also been to the municipal committee's family compound for a secret reconnaissance, disguised as a rag-and-bone man. Huang Bingyan discovered that access to the compound was strictly controlled, with cameras everywhere. Another problem was that Xue Zhiheng rode in an Audi A6, which was very fast, and the van Huang Bingyan drove was too slow to keep up – as he had discovered on several occasions. The matter was temporarily put on hold.

Later, Jiang Baoguo had the good fortune to go to Mei Village and meet Liu Jinding, the executive deputy mayor. Through Deputy Mayor Liu, he became a member of the dinner club. After many dinners there, his attitude changed, and he felt that he had some hope of promotion again. So he dropped the matter completely, although he still found uses for Huang Bingyan.

Everything stemmed from that dinner. After Jiang Baoguo had challenged the county director, Tang Mingsheng, at the Meiling Club, Liu Jinding took him to one side. The two drank another bottle of wine, getting heartily drunk in the process. In their cups, they pledged eternal brotherhood, lamented the fact that they had not met earlier and indulged in a lot of intimate conversation.

After that, Jiang Baoguo made a particular point of inviting Liu Jinding for a drink. They took a bath at the spa after dinner, then summoned a girl to their private room for a "little massage". When the two of them were alone in the room again, Jiang Baoguo said: "Mayor Liu, my brother, I want a transfer. I'm so frustrated, I am suffocating to death. Can you help me move?"

"Brother, there's no problem at my end," said Liu Jinding, "but it depends where you want to move. If it's in the city, I don't have the authority. You'd have to ask Xue Zhiheng, as he has the final say."

"I'm not going to pretend, Brother, Xue Zhiheng is a problem. That bastard has mortally offended me, and you just wait and see, I'm going to settle that account sooner or later! Can you transfer me out into the province? That would do fine. I just don't want to be under Xue Zhiheng's control."

"At your rank, if you want promotion, you'll have to talk to the old man. That's why I asked you to join this dinner club."

"I'm not on familiar terms with the governor, Brother. I've been to a few dinners, but I haven't dared say anything yet. You are his student. Please talk to him about me, I beg you! I will never forget it even when I am old and toothless!"

"I can talk to him. That's not a problem. As it happens, he has a difficulty of his own. Do you think you can help with it?"

Jiang Baoguo slapped his chest and said: "I, Jiang, will go through fire and water to help. I will not hesitate!"

At this point, Liu Jinding lowered his voice and said: "Brother, you've got eyes to see what's going on. You know Number One is on the way up and will sooner or later make it to Beijing and the State Council. We must make sure he is not troubled in any way."

"Yes, yes, I understand."

"It's not a big deal. A former nanny is embarrassing the old man... He's certainly going to make it to the Central Committee one day, and she can't possibly go to Beijing as his wife. It would be beyond a joke. She would be a real embarrassment. Too shaming."

Jiang Baoguo gestured dismissively and said: "If a nanny gets above herself, you just get rid of her. Get rid of her!"

Liu Jinding gave him a sidelong look. "It has to be done very carefully. Very cautiously."

With the wine swirling around inside him, Jiang Baoguo said: "It's got to be done, and done cleanly. Leave this to me. I've got an underling who can do the job."

"However you do it, you still have to be cautious. I think it would best for her just to leave."

"Leave?"

"That's what I said."

"What do you mean, 'leave'?"

Liu Jinding remained somewhat vague: "Leaving means disappearing. You don't have to worry about money, I'll give you a bank card number you can use."

Just like that, they had reached the crux of the matter. Jiang Baoguo politely offered Liu Jinding a toothpick, which he took and put in his mouth. The two looked at each other. Jiang Baoguo said: "This matter could go either way, don't you think?"

With the toothpick in his mouth, Liu Jinding said vaguely: "Don't worry, Number One will look after you."

The two men had two further "meals" together, at which they found themselves even more in harmony. But after they were arrested, their stories differed greatly, and they had to retract their confessions over and over again. To start with, Liu Jinding tried to keep his hands clean by claiming he had just passed on a message and didn't know anything else. But as time passed, he kept changing his story. For a while, he said that Li Delin had called him and wanted to cancel the action. Then he said that Li Delin didn't know about it, and that it was all down to Jiang Baoguo alone... Liu Jinding had always hoped he could protect Li Delin. He felt that saving his master was his last hope. However, on the question of how to get Xu Ya'nan to "leave", his explanations differed completely from Jiang Baoguo's. In the end, the two of them turned on each other.

Given the situation, Li Delin could no longer deny the relationship.

TWO

AFTER ENTERING THE RED MANSION, Li Delin's hair turned white overnight.

Of course, he was "invited in" and given special treatment. He wasn't forced to change his clothes on the spot, but even so, he was still very uncomfortable to be surrounded by four rubber-lined walls.

He just sat there all night as his head seemed to blossom with snowy white hair.

Nonetheless, his arrogance was still with him in the interrogation room when he saw Helian Dongshan. Yes, after all, he was a PhD who had studied abroad. He had been a deputy governor for many years, and there was still something about him that seemed to give him strength. Before the interrogator could speak, he said: "Are there any cigarettes?"

Helian Dongshan took out a cigarette, and was just about to pass it over when he heard Li Delin refuse it, saying: "I'm sorry, I only smoke Zhonghua... I'm sorry, I'm not being fussy. They're just what I smoke. It's a habit I got when I was studying in the United States, and the only Chinese cigarettes you could get over there were Zhonghua."

Helian Dongshan took the cigarette back, hesitated for a moment, then said to one of the other policemen in the room: "Go and buy him a pack."

After getting the cigarettes, Li Delin smoked two in a row. Afterwards, he looked up and said to Helian Dongshan in a superior tone: "Do you know what a seed is? A seed is one of the organs of a plant. The growth of a seed requires a process, the result of long-term evolution and the highest manifestation of sexual reproduction in plants. This falls within the category of aesthetics. It may well be the case that you simply don't understand–"

Helian Dongshan choked off a laugh and said: "Lao Li..."

Li Delin didn't wait for him to ask anything, but said proudly: "Let me tell you, I am working on six major projects for the United Nations' Food and Agriculture Organisation. Each one is worth several hundred million and you've got me sitting here! Do you want to ruin all of them?"

Next, he gushed: "Do you know how much damage this will cause to the country? Do you know how the United Nations will treat this matter? I am their representative, the representative of the Food and Agriculture Organisation. If you keep this up, the United Nations will send a diplomatic note. Do you understand?"

"Listen to me, Lao Li. Are you Chinese or not?"

Li Delin stroked his hair, made a slight calming gesture with his hands and said: "No, you let me finish! Then you can ask me whatever you want, no problem. I will tell the whole truth. But I have a demand, or rather, a request. Please give me another six months, six months. I only need six months, so I can finish the cultivation of Huanghuai Number One." He lowered his voice and murmured: "It's my life's work. I've got to see it through."

Helian Dongshan looked at him in silence, with mixed feelings in his heart, and he didn't know what to say for a while. This person, this man... what a pity!

Li Delin went on, still arrogantly: "I know that you, none of you, are actually in charge of this. Go and ask for instructions. Ask the Provincial Party Committee or even the central government. I am sure they will give me this time."

Helian Dongshan shook his head, looked at him quizzically for a long time, before saying: "You're talking about growing seeds?"

"Yes, I am engaged in bioengineering, or breeding."

"With everything that has happened, you still have the nerve to talk to me about seeds?"

"It is an academic field of study," Li Delin said boldly. "It is called seed science."

"Oh, I see, and you are saying that China can't produce good seeds without you?"

"That's not what I mean. I have been working on this for nearly thirty years, and I hope to produce a particularly fine type of seed from the Huanghuai Number One. I am just one step away. Have you heard of Huanghuai Number One? It is a double-eared wheat. A wheat plant that can bear two ears of wheat per head. If I'm successful, it will be a miracle for mankind. With double-eared wheat, the yield per *mu* will be doubled in existing conditions, and in a country like ours, no one will ever starve to death again."

Li Delin looked up at him and continued: "The authorities have ring-fenced ten billion yuan for the project. Do you understand? It's all about food conservation. Someone your age knows what it is to go hungry. It's not pleasant, is it? Back in those days, when we were young, hunger was hunger and society was clean and pure. Frankly speaking, it's not clean and pure any more. I am not alone in thinking this, am I? So I am begging you, hurry up and ask for instructions. I only need six months."

Helian Dongshan was silent. Li Delin's words had really moved him. Yes, for those born in the 1950s, society was clean and pure in the early years. While they weren't too sure what was going on in the upper echelons back then, at least, as Li Delin said, the bottom of society was clean. But now? Whatever the case, looking it as a criminal investigator, just because someone was an expert in wheat, was that any justification for being exempt from the law? Of course not. It was a joke!

Helian Dongshan no longer showed him any mercy. He shouted sharply: "Wake up, Lao Li! Look around you! What is this place?"

Helian Dongshan had prepared carefully before starting to question Li Delin. He thought he had considered everything, but he hadn't anticipated Li Delin making such a request.

He continued sternly: "Lao Li, let me tell you the truth. What you have requested is not completely beyond the realms of possibility. If we were living in special times, like the Great Famine, you might be given an amnesty from the very top. It is still quite likely that you might be given some leeway outside the law, just like you said, to let you continue your research into your double-eared wheat, but first you have to plead guilty and go through a certain legal process so you can be determined to have atoned for your crime through meritorious service. At the moment, you are pleading not guilty. I advise you to forget that idea."

Li Delin's *qi* deflated. The corners of his eyes were covered with fine wrinkles, like crumpled rags covered with dust. Suddenly, he looked unimaginably old. His spirit was gone. He sat there, exactly like a pile of ash. This pile of ash was left behind on a shelf, and he was hanging onto that shelf for all he was worth.

Helian Dongshan felt a little sorry for him. Softening his tone, he said: "Lao Li, you are an expert and a senior cadre. Let's you and me talk about it."

Li Delin sat blankly, then suddenly raised his head and exclaimed: "Oh, oh oh."

"Do you remember? When I was in middle school, there was a text called 'Liang Shengbao buying rice seeds'. That text–"

"Remember? Of course, I remember! That text is taken from Liu Qing's novel *History of Entrepreneurship*. Yes, he was really poor at the time. He couldn't afford to stay in a hotel when he was travelling and only drank two-cent bowls of tea."

"Do you think there are still people like Liang Shengbao, Lao Li?"

"I said that in those days, society was clean and pure. That was true, of course it was. Now..." He shook his head, then lowered it and murmured: "Now, we are not clean or pure any more."

"Lao Li, I know you are an expert in seed research, and you have contributed a lot to the country. It is not easy for someone from three generations of farmers to get a PhD in the United States. Let's have a talk. I have something to ask you: has the country offended you somehow?"

Li Delin was taken aback, raised his head and stared at him, not knowing what to say.

Helian Dongshan continued: "It is a fact that, from elementary school, through junior high school, to high school, you have an exemplary academic record, and you went to school for free. Back then, you had a certificate issued by your village, giving you free tuition. This is a fact, isn't it? You went to university on a full bursary. This is also true, isn't it? You went to study in the United States on a public scholarship. Do you know how much was spent on you? You were studying for a PhD in biology for three years and the tuition had to be paid for. The cost of living was eleven hundred yuan per month, but you were actually getting nine hundred and seventy US dollars. Not counting the air tickets, that is equivalent to at least one hundred thousand yuan a year, no small amount at that time! So you work it out. How much of the country's money did you spend? Of course, it is true that you were very frugal and hard working at the time."

As Li Delin listened to him, he seemed to be lost in his memories. He murmured: "I want a cigarette."

"Let's talk about now, in your role as a provincial vice-governor. We won't even consider the salary. Let's just look at the perks. You have a dedicated car for your sole use. Currently it's an Audi that costs about six hundred thousand yuan. You have changed car three times. The first one was a Nissan Bluebird, and the second was a Volkswagen. The annual insurance and maintenance costs for each car is at least sixty thousand yuan, and a special chauffeur has a monthly salary of at least four thousand yuan plus a business trip subsidy, so that's about fifty thousand to sixty thousand a year. You have a driver and full-time secretary who take care of all aspects of your life. Whenever you go out, no matter where it is, you are welcomed. In addition, there are various other allowances for housing, medical care and so on... Lao Li, there is one thing I don't understand, and it's really puzzling me. If you have reached these heights, why bother to murder someone?"

Li Delin sat stunned for a long time, then suddenly woke up and murmured: "I didn't murder anyone, didn't kill, no, no..." Then, he lowered his head and muttered to himself: "When the wheat is yellow, there is no sound, and when the hair is grey, there is no sound either. Why should I believe it?"

At this point, the lights in the interrogation room were turned on, and all kinds of bright light suddenly hit Li Delin. His eyes squinted, and a thin film of sweat appeared on his forehead. The sweat beads were like small bugs that had gathered, squirming slowly and forming a winding stream along the wrinkles. His hand stretched out convulsively and he pleaded: "Please, let me smoke another cigarette."

For about ten minutes, Li Delin was sitting alone in the light. He shrank subconsciously under the strength of it, as if frozen. His cigarette was finished and the ash fell silently to the floor.

After a while, the lights dimmed again. On the wall opposite Li Delin, a white screen unfurled silently. The screen was lit up and a vehicle appeared, a white Jinbei minivan. The camera slowly zoomed in on the minivan and fixed on the licence plate: Shaanxi A7563. Then, there were enlarged, frame-by-frame images that rotated into position: the same Jinbei on the campus of the University of Agricultural Science and Technology; in front of the university's library; an alert but surprised-looking Xu Ya'nan turning to look before getting into the vehicle; the Jinbei minivan passing through the provincial expressway toll gate; a close-up of the front licence plate: Shaanxi A7563; the minivan exiting at the Dongxia toll gate; another close-up of the licence plate: Shaanxi A7563; then the minivan as it appeared in the oak woods of Laoyeling, burnt-out and almost unrecognisable; the close-up of the licence plate showing just a piece of blackened iron with letters...

Then, the rippling blue water of the reservoir appeared on the screen, and once again close-up shots revolved into position. Close-ups of the sack being held up, soaking wet from the reservoir, and then falling to the ground and inside it was a dead body, a bloody corpse. Then a DNA certificate with the seal of a testing agency. The shot slowly focused in on the large red seal, followed by the certificate itself: after a series of English letters and the supporting data, the last three characters were "Xu Ya'nan".

The lights dimmed again, and sequences of the interrogations of the suspects appeared on the screen. The first was of the killer Huang Bingyan. He was clearly answering questions in the interrogation room, but there was no sound. The second showed the killer's accomplice, Hong Xiaohe, under interrogation. The third showed the witness Zhou Shen being questioned. The fourth was Jiang Baoguo, shot during interrogation and with him answering questions, but again there was no sound. The fifth showed Liu Jinding being interrogated. The camera angles changed many times, but still without audio.

Dropping onto the screen like miniature bombs were a series of familiar telephone numbers. After each group of numbers, there was a single word: "success". The word appeared four times in a row after the phone numbers. When the last huge "success" appeared on the screen, the receiver's location was prominently indicated above it: Beijing.

This mobile phone number in Beijing was clearly shown. The camera zoomed in until the number filled the entire screen.

When the screen was illuminated again, it was blank at first, followed by the sound of weeping, loud weeping. The image of a boy appeared on the screen. He was a little over four years old and was crying out: "Mummy! Mummy! Mum..." When the screen froze, there was only a pair of eyes left, the child's eyes. They were looking straight ahead, tears streaming down his cheeks, and full of sadness and fear.

Reacting to the images, Li Delin stood up suddenly, took off all his clothes and stood naked, shouting: "Look, she beat me, bit me, pinched me, I'm covered in..."

At this point, Helian Dongshan seemed to hear the sound of an explosion. His eyes went dark as a cloud of smoke appeared. He suddenly realised that Li Delin had disappeared in the smoke. He stood up, rubbed his eyes and yelled: "Hey!"

Li Delin had simply disappeared. That person who they held in such high regard; that person in the suit and tie who they often saw on the television giving them instructions; that expert who enjoyed special treatment from the State Council, had suddenly disappeared.

The interrogation room went quiet.

In fact, he had not disappeared. Li Delin was squatting on the concrete floor after taking off his clothes. He was engulfed with shame. He knew that he had nowhere to hide. He squatted naked on the ground, like a pile of ash after the fire had gone out.

Helian Dongshan was exhausted too. He had been on the case for too long, and he also fell to the ground in a faint.

THREE

"Project One" was finally closed.

For more than five months, a group of detectives had been absorbed in the case, day and night. All of them were stressed, and they hadn't even had time to catch their breath. Now that the case was over, it stood to reason that everyone should celebrate. The whole task force was on temporary transfer, so the very least the office could do was invite them for a meal. In the event, it was agreed early on that the executive deputy head of the Provincial Public Security Bureau in charge of this case, Lao Wan, should attend in person. He called Helian Dongshan specifically to say that not only was everyone to be celebrated for their meritorious conduct, but he also wanted to bring Vice-Governor Qiao to toast everyone individually, and to express appreciation to all the comrades of the task force on behalf of the provincial bureau.

However, things suddenly changed. Executive Deputy Director Wan Haifa, who promised to come to the celebration banquet, was suddenly unable to attend due to a diary change. He asked his secretary to call and say he was out of town, and he was afraid that he would not be able to get back in time. He personally posted his apologies in two messages in the message box. As the person in charge of the task force, Helian Dongshan was very upset when he learnt the news, but he wasn't going to spoil everyone's enjoyment. "If the boss can't come, he can't come," he said. "We still have to eat. It's my treat. We'll eat by ourselves."

However, what Helian Dongshan could never have suspected was that Deputy Director Wan, who had suddenly gone back on his word and was not attending the celebration banquet, had not left town at all. At that very moment, he was sitting in the office of Vice-

Governor Qiao, whose other position was director of public security. Moreover, Deputy Director Wan was banging the desk at that exalted official and shouting angrily: "This is just like killing the cat when the mice are gone! From now on, who is going to... how can this be happening? I don't believe it! You can strike me down dead, but I don't believe it!"

Vice-Governor Qiao looked at the *shuanggui* order on the table and said: "Lao Wan, this is not a question of believe it or not, it is an organisational decision. I don't believe there is any problem with Comrade Lao He, but since someone has made a report, and the top brass have approved it, it has to be investigated."

"He's being framed!" Lao Wan said angrily. "It's a stitch up!"

"Then we need to find out what is going on. Only then can we restore Comrade Helian Dongshan's good name. Go ahead, you're to take it on personally."

"I'm not going to. I'm not going to get involved. Just what is this?"

Vice-Governor Qiao thought for a while and said: "That will work fine too."

So four hours later, Helian Dongshan, who had just been drinking the celebration wine, was served with the *shuanggui* order. When Helian Dongshan emerged from the Red Mansion, he was blindfolded and taken to another *shuanggui* base. What happened was beyond his wildest imaginings. The officer who served him with the order was none other than Xing Zhibin, the young "apprentice" he had previously supported. After seven years of absence, Xing Zhibin was now a deputy division-level inspector of the Provincial Commission for Discipline Inspection. When Xing Zhibin unfolded in front of him the "double regulation order" with the large red seal, he said: "I never expected this, my old commander. Still, everyone gets what they deserve eventually."

Xing Zhibin was not really a narrow-minded and intolerant individual, but he had never forgotten the sight of his parents seven years ago, kneeling in front of Helian Dongshan begging for his future. The image was still vivid. Back then, Helian Dongshan only said two words: "Get up." How could he forget? Nobody could forget that.

Helian Dongshan was very surprised. From Xing Zhibin's tone of voice and expression, he realised that that the person he had so desperately worked to protect had completely misunderstood him. He said nothing. There was nothing to say.

Even though Xing Zhibin was indeed an apprentice under the wing of Helian Dongshan, he was initially demoted to a suburban police station. But then, with some help from relatives, he was seconded to the Municipal Commission for Discipline Inspection. It was during his time assisting the commission that he successively closed several major cases assigned to him, so his secondment became an official transfer. Since the case against Helian Dongshan had been approved by the top brass, it was considered a key case, and Xing Zhibin was brought in to take charge of it.

The investigation of the case against Helian Dongshan for the "acceptance of bribes" only lasted four days. During the first three days, Xing Zhibin, as chief investigating officer, had been silently watching his former teacher, observing him from different angles. Sometimes, he stood behind him. Helian Dongshan knew that his eyes were boring into his back... Xing Zhibin was deliberately imitating Helian Dongshan's interrogation style. He had been observing him for three days, and Helian Dongshan had not spoken.

Following the *shuanggui* order, Xing Zhibin told someone to give Helian Dongshan a stack of blank paper. But three days later, the stack of blank paper remained on the table, and he hadn't written a thing. On the fourth day, when Helian Dongshan was taken to the interrogation room, Xing Zhibin asked: "Have you thought about it?" Helian Dongshan replied: "I have thought it over." But just as he opened his mouth to speak, a mouthful of blood spilled out. All Xing Zhibin said in response was: "Go and see if he's faking it!" A second mouthful of blood spurted out and Helian Dongshan fell to the floor, unconscious.

He was rushed to the hospital to be resuscitated. After a series of tests, it was found that he had had a cerebral haemorrhage. After three days of emergency treatment, he gradually came round. When Wan Haifa, the executive deputy director of the Provincial Public Security Bureau and a member of the Standing Committee of the Provincial Commission for Discipline Inspection, hurried over, Helian Dongshan just opened his eyes. Wan Haifa held his hand, and the two men looked at each other in silence.

In fact, there were two reasons for Helian Dongshan's sudden cerebral haemorrhage. One was that he had invested too much in Project One, and five months of continuous investigation had got the better of him. The second and more important reason was that he couldn't stand the look in Xing Zhibin's eyes. There were too many "termites" in those eyes, glowing like little white dots. Multiple hidden meanings could be seen in those termites: they were condescending, gloating, full of old-fashioned resentment for past injustice and the dispassionate hatred of a cat for a mouse. That look was as deep as a well, a well seething with termites and chilli peppers, with time and with iron nails. His apprentice had turned into his enemy. What else was there to say? For Helian Dongshan, that look was lethal, and where it hit him hardest was in his dignity. His dignity as an old pre-trial investigator was everything to him, and he simply couldn't stand it.

(Later, when Helian Dongshan walked out of the *shuanggui* interrogation room, he cited Xing Zhibin's eyes as the main reason he did not cooperate. After that, he avoided associating with anyone with "Xing Zhibin eyes". Of course, sometimes, when alone, he would also reflect on who it was Xing Zhibin had learned that look from.)

Helian Dongshan was suddenly subjected to the *shuanggui* investigation principally for two alleged crimes. One was "accepting bribes". According to the informer, Helian Dongshan's son had just graduated from university and had bought two properties in a prime location inside Beijing's third ring road. These two properties were purchased at the low price for the time of 1.2 million yuan – according to the report, a fifty per cent discount when buying a house was the equivalent of a free gift. If calculated at current market value, the properties were now worth at least 12 million. Judging by Helian Dongshan's financial circumstances, a serious discrepancy existed. Even back at the time of purchase, 1.2 million yuan was not a small sum. Where did he get so much money? If the current market value was applied, any bribes taken by Helian Dongshan would amount to more than 10 million yuan! It was a big case. Helian Dongshan's other alleged crime was "rape", along with the lesser charge of inappropriate relations with a work colleague. Someone reported that he had seen one of Helian Dongshan's female juniors sitting on his lap. This relationship was regarded as corroboration of the rape accusation, as it was an indication of existing bad character. According to the report, Helian Dongshan used his position to rape the wife of a suspect in the course of an investigation. Of the two crimes, it did not matter which was proved, as both were felonies.

After visiting Helian Dongshan, Deputy Director Wan left with a heavy heart. He made an exception to his normal behaviour and called the handler of the Helian case. He said down the phone: "Please come to my office, Comrade Xing Zhibin." He put the phone down before Xing could reply.

When Xing Zhibin arrived at Deputy Director Wan's office, it was already evening. The office door was wide open, and he saw Wan sitting ashen-faced on a leather sofa. Xing Zhibin entered the room and called out: "Xing Zhibin reporting, sir!"

Deputy Director Wan glanced at him and said: "Sit down, sit down."

Xing Zhibin sat down on the edge of the sofa next to him, took out a small notebook and pen from his pocket and said: "Please give me your instructions, Director Wan."

"According to the regulations," Wan Haifa said, "only departmental heads should intervene in cases. I am breaking that rule today but let me make one thing clear. I am not seeking a favour from you, I just have something I want to talk to you about. You can put it on record."

Xing Zhibin sat up straighter and said: "Go on."

"Has Helian Dongshan confessed?"

"Not yet, no. He is very stubborn."

"I asked you here to tell you that you must investigate this case thoroughly. You must make sure the truth comes to light. If there is a problem with Helian Dongshan, you should do everything according to the regulations. If someone has framed him, make sure it is uncovered and you prove Helian Dongshan's innocence."

"Is that all?"

"That's it."

Wan Haifa looked at him and said: "Put away your little notebook."

Xing Zhibin was taken aback, and reluctantly put the notebook and pen back into his pocket. At this point, Wan Haifa said: "Do you know why I made an exception and sought you out?"

Xing Zhibin shook his head.

"Do you hate me?"

Xing Zhibin was momentarily stunned. He didn't know what Director Wan meant.

Wan Haifa waved his hand, indicating he didn't need to answer. He went on to say: "Late one night, eight years ago, a man knocked on the door of the head of the Huanghuai City Public Security Bureau. He came to intercede for a young policeman. He said: 'Director Wan, this is a conspiracy. He is being framed.' I will tell you now, quite frankly, that I was under great pressure from above, and I couldn't take it any more. To put it bluntly, your case had already been decided before it hit my desk. The man told me: 'You must stand up to them. You can't ruin a young man's future.' I'm telling you now that that person who forced his way into my house late that night was Helian Dongshan."

There was a long silence in the office.

Finally, Wan Haifa said: "Let me repeat, I'm not asking for any favours. I just want you to look at the facts and find out the truth." Then he gestured in dismissal and said: "You can go now."

Xing Zhibin stood up, saluted and walked out in silence.

FOUR

AFTER THE PROJECT NUMBER ONE CASE WAS CLOSED, Li Delin was transferred to the Provincial Detention Centre. It was different from the *shuanggui* base, as it was a proper prison. At the *shuanggui* base, it was one person to a windowless cell and no interaction was allowed with anyone. At the prison, there were windows, but they were small and high up. Every day, when the sun shone in, it was as though rays of sunlight were being refracted by a mirror into myriad petals. Other than being let out for exercise, all he had to do was look at the sunlight. In there, he was simply "0561".

There were only three prisoners in the cell, and they all shouted "Reporting!" when they went in and out of it. He was 0561, and with him were 0452 and 0376. It would be justifiable to say that he was under observation in the cell. 0452 was accused of rape and 0376 was accused of bribery, neither of which were regarded as serious crimes. The two of them wore yellow tabards, which meant they were on remand. He wore a red tabard as he had already been convicted. He knew that the others had been put there specifically to monitor him, or maybe it was to guard him against "accidents". So apart from smoking, he had nothing to do with them.

Sitting in the cell, wearing shackles and handcuffs, Li Delin had been pondering the question: how did he get to this point? When did the process that got him there actually start?

Whenever he closed his eyes as he lay facing the wall, a boundless field would appear in his mind's eye. He had taken to muttering to that field.

He saw a large bowl. Blue rimmed, coarse porcelain, with a gap in the rim; his tongue swept over the rim, again and again. There was a moon in the bowl. He used his tongue to fish for the moon time and time again... The blue-rimmed bowl was so clean, as clean as if it had just been washed. The wind had colours: sometimes yellow, sometimes black, sometimes purple. The wind was also curved. When the wind passed across the sky, it said in an arc-shaped voice: "My baby, are you ravenous? Here's a big bowl of sticky rice. It's enough for two, so share it with your dad." Then a fire appeared in the sky turning every tile of the cell red, and the red spread and spread until it turned into a desert. An oasis appeared in the desert, and another voice could be heard: "This is Israel's Famine Relief Farm Village, with the most advanced drip irrigation technology in the world... Will you have coffee or red wine, sir?"

He saw a pair of chopsticks growing in a field. The chopsticks trotted to the edge of the field, skipping like monkeys coming down from the branches. One chopstick was broken into two pieces, one long, one short. A voice said: "Don't you like noodles, then? Aren't there enough in this pot for you to slurp down?" There were also two black-and-white twisted buns threaded on the chopsticks, more black showing than white. A pair of very rough, cracked hands was peeling off the white parts, layer by layer, and throwing them into a bowl. A voice said: "We can't waste the good stuff! Just get on with your food." Why were there lights on the chopsticks? There were rows of lights, and the lights said: "You are a Chinese. You've been looking for ages, why don't you buy anything?" The price list read: $1.12, $1.26, $1.58, $2.56, $3.58... $5.99. A voice said: "Damn, how long is it since you last ate noodles? Pick an expensive one. Go for it and pick an expensive one. Try the most expensive instant noodles in New York!"

Heat some water on the electric ring but when they're cooked, all that is left is half a bowl of butter soup that is rancid and nasty. Fucking American instant noodles! A waste of $5.99.

He saw a stone roller, the sunlight dancing on it. A black bullock, a yellow bullock, a draft team muzzled in the sunlight, rolling away across the field. The roller pressed against the ears of wheat and rolled the grain out. The horns of the black bullock were quite long, and one of the horns of the yellow bullock was broken. The two always bumped into each other when they turned. The whip whistled through the air, with a crack crack, but it didn't hit the black bull. A voice said: "It's shitting, the black one's shitting! Scoop it up, hurry up and scoop it up... use your hands, you little prick! Use your hands! You have to have dung if you're growing flowers." "Dong, Dong, Dong." The school bell rang, and the primary school teacher pointed at the blackboard with a pointer and said: "Read it again: 'E Ou-Ou, Huang Ou de Ou!'" The students chanted: "E Ou-Ou, Huang Ou de Ou!"

He saw cooking smoke, a line of cooking smoke. At noon, as the sun was shining out of the oily sky, the cooking smoke curled up over the village, drifting from east to west, slowly dispersing in strands. It came from steamed buckwheat nests made in Da Huai's home, with sweet potato noodles and corn noodles, both types, yellow and sweet. The noodles rolled out in Da Wei's home, sweet potato leaf noodles dipped in sesame oil, dipped in the oil with chopsticks, at least three deep dips! The cornmeal cakes baked in Uncle Shushan's home, yellow and fragrant. The sweet potato rolls from Wenxiu's home with radishes, red and sweet. Yellow flour porridge with lumps of mustard from Mai Ren's home where sizzling oil filled the yard. Erqiu's home had a guest so there was a banquet of bean curd. The tofu was deep-fried, accompanied by fried vermicelli and cabbage. One large bowl per person, with a knotted dough steamed bun. Erqiu's father jumped up and down and shouted: "Get them done! Hurry up! We haven't got all day!" Erqiu Niang picked up a rolling pin and chased him out with it, saying: "We've got guests, haven't we? What's the matter? Are you afraid there won't be enough for you?"

He saw a hare. The hare's ears were sticking up like antennae. Suddenly it turned round with a jump, crossed the bean field, darted over the corn field, tripped on a ridge, rolled over and was up running

369

again. A voice said: "Stop it! East! It's running east! Dahuai, where's your gun?" The dust flew into the sky in a cloud. Thump, thump, thump. The sound of footsteps and the hare disappeared. There was a chattering noise... "Fuck it!" Da Huai said. "It's got a store hole! God, autumn's over and it's got a store hole! Fuck it, it's got our wheat in there! At least two catties of wheat! Quick! Dig it out!" In class, the professor said: "Li Si said: 'How can you lead the yellow dog out of the eastern gate?' Which of you knows the meaning of this sentence?"

He saw the reception party with their bicycles, riding in pairs, two by two. There were safflowers hanging on the bicycles, and safflowers on the chest of the bride. Red ribbons adorned the breast of the groom. Firecrackers exploded as the bicycles entered the village. A voice shouted: "First kowtow to heaven and earth, then kowtow to your parents and ancestors." Later, the courtyard was full of greedy, grease-stained mouths. This was a villager's wedding. Basket after basket of steamed stuffed buns were brought out, along with a pot of braised pork with tofu and noodles. A voice said: "Mix it! Mix it strong! There's more than enough for today!" When the moon rises, he gives a great belch, has a good long piss then squats down under the eaves to listen to the bridal chamber... A voice said: "It's midnight, and I haven't heard a word." Another said: "I heard a tinkling sound. There's a chamber pot in the room." Listening and listening, as the moon's smile faded. Suddenly, a voice said: "This must be the Japanese 'body feast'! Beautiful to look at and delicious to eat!"

He saw the melon fields. The moonlight filled them, shining with a blue aura. The round watermelons were oily black. A voice said: "Quiet! Wait till you can hear the old devil snoring, then crawl in." Another voice said: "No point in that, his eyes are like a turtle's. We'll never get past him! You go east and I'll head west. We'll wait till he's having a piss, then we'll snatch one and run away. He'll have his pants in his hand and be unable to chase us in two directions at once. He'll never catch us..." How sweet that melon was! Every bit of it, sweet as sweet! Then the sound of the whip rang, and the whip said: "Beat his arse to pieces! See if he steals any more melons!" Professor Weiner stood, full of energy in the classroom, stretched out a big hairy hand, and pointed at him and shouted: "You! Chinese fellow! Do you have any desires? What are your desires?"

He saw a hayrick...

No, he shouldn't give up the wheat. In fact, what Li Delin liked best was to sit alone on the edge of a wheat field, light a cigarette and stay there silently as if in conversation with the wheat. It was a heart-to-heart, wordless communication. Yes, he would sit on the ridge next to the wheat field, take off one of his cloth shoes, put it under his buttocks, and with his bare foot, rub the hot soil of the ridge with his toes, smelling the sweet, sentimental, familiar fragrance of the wheat and just sitting silently. Those were the most pleasant moments of his life.

From when he was little, he had grown up on the edge of a wheat field, and it was wheat that gave him his dream. He had wheat first, then life. He had been able to walk step by step through his life until now, all thanks to the wheat. Now that he had given up his wheat, there was nothing left. He seemed to hear the wheat weeping. It was weeping for him.

He said: "When the wheat is yellow, there is no sound, and when the hair is grey... Why did I believe it?"

"Lao Li," 0376 asked, "what's that sutra you're reciting?"

FIVE

THE WINTER THAT YEAR WAS VERY COLD. It started snowing just after November, and a blizzard swirled in the sky.

The day Wang Xiaomei went to visit Li Delin, it had just snowed. The snow had fallen heavily, and everywhere was white, much like her state of mind.

After Project Number One entered the judicial process, it went through a preliminary trial, a review and a retrial. The judgments on the other prisoners were very consistent, and only differed for the principal culprit Li Delin. When studying Li Delin's judgment, the opinions of the Provincial High Court's Review Committee on the sentence appeared to be divided. One opinion was for the death penalty and the other also proposed the death penalty, but suspended. The opinion that insisted on the death penalty stated: the nature of the crime was so bad and the social impact so huge, anything short of the death penalty would anger the citizens. The opinion that insisted on the suspension of the death penalty said: although this person was at the centre of the crime, the only evidence against him were the frequently changed confessions of his co-accused, and he himself did not directly participate in the murder. Moreover, this person is a famous agricultural scientist well-known at home and abroad. His Huanghuai Number One was a national key research project and might make a great contribution to the country. It was recommended that the sentence be one of execution with a reprieve, to give time to consider all the ramifications. The two opinions were delivered at the same time, and the instruction came back from the highest level. It consisted of a total of ten words: "The man is scum. Only execution will satisfy the people."

After the final judgment was issued, the Provincial High Court sent someone to the detention centre to announce it to Li Delin.

Vice-President Sun said courteously: "Lao Li, I have to inform you that the ruling has been delivered."

Li Delin asked eagerly: "Is there any change?" Vice-President Sun shook his head. Li Delin asked: "Weren't the materials for my appeal delivered to them?"

Vice President Sun said simply: "Rejected. The original sentence is upheld and the death penalty is upheld." Then, he motioned to a staff member to read the review verdict to him face to face.

Li Delin lowered his head and was silent. After a while, he raised his head and said: "I... I have a request."

"Go on."

"I want to see someone."

In the past, they had worked together in the same province, and Vice-President Sun had reported to Li Delin on several occasions. His impression of him had always been good. He hesitated and said: "If it is a family member, I think it will be OK."

"Not a family member, but... a staff member of the Meiling Agricultural Bureau."

"What is their name?"

"Wang, Wang Xiaomei."

"A woman?"

"A woman."

Vice-President Sun smacked his lips, shook his head and said: "It's not a family member. According to the regulations, it's not permitted. What about your child, Lao Li? Don't you want to see your child?"

Li Delin hesitated, closed his eyes and thought for a while. Then he shook his head, and said: "This is my only request."

Vice-President Sun was silent for a long time. Finally, he said: "I think you can... you can see her. I'm in charge of this and I say you can see her."

When she was told, Wang Xiaomei hesitated. She was under too much pressure. After Li Delin was arrested, various rumours swirled around Meiling. As the saying goes, nothing can be kept secret forever. Gradually, the rumours were aimed more and more at her. People labelled her as the "little mistress", the "sugar daddy's little mistress" and "little number three" who broke up the family. Whenever she went out, they would surround her and point at her. Some people who had been after her in the past, especially her ex-husband, had spat in her face, cursing her: "Slut! Baggage!" She endured it all. What else could she do?

A telephone call from the Provincial High Court came through. It said that Li Delin wanted to see her for the last time before being executed. Until that call, everything had been guesswork and supposition, but that was all over now. She was exposed to the full glare of daylight. Was she going to go?

By now, the result would be the same whether she visited or not. She thought about it for a day and a night, and in the end, she went. I don't care how it looks, she said to herself.

The sky was all white with snow. On the way there, she wrapped her face tightly with a scarf, leaving only a pair of eyes showing. Although she didn't care what people thought of her, she still preferred not to be recognised.

Wang Xiaomei met Li Delin in the office of the director of the detention centre. When they met, Li Delin's fetters had been taken off, but the handcuffs were still on, and he was wearing a red tabard with the words "Constant Surveillance" printed on it. A file of armed police stood outside the door, as if expecting some mighty enemy. The director, who seemed to be a reasonable kind of person, led her into the office, and then said: "You two have a talk."

Li Delin knew in his heart that he could not blame this woman. After all, he had only known her for a little more than four years. From beginning to end, Wang Xiaomei had never questioned him. And now she had still come to see him, which showed just what kind of a woman she was. But what about him? In front of her, he saw what a small, insignificant man he was. It was not something he had recognised before, but when Helian Dongshan interrogated him, he had suddenly collapsed under the weight of everything he had done. Out of his mind with fear and desperate to plead his innocence, he had torn off all his clothes; that was when he saw how small and insignificant he was. He had squatted on the ground looking for a crack to crawl into. Then, he finally understood that once he took off the cloak of deputy governor, he was just a "child of the yellow earth".

Life is finite. What was meant by the saying "One misstep gives rise to eternal hatred"? Well, now he understood what the ancients meant, and it was being visited on him. It was true that he had never thought of killing anyone. If he had known that he was going to turn out to be a murderer, he would never have travelled thousands of miles to study for a PhD in America. You don't have to study hard to be a killer, do you! But now it was too late to say anything.

Yes, it was too late.

Li Delin and Wang Xiaomei looked at each other in silence for a long while. Finally, Li Delin said: "So how are you?"

"I'm OK."

"It's snowing. Is it making walking difficult?"

"It's OK."

"How is the wheat growing in the field?"

Wang Xiaomei looked at him in surprise, as if she had suddenly understood something. "There was a drought first, but it recently snowed twice."

"I'm sorry, Xiaomei. I've been sentenced to death, and I'm going to be gone soon. I shouldn't have invited you. On the one hand, I was afraid of tarnishing your reputation, but on the other, I... I still want to tell you something."

"Go on."

Li Delin glanced at the door and said quickly: "I have a notebook with a blue cover. It is the record of my years of studying double-eared wheat. That is, all the test records on Huanghuai Number One. I remember it was released from the evidence. It's in Mei Village. You know my office in there? Only you have the key to that office. You took it, do you remember?"

Wang Xiaomei nodded.

"That notebook is my life's work and I'm handing it on to you. If, and I mean if, you are willing to continue the research, then cultivate Huanghuai Number One. My only condition is that if it is successful, let me know when it happens."

Wang Xiaomei nodded again and said: "I'll remember."

Faint tears were showing in Wang Xiaomei's eyes. "I brought you two packs of cigarettes and some fruit," she said.

"You know I only smoke Zhonghua."

"They are Zhonghua."

Li Delin let out a sigh of relief and said: "I don't have long left. I'll only get through a few of them." Then he added: "You should go..."

Wang Xiaomei said through her tears: "Remember *The Old Man and the Sea*?"

"I am no longer worthy to talk about that book."

"He... failed."

"Yes, he failed, but he was only defeated. I became a criminal."

Wang Xiaomei didn't know what to say. "I just saw the sadness in it... it's really a sad book."

After that, she stood up abruptly and said: "I'm leaving now."

"Yes, you should go." He stood up as well.

Li Delin stood there, watching Wang Xiaomei walk out of the director's office, into the yard and then step by step towards the large iron gates in the distance. The sky was clear, the snow was orange in the light of the setting sun. Draped in orange splendour, she walked across the prison yard, hips swinging, and leaving a line of white footprints in the ground. It was very beautiful.

Then the bell rang, trilling rapidly. It was the exercise period.

Three days later, Li Delin was executed.

He was the first prisoner in the province to be executed by lethal injection. Judicial departments from all over the country sent a number of people to observe from behind a large glass window. It could be said that this was the last piece of preferential treatment he received while in office.

After Wang Xiaomei retrieved the blue diary, her heart was constantly a flutter, like a baby rabbit, and she couldn't sleep at night. She started to take Valium again, first two tablets, rising to a maximum of six at a time, but she still could only sleep for two to three hours. And even when she did fall asleep, she would wake up suddenly, because, as long as the light was off, a dark shadow would appear in front of her bed. It disappeared as soon as the light was turned on. If it was turned off again, the shadow would reappear. And every time, over and over again, it asked: Has it been propagated yet?

Wang Xiaomei tried not to go out in the provincial capital. When she couldn't avoid it, she would wrap her head and face in a scarf and put on a big mask. But she was often recognised, and once that happened, she could feel the eyes boring into her back.

At this time, Xie Zhichang made a special trip back to Meiling to see Wang Xiaomei. He brought a really heavy present with him. He put it down and said: "Chief Wang, I heard that you made a special trip to see Governor Li, so I came as soon as I could to say how much I respect you." Wang Xiaomei said nothing. Xie Zhichang continued: "I also heard that you now have a book in your possession that happens to be Governor Li's diary." Wang Xiaomei remained silent. Xie Zhichang continued: "Well, I have rented you twenty acres of land in the outskirts of the county and built a house where you can live. It's quieter there and no one will harass you." Finally, he produced a contract. It was in relation to Huanghuai Number One. If it succeeded, Xie Zhichang wanted half the shares in any company.

So Wang Xiaomei resigned from her job, sold her house in the city and moved into the small villa. She had twenty acres of land and started experimenting with Huanghuai Number One, using Meiling Number Seven as the female "parent". However, once she started living in the country, she encountered a lot of problems and was becoming quite desperate. She simply didn't know whether she could propagate Huanghuai Number One.

She knew that ghostly spirit would always be with her. One night, she had a dream. She dreamed that Huanghuai Number One had ears: not double ears, but twelve ears! A huge, tree-like wheat stalk standing tall in the field like a solitary pillar. Then, a strong wind sprang up and it blew, and it howled, sweeping all the wheat ears away in an instant. When she woke up, she heard the rooster crowing, and knew it was dawn.

SIX

IT WAS MORE THAN TWO WEEKS before Xing Zhibin interrogated Helian Dongshan again.

After spending some time preparing, Xing Zhibin demonstrated what a seasoned professional he was. Despite what Deputy Director Wan had told him, his face still showed no trace of emotion, nor did he even hint at any concern for Helian Dongshan. Those "termites" were still in his eyes. But there was a softening of tone in the interrogation, as he changed to using the more respectful form of the pronoun "you".

Helian Dongshan was in a wheelchair when he was questioned. He had planned to keep silent, feeling that this whole process was an insult to him and a challenge to his personal dignity. He had been involved with pre-trial investigation all his life. He was born to interrogate prisoners, but now he had become the subject of the investigation, and he couldn't accept that. However, after he had been resuscitated following his stroke, he was lying handcuffed to a hospital bed. He had a lot of time to think... He knew that, as long as he kept silent, it would be impossible to verify the authenticity of any report in which he was named. Moreover, without details, this was likely to become an "unsolved case". Once it was labelled as that, the most that would come of it would be that it was shelved with the words: "A crime was committed but there is no evidence." If that was the outcome, he would be like a stained bedsheet that could not be cleaned. His reputation would be forever tainted.

Xing Zhibin asked: "Are you in better health now, Lao He?" Helian Dongshan just grunted.

Xing Zhibin went on: "What are your thoughts about the matter now? You're an old investigator yourself, so let's not go through all the rigmarole and just talk openly. Let me be clear, you have to explain yourself. If you don't, the case will never be settled. So first of all, what's going on with the property in Beijing? Where did the money come from?"

He finally understood about the set of keys that had been sitting on the corner cabinet. The keys that were slotted on one side, and claimed to have advanced Japanese, German, Italian and American technologies. The keys that he had been suspicious of all along, had now become a breakthrough point.

Helian Dongshan was silent for a moment, then replied: "The child told me about the fucking apartments. I heard there were two. As for where the money came from, I don't know. My son went to college. I only provided tuition and miscellaneous fees plus living expenses: sixteen thousand a year. Eight thousand was tuition and miscellaneous fees, and eight thousand was living expenses. In the first year, I took it to him personally. The rest of the time, I mailed it. This is all well documented. In addition, his mother went to Beijing to see him and took six thousand. That's how much money his family gave him. As for the money for buying a property, I don't know where it came from. If it was stolen, then you'll have to investigate that for yourselves. Or you could just ask him."

In truth, he was too embarrassed to say that his son was playing "games" for a living. But he also knew that no one would believe him anyway.

"All right, that's what will go on record," Xing Zhibin said. "The second charge is rape. Someone reported that you used your official position to rape a member of the family of a prisoner in your charge. What is more, we have the victim's own testimony. What do you say to this charge?"

Helian Dongshan raised his head, smiled and said: "Rape? You're going to have trouble making that stick! Who did I rape? When? Where?"

"Can't you remember? Then let me remind you. You were the presiding investigator on the 'July seventh guns case'. The case was tried at the Blu-Ray Hotel. Do you remember?"

Helian Dongshan thought for a while and said: "Oh, you mean the case I did eighteen years ago? That case was investigated for eighteen years and now this is another eighteen years. You're saying I raped a woman eighteen years ago and she's only reporting it now? Do you actually believe that?"

"Do you remember a woman named Yao Yi? She says she knelt in front of you begging you to save her husband. You promised that he would not be sentenced to death." Then, Xing Zhibin suddenly played his trump card: "Let me tell you. The woman still has the key piece of evidence against you: a piece of her underwear!"

Helian Dongshan quickly recalled the facts. The July seventh gun case, Wei Shaohua's case, did indeed involve such a woman. She was Wei Shaohua's mistress in Shenzhen, not his wife. This woman was at least twenty years younger than the armed robber, Wei Shaohua. She was young, beautiful and very fashionable. She had flown over from Shenzhen with a pot of soup. At the time, he had been moved by her behaviour. And yes, some of the other details were true too: she did kneel in front of him and entreat him... At this point, Helian Dongshan broke out in a cold sweat. Eighteen years had passed. What kind of power or influence had brought this woman scurrying forward with false accusations?

Helian Dongshan fell silent.

Xing Zhibin said: "There is another issue about your connection with women. Someone reported that you had a relationship with Hu Xiaoyue of the pre-trial division of Huanghuai City Public Security Bureau. Someone saw the two of you hugging in the office, with her sitting on your lap. She was transferred because of you. Are you going to admit to this one, Lao He?"

Helian Dongshan remained silent. Yes, Hu Xiaoyue was a young woman who had just been assigned to the pre-trial division after graduating from university. She was quite plump and well-built. She walked everywhere at great speed, like a cannonball erupting out of a barrel. It seemed she had followed a couple of cases and had probably heard about some of his achievements in the bureau, so had developed a kind of crush on him. One evening, she had rushed into his office, sat down on his lap and hugged and kissed him, murmuring: "I really like you, Teacher He. You..." Yes, it was true, and if that was true, then the charge of rape was only a short step away. In other words, this charge could be used as strong evidence of his predisposition to rape. A beautiful young woman sitting on your lap? What did that mean? Confess that your relationship with her was out of the ordinary! Whatever the case, having a young girl sitting on your lap can't have left you completely unmoved. Unless you're not a man, of course. Is that what you're saying? By this reasoning, if he couldn't keep his hands off his subordinates, then he was highly likely to rape a prisoner's wife. If they linked the two things together like this, it didn't leave him any way out.

Helian Dongshan suddenly felt that the scale of this "game" was too big for him; too big to work out who he had offended and was now out to get him. Who had that kind of power, to be able to fit him up so quickly? He thought about it and decided that if it came down to criminals he had convicted, then the biggest case he had handled was Project Number One, which had just been closed. But the main perpetrators of this project had all been arrested, hadn't they?

What Helian Dongshan particularly wondered about was why, for no apparent reason, this girl Hu Xiaoyue had come rushing forward to frame him, with no regard for her own reputation. What had happened that evening was still vivid in his mind's eye. He remembered being on the night shift when the doorbell rang and the girl burst in. Soon, she was indeed sitting on his lap. His heart rate accelerated. Hu Xiaoyue put her arms round his neck and murmured: "I really like you, Teacher He. You are my idol. I really admire you..." He had jumped up at that point, not least because the smell of her perfume was so strong it almost made him vomit. Later, he found out the perfume was made by Dior and it was called Poison. It contained Malaysian pepper, lily of the valley, cinnamon and ambergris... but, deep down, really none of that was important. The important thing was that he was afraid. To be quite frank about it, at that time he used to go to foot spas and massage parlours... he was no saint and subject to the same human passions as anyone else. He couldn't say why he was afraid that a beautiful girl was sitting on his lap. But he was very much a man of the times, and, as such, he was afraid at that moment. And, of course, he couldn't be sure that, if the girl had been wearing a lighter perfume, or had sat on his lap a little longer, he might not have... But he had jumped up in less than ten seconds and said: "Child, I'm old enough to be your father. This is not right, OK? Someone's calling you. You'd better go. Go now!" Could it be that, that the girl hated him for it?

Finally, Helian Dongshan raised his head, looked at Xing Zhibin, and asked: "Is that all?"

"Isn't it enough?" said Xing Zhibin.

"You are experienced in pre-trial investigation, so you'll be familiar with the term 'partial truth'," Helian Dongshan said. "If there is no such partial truth here, you have no reason to *shuanggui* me. First, my son did buy two apartments in Beijing, and he bought them cheap. As for where the money came from, you'll have to conduct a thorough investigation and find out. I'm not worried about that. Second, in the course of the July seventh gun case, the woman did fly up from Shenzhen, and she did kneel in front of me and entreat me, at the Blu-Ray Hotel... But for her to suddenly come forward and accuse me of rape eighteen years later... well, there has to be a reason for that. As for you, you can find out whether the evidence is reliable or not by doing a DNA test. But it has been eighteen years and it may not be possible. That would make it an unsolved case, wouldn't it? You know the result they want, but it leaves you in a difficult position, doesn't it! Why has she come forward to report me now? That's the question you must investigate and resolve. Third, yes, Hu Xiaoyue did sit on my knee, that is a fact. Girls are very free and easy these days, and I can't be sure that she wasn't acting maliciously, but there has never been any kind of relationship between us. I suggest you start with Hu Xiaoyue to find out what has made her stand up and sully her own reputation. Check it all out. There's nothing more for me to say. If you investigate all this thoroughly, even if I am sentenced to death, I will still bow in respect before you. Please remember my words."

"That's your attitude, is it?" Xing Zhibin was longer using the polite form of "you".

"Yes, it is."

"It seems that you are going to hold out to the end?"

"Let's find the evidence. I'll only bow my head to the evidence."

Xing Zhibin felt that the current stalemate wasn't getting him anywhere, so he said: "All right, you just think about it some more." Then, he gestured to the man sitting next to him. "Take him away."

Xing Zhibin still put a lot of effort into his investigations, and he led them himself, taking his team to numerous locations to sift the evidence case by case. What he found out frightened him. The case was a veritable maelstrom that threatened to suck him in too!

Twenty-one days later, when Xing Zhibin took the initiative to report the case to Deputy Director Wan, his face was very solemn, even anxious.

Wan Haifa asked: "Did you clear it up?"

"It's a very serious problem, Director Wan," Xing Zhibin replied.

"Explain what you mean by that."

"There is a lot of background to it."

"Go on."

"First of all, with the question of the apartments, we checked all the procedures in Beijing, and also checked all Helian Xichu's bank accounts. He's Helian Dongshan's son. We found no substantive problems. Helian Xichu bought the apartment with the money he earned selling weapons–"

"Wait a minute... selling weapons? What kind of weapons?"

"Virtual 'weapons' for computer games."

Wan Haifa breathed a sigh of relief.

"As for the preferential price, it took place too long ago and it's not clear who was involved. I checked all the property purchase contracts of the real estate company, and a whole group of people were getting preferential prices, not just him."

"All right, go on."

"Second, the rape. Again, it happened too long ago and DNA is no use. We went to Shenzhen but couldn't find any witnesses. The woman named Yao Yi left the country ten days ago and went to Macau with her husband. Lots of sources told us that she had got remarried to a gambler. He is an addict and has lost a lot of money. He has creditors everywhere. But not long ago, someone came to Shenzhen looking for her. Rumour has it she was offered three hundred thousand for her testimony."

"Can this be verified?"

Xing Zhibin shook his head. "No, we couldn't find any witnesses. We're just going on what the neighbours told us." He continued: "The third thing is the business with the girl. We found Hu Xiaoyue. We got to work on her and she finally told the truth and said that someone had forced her into doing this. If she didn't give her testimony, they would publish some of her details on the internet and show some of her photos to her new husband. In addition, when she got married, she was given a red envelope containing fifty thousand. She admitted that she had never had any kind of relationship with Helian Dongshan."

"Oh! So what are you going to do?"

"Ordinarily, since there is no firm evidence, we would close the case. But there are some new problems."

"What the hell are you on about?"

"The prosecution approval document has been sent to us and there are new charges that have come back from Beijing."

"What new charges?"

"This time there are six counts. One of them is that he knowingly broke the law and tortured a suspect to extract a confession by burning his face with a cigarette."

Wan Haifa smiled and said: "Isn't this... isn't this something to do with you?"

"Yes, that's what attracted my attention. I went to Beijing specially, and by pulling some strings, I got some information on it. It's very serious. It's not just one family that informed on Helian Dongshan, it seems to be four. They joined forces to press charges: the Bai family, the Liu family, the Xie family and the Jiang family, plus all the villagers from two villages who also put their fingerprints to the charge... They're in two groups: one in Beijing to file the complaint, and the other to collect evidence in the city and the province. We're told that the evidence was all bought with money. Anyone who provided evidence of Helian Dongshan's illegal or criminal offences was paid according to the seriousness of the offence. Rape was worth three hundred thousand yuan and amounts of ten thousand, thirty thousand, fifty thousand and eighty thousand were given for other offences. All the villagers had to do was to put their fingerprint on the complaint and pay a hundred yuan. According to reliable sources, the Liu family recently sent a prize potted flowering plum tree up to Beijing... this is some kind of concerted attack, Director Wan."

Wan Haifa was silent for a moment, then said: "Crazy! Totally crazy! Can you do anything about all this?"

Xing Zhibin shook his head. "No, there are too many people, and the area involved is too large. Sooner or later, Director Wan, we're all going to be caught in this net."

Wan Haifa was silent for a long time. He knew that the Xie family had hundreds of millions in assets. The Bai family, the Jiang family and the Liu family all had backgrounds in officialdom and a network of connections that went very deep. There were also all those farmers who paid a hundred yuan and provided their fingerprints. Once all that was put together, it was an overwhelming force... Finally, he slapped the table and said: "Release everyone! Write a report on the case but let them out first. I will report to the Provincial Party Committee on exactly what is going on."

On the twenty-seventh of the twelfth lunar month, three days before the Spring Festival, Helian Dongshan walked out of the *shuanggui* base. He was the first contemporary official of recent times to emerge from the place an innocent man. Consequences were still going to follow, but at least he was out of there.

That afternoon, as he walked out of the *shuanggui* base leaning on a cane, he stood in the snow and saw his son, Helian Xichu arriving in a Mercedes-Benz to pick him up. He was told that his wife had completed the retirement formalities on his behalf, and his son was going to take him to live in Beijing.

Finally walking out of the *shuanggui* base should have been a happy experience, but Helian Dongshan was full of sorrow. He was a "clean" person or, at least, he had always considered himself clean, but now he learned that so many people had come forward to accuse him! How could that be? You couldn't say they were all bad people just because they had paid their money and provided their fingerprints, could you? No, all you could say was that they were not people of good faith. Why was that?

He also had to admit that if it were not for Deputy Director Wan doing his utmost to protect him, and if it were not for Xing Zhibin's "final favour", he would never have been released. That was what saddened him the most. He always knew he was innocent and believed that he would be able to survive the ordeal, and that was what had kept him going. However, when he was released, the words of Xing Zhibin made him feel even more uncomfortable: "Teacher, I remember your kindness. We tried our best." It was these words that left him feeling so desolate.

So out he came, but when his son and wife walked towards him, he stopped. Helian Xichu was already a made man, and Helian Dongshan saw condescension in his eyes. In fact, the expression was really one of acceptance and even compassion. He looked at his father unabashedly, effectively saying: You are old and outdated, and you just have to accept it. Suddenly and emphatically, Helian Dongshan drew a line in the snow with his walking stick. It meant he was severing relations with them.

Undeterred, his son Helian Xichu said, in a loud, confident voice: "Listen to me, old man. Let me tell you. What I do is not 'computer games'. It's called artificial intelligence."

Helian Dongshan sniffed disdainfully.

Even in the 21st century, in the internet age, Helian Dongshan still stubbornly believed that his son's money was dirty. He knew they were still on his tail, and he didn't want any more involvement with them. Yes, he saw danger all right, but he didn't know who the enemy was.

He turned away, leaning on the walking stick Xing Zhibin had given him, and hobbled off in the other direction.

The snow was still falling.

SEVEN

IT WAS TIME FOR THE WINTERSWEET PLUM to show its glory.

The ancient-boled tree known as both Butterfly Transformation and the Two-Sided Reclining Buddha was transported to Beijing by a special vehicle sent by Xie Zhichang. Naturally, it was carefully looked after along the way. Whenever the driver stopped at the expressway service areas, he remembered to water it. Of course, he didn't dare give it too much, and just moistened it instead. After arriving in Beijing, it was covered with plastic film because of the cold weather. As a result, this ancient tree, with a history of three hundred years and known as The King of Chinese Plums, finally saw the proper light of day after twenty-two years of careful nurturing by the master gardener Liu Quanyou.

Butterfly Transformation was revealed to the world in the Kyushu Flower Market in Beijing, where it caused quite a stir. On the same day, a tabloid reporter wrote the story of "The King of Plum Tree's entry into Beijing", and it specifically noted the day when it bloomed. After that, it was quietly sent to a courtyard residence.

Xie Zhichang sent Butterfly Transformation to Beijing because the matter he wanted handled was a very big deal. His only request was to get Helian Dongshan sent back to prison with no chance of release. This was not his project alone. Many other people also had an interest. They all knew that Helian Dongshan was not only pure poison to them, he was also very stubborn, and never let go of whatever he got his teeth into.

Huanghuai had long been approved as the site for a world flower market. This multi-billion-yuan project had already attracted several billions of investment in its preliminary stages. The money came not only from the government, but also included investment capital from Hong Kong, Macau and Chinese businessmen in Southeast Asia. These foreign investments were acquired with great difficulty, and the Huanghuai City Government had also guaranteed the project with credit. But now, Project Number One had led to so many arrests, with even the deputy governor sentenced to death... If the case continued to be investigated like that, an awful lot of things were going to come to light. It had already progressed from the "June 29th railway incident" to the "gold shop arson" and on to the "case of the murdered wife". Unchecked, Xie Zhichang would sooner or later be uncovered as the mastermind. Once Xie Zhichang became involved, the billions of yuan of early investment would be wiped out. Then, as guarantor of the project, the Huanghuai City Government would be implicated. Once the government became the defaulting party, it would have to compensate all the foreign businessmen for huge losses. Then there were the flowers that had already been planted, the florists hired and the huge commercial buildings already constructed... the economy of Huanghuai would be hit hard, maybe even crippled. There were some high-up officials in Huanghuai who also believed that Xie Zhichang should be protected for the time being. It was not that he should get away scot-free, but nothing could happen until the project had been fully landed.

Because of all this, Xie Zhichang managed to escape. In Huanghuai, there was nothing he could not do. He had helped so many people... but there were some things that he regretted very much. But he had come so far and could not afford to look back. So on the one hand, he spent money hiring agents, and arranged for the Bai, Jiang and Liu families to come together and go to Beijing time and time again to file complaints. He was hoping he could settle the case with his spending power. On the other hand, he drew on a very important relationship. This time, when he came to Beijing, he not only brought Butterfly Transformation, he also brought a lot of cash. He thought that even if the case itself couldn't be resolved, the underlying matter could, at least, be put to rest.

After Butterfly Transformation was taken to the courtyard residence, it was respectfully "invited" into a greenhouse, and carefully tended. The day for its flowering had long been determined and the event was guaranteed by Xie Zhichang, the president of the Flower

World Group. However, on the day when it was scheduled to bloom, no flowers appeared. Not only did it fail to bloom, there were even signs of the whole tree failing. The bole of the so-called "Two-Sided Reclining Buddha" began to crumble to the touch…

When Xie Zhichang came again with a gift, he was politely turned away. But as the front door was closed, the family's nanny called after him: "Swindler!"

Xie Zhichang was stunned. He didn't know what the problem was, but after making many inquiries, he finally found out. The Butterfly Transformation he had sent there had not bloomed as promised. When he took the phone call telling him this, Xie Zhichang wiped the sweat from his forehead, and told his agent: "It's OK, it doesn't matter, there is still something that can be done." He made another phone call and arranged for a special car to pick up master gardener Liu Quanyou. The man had nurtured this tree, slaving over it for twenty-two years, and he must have a way to make it bloom.

The eighty-two-year-old Liu Quanyou was eager to save his son, who was still in prison, so he came without any argument. However, when Xie Zhichang led him into the red-walled hutong, he suddenly stopped. He squatted on the ground and wailed.

He had seen it. He had seen a little food stall at the entrance to the hutong selling *hulatang*, and in the flames under the pot of soup, there was the rotting stump of a plum tree that had been split in two and was crackling and burning in the cooking fire.

The smell of winter plum screeched through the air!

That afternoon, Xie Zhichang received a mysterious phone call. A voice told him that Helian Dongshan had been called in by the Central Commission for Discipline Inspection. Xie Zhichang said excitedly: "OK, this is a good thing! Has he been arrested again?" But the other party said: "It is not good, Lao Xie. He has not been arrested. He was invited up to Beijing by the commission. I've heard he is going to be hired as a supervisory commissioner." When he heard this, Xie Zhichang felt as though he had been coshed.

After a short while, he received a text message. When it came down to it, he had been very public-spirited and helped lots of people, so it was natural that plenty of folk would want to warn him. He looked down at his phone and saw that the message consisted of eight lines of poetry: "The oriole is holding a yellow flower and fluttering against the eaves. It wants to thank its Lord for his great kindness and ask how it can repay it. With bejewelled sword and clothing worth a thousand gold pieces, he ascends to his lord's white jade hall; he himself serves the Lord of the Central Plain and at home has dancing girls from Handan."

This message was sent by Su Canguang, former director of Huanghuai City Cultural Bureau, current vice-chairman of the CPPCC and a gifted graduate of Peking University. Xie Zhichang stared at the message for a long time, asking himself what it could mean.

As all this was happening, cars and pedestrians were coming and going on the streets of Beijing. The human face is like a mirror: people reflect each other, but no one can see themselves. There was no haze that day, the sun was bright, but when the wind blew, the cold was icy.

AFTERWORD

THAT BUTTERFLY, the one lying on the rails, is it awake? To be honest, I don't know.

On the Central Plain, the word "客" (*ke*) is used as a kind of honorific. In the upper register of its use, it applies to anything from bureaucrats to religious types and mystics and magicians of all kinds, to sons-in-law, to teachers. Lower down, it could be used for family and relatives, good friends and even street pedlars and the like; anyone who comes through your door is essentially 客. In the great sea of people and traffic, to-ing and fro-ing, who would not be considered 客?

As I have said many times, I have been writing about "the relationship between soil and plants", and people are my "plants". This novel has taken a little over two years to write but has been as much as ten years in the making. On the surface, it could be considered a work on the subject of anti-corruption. I have written about a case involving officials on the Central Plain. In fact, what I am writing is the spiritual ecology of a specific region. I started this book writing about a "flower man". The whole story is set in motion by him, a man who sells flowers, starting from a flower market in a small town, and leading on to a whole catalogue of people and stories. That is why the novel is called 平原客 (*pingyuan ke*): *A Man of the Plains*.

I remember back in the early 1980s, when I first transferred to the provincial capital, my life was very plain, and whenever I felt greedy and wanted to indulge myself, I ran over to queue up at the He Ji Braised Noodle Restaurant in the city centre near the Erqi Pagoda. There was always a long queue outside. At that time, people cheered up their lives by eating a bowl of braised noodles or some such thing. The restaurant's delicious noodles were served with a large ladle, one ladleful per bowl. Add some searing hot chillis and they would make the sweat start to run all over you. I remember that it was forty-five cents a bowl at first, plus a couple of food coupons.

Later, noodle restaurants sprang up everywhere. They served many different types of noodles, with anything that moved on the ground, in the sky or in the sea being thrown into the pot... so much variety you never knew what to choose next. As people started to look for ways to feed and clothe themselves, in the blink of an eye, emerging like bamboo shoots after the rain, "hair salons" and "foot spas" suddenly appeared on the street. Red lanterns were hung in front of the doors, attracting the eyes of so many passers-by. Later, there were bath houses, karaoke bars and the like. For a while, I used to hear about a whole army of 100,000 girls moving either north from the south or south from the north to "wash hair" or "wash feet". They were making a lot of money too. Later, the girls were displayed in all their tender-fleshed loveliness, with their own number discs attached to skirts as filmy as cicada wings, and they shook their heads in time to the provocative music, just waiting for you to choose. Could it be that one passer-by or another, in that great crowd of rubberneckers, might want to take a proper look? So yes, maybe someone did actually go in? Could it be that the so-called "army of 100,000 girls" only corrupted a single passer-by? Or did each girl corrupt one person? How many would that make?

For about ten years, I followed a case that took place on the Central Plain. It involved a provincial deputy governor who killed his wife. The man had studied hard since he was a child, and after he was admitted to the university, he went to the United States for further studies and became known an expert official who studied in America. But he hired an assassin to kill his wife and was sentenced to death. I once went to his hometown to interview the residents, but it turned out they didn't hate him for being a murderer. They told me he was a good person, and it was all because of his bad *feng shui*. His house had become a "sinkhole of bad luck". Such a person is not a bad person in essence, but why, in the end, should he hire an assassin?

The deputy governor's second wife was originally his household's nanny and was also the child of a peasant family. She was probably chasing the good life. It was when she finally became the governor's wife that war broke out. The two became deadly enemies, and she fought stubbornly, becoming more and more courageous right up to her death. Why was that?

For more than ten years, I followed the fortunes of a flower grower on the plain. His ancestors had been flower growers for generations and were known as the Hunchback Family Clan. I know that people who grow flowers are kind and beautiful beings. He later became a famous local "master gardener". He was always experimenting with grafting, and he cultivated the plants into "fairy sprites" that would bloom at a time of his choosing. But as far as onlookers could see, he was most proud of raising a son who was promoted to mayor, and he became the "father of the mayor". However, the mayor also came to grief later on. Why was that?

For at least ten years, I also followed a pre-trial investigator of the Public Security Bureau on the plain. For a time, he was regarded as the number one investigator in the world. Nicknamed "Blade", he looked at the world through narrowed eyes. Using those eyes as a weapon, he solved many big cases that no one else could break, but he ended up being investigated himself. And he had an enemy: his own biological son. Why was that?

So in the era of a unified society, we yearn for diversity; and in the era of diversity, we miss purity. When social life becomes unified, does that not lead to purity? But purity itself can easily lead to extremes. When social life is diverse, and diversity leads to abundance, it is easy for it to fall into chaos and turmoil. This is a paradox. In short, for human society, the only thing that is eternal can be summed up in one word: change.

It has started. The wheels are rolling forward. That butterfly, the butterfly lying on the rails, is it awake?

ABOUT THE AUTHOR & TRANSLATOR

Li Peifu, born in 1953 in Xuchang, Henan province, is the author of twelve novels focusing mostly on rural life in his native Henan. He is best known for his Plains Trilogy, consisting of *Door of the Sheepfold* (1999), *The Light of the Cities (*2003*) and The Book of Life (2012)*. His works have successively won national awards, including the 9th Mao Dun award and the People's Literature award for *The Book of Life*. He has been selected as a National First-Class Writer by the Chinese Writers Association.

James Trapp has an honours degree in Chinese from the School of Oriental and African Studies, University of London, with special papers in pre-Han archaeology and early Buddhist sculpture. After graduating, he spent ten years as an art dealer. He then refocused on making Mandarin accessible to young learners. He has published China-related books on characters, proverbs, astrology, science and technology. His translation works include new versions of Sunzi's *The Art of War* and Laozi's *Daodejing*, and, for Alain Charles Asia, Wang Hongjia's *Final Witness* and Ma Pinglai's *The Elm Tree*.

ABOUT **SINO**IST BOOKS

We hope you enjoyed this exploration of hard graft and justice in China's Central Plain.

SINOIST BOOKS brings the best of Chinese fiction to English-speaking readers. We aim to create a greater understanding of Chinese culture and society, and provide an outlet for the ideas and creativity of the country's most talented authors.

To let us know what you thought of this book, or to learn more about the diverse range of exciting Chinese fiction in translation we publish, find us online. If you're as passionate about Chinese literature as we are, then we'd love to hear your thoughts!

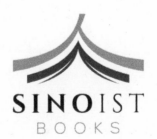

SINOIST
BOOKS

sinoistbooks.com
@sinoistbooks